The Assassin's Gift

The Emperor's Conspiracy

Claire Leggett

BANTILLY
PUBLISHING

The Assassin's Gift: The Emperor's Conspiracy 1

EPUB format: 978-1-925696-49-3
Mobi format: 978-1-925696-50-9
Print: 978-1-925696-51-6
Large Print: 978-1-925696-52-3
Hard Cover: 978-1-925696-53-0

Cover design by Lana Pecherczyk
Edited by Ann Harth
Proofread by Teena Raffa-Mulligan
Map by Shona Husk

If you know the enemy and know yourself you need not fear the result of a hundred battles.

Sun Tzu

About the Author

Claire Leggett has loved dragons, magic and everything fantastical since she read The Enchanted Wood by Enid Blyton. As a child she used to sneak to the bottom of the garden in the hope of finding fairies. Alas she never found any, so she brought them alive in her own imagination. Her stories are full of magic, adventure and escape.

When Claire's not writing she can be found creating her own handmade journals, swinging on a sidecar, or in the garden attempting to grow something other than weeds.

Claire lives in Western Australia with her husband, who loves even her most annoying quirks, and is currently learning how to crochet.

You can connect with Claire by joining her reader group.

(http://www.claireleggett.com/reader-group/).

Also by Claire Leggett

Fantasy
The Emperor's Conspiracy
The Daughter's Duty
The Assassin's Gift
The Healer's Curse
The Servant's Grace

Claire also writes contemporary romance and
romantic suspense under the pen name Claire Boston.
www.claireboston.com

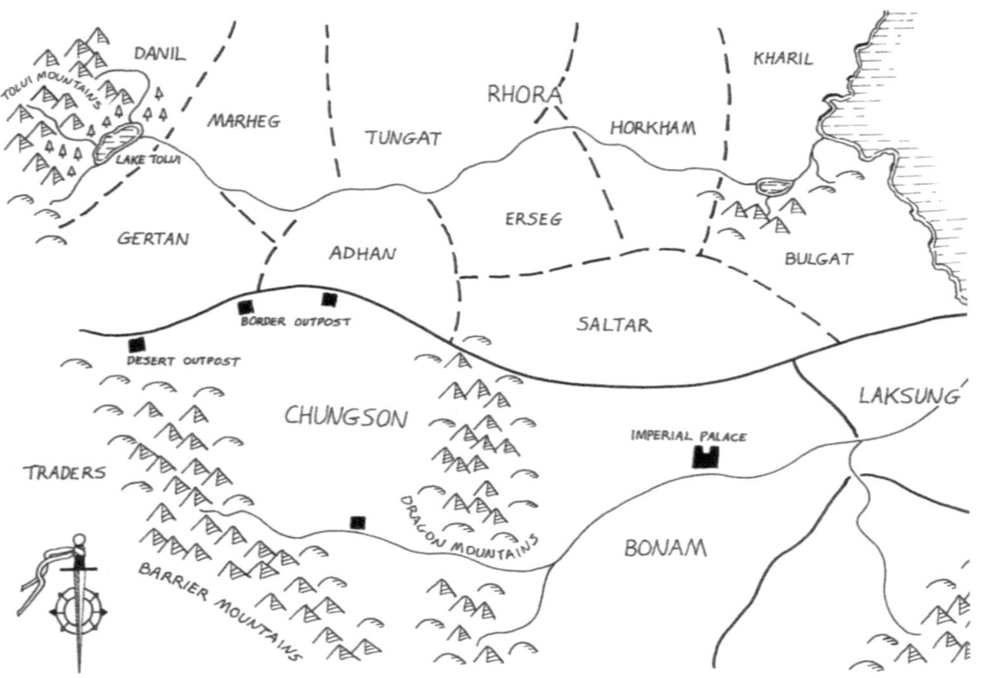

TOLUI MOUNTAINS
DANIL
LAKE TOLUI
MARHEG
GERTAN
RHORA
TUNGAT
HORKHAM
KHARIL
ADHAN
ERSEG
SALTAR
BULGAT
LAKSUNG
IMPERIAL PALACE
BONAM
BORDER OUTPOST
DESERT OUTPOST
CHUNGSON
DRAGON MOUNTAINS
BARRIER MOUNTAINS
TRADERS

Chapter 1

Today she would kill a man. That fact dominated State Princess Lien's thoughts as she walked over the bridge into the emperor's garden seeking solitude.

She paused under the shade of the Maidenhair tree, ran her hand over the rough bark. The tension in her shoulders eased as she inhaled deeply and enjoyed the quiet and relative privacy of being surrounded by plants.

But someone was always close by, watching her, being there for her every whim, but unable to give her what she truly wanted.

Kew pranced from bush to bush, enjoying the freedom of the outdoors, away from the disapproving gaze of others who believed dragons should be dignified at all times.

Lien glanced over her shoulder. Her servant's smile vanished and disinterest replaced it. A good reminder that at any minute Lien might round a bend in the path and meet the empress, or one of the emperor's concubines. It was inappropriate to run or frolic, inexcusable to make friends with someone of a lesser class. As a State Princess her behaviour had to be beyond reproach.

She brushed her fingers over the leaves of a peony bush, enjoying the soft texture, before tucking her hands into the sleeves of her long gown, touching the sharp points of the daggers hidden there. She'd come here for contemplation, to centre herself before her task later that morning.

It was a huge honour to have been chosen by the emperor for such an important task. It proved he believed in Lien and trusted her completely. And finally she would come face to face with the barbarians who had killed her family. Eighteen years was a long time to wait for justice.

She moved towards the Pavilion of the Ancestors, passing by the Pavilion of Purity where several of the emperor's concubines sat having tea. Yu deliberately turned away from her. Lien ignored the pinch in her heart. In the five years since she'd defeated Yu in training in front of the emperor, Lien had been shunned in the women's quarter.

It no longer mattered. Her task today would show everyone how important she was to the emperor, would raise her status above orphan.

Afterwards she'd be invited to events, be included in palace life.

The rich red posts of the Pavilion of the Ancestors contrasted sharply with the lush greenery surrounding it. Lien paused. A palanquin sat outside surrounded by servants. Someone was already inside.

Lien needed solitude and she desperately wanted to communicate with her parents, to calm the concerns in her mind. Her cousin, First Princess Fen appeared at the doorway of the pavilion and Lien ducked behind a tree. She couldn't afford to be distracted and Fen's frivolous delight about palace gossip could take hours.

Fen walked down the pavilion steps and screeched at

one of her servants. "Where is my parasol? The sun must not touch my skin."

The servant hurried to obey and Fen slapped her. Lien winced at Fen's lack of honour. Thankfully her cousin spent most of her time learning court etiquette with the empress, whereas Lien was busy with the special role the emperor had given her. In fact her cousin, First Prince Kun was the only relative she regularly interacted with and only on the training ground. Kun had pushed her to worker harder, longer, but barely acknowledged her in public, as no one could know they trained together.

After Fen left the pavilion, Lien approached, lit incense at the doorway and knelt in front of the statues representing her father, mother and brother. Kew settled by her side. Today she would avenge them. Today she would kill the man responsible for their deaths, for taking them from her when she was just five years old.

She closed her eyes, prayed for them to help her, to guide her hand and give her the strength to take his life.

Her stomach swirled with nausea, an unbecoming sensation which betrayed her twelve years of training.

But she had never killed before.

She inhaled and the strong, spicy smoke of the incense triggered a memory. Kneeling here with her parents and Bao, honouring her grandparents. It had been a hot, summer's day and the smell had drawn flies buzzing around them. Bao had killed one.

Her mother's words. "Bao! You do not get to choose when something dies. Only God has that right."

Lien opened her eyes, dread curdling in her stomach. Was the memory a message from her parents? Should she not kill the khan as the emperor had ordered?

But the emperor was God's representative on earth.

He condoned it. She glanced up, but the paintings of her grandparents no longer hung there. When had they been taken down?

Kew sent her a pulse of support, followed by the thought someone was searching for her. It must be time.

She must do as the emperor bid.

She clenched her teeth, taking another moment to visualise Bao's cheeky smile and then rose to her feet, tucking her hands into her sleeves, the cold, hard metal daggers a symbol of the strength she needed. As she exited the pavilion, her servant rejoined her at a discreet distance.

Another servant hurried towards her, dressed all in black, and bowed. "State Princess Lien, the emperor requests your presence in the Hall of Clarity."

Her heart leapt, but she simply nodded. "Of course." She followed the servant through the garden and towards the large Gates of Heavenly Virtue which separated the private quarters of the imperial palace from the public section.

Kew stayed by her side, now sedate, her head held high and her skin a bright red to match Lien's gown.

This was it. No time for doubts. This was Lien's duty, her chance to prove to the emperor she was worthy of all the hours he'd put into her training, that she was worthy of being one of his bodyguards.

The servant showed her into a private room off the main hall. His Majesty the Emperor, Son of Heaven, Zi Xue of the Bonamese sat behind a desk and beside him stood Master Ying, her mentor and the general in charge of the Office of Internal Scrutiny. Nerves fluttered in her chest as she kowtowed, her pulse thumping against the cold, polished parquetry floor. It had been months since she'd been in the same room as the emperor. His personality, his power always exuded from him, filling the whole room. She was lucky to even be in his presence.

"Stand." The emperor's voice was deep, the same rich tones as her father's had been.

Lien obeyed, keeping her head lowered, not looking directly at her uncle, but her heart filled with pride and joy. He was their leader, their saviour, keeping the Bonamese safe from the Rhoran horde and protecting them, giving them the best life possible. He had taken her in after her parents' deaths, had nurtured her and when he'd discovered her gift, he'd given her a most noble task.

His faith made her work hard to be the best. And though she rarely saw him when he visited the training grounds, Master Ying always passed on his praise to her.

The emperor couldn't have a favourite.

Inwardly she smiled, though her expression remained impassive.

"I am pleased you are wearing the gown," the emperor said.

She inclined her head. "You asked me to, Heavenly Majesty."

"You have the knives?" Master Ying asked.

In response she withdrew the blades from the special inserts in her sleeves and showed them to her master.

"Good. The Rhoran are approaching the palace," Master Ying said. "Time to get into position. You know what to do?"

"Yes, Master. Are the archers in place?"

"Of course." His tone carried a hint of steel. She shouldn't have questioned him.

"The khan will be at the front." The emperor was

grim. "This must go according to plan."

"Yes, Heavenly Majesty." He must love her to allow her to avenge her parents. It had also been his brother who had died. But she had one concern. "Will his death not dishonour you for breaching the emissary treaty?"

"You will not mention I ordered this. You will respond to something that will happen inside."

Before she could ask what he meant, her master said, "Follow me." He headed towards the door and Lien followed. To ask more questions after being given an order was disrespectful. Kew moved ahead of her between Master Ying and Lien, her pace steady and alert.

They moved into the immense Hall of Clarity, its high, lofted ceilings arching above supported by majestic polished wooden columns, each intricately carved with a Kixi, the guardian of the Gates of Heaven. Government officials murmured to one another as they stood around the edges of the room, their navy-blue uniforms pressed to perfection and not a hair out of place. No hint of the archers in the room.

Lien stood at the base of the emperor's dais, below the impression of the emperor himself, the embodiment of God, the features so realistic one would believe God had turned him to wood. Only the current emperor's visage was ever displayed, only he was the hand of God. Directly in front of her, the massive double doors would soon open to admit the barbarian she had to kill.

She focused on the delicate mosaic on the polished wooden parquetry floor. The perfect pattern, not a tile out of place, showed the superlative talent of Bonamese craftsmen.

Incense burned around the bottom of the dais, a musky scent filling her nose and making her eyes water.

She preferred the fresh air of the Imperial Garden, but she would never tell her uncle.

"All bow for His Majesty the Emperor, Son of Heaven, Zi Xue," a courtier announced.

Lien kowtowed as the emperor entered the room and crossed in front of her, his own pet dragon by his side, and then moved up the stairs of the dais to his throne.

"Stand."

As Lien obeyed the emperor, she raised her eyes briefly, a movement too quick for anyone to see. One man glanced at her, his brow furrowed in confusion. The state princess was not usually present for political matters.

They would find out why soon enough.

The emperor's dragon slithered around the bottom of her gown, blending in with the rich red, and then pounced on Kew, ready to play. Lien's heart caught in her throat as the two dragons rolled around on the ground snapping and growling at each other. Some officials laughed.

This was not dignified.

Stop!

Lien sent the visualisation to Kew and her dragon responded, climbing off the emperor's dragon and coming to stand by her feet. The emperor clicked his fingers and a servant rushed over, kowtowing.

"Take the dragon out."

"Yes, Your Imperial Majesty." The servant sprang to his feet and made shooing motions with his hands to Kew.

Go with him.

Nothing should upset the emperor today and Lien's task was too important for her to be distracted by Kew.

There was the occasional rustle of clothing as people

shifted, tired of waiting. The Rhoran should have been here by now and it was sacrilegious to keep the emperor waiting. They were a rude and uncouth people, but even this was far from what she'd expected. The emperor would be furious.

Then again, she was in no hurry to take a life.

Nerves skittered over her skin. Focus. Visualise. Be calm.

In her mind's eye she visualised her favourite memory. Sitting around the dining table with her family, her father at the head, his shoulders shaking as he laughed about something, and Bao's echoing raucous laugh. Her mother, ever the lady, smiling in delight, her eyes sparkling.

Warmth filled Lien.

"The Rhoran are here, Heavenly Majesty."

Lien's chest tightened as the mood in the room changed instantly. The emperor's dragon changed colour, flowing from moss green, through grey to blood red in response to the emotions of disgust, anxiety, abject fear.

Weak.

They shouldn't fear some nomadic barbarians who raided their borders if the Bonamese didn't pay them tribute. They were Bonamese, the most civilised people in the world, and the imperial palace was the centre of the universe.

But with so many weak officials, was it any wonder the Rhoran demanded whatever they wanted?

At least her uncle was doing something about it.

She lifted her gaze as the huge red, wooden doors opened and a group of ten Rhoran men entered, the man Lien assumed was their leader at the front. He was taller than the rest of the barbarians, perhaps two hand spans taller than herself, and wore his brown, shoulder-length hair loose like a drunkard. His skin was the tanned colour of a peasant who spent his days in the sun, far darker than hers. The Rhoran weren't civilised enough to change their environment to suit them.

He wore a long-sleeved dirty yellow caftan tied with a thick unsightly sash around the waist and loose pants underneath, all made from some rough cloth. No sign on any of the men of the silk they demanded as tribute.

The party walked down the centre of the hall and stopped at the base of the dais, but did not kowtow as they should.

How insolent! Her fingers clenched inside her sleeves.

Prime Minister Cong's voice rang out. "His Majesty the Emperor, Son of Heaven, Zi Xue of the Bonamese permit me to introduce the Khan Temur, leader of the Rhoran, here to receive tribute as your vassal."

Why did the emperor insist on playing these games? The Bonamese were stronger, smarter and richer than these nomads. All their other vassals paid tribute rather than received it.

No, she should not question the emperor. He knew best, which was why she would kill the khan today and show everyone her worth.

Lien raised her eyes fractionally as the emperor's dragon slid past the khan, reflecting a dark grey. The khan was wary. It was surprising he had any inkling of the dangerous position he was in. The Rhoran weren't known for their intelligence. Lien glanced at the men behind him. The warriors were alert too, their posture stiff and hands resting where their sabres would be if they were permitted to be armed in the emperor's presence. They didn't like being here, that much was certain.

Good.

"Welcome to my home, vassal Temur," the Emperor said.

Lien focused on his words. She needed to be ready.

"We are grateful you have opted to travel the distance to receive the gifts we bestow upon you."

"The honour is ours." Temur's voice was deep, with a hint of sarcasm in it.

The nerve of him. This man had ordered the raid which had killed her parents. He had no honour, he didn't deserve to live.

"We have gathered some of our finest silk," the Emperor continued and a servant carried in a bolt of silk for the barbarians.

Temur fingered the fabric. "It is fine indeed." His Bonamese was fluent with only a hint of accent but his tone grated on Lien's nerves. How could he be so insolent in front of the emperor of the world?

"In addition to the textiles, we have silver, sheep and several cartloads of rice." Xue's tone was benevolent.

"Your generosity is magnificent," Temur replied.

No one could be rude to the emperor. Lien fingered her knives. It would be a pleasure to kill him.

But time was running out. The barbarians had refused to dine with the emperor and the Heavenly Majesty was not offering anything else. Had she missed her cue to kill him? Her throat closed over. Maybe she had ruined everything.

What would Master Ying tell her? She needed to be alert to every opportunity. Temur was only one step below her and two arm lengths away. She could be beside him before anyone blinked.

"There is one last thing," the emperor announced. "I wish to give you one of my greatest treasures."

What was he talking about? Lien wanted to look at him, but she kept her eyes lowered as expected. He hadn't told her anything about a treasure, only what was in the tribute. Her fingers dug in to her arms where they crossed.

Relax.

"I wish to give you my niece, State Princess Lien, for your wife."

Shock speared through Lien like a lightning bolt and her head whipped up to stare at the emperor. What? He raised his eyebrow and she returned her gaze to the ground, composing her expression like the perfect woman. Every nerve in her body jumped, the hairs on her arms stood alert. Why would he do this to her?

How had she displeased him?

"You do me great honour, Emperor Xue." Temur's voice again. "Please allow her to approach so I can admire her."

The admiration in his voice crawled over her skin, but Lien relaxed, her body at once calm. How could she have been so foolish? This was the opportunity her uncle had mentioned—her chance to kill the barbarian.

"Princess Lien, you may approach the khan."

"Yes, Heavenly Majesty." She kept her voice meek as she walked towards the barbarian, her face lowered, while her fingers withdrew the knives from their pockets. She gripped them and waited for her moment.

She had to get her timing right. The archers hidden around the room needed to aim for the remaining Rhoran men. The emperor didn't want her to expose her gift by killing all the men herself even though she would be quicker than the archers.

Her pulse raced as she stopped in front of Temur. She would show these men what she could do, she would free the Bonamese from the Rhoran tyranny.

"Let me see your face." Temur raised her chin with one hand.

His touch was gentle, his fingers warm. Her skin tingled as Lien lifted her eyes, past his dark lips surrounded by laughter lines, over his crooked nose, to his brown eyes showing compassion.

Her heart jumped.

He knew she didn't want this, but he could not refuse her. To refuse a Bonamese princess would give the emperor a legitimate reason to declare war.

He was also young, far younger than she expected, perhaps only a half-score older than her. Too young to have been responsible for the attack on her parents.

Could the emperor be mistaken?

No, it wasn't possible, he was the embodiment of God, he knew everything.

She had to kill Temur, yet still she hesitated—now she was so close, her skin warm from his touch, seeing the life in his eyes, her mission became real. He was no sand-stuffed sack. He was human, just like her, and would have family to grieve for him, as she still grieved for her parents and brother. The reminder of her family strengthened her and Master Ying's instructions flooded her mind—strike fast, strike true. Lien withdrew her blades as a shout rang out behind her. She didn't turn. It was probably the general giving the archers the command to aim. She braced herself.

It had to be now. She could kill him.

Temur grabbed her arms, his eyes wide, focusing on something behind her and he swung her to the left as the most horrific pain she'd ever experienced sliced its way through her back.

Agony shot through her body, pushing thought from her mind and filling it with a pain she couldn't ignore. Lien groaned. What had happened? The world faded aside from the pulsing heat in the base of her back. Everything hurt and her legs wouldn't support her. The knives fell from her hands, clattering to the ground. No. The barbarian would see them.

"Seize him," the emperor's voice rang out.

Seize who? Her mind clouded with pain and Temur's strong grasp held her immobile. He lifted her up and passed her to one of his men. "Make sure she doesn't bleed over the tribute."

Bleed? She glanced back. Temur clenched his jaw, his face red, his hand going to where his sabre should have been. The rest of his men surrounded him in a protective circle, and in front of him a Bonamese official was held by two guards, a sword covered in blood on the ground.

Her blood?

The emperor's face was stony, his eyes chips of ice. His dragon slithered over his feet radiating a colour she'd never seen.

She had failed him. Confusion, despair and pain closed in until the darkness claimed her.

~*~

Lien woke lying face down, her face buried in soft, dusty fur. She shifted, but her limbs were tied down, splayed out from her stomach like a star. Her body tensed, the hairs on her arms standing on end.

Where was she?

Fear fought the fatigue dragging her back under and she pushed through the sludge as she mentally checked herself. Under the thick, course fabric covering her she was naked. Panic pushed to take control but she refused to let it.

She visualised her father's face, his deep brown eyes, his wide smile and as her heart rate slowed, she focused on her body.

Her lower back throbbed with a piercing ache, and

she squeezed her eyes closed.

The Rhoran had come. The emperor had betrothed her to the khan so she could get close enough to kill him. And instead of succeeding, she'd been stabbed in her own home. Her skin flushed hot, tingling throughout her body.

How was it possible? Her home was her sanctuary, but it was a Bonamese official who had stabbed her.

He must have been aiming for Temur—a novice to miss so badly.

Then one of the Rhoran men had carried her away, instead of taking her to a palace healer.

Vague memories flashed through her mind of waking in pain, lying in a cart as it jolted over the ground. Searing agony as she was lifted down when they'd reached their destination.

She was in one of the Rhoran camps.

Her breath caught in her throat. She had to escape. The khan had surely noticed the knives fall from her hands and would be waiting for her to wake so he could torture her before he killed her. The barbarians were vicious with their enemies, cutting off their heads or allowing their herds to stampede over them. Her family had been fortunate their deaths were quick. They had drowned crossing a flooded river to escape the Rhoran.

She wouldn't go easily. As long as they untied her, she could defend herself, and escape. Her heartbeat slowed.

But how would she find her way back to Bonam and the imperial palace? She'd never been further than Jung Li's Dumpling House on the edge of the city. She wouldn't survive crossing the sparse steppes alone.

She opened an eye. Dark aside from the candlelight which glowed somewhere off to the side. It must be night—the best chance for her to escape.

Soft footsteps sounded behind her and an accented female voice said, "You're awake. Don't be afraid, you're only tied down so you wouldn't reopen your wound. I'll get you something to drink."

Lien tracked the short, stocky woman's movements over to a low table with a bowl of liquid on top. Lien tested her restraints, they gave slightly allowing her some movement, but not enough to defend herself.

The woman brought over a ladle of the liquid, lowering it towards the bed. Lien wouldn't drink it. It could be drugged or poisoned. "No—" She lifted her head as she spoke and pain shot through her lower back, making her dizzy. She opened her mouth, tried to scream but her mouth was too dry for sound. Before she closed it, the woman poured the liquid in.

Lien swallowed, her body demanding the fluid, and then lay down panting as the pain spread out across her back. She groaned.

"Let me get someone to check your back and take the ties off." The woman hurried away.

Nausea swelled in Lien's stomach, but she gritted her teeth, ignoring the dizziness. This was her chance. She tugged on the rope on her wrist, the fibre burning her skin.

A door banged and she froze.

"You're awake."

He spoke the Rhoran language, but Lien recognised the deep warm voice. Her skin prickled. The khan, Temur.

She said nothing. Best let him lead the conversation to discover how much he knew.

"I thought you might not wake after all this time. You've been very ill. The poison took time to work its way out of your system."

Poison? She twisted her head. Temur stood just

inside her peripheral vision, his dark brown clothing making him more of a shadow than a person. He towered over her and though his arms hung loosely by his side, tension surrounded him and he exuded power in the same way Master Ying did—confident and terrifying. She froze.

"Please forgive the restraints. You thrashed about while you were healing and kept reopening the wound." He walked around her bed and squatted in front of her, holding something up for her to see.

Her knives.

All her years in the palace women's quarters had made Lien an expert at showing no reaction to veiled and not-so-veiled barbs, but inwardly she flinched.

"And you were going to kill me." His eyes were hard. "Did the idea of marrying me so upset you, or was it the emperor's plan all along?"

Her heart galloped. She would not tell him the emperor's plans even if they tortured her.

Temur stood, lifted the bed coverings, and a cool breeze wafted over her naked body. What would he do to her? Lien struggled to free her hands, ignoring her back screaming in protest.

"Calm yourself." He cut the ropes at one wrist and ankle, dropping the cover back in place. "I thought you might like to move around."

She stilled. He was letting her loose?

Turning gingerly to her side to face Temur, she clutched the cover to her chest.

"I don't believe you'll try to escape. You're naked—" He smiled. "—and you've reopened your wound with your struggling." He went to the only door of the round tent and spoke to someone outside. Aside from the small table, there was little other furniture in the room, and only the ladle and bowl she could use as a weapon.

She rubbed her freed wrist against her side and circled her ankle as needles rushed through her skin. She gritted her teeth and reached for the restraint on her other hand. Her back spasmed, pain blooming from the stab wound and with it something warm ran over her skin. She jerked her hand back. Bleeding wasn't good. How much damage had she sustained? How had it weakened her?

Temur's eyes met hers. Lien remained still while her heart thumped as if she was in the middle of an intensive training session. The khan walked forward, jiggling her knives in his hands. Would he use them?

He passed around the end of the bed, out of her vision and she twisted, clenching her fist, ready to punch. He lifted the blankets, cut the remaining restraints and dropped the covers back in place.

She relaxed her hands.

"There are men throughout the camp. I suggest you stay where you are."

His threat wasn't subtle, not that she expected it to be. But she could protect herself against any man.

Lien sat up, wincing at the pain and wrapping the coarse sheet around herself. A different woman, taller and slimmer than the first, entered the tent carrying a basket and Temur turned to leave. "Geriel is one of our healers. She will tend to you, but if you harm her, I will kill you myself."

Lien raised an eyebrow. "You're not staying to watch?" Her tongue tripped over a few of the Rhoran words and she swallowed to get moisture back in her mouth.

"Here we give our women the privacy they deserve." He closed the door behind him.

She stared at the closed door, her mouth open. That wasn't what she'd been taught. The books Master Ying had given her said the Rhoran treated women like possessions, selling or trading them at will. Top Bonamese scholars had written them so they couldn't be wrong.

"I understand you're frightened, but Temur is a good man. You'll be safe here." Geriel was Lien's height and around her twentieth year, only a few years younger than Lien. A simple plait tied back her long, dark hair and her dress was a surprisingly pretty blue, tied with a yellow sash and with blue pants underneath. She wore no makeup and her movements were too big to have the grace and poise of a Bonamese woman, but her eyes showed compassion.

"Lie down while I examine your wound."

Lien assessed her. Some Rhoran women rode to war with their men. Maybe Geriel wasn't a healer. Only men could hold such an esteemed position in Bonam. She could be an assassin like Lien. Slowly she lay down, facing the door.

"You've reopened the wound, but it's been healing." Geriel prodded Lien's back, holding a cloth to the wound for a minute and then putting foul-smelling ointment on it. "Sit up and I'll wrap a bandage in place so you can move around."

Moving carefully, Lien sat on the edge of the low bed, holding her hands over her breasts while Geriel wrapped the bandage around her torso. The air was warm enough for it not to be unpleasant, but at any moment someone could walk through the door.

"Temur brought you some clothes." Geriel pointed to the table where a pile of bright red clothing, the traditional dress, sash and pants of the Rhoran lay. "They're nothing like the silk gowns you're used to, but they will serve you well out here."

They wanted her to wear the rough peasant cloth?

The idea of dressing like the barbarians gave her chills and she almost refused, but the lessons of Master Ying rang in her ears. *'Everything can be of use to you.'*

She wouldn't get far naked. "Thank you." She stood and waited for Geriel to bring her the clothes.

Geriel frowned and then picked up the outfit. Lien stepped into the pants as the healer held them open and then raised her arms for the dress. She flinched as her back twinged, but didn't say a word.

Geriel tied the sash and then took a crude bone comb and untangled the knots in Lien's long black hair before plaiting it. Lien suppressed a shudder. She would look like a peasant. The Rhoran weren't sophisticated enough to do the beautiful, elaborate hairstyles of the Bonamese. At least it would be less cumbersome if she had to fight her way out of here.

"Sit down and I'll bring you some food." Geriel gestured to the cushions surrounding the table and left.

They would guard the door but there had to be another way out of here.

Lien strode around the yurt, running her hand over the thick felt with its wooden lattice structure underneath. It would be difficult to get through. Embroidered pictures hung at intervals, one of a group of deer and another of the steppes. The quality of the work was exquisite. Had they been part of the Bonamese tribute?

She reached up to check the initials at the bottom and her back twinged. Focus. She was injured in the enemy camp, and Temur would retaliate in some way for her assassination attempt.

Her failed attempt.

Her only excuse was the betrothal had shocked her.

If only the emperor had discussed it with her beforehand... She could visualise Master Ying shaking his head, see his cold stare and lips pressed together at her excuses.

Had the emperor changed his mind? Maybe he'd decided a strategic marriage would be better to temper the Rhoran's actions. Or perhaps it had simply been the opportunity he'd spoken of for her to get close to the khan.

Confusion filled her.

The only thing she was sure of was that she hadn't reacted fast enough. She had been as useless as all the weak officials in the hall.

Her eyes watered and she looked up, blinking the tears back. A beam spanned the distance between the wall and the four long wooden poles supporting the circular apex of the tent—the only part of the yurt not covered by lattice. A rope attached to the fabric was tied to one of the poles. It was a space big enough for her to fit through. Escape.

She would return to the palace and find out what the emperor wanted of her.

She gripped the rope as the door opened. Dropping it again, she ran her hand over the simple carving on the pole, pretending to admire it. Temur entered, carrying a steaming bowl of something smelling meaty and delicious.

Her stomach rumbled.

She stepped back, shifting her body to the side, taking a defensive pose.

Temur paused, looking her up and down. "The clothes suit you."

Ignoring the insult, she inclined her head. "Thank you."

Temur nodded towards the table. "Please sit down and have something to eat."

Why was he being so nice? Courtesy was not part of

their natural behaviour. But she would pretend she believed he was genuine. A meal would give her strength for her journey. Lien knelt on a soft, square cushion and waited until Temur had set the bowl down and seated himself opposite her before asking, "Is it customary in the Rhoran culture for the khan to serve food to his prisoner?"

"No. But it is customary for a man to serve his bride-to-be horse-head soup."

Lien glanced down at the bowl in front of her. No horse's head floated in it.

Temur burst out laughing, his rich tone flowing over her and tugging at something in her chest.

She frowned. "I do not understand what is funny."

"I don't mean to laugh, my *bayar*, but the shock on your face was too much." He chuckled. "Taste the soup. It's delicious."

Her body tensed. He'd called her his joy. No one had called her anything but her name since her brother had died eighteen years ago. It was too… intimate. She shifted in her seat as she examined him. The lines around his eyes and mouth were more pronounced as he smiled with genuine humour.

She couldn't remember the last time she'd seen someone smile without restraint.

Odd.

She focused on the soup. The smell coming from the bowl was enticing, thick and meaty, but the food could be drugged.

Should she refuse to eat?

No, she had to get her strength back and hunger gnawed at her stomach.

No way to be subtle about her concerns. "Is it drugged?"

His smile vanished. "No." He took the spoon and

dipped it into the soup, eating several mouthfuls. He handed it back to her.

She hesitated. The spoon had been in his mouth, but there was no other cutlery.

Should she make a fuss?

He watched her. Testing her. Judging her.

She had to eat. Dipping the spoon into the bowl, she then took a small sip. The meaty broth slid down her throat and hit her stomach which danced in celebration. Rich, delicious. She ate more, trying to contain her eagerness.

"Slow down, you don't want to make yourself sick. You've not eaten for a quarter moon."

She froze. A quarter moon. A lot of distance could be covered in that time. How could she have so few memories of it? She rested the spoon in the bowl. "Where am I?" And where was Kew? Had her dragon been left behind?

"You're in my camp."

"And where is the camp?"

"On the steppes. You're quite some way from the imperial palace. The emperor can't reach you here."

What was he implying? Lien ate more soup, this time chewing the tender meat chunks which melted in her mouth as she waited for him to continue.

"You will be safe here as my wife, under my protection, as long as you do nothing to harm the tribe."

He couldn't be serious. "You still wish to marry me after I was going to kill you?" At the palace any assassin would be killed immediately.

"An assassin wife could have its advantages," Temur said.

So she would be a tool for him. Who did he expect her to kill—her uncle? Never.

The idea of having to stay here and live with these barbarians made her stomach curdle. Shaking her head, she asked, "What makes you believe I won't kill you the first chance I get?"

"Two things. You would be dead before you reached the outskirts of the camp and you have nowhere else to go."

He did not understand her abilities. She didn't need a weapon to defend herself. "I could return to the imperial palace." The emperor would be pleased she had succeeded in her mission without damaging his honour.

Temur raised an eyebrow at her. "Why would you want to return to the man who tried to kill you?"

Chapter 2

Lien's whole body tensed and her pulse thudded in her ears. What in the emperor's name was he talking about? Was this his attempt at playing mind games with her? If so, it showed a remarkable lack of sophistication. He couldn't think she would believe him. The emperor was truth. "I don't understand."

He studied her. "What can you remember of our audience with the emperor?"

She hesitated and chose her words carefully. "The emperor betrothed me to you. You asked me to come closer, so I approached. Someone shouted." She'd assumed the general was ordering the archers to aim. "Then I felt the pain in my back. You gave me to one of your men, and told him to make sure I didn't bleed over the tribute!" How like a barbarian to care more about goods than a person's life. She breathed in and out twice to regain her centre.

"Is that all?"

She didn't like his expression. It was as if he was secretly laughing at her. She'd said nothing funny.

Lien reviewed the event again. He had looked behind her, had moved her. Had used her as a shield. Just what she'd expect of a barbarian. "You moved me into the path of the sword."

"No, I tried to move you away."

He was a terrible liar. There was no reason for anyone to stab her.

"An official ran out, holding a sword and yelling. I wasn't fast enough to shift you away." Temur waited for her response.

It made no sense. Temur had had plenty of time to make up his lie and this was the best he could do? She indicated for him to continue.

"After the official stabbed you, court guards surrounded him and took him away before I could question him. They told me he was killed trying to escape." Temur frowned. "The emperor said the official was in love with you and couldn't bear for you to marry me."

She didn't interact with any officials. She rarely left the inner palace. "What was his name?"

"Li Ping."

The name was unfamiliar and she hadn't recognised him.

"Why did you take me away? The healers at the palace are well trained." And why hadn't the emperor stepped in to help her?

"The palace wasn't safe. Someone had tried to kill you—someone who shouldn't have been armed in the emperor's presence."

Her throat tightened and Lien struggled for air, but she kept her face expressionless. Temur was right. The only people allowed to carry weapons in the Hall of Clarity were the men guarding the emperor.

She stared across the room at the embroidery on the wall as she reviewed the day.

The emperor had probably armed more men to kill

the Rhoran if the archers failed. He wouldn't want any survivors telling what had happened. This Li Ping must have been too eager to carry out his duty.

"Can I tell you what I think?" Temur asked.

Lien nodded. His point of view would be interesting.

"I believe someone ordered Li Ping to silence you, but he acted too soon. He should have waited until after you had killed me."

Lien wanted to scoff. The emperor didn't want her dead. She was his secret weapon, his family.

"Li Ping wasn't in love with you."

Temur's voice brought her out of her thoughts. "I am not sure."

"I understand why the emperor would want me dead, but why would he want to kill you?"

She shook her head before she could stop herself. If he was going to persist with this lie she needed to pretend to believe him. The emperor was the closest thing she'd had to a father since her own had been murdered when she was five.

"The sword was poisoned with dragon's fire."

Of all the poisons he could have chosen for his lie… dragon's fire was one of the deadliest. No one survived the long, tortuous agony of the poison. It was fatal.

"How strange."

Temur examined her. "You don't believe me." He sighed. "We need to set some rules. You don't want to be here, but I can't let you leave or kill you without the emperor faking offense and declaring war, so I have a proposition for you."

Lien waited.

"I understand the Bonamese have a great sense of honour and when they promise something they stand by their promise—is that true?"

She nodded. Without honour they were nothing but

barbarians—like him.

"Then I want you to promise me two things: you won't harm or betray my people and you will always tell me the truth."

She shifted in her seat. It didn't sit well with her to make deals with the Rhoran, but he showed remarkable trust in her word. If she made the promise, she might not be able to carry out the emperor's orders when they were clarified. She needed more time. "And what do I get in return?"

"You will be welcomed into my tribe as my wife and we will protect you from the emperor."

His wife. Is that what the emperor wanted? Did she have to marry the khan and stay here for the rest of her days, become one of the uncouth? She shuddered. "How do I know your promise is worth anything?"

"You think little of the Rhoran, don't you?" Temur stared at her.

"I've not seen many examples of your honour."

"No, I suppose secluded as you are in the imperial palace you aren't told what goes on at the border. You only hear the stories the emperor wants you to."

How dare he! "Are you implying the emperor would lie? You have said you will take my promise on my honour and you are suggesting the emperor has none." Her outrage made it difficult for her to form words. "He is the embodiment of heaven on earth." The emperor was everything good in this world.

Temur held up a hand. "We could argue the point for days," he said, "but it wouldn't get us anywhere. I will leave you to consider it overnight." He stood and left the tent.

Lien stared after him. Was he leaving her here, untied and unguarded?

Foolish man.

She stood up, wincing at the pain in her back. Not the wisest idea for her to leave while she was still injured, but she might not get a better chance. Bonam was somewhere south of here, and the North Star would show her which direction to go. But how far was it? Setting out on foot, with no food or water would be dangerous. Although the Rhoran had many horses, she couldn't ride or communicate with the beasts.

And then there was the question of whether the emperor wanted her to stay.

Her duty was to do as the emperor bid, but he'd given her contradictory orders. Had the betrothal simply been an excuse for her to get close to the khan, or was it supposed to supersede the assassination orders? His enigmatic comment hadn't been helpful.

Lien sat on the edge of her bed. If she returned home and the emperor wanted her married to Temur, he would be furious. To disobey meant death.

If she stayed at least while she healed, she could do some good. Living in the camp, she could discover their vulnerabilities and tell the emperor how to exploit them. Then he could bring the Rhoran into his empire as he'd been wanting to do. She'd ask Temur for permission to return to the palace before the wedding to collect her belongings, she'd speak to the emperor, and he'd clarify his orders.

The solution was perfect.

Relief washed over her, swamping her in fatigue.

Suddenly exhausted, she lay down on the bed and fell asleep.

~*~

"Princess Lien, Temur would like to break the fast with you."

The strangely accented voice broke through Lien's

consciousness and she opened her eyes. A Rhoran face filled her vision and she flinched away, arms up in defence before everything came rushing back to her. She pushed herself up and winced at the pain in her back.

"Sorry, I didn't mean to startle you," the woman said. "My name is Erdene."

A stocky, unattractive woman by Bonamese standards, though her pretty brown eyes were full of concern. Was she a servant?

Lien held out her arm to get Erdene to step back. What had she asked? Something about breakfast. "If you help me freshen up, I would be pleased to dine with him." She had to learn about the Rhoran and quickly. She didn't want to be here for longer than necessary. "Where will we dine?"

Erdene fetched some pouches from the table. "In Temur's tent."

Lien frowned. "Should a servant not address the khan by his title rather than his name?"

Erdene glanced at her. "I'm not a servant." She tucked one sweet-smelling pouch into Lien's belt. "We have no servants, everyone has a role in the tribe. The Rhoran elect our leader and therefore he is treated the same as any other member of the tribe. We only use his title for formal occasions."

What an unusual concept. God hadn't favoured the Rhoran like the Bonamese, but this was a fair system. She never would have expected it from them.

Erdene chuckled. "Besides, he's my baby brother. There's no way I'd give him the satisfaction of grovelling to him."

Lien examined the woman, recognising the same warm brown eyes. "But surely as his sister, you shouldn't be serving me." Did the Rhoran demean their leaders this way?

"If I can't help my future sister, who can I help?"

A sister. Lien had longed for family for so many years. But not with the barbarians.

Lien studied her. There had to be more to it. Kindness meant they needed something in return. She'd learnt that the hard way.

Erdene touched her arm. "Living here will be a shock to you, but trust me, my brother will take care of you."

Lien shifted away. It was forbidden to touch any member of the imperial family without express permission. Yet Erdene meant it to comfort, something Lien had survived a long time without. Lien didn't trust herself to speak, so she nodded.

"Come on. Let's not keep Temur waiting." Erdene left the tent.

Lien followed her slowly, her back more painful as she moved. She flexed her muscles before exiting the yurt, ready for any attack. Bright light assaulted her and she squinted, but no one else was around, not even a guard or escort. As Temur's betrothed she should have a bodyguard—if he meant what he'd said last night.

Directly in front of her was the back of a large, round white tent and next to it another one. In fact they were all an identical size, with white felt walls and each door facing the same direction. The only difference between them was the doors. They were all patterned and painted in different colours. The designs appeared to be complex but Lien didn't have a chance to examine them to check if they were copies of Bonamese designs.

With enough space between the yurts to give each home privacy, each row was positioned at a slight offset to its neighbour which meant people had to zigzag their way through the camp. A good defensive strategy. No one attacking would get up the momentum to charge.

The dirt path between the tents was well trodden; no civilised paving here, no manicured gardens, or pavilions for contemplation. Nothing as far as she could see but tents and dirt. Smoke from hearth fires wafted out of the tent apexes and she wrinkled her nose at the grassy smell.

People moved around going about their morning business. They all wore the caftan, sash and pants common among the Rhoran, the only difference being the women braided or plaited their hair while the men left theirs loose.

A shriek pierced the air and Lien froze as a small girl stumbled, and narrowly missed crashing into her as she looked over her shoulder at another child chasing her.

Ugh, there was no decorum here. They needed discipline. Erdene simply smiled. Didn't she understand children needed structure? They had to learn the correct behaviour when they were young, otherwise they would never get a respectable job when they were older.

"You can't catch me!" the girl yelled.

The words resonated something deep within Lien's memory. Another time, another place, another set of children. Her brother Bao, and his best friend, Jie chasing her through the imperial garden, the rush of excitement, the thrill of being the centre of their attention.

She blinked. Surely she would never have been so unruly. The empress would not have stood for it. Children were rarely seen in the women's quarters and certainly never heard. She must have been mistaken.

"Lien, are you coming?" Erdene asked.

Lien nodded and followed the woman, passing an older child carrying a bucket of milk back to her tent. That was better behaviour.

A couple of adults smiled at her as she walked past. She stiffened and swallowed the insult. Things were different here. In the imperial palace they would have averted their eyes, not daring to look directly at a princess. She needed to note all the differences, needed to record them for the emperor.

Erdene led her to a yurt in the camp's centre and opened the door. Lien stopped at the entrance to allow her eyes to adjust to the dim light.

Temur sat on a cushion on the ground at one end of a table and next to him sat an older couple and a man Lien recognised from the imperial palace. He was the man Temur had passed her to after she had been stabbed. He had *handled* her.

The khan stood in one fluid motion, remarkably graceful for his size, and approached her to take her hand.

Her chest fluttered, probably a nauseous reaction.

"I am delighted you could join us, my *bayar*. Let me introduce you." He led her over to the table.

She wanted to snatch her hand from his, but courtesy forbade her.

"These are my parents, Bolormaa and Mongke."

Parents? Of course, they elected their leader and so his parents could still be alive. Had either of them been involved with her family's death? They were the right age.

Lien pushed her suspicions aside and allowed her training to take over. "It is a pleasure to meet you." She put her hands together and bowed, wincing slightly at the pain.

Bolormaa scrambled to her feet, a stocky but smaller version of Erdene. "Child, don't be so formal. We will be family." She came around the table and extended both arms before her.

What was Lien supposed to do?

She reached out her hands and Bolormaa put her arms on top of them before standing on her toes to smell Lien's hair. "Welcome." Bolormaa hugged her.

Lien stiffened as Bolormaa squeezed her and an earthy herbal scent enveloped her. The last time someone had hugged her was when Jie had snuck into the inner palace after her family had died and they had comforted each other, crying at their loss. She lifted a hand to her hair as Mongke stood and repeated the greeting. "Welcome, child." His smile was the same as Temur's.

She stepped back, needing the distance. A small part of her wanted to hug him back, to bask in the affection, but it wasn't right. It wasn't appropriate.

Temur watched her.

She clasped and unclasped her hands. "Thank you for your warm welcome." Was this how families behaved here?

Temur held her hand again and indicated the man who still sat. "This is my sister's husband, Amslan."

She tensed as he stood, towering over her, his wide chest full of muscle. A warrior with his guard up. He gripped her forearms, his fingers digging into her skin. "Welcome." Though his tone was warm, his eyes were cold and suspicious.

This was the reaction she had expected. She nodded to him and relaxed. "Thank you."

Temur frowned at Amslan.

"May I sit?" she asked. It wouldn't bode well to cause tension between the two men so soon.

"Of course." Temur gestured to the cushion next to him and she knelt between Erdene and Temur.

He handed her a bowl filled with meat, dried milk biscuits and some kind of grain. She had no experience with Rhoran food or traditions, did not know what was acceptable and taboo.

He poured liquid that looked like watered down milk into the bowl, and then handed her a spoon and fork. The others likewise dished up their servings and ate. The khan didn't need to give his permission to eat.

At the palace no one dared to breathe in front of the emperor without his say-so. This more relaxed culture would take getting used to. Not that she would stay for long.

Lifting the spoon to her mouth, she tasted the unusual sweet and savoury combination. Nice. Anything would taste good because she had had little to eat.

Bolormaa cleared her throat. "Our spiritual leader is contacting the Gods and Goddesses to discover which auspicious day you and Temur will marry. We will need to gather the tribes and arrange your wedding clothes."

It was too soon to discuss returning to the palace for her things. They would get suspicious. "Of course," she said. "I will need to learn the traditions of the Rhoran as I find myself unfamiliar with your ways."

"Erdene and I will be delighted to teach you, my dear," Bolormaa said. "We shall start after breakfast, if you like—while we're embroidering."

"I would like to show Lien around the camp," Temur said. "You may have her tomorrow for the whole day."

Lien kept her eyes on her bowl. He would ask her to make those promises. She needed to work out how to keep them and report back to the emperor.

"All right. You must find her a horse as well."

Temur nodded.

The discussion changed to the horse herd and Lien listened, but she understood little. Their chatter reminded her of the one clear memory she had of dining with her own family. Meals had been a time of silent contemplation since they had died.

Finally Erdene stood. "We must get to work." She gestured to Amslan.

"Yes, you're right, daughter," Bolormaa said and together the four of them left the tent leaving Lien alone with Temur.

Her skin prickled. Without the others here, he seemed so much closer. His presence filled the room and her senses. She shifted to the side. "Why do you wish to marry me?"

"I don't." Temur's lips pressed together.

She blinked. She appreciated his honesty. "The emperor will not know if you don't and there must be plenty of Rhoran women who would be pleased to take the role."

"I'm as trapped as you are. The emperor insisted I bring you when I next return for our tribute and my spiritual advisor tells me the Gods approve."

Her heart jumped. The emperor wanted her back.

"So we need to discuss those promises," Temur continued. "I need to protect my people."

She focused. "What were they again?"

"Two things: you won't harm or betray my people, and you will always tell me the truth."

The only person she was meant to harm was the khan himself. "Very well. I promise I won't harm your people, or betray them, and I will always tell you the truth, though I won't promise to always answer your questions." She paused. "Are you not concerned I may attempt to kill you again?"

"No. You promised not to harm my people and killing me would do that."

Her stomach sank. She hadn't considered that. The

emperor would not be happy. "Will your people accept me when I tried to kill their khan?" She shouldn't be talking herself out of the marriage. The emperor wanted it and would surely annul it when she returned, but married people did things together, things she would have to do with Temur. The hairs on her arms stood on end.

Temur looked into her eyes. "Only Amslan knows and he has promised to keep the secret."

It explained Amslan's attitude. "Very well."

He stood. "Now I have your promises, let me show you around the camp."

Lien hesitated before taking the hand he offered, allowing him to help her stand, pain shooting through her back. His goal might be to protect his tribe, but there would be a catch somewhere. She needed to be alert.

"Geriel says your back is taking longer than normal to heal," Temur told her. "I suspect it is because of the poison."

He continued to lie. She should have asked for some promises in return. Not that she would believe him if he promised to tell the truth. "It is uncomfortable." She didn't like her inability to move freely.

"This way." He tugged her hand and led her through the camp. People waved at Temur as he walked by but didn't stop him. He had no guards. What if someone attacked him?

The emperor would never walk amongst the commoners, and never leave his palace without a large contingent of soldiers.

"Each family has its own yurt," Temur said bringing her attention back to him. "But we share a lot."

He pointed to a larger tent than most. "We go to the gathering hut to sort out differences of opinion or as a place outside our homes to gather and socialise. It's considered neutral ground."

The Rhoran were reputed to be feisty so it made sense for them to have a safe place for discussions.

"Next to the gathering hut is the spiritual centre. Solongo is our spiritual advisor and will set the date for our wedding. Small ceremonies take place inside the centre but weddings are held outside."

The spiritual centre had a red roof to make it easy to distinguish from the other yurts. She committed the knowledge to memory.

"Over there is the supply tent where we keep the emperor's tribute until it gets shared between the tribes, and next to it is the healers' tent."

He was being so open about everything. She needed to test him. "How many tribes are there?"

"Ten."

It confirmed what she'd been told. "How do they know to come and collect the tribute?"

"We send word."

She itched to ask how, what kind of communication system they had, but it would be too obvious. If the emperor knew how to find each tribe, he could bend them to his will, make them part of his empire. A light breeze sprang up, blowing dirt over her shoes. Lien sneezed and grimaced. She would have to find someone to wash them. "Where are the wash rooms?"

Temur laughed and stopped at the edge of the camp where shaggy goats, sheep and horses grazed in pens. "Tell me, Princess, where is the nearest water source?"

The steppes were an endless undulating sea of dry, yellow grass. The sun beat down on them and she shaded her eyes. No line of trees which would signal a river or lake. She shook her head. Amazing anyone survived out here.

"We have little water on the steppes. To the south of the camp there is a small stream we use to water the animals and for drinking and cooking. It is too valuable to use for bathing. You will have to get used to washing your face and hands with only a little water."

She stared at him. No bathing? But with all the dust she would smell. How could anyone live like this?

"Can you adjust to such a barbaric way of living?" Temur asked, his tone mocking.

He thought her vain. She could deal with anything the barbarians could, though it was clear the Bonamese were far superior. Her people had the expertise to move rivers to where it suited them, rather than moving to suit the environment. However Erdene and Bolormaa hadn't smelled. They had appeared clean and presentable. Lien faced Temur. "I believe I will."

At least until she returned to the palace.

Chapter 3

Temur waved at a short, squat man with dusty brown hair and bowed legs who groomed a dirty, black horse. The man said something to it and the horse pushed its head into his shoulder and snorted. Lien shuddered. He let that thing breathe all over him.

"How are things, Sukh?"

"Satisfactory." Sukh didn't bow or even stop grooming as he answered. "A couple of horses need wounds dressed, but nothing serious."

"Good." Temur introduced them and Lien resisted the urge to grimace as the man placed his arms on her outstretched ones and then smelled her hair. The horse was less than an arm-length away, close enough to bite or kick her. She wrinkled her nose at the smell and shifted to the side to put Temur between her and it.

"I would like you to find Lien a horse."

What was she supposed to do with a horse?

"Have you ever ridden before?" Sukh evaluated her.

"No, of course not." At his amused expression, she added, "The imperial family had palanquins."

"We'd better teach you immediately, so you don't slow us down. A gentle mare like Batu will be good for you. Why don't you come over and let me introduce you?" He patted the rump of the horse he'd been grooming.

They wanted her to touch the horse, to ride it? Only soldiers rode horses and she'd never been allowed near them. A state princess had no need and they weren't part of her training. But horses were a big aspect of the Rhoran culture, and if she had one, it would help her escape.

Temur took her hand. "Don't worry, she's as gentle as a lamb."

Lien knew nothing about lambs, gentle or otherwise. She ignored the warmth of his hand on hers, his frequent invasion of her personal space. The Rhoran were so affectionate with each other—smiling, laughing and teasing. Not controlling one's emotions was a sign of a less civilised people. She couldn't be lured in by it, no matter how much Temur's easy affection reminded her of happier times when her family had still been alive.

She allowed him to lead her to the horse.

"Hold out your hand and let Batu smell it," Temur told her.

And let it bite her? She examined the animal, and its dark brown eyes peered back at her without a concern in the world. An animal would not be superior over her. She raised her arm, palm down under the horse's nose.

The horse sniffed it, bumping it a little.

"That's it," Sukh said. "Now rub her chin. She likes it."

Lien gently rubbed the horse's chin, searching its eyes for any sign it would bite. Its muzzle was so soft, like velvet, a fabric so rare she'd only seen it once. Batu's hair was such a contrast from the cold, scaley hardness of Kew.

Sadness settled over her. What had happened to Kew? Was she still at the palace wondering where Lien had gone?

"Looks like you'll be great friends," Sukh said as he slipped on the bridle. "Let's get you up on her back."

Her heart beat a rapid tattoo. Was he mad? "It doesn't have a saddle." The empress had spoken about how dangerous horses were. They were unpredictable, there was no control.

"If you can ride a horse bareback then you can ride it with a saddle," Sukh told her. "No point learning twice."

He had to be joking. They wanted her to get on a horse with nothing underneath her.

She studied both men. It could kill her and if she fell off and died, the emperor wouldn't punish them. They both watched her, their stances relaxed, eyes patient. Even with her injury, she could protect herself. She straightened. "How am I meant to get on?"

"Eventually you'll mount like this." Sukh clasped a handful of the horse's mane, took two small steps and swung himself up on to the horse in one fluid motion. He grinned before sliding off. "But for now, I'll give you a leg up."

Her training would allow her to follow his example but she couldn't reveal her skills, even if it meant allowing the man to touch her again. "What do I do?"

He cupped his hands together. "Grab some of her mane and then put your left foot in my hands. I'll give you a boost and you swing your other leg over her back."

Lien nodded. The mane was coarse and greasy, but long enough for her to get a good grip. She placed her foot in Sukh's hand, he boosted her up and she swung her leg over, the wound in her back twinging as she did so. Batu shuffled forward a couple of steps as Lien settled and she clung to the mane. The horse's back was a little bony and she shuffled back where it was softer.

It hadn't appeared so tall when she'd been standing next to it, but now, up here, the ground was a long way away. It was like balancing on a log—she could fall either way. One prance from the animal and she'd be in the dust.

"Well done." Temur smiled. "I'll leave you to your lesson."

Thank the ancestors. Her gaze followed him as he walked back towards the yurts, calling out greetings to people. Nothing he did was what she expected. What game was he playing?

"Let's walk." Sukh clicked his tongue and led Batu forward.

Lien tightened her grip on the mane as the horse moved under her, a strange almost swaying motion.

"Wrap your ankles around her belly so you don't slide off." He grinned. "And relax. I won't let her go."

He held the reins loosely which would do nothing if the horse bolted. Maybe that was the point.

Still, riding was her only mode of transport out on the steppes, so it was important she learn. She shifted to gain a more comfortable seat. Batu's ears flickered back and then forward again. There was a definite awareness.

"Now, let go of her mane and put your hands out to the side. Balance is one of the most important things when riding."

Lien focused on her breathing, remembering her lessons with Master Ying, and let go of the mane, slowly bringing her arms out to her side. She would not let her fear show.

Batu shook her head, dislodging some flies, and her body quivered. Lien's heart leapt to her throat, and she gripped tighter with her thighs, keeping her focus straight ahead. Batu broke into a jog.

Lien jolted and lunged for the mane.

"Woah," Sukh said. "Relax your legs, Lien. Tightening them only tells her to go faster."

Every muscle in her body wanted to cling to the animal, but she forced her legs to relax.

"Very good." Sukh nodded. "You're ready to direct her." He stopped walking and Batu followed suit.

She wasn't convinced. The animal had gone faster because of a signal Lien hadn't realised she'd given.

Placing the reins over the horse's head, Sukh left them lying over its neck. "Don't hold on to them yet. I want you to do this using just your legs."

Lien lowered her hands to her lap.

"To move forward, nudge her with both heels. To make her stop, lean back and if you want her to turn, nudge her in the direction you want to go. Understand?"

It didn't sound too difficult. Lien nodded and nudged Batu with both heels. The horse moved forward.

Ha! She'd done it.

"Good. Now make her stop."

She leaned back and the horse stopped. Impressive. Batu was well trained.

"Next we'll turn," Sukh called as he walked some distance away. "I want you to circle me and return to where you are now."

Lien prodded the horse and walked towards the horse master. Batu's sway was rhythmic, kind of lulling, and the warmth of her hair under Lien's thighs connected them, making them one. As she came closer she nudged Batu's left side and the horse almost hit Sukh, but at the last moment she shifted, clearing the man and Lien nudged Batu's right side to make her circle to where they had started. She leaned back to stop the horse.

She had controlled this animal. Such power. Batu could help her escape.

Sukh jogged up behind them. "Your balance is amazing. Let's get you trotting now."

His praise washed over her like a refreshing stream, the same feeling as when Master Ying had told her the emperor was pleased with her progress. Lien's chest tightened, not in fear but in excitement. She would master this quickly.

Some time later, Sukh called a halt. "That's enough."

Lien let out a sigh of relief. Her mind was so full of all she had learnt that it ached almost as much as her thighs and back did. Trotting had been much more challenging than walking and it had taken her some time to master the sitting trot. The wound on her back had pulled, and her bottom was bruised but she ignored the pain. Show no weakness.

She slid off Batu and gave her a pat. She wasn't so bad. Batu butted her head against Lien's shoulder, knocking her back a step.

"She likes you," Sukh said.

Pleasure filled her. It appeared she had an affinity with animals whereas humans were so much harder to please. As she moved to go, Sukh stopped her. "We're not finished yet. You need to learn to take care of her." He handed her a brush.

Lien frowned at him. "Is that not your job?"

Sukh laughed, loud and raucous, so like the laugh of her brother. She stared at him. It had been so long since she'd had such vivid reminders of Bao, and she'd had two since arriving here. Strange.

"You have a lot to learn about us, Princess." He chuckled. "Without our horses we wouldn't survive out here. They are our transport, our trade and at times our food and shelter. They are an extension of who we are and we take care of them because they are family. You need to learn how to groom Batu, how to recognise signs of illness, unhappiness, exhaustion. If she fails then you shall fail."

Lien curled her fingers around the brush. Again she adjusted her concept of the Rhoran. They considered no task menial and no one was above helping.

It intrigued a tiny part of her. She'd loved being part of the secret bodyguard, being taught how to shoot arrows and fight. It made her think and stretch herself. It helped her grow. It was the only place she'd been encouraged to learn.

Elsewhere, the emperor had discouraged her inquisitive nature, particularly after Kew had hatched. "Show me how."

Sukh placed a hand over her hand which held the brush and pressed it against Batu's hair, running long strokes down Batu's body. He pressed firmly, but was not rough and after a few strokes he let go for Lien to try on her own.

"I brush her whole body?" There was so much of it.

Sukh nodded. "Look for any cuts, or insect bites, anything that mars the coat."

She did as he instructed, using long strokes to brush the horse and examined her for any injury. When Sukh was satisfied, he explained how to check the hoofs.

Lien forgot her fear as she bent and picked up Batu's front leg and examined it as Sukh showed her.

"That's enough for today." Sukh slapped Batu on the rump and she trotted back into the herd.

"You did great, Lien," he said as he led her through the camp. "Tomorrow we'll work on cantering."

She wasn't certain her body would handle it, but she

inclined her head. "Thank you for your guidance, Sukh."

He waved and walked off.

Her hands were filthy and she smelled like horse. A long hot soak in a bath would be bliss—and impossible here. With no water how on earth would she get clean?

The lamps were lit in her tent and Erdene sat at the table stitching. Lien paused inside the door and scanned the rest of the room for intruders.

Erdene placed her work aside. "Temur asked me to wait here for your return. He said you'd want to be shown how we keep clean."

Seize every opportunity. "Yes, please."

Erdene walked over to the table where a bowl of water sat next to a pile of clothes, a few small bottles, and embroidered bags. "Temur sent you more clothes."

Something fresh to wear would be nice.

"The bowl here is your ration of drinking water. You may do with it as you will. I often use a little to wash my face."

Temur's sister was pleasant, but she was Amslan's wife, and he didn't trust Lien. She needed to be careful. "Why don't you drink first? You've been busy with your sewing."

Erdene glanced at her in surprise. "The water is precious."

Temur might want her alive, but others may not agree with him. "I *insist*."

Erdene's eyes widened and then she nodded. "As you wish." She dipped the ladle in and drank the water.

It was safe.

"We need to clean up for dinner. There will be a communal meal to celebrate your betrothal." Erdene smiled at her. "I'm so pleased Temur is finally getting married. I've always wanted a sister."

Lien blinked. "So have I." The words sprung from her lips unbidden. A sister, or her brother alive again, was all she had prayed for. This was an aspect of her betrothal she had not considered. She would have a new family. Her heart twinged. Family here was so different from the palace.

But these people were barbarians.

"You don't have any sisters of your own?"

"No. A Rhoran raiding party killed my only brother and my parents when I was five." Sorrow strengthened her resolve. Those who took part would be old by now. Did they come from Temur's tribe or one of the other Rhoran tribes?

Erdene's mouth dropped open.

"The emperor raised me." Or rather his servants had. He was far too important to spend time on one young girl.

"I am sorry. May they ride endlessly over the steppes."

It was probably considered a positive sentiment for the Rhoran and after her lesson today, the idea of riding Batu across the steppes wasn't an unpleasant one.

"You can use this as a face cloth if you like." Erdene took a cloth from the table and handed it to her. "These bottles contain different scents which the traders from across the mountains have given us. You may choose whichever you like." She slid the bottles towards Lien. "I use a combination of the scent and these bags of herbs." She indicated a small embroidered bag hanging from her belt.

Erdene didn't smell unpleasant. Lien dipped the ladle into the water bowl, drinking deeply and using the last bit to wet her face cloth. She washed her face and hands before handing the cloth to Erdene to hang up to dry. Then she removed the lids from the three small bottles and sniffed. The first was too strong, a nutty, spicy, more masculine scent and the next made her eyes water it was so sweet. The final scent immediately transported her back to the palace, to her cosy bed she'd slept in as a child, and her mother bending to kiss her goodnight. Tears pricked her eyes. How could a scent remind her so vividly of something she'd forgotten? This was the scent of love and home. "I'll take this one." Dabbing a little on her wrists and neck, she then carefully replaced the lid.

Scents like these were rare and expensive. "Where did you say you got the fragrances from?"

Erdene hesitated. "Across the mountains."

She hadn't known the Rhoran traded with anyone outside their own tribes. It was something to tell the emperor and Master Ying.

Lien reached for the embroidered bags which contained herbs and spices, some familiar and some not. She chose one she liked and put it to one side.

As she changed her clothes, she asked Erdene, "What will happen tonight at the communal dinner?"

"Lots of eating, drinking and singing." Erdene smiled. "Some may even dance. The tribe will offer their well-wishes and raise a prayer to the Gods and ancestors to bless you both."

"Do I need to say anything?"

Erdene shook her head. "If you're ready we will head to the fire now."

Lien wanted to lie down for an hour and rest her thighs which throbbed from the horse-riding, but she often did things she didn't want to. "You may show me the way."

She needed to learn everything about the Rhoran.

And then the emperor could defeat them.

Chapter 4

Dusk had fallen, and the sky glowed red as the sun sank below the horizon, bathing the camp in a warm light. Lien walked next to Erdene to the communal fire in the large open area outside the spiritual tent. Hundreds of people sat in smaller groups chatting to one another. Lien's muscles tensed. It must have been most of the camp. She was completely outnumbered. Even her gift wouldn't help her if they trapped her. She couldn't let her guard down, no matter how nicely they treated her. Master Ying had taught her some enemies liked to pretend to be friends before they attacked.

Erdene led her to Temur who sat by the fire. Lien nodded a greeting and knelt next to him on the horsehide rug, sitting back on her heels.

The fire burnt in front of her, though no wood was on it and the smoke reminded her of the grass steppes. Above the fire a hunk of meat, possibly sheep, roasted, staked there by a crude rotisserie.

Bolormaa sat down next to her, legs crossed in an unseemly fashion. "I have discussed the wedding with Solongo and she has consulted the Gods and Goddesses. The date has been set for a little over a moon from now. This will give us time to embroider your wedding clothes and for the other tribes to arrive."

A little tremor fluttered in her stomach. So soon? A wedding for the Bonamese imperial family took months to prepare. It didn't give her much time to gather information and then return to the palace.

"Tomorrow Erdene and I will show you how to do our style of embroidery and we can start with your clothing." Bolormaa paused. "I know nothing about Bonamese wedding customs. Is there something you would like to include?"

Lien blinked. How considerate of her to think of Lien's heritage. "I am not sure," she said. "I will think about it and tell you tomorrow." She needed to come up with her excuse to return to the palace.

"Of course, dear." Bolormaa patted her knee. "I hear Sukh gave you riding lessons on Batu. She's one of our best. I had my eye on her myself."

Lien stiffened. Was Bolormaa the equivalent of the empress while Temur was unmarried? If so, it made her a powerful woman and not someone to trifle with. "My apologies if I've taken your horse." Did she need to give it back?

Bolormaa chuckled. "She is not mine. My horse still has a few more years in her yet and by then there'll be more to choose from. Sukh's gift is knowing which horses should be mated together. That's why they are so sought after by the other tribes."

An older woman stood on a small raised platform, her face wrinkled with age but with a youthfulness about her. She pushed her long plait over her shoulder where it fell far below her waist and banged a long wooden stick decorated with fur and feathers on the platform to get the tribe's attention. Everyone fell silent.

"Solongo is our spiritual leader," Bolormaa whispered to Lien.

"Our beloved khan has chosen a wife," Solongo announced and the tribe cheered. Temur raised his drink in acknowledgement and grinned at Lien. Something in her chest squeezed painfully. She didn't like it.

"The Gods and Goddesses have blessed the union," Solongo continued. "Princess Lien comes to us from the Bonamese, a different culture and a different place. She is not yet conversant in our ways." She smiled and Lien forced herself to smile back. "We must all remember to be patient, to be understanding and to take the time to teach her if the opportunity arises. She will be one of us and we do not let members of our tribe wallow in ignorance."

Lien stiffened. She was not ignorant. She was well educated, could speak several languages and knew more about military tactics than any of the women at the palace. Temur stroked her knee with his thumb, a small movement, perhaps meant to soothe, but it did nothing of the sort.

The sensation shot through her, heating her, making her hyper aware of every swipe. The intimacy was shocking and made it impossible to focus on the spiritual leader's speech. All her attention was on the movement on her knee. She desperately wanted to swat it off, but it would show him it disturbed her.

"Lien will be our mother, just as Temur is our father." Solongo faced Lien. "I welcome you to our tribe, Lien Mother, and give you my blessing." She walked over taking something out of a pouch on her belt.

Lien tensed, ready to defend herself.

Solongo stretched out her thumb covered in something sticky and smeared it on to Lien's forehead.

What should she do now?

Temur raised his drink and called, "To Lien, our mother." He drank and handed the cup to Lien.

The tribe echoed his words and they all drank from their cups. Lien glanced at Temur. He motioned for her to drink as well. She lifted the cup to her mouth and sipped. The fiery liquid hit the back of her throat, causing her to gag, her eyes wide. It couldn't be poisoned if Temur had drunk from it. She forced herself to swallow, her eyes watering.

The whole tribe cheered.

"It is time to eat," Temur announced.

Immediately people moved, some to cut the meat, others to stir pots next to the fire. Children danced from foot to foot in excitement, waiting for their turn.

Lien's throat burned.

Temur turned to her. "I should have warned you about the litak. It's strong."

An understatement. Before she could comment, Erdene offered them both a plate full of food. Even with the light of the fire, everything looked like dark lumps.

Bolormaa tapped her on the arm. "Let me tell you what you're eating," she said. "These are mutton dumplings, and roasted goat." She pointed to two of the lumps. "Then there is a yoghurt dipping sauce and cheese."

Quite a variety. They managed well despite their nomadic lifestyle. She tasted a dumpling and although the Rhoran didn't use the same spices as the Bonamese, the food was delicious.

Which was contrary to everything she had been taught.

How could her teachers and Master Ying be so wrong?

Were the misunderstandings between the two countries because of a lack of knowledge? If so, she had to take what she learnt back to the emperor. Perhaps she could bring peace to their lands, stop anyone else losing their loved ones.

When the food had been cleared away, some of the tribe brought out drums and other musical instruments—stringed lutes, zithers and some strange instrument which went in the player's mouth—and played. The music, if it could be called that, was unlike anything Lien had heard before. Rhythmic, loud and primal notes made Lien wince, but as the music washed over her she caught herself patting her thigh in time to the beat. The dancing was raw, with no grace, and yet Lien couldn't look away.

Suddenly someone screamed, a high-pitched squeal of terror, and instantly the music fell silent and people stood, drawing their sabres. Lien leapt to her feet and Temur pushed himself in front of her. "Stay behind me."

He wanted to protect her?

She shook her head and reached for her knives— which she no longer had. It didn't matter. She had her skills.

"Dragon!" someone yelled.

Through the crowd was a flash of green and Lien felt a familiar pulse.

Kew.

"Stop!" She pushed past Temur, feeling the confusion, fear and determination Kew sent to her. "She won't hurt you."

No one heard her.

A ring of people surrounded Kew, their weapons all

pointed inward. If Lien wasn't fast they would kill her dragon.

She ran, applying her speed, slipping between people into the circle. Amslan swung his sabre at Kew and the dragon opened her mouth to breathe fire…

"No!" Lien threw herself in front of Kew as the sabre came down.

She grabbed Amslan's wrist with both hands and dropped to her knee with a jolt as she halted his sabre. His eyes widened with shock.

Ancesters. What had she done? He was already suspicious enough.

She dropped his wrist and checked Kew as the dragon climbed onto her lap and licked her. Love radiated from her and Lien hugged her. *What are you doing here? How did you find me?*

Kew stiffened and her skin changed to black, a sign of a threat. Lien spun around as Temur entered the circle. The whole tribe stared at her. "It is all right," she said to both Temur and Kew, stroking Kew's scaly skin to relax her. "Kew is my dragon. She was searching for me."

"We don't get many dragons out here," Temur said.

"She won't hurt anyone." The faces around her held expressions of wonder, doubt and fear, and as Temur stepped forward Kew growled and blew smoke out of her nose.

Kew projected images and emotions into Lien's mind. "She is angry at you for taking me away," she explained.

He hasn't hurt me, she projected to Kew.

Kew glanced at her and then back at Temur before crawling off Lien's lap and taking a couple of steps towards Temur.

"She wants to meet you." Lien stood. "Kneel and

hold out your hand."

Amslan stepped instantly to Temur's side and Kew took a few steps back, growling, her whole body tense.

"You're scaring her, Amslan," Lien told him. Kew wouldn't hurt Temur unless threatened.

"Put your sabre away, brother," Temur said. "Join the rest of the circle."

The camp was silent. All eyes were on Lien, Temur and Kew and the children had squeezed through to the front and sat cross-legged, watching with amazement. Being the centre of attention was not what Lien wanted.

Temur got to his knees and Lien knelt next to him, keeping attuned to Kew's feelings. Kew waited until Amslan joined the crowd before she trotted to Temur and sniffed his hand. After giving it a quick lick she curled up next to Lien and yawned.

Temur shook his head as if he didn't believe it.

"She's exhausted," Lien said. "It must have taken her days to travel here. Do we have some leftover meat I can give her?"

"I'll get it," one boy yelled and ducked off to fetch the food.

"Why don't you take Kew to your tent to eat and rest, and then join us back here?" Temur said. "I'm sure everyone wants to know how you tamed a dragon."

He wanted her to tell her story. No one had ever asked her to. Lien nodded and got to her feet, nudging Kew to do the same. When the boy returned, Kew took the meat from him in her mouth and Lien led her to her tent.

Stay here. Rest. I will return later.

Kew growled.

Really. I can protect myself. I won't leave without you. I promise.

Kew dropped the meat on the floor and began to chew it. Lien smiled. She wasn't alone anymore. She had one ally in this strange place, someone who would protect her.

Back at the fire, everyone spoke about the dragon. The children begged their parents to let them see it. As they spotted Lien they sat down. Temur took her hand and led her to a stool on the platform.

"It is tradition when a tale is being told, the storyteller sits here and has the tribe's undivided attention."

She would be above the tribe, a clear target. In the dark she wouldn't notice anyone take aim, wouldn't have much time to react.

Temur waited.

Her skin prickled as she sat.

"Tell us how you first met Kew," Temur suggested.

"Kew is one of the cultural differences Solongo mentioned earlier." She forced a smile as she gazed around the group, the firelight flickering off people's faces. "At the imperial palace, the emperor and each member of his immediate family have a dragon. I don't remember a time when a dragon wasn't at court." She had once sat on her father's lap as Manalin, his own dragon, lay at his feet. "I was five when Kew hatched." It had been only a few moons after her family had died, and she had been desperately lonely. No one at the palace would talk to her about them and they told her to be quiet if she raised the topic.

"One evening I went to visit her egg before going to bed and her shell had cracked." She shouldn't have been anywhere near the eggs. They'd been kept in a forbidden area of the palace, but Bao had taught her how to sneak around unnoticed and she'd wanted to see them. "I waited and her nose poked out and then her head." Lien smiled. "She wore her shell like a helmet." One of the little girls seated in front of her giggled and the sound tickled Lien's heart. Lien focused on her. "Her front feet came out next and then she leapt forward, into my arms." She'd nearly dropped Kew, she'd been so slippery. "We bonded instantly." When the emperor had found out, he'd been furious. He had banned her from visiting Kew, except, "She wouldn't go to anyone else and wouldn't eat if I wasn't near her. We have taken care of each other since then." The emperor hadn't spoken to her again until she was eleven and he'd discovered she had the gift.

"Where did the egg come from?" Amslan asked.

Lien glanced at him. "I don't know. I imagine one of the other dragons laid it." Was it wrong she didn't know who Kew's dragon parents were?

"Convenient."

Was he implying they shouldn't have dragons? Lien bristled but before she responded Temur touched her shoulder. "It is getting late and Lien is still recovering from her injury. We can ask her more questions and meet Kew in the morning."

She let out a quiet breath. She wanted to discover what Kew had been up to, talk to her about the emperor.

A few children mumbled complaints as Temur helped Lien down from the platform. He accompanied her back to her tent.

"It took an amazing amount of foolishness to get between Amslan and your dragon," Temur said.

She tensed. How dare he call her foolish?

"He could have killed you." He took both her hands in his. "I did not protect you as I should."

A warm glow lit in her belly, but she squashed it. Amslan wouldn't have harmed her, she was too quick for him. "You need not apologise." He was touching her again and she was acutely aware of how alone they were.

Temur rubbed his thumbs over the back of her hands. "How many more surprises have you got for me?" He tugged her closer, and heat radiated from him. She stared at him as he leaned in and kissed first one cheek and then the other.

Her breath caught in her throat. Heavens. The simple brush of his lips against her cheeks sent her insides dancing and flipping around.

"Goodnight, *bayar*." He walked away.

Lien stared after him. What was wrong with her? He was Rhoran. She should be revolted, not staring after him like a love-sick fool. It must be because it was her first kiss. She fumbled with the door latch, her breath unsteady. Stepping into her tent she closed the door behind her and leaned against it.

She would not be seduced.

She would accomplish her mission.

If only she was certain what it was.

Chapter 5

Lien woke the next morning to the smoky snores of Kew lying on the floor next to her bed. She grinned at the familiar noise and smell and sat up, stretching the kinks out of her shoulder. Outside voices murmured around the door to her tent. A lot of voices.

Quickly she freshened up and then opened the door. Relief filled her as she stepped outside. A mass of children clustered around her, pushing and shoving each other, and shouting at her, all their voices blending together into incomprehensible noise.

Lien raised her hands to fend them off, her muscles tense. Surely there hadn't been this many children in the camp last night.

They were too close, she could barely breathe. Wasn't anyone going to help her?

Her eyes met Temur's. He watched from a distance, assessing her, his arms crossed, his stance casual. Determination swept through her. Some children wouldn't overwhelm her, even though she had no idea how to deal with them.

She inhaled deeply. "Quiet, please." She didn't raise her voice, but they became silent. She blinked. "What do you all want?"

A young boy tugged on her sleeve. "We want to see your dragon."

Oh. "Kew is still resting. She needs more food if one of you could show me where I can get it."

A small hand tucked into Lien's and she looked down into the round, smiling face of a girl about six or seven. "I'll show you where it is, Princess."

Lien's heart softened.

"Oh, Shuren. That's not fair," one of the older children complained.

"You all have chores to do," Temur said.

Lien looked up, her pulse racing. He stood only a few yards away.

"Yes, Temur," the children chorused and dispersed, except for the little girl holding Lien's hand.

"Shuren, there is leftover meat in the supply tent. Show Lien to it and then go home before your mother wonders where you've got to." He smiled at Lien. "When Kew is fed, would you join me in my tent?"

"Of course." What did he want? Would others be there?

Shuren tugged her hand as he walked off. "Come on, it's this way."

They walked in silence, though Shuren kept glancing at Lien. Finally the little girl said, "You're very pretty."

"Thank you."

"Mother says that's why Temur is marrying you because you can't even ride a horse." Shuren frowned at her in disbelief. "But *everyone* knows how to ride, don't they?"

Lien swallowed her laugh. Of all the problems she'd expected to deal with, a disbelief in her inability to ride was not one of them. "Sukh is teaching me to ride," she said. "Where I come from the imperial family are carried in palanquins."

"What's that?"

"It's a litter—" at the girl's confused expression she added, "a large wooden box with seats inside which is carried on poles by four or more people."

"You treat people like horses? How strange."

Lien paused. The girl was right, the bearers were treated like beasts of burden. She flinched at the traitorous thought. The Rhoran were not better than the Bonamese.

"It's OK. If Father is teaching you, you'll learn soon enough." Shuren opened the door of a tent and walked over to the pots lined up on a table. She peered inside them until she found the one she wanted. "Here you go."

Lien glanced at the large slab of cooked meat. She picked up the pot, and grunted at the weight. The handles were narrow making it difficult to carry. Taking small steps, she followed the child back outside.

"I'd better get back to Mother. I'll see you later." With a wave, Shuren ran off.

The pot was getting heavier by the second. So many people were around, but she would do it herself, show them she didn't need any help.

The distance back to her tent felt as if it had doubled. Her arms burned and she walked as fast as she could without using her speed. Finally she reached the door and pressed the pot against it, taking some weight from her arms. She puffed as she examined the latch. She would have to put the pot down to open the door.

"Let me help." Temur reached around her.

She jumped and braced the pot as the door opened. Where had he come from?

Lien hurried inside and placed the pot on the table. She sighed in relief. Composing herself and controlling the shake in her arms, she turned back to him. "Thank you."

Kew jumped off the bed and trotted over, stretching up to sniff the pot.

"No one will think less of you if you ask for help, *bayar.*"

Liar. At the palace she'd had to be perfect and still she'd been judged, and here was no different—Shuren's mother had already judged her based on her appearance. The Rhoran would make comments behind her back about how pampered she was. She wouldn't allow anyone, let alone these barbarians, to look down at her. Lien lifted the lid off the pot and moved the container to the floor so Kew could eat. "Did you want to see me about something?"

"I came to help. If Kew is all right by herself, I thought we could eat together."

Of course he would wait until the last moment to help her. "She will be fine."

Temur took her hand and led her from the tent.

~*~

After breakfast Bolormaa and Erdene took Lien to the gathering hut. The tent was at least twice as big as the other yurts and had half a dozen tables inside. The centre fireplace was unlit. Fletchers took over one table, their hands moving fast as they tied feathers onto the shafts. Bolormaa called a greeting to them as she settled at the table across the room and handed Lien some emerald green fabric. "This will be your wedding jacket."

She showed Lien the design and the stitches to use. It was similar to the embroidery she'd learnt at the palace and she had no trouble following Bolormaa's instructions. When she glanced up from the work sometime later the tent was almost full. Leather workers sat at one table making bridles and saddles, craftsmen and women sat at another making instruments, and another table held people spinning wool.

"Does everyone have a particular skill?" Lien asked.

"Yes," Bolormaa answered. "Each person has one thing they specialise in, though we all must learn the basics of how to do everything."

"My fletching is terrible," Erdene said. "I used to sweet talk Cheren into making my arrows." She frowned. "But he's been missing a while now."

Missing?

"We'll get someone else to teach you when it's time," Bolormaa said. "Unless you already know how?"

Lien shook her head. "What is your specialty?"

"Embroidery." She smiled. "You're in safe hands."

Lien couldn't help smiling back. These women were far more welcoming than the women in the palace. Which reminded her she had to learn more about them. "Are all the tribes coming for the wedding?"

"Of course. Temur is khan over them all and his wedding is an auspicious occasion," Bolormaa replied.

Would she have a similar powerful position? She doubted it. The empress only took charge of the women in the palace and the Rhoran didn't have a similar hierarchy. Not that she planned to stay. "Who is in charge of the other tribes?"

"Each tribe has leaders, a symbolic mother and father who work with the elders and spiritual advisors to make day to day decisions for the tribe. They rule on Temur's behalf."

An interesting concept.

"You'll meet them soon enough," Erdene said. "The messengers will reach them in time."

The steppes were so vast and the Rhoran always

vanished after they raided. "How will the messengers know where to find them?"

"Each tribe has its own area and we leave signs to show which direction we are travelling."

Vital information for the emperor. "What do they look like?"

"Many things—depending on what we have available. Temur will teach you how to recognise them after you are married," Erdene said.

Lien wanted to insist, but it would seem strange. "How long do you stay in one place?"

A woman who looked like the healer, Geriel, came over to the table. Maybe her mother. "Are you teaching Lien about our tribe?"

"Yes," Bolormaa said. "Would you like to join us, Odval?"

"Why don't we gather in a circle so we can all contribute?"

Around the tent, people stopped what they were doing.

Erdene beamed. "What a great idea."

In almost no time they had rearranged the room so everyone sat in a large circle, all attention on Lien. Her skin tightened. She didn't like having all eyes on her.

"What was your last question, child?" Bolormaa asked.

"How long do you stay in one place?"

"It depends on many things," Odval said. "The weather, the availability of food and water, and what is happening in the other tribes. We are always careful not to stay too long in any one place as we don't want to exhaust the resources." She was making something with long strips of leather—maybe a bridle for a horse. Her hands moved deftly and she didn't glance down, but the work was good.

"Do you enjoy travelling all the time?" Lien didn't understand it. The Rhoran were more intelligent than she'd been told, and they could make their lives more comfortable.

"It is our way." Erdene smiled. "You may think it strange, but for me, to be trapped in a town with all those walls around me would be torture. I need the fresh air and the freedom of the steppes."

The walls had sometimes felt constrictive to Lien too.

"Is there anyone you would like to invite to your wedding?" Bolormaa asked.

Lien looked up, and then hissed when she pricked her finger with the needle. Blood welled on her finger tip. She didn't want to get it on her embroidery but she didn't have a spare cloth.

"Oh, you've pricked your finger," Erdene said. "Just suck it before it gets worse."

Lien hesitated. Her stomach rolled, but everyone was watching. Bracing herself, she sucked her finger. It tasted metallic and when she took her finger out of her mouth it had stopped bleeding.

Bolormaa still waited for an answer.

She was no longer close with Yu and the idea of her travelling to the steppes for Lien's wedding was so comical Lien almost laughed. The Bonamese wouldn't acknowledge her after she married—if she married. The only people she would have loved to have at her wedding, whomever she married, were her parents and Bao and that wasn't to be.

She straightened. But there was Jie. She'd run into him only a few years ago when he'd become an officer in the army. He'd told her to contact him if she ever needed anything. What would he say if she invited him to her wedding?

A moot point. She didn't know where he was, had no idea what kind of man he'd become. She shook her head. "There is no one." This was her chance to plant the seed. "However, there are a couple of items I would like to fetch from the palace beforehand if it is possible."

"What things?" Erdene asked.

"I left with none of my belongings, and I have a few of my parents' things that I would like to keep."

"I'm sure we can arrange something," Bolormaa said. "I'll talk to Temur."

Lien smiled. "Thank you."

"We must consider the wedding ceremony," another woman said. "Tradition requires Temur to ask permission from Lien's family and collect her from her own tribe."

Erdene glanced at her, her expression apologetic. "Lien's family died when she was young."

"I will speak to Solongo about it," Bolormaa said. "Perhaps an adoption and I'm sure with all the other tribes arriving, we can form a separate camp for the wedding."

"There'll be no shortage of people wanting to adopt her," Erdene said.

Lien focused on her sewing, each stitch slow and perfect. Adoption. People wanting her as part of their family. Her throat constricted. Isn't that what she'd always wanted—a family of her own? But never with these people. They had been the enemy, the barbarians at the border for as long as she could remember. They were the reason she didn't have a family of her own.

But seeing them all together here, a caring community, she couldn't reconcile it with the stories Master Ying had told her.

There'd been no one left alive to say exactly what

had happened to her parents, but the arrows in their bodies and on the ground had been Rhoran. And they'd been deep in Bonam territory, close to the border of Chungson.

Which made no sense from the things she'd learnt. Perhaps it had been different eighteen years ago. She couldn't ask without sounding accusatory.

But one thing was clear. Master Ying's information about the Rhoran was incorrect. She had to return to the palace, tell him everything she'd learnt, and maybe the hostilities could end.

Maybe she could save another person from the heartache of losing their family.

Maybe she could stop the fighting.

When Lien's fingers were sore from the embroidery, Bolormaa called a stop. "We need to prepare dinner."

Cooking? She didn't have the slightest idea how. Lien packed up her work and followed Temur's mother back to Bolormaa's tent.

The layout was the same as the other tents she had been inside. Coloured cushions were scattered around the low table and a deep red curtain separated the sleeping and living areas. The carvings on the wooden poles holding up the centre of the room were magnificent and Lien ran her hands over them.

"Your home is lovely," she said as Bolormaa lit the central fire.

"Thank you. Ask Temur to carve the poles for your home."

Lien glanced back at the woman. "Temur carved these?"

"Yes."

The workmanship was exquisite. "Is this Temur's talent?"

Bolormaa laughed. "No. Temur is good at everything. Now, let's prepare dinner."

Cooking was much harder than Lien expected. She had never been allowed near the kitchens. Food had been prepared and delivered in easy to eat portions.

Now she stared down at the raw slab of meat in front of her and her stomach rolled. What kind of magic would she have to work to make this thing edible?

Bolormaa handed her a knife. "Cut it into bite-sized chunks."

Lien hesitated before taking it. A weapon. It was a good weight, and she tested the sharpness against her finger, hissing as it cut. Bolormaa was foolish to trust her. She wasn't even looking as she bent to get something out of a trunk. Lien could kill her in an instant.

Not that she wanted to. But no one at the palace would trust a Rhoran in the same way.

She stared down at the soft, dark red meat in front of her. Focus. She hacked down, the knife biting into a small section of the flesh. So far so good. She hacked again and this time the knife sliced all the way through, the small off-cut flying off the table and on to the ground. She screwed up her nose, with no desire to touch the raw meat.

With a sigh, Bolormaa bent down and picked it up. "You've never cooked before have you?"

"There was no need."

Bolormaa nudged her out of the way and took the knife out of her hand. "You cut it like this." She sliced through the meat using a sawing action, holding it steady with her other hand.

Lien shuddered.

"You have clean hands and you can clean them

again afterwards," Bolormaa said.

Lien took back the knife and followed Bolormaa's example. She winced as the knife bit into the flesh, slicing through the meat. Was this what it would have felt like if she'd stabbed Temur?

Her stomach swirled. She couldn't imagine killing him now. Not after they had spoken, shared a meal and he had been kind to her.

Was she too soft?

What would she do if the emperor wanted him dead?

No, he would change his mind when she told him all she had learnt. When she finished chopping the meat, she put down the knife and wiped her hands on the towel Bolormaa passed her.

"Don't worry, you'll get quicker with practice." Bolormaa threw ingredients into a pot heating on the hearth. Many of the items Lien had never seen uncooked. She barely recognised them, how would she remember what to put in?

"I'll write instructions when we are done."

She'd been so sheltered at the palace. If she'd been left on her own she would have starved to death or poisoned herself. Her ignorance had to end. She asked myriad questions until Bolormaa pronounced the dish was ready.

"Why don't you find Temur and Mongke?" Bolormaa suggested. "Tell them dinner is ready and I'll clean up."

Stepping outside, Lien took a deep breath of the evening air. It was fresh, a little dusty with the hint of livestock, but still pleasant. Even with the top flap open, the tent had been warm and stifling. She headed towards Temur's yurt and stopped outside when she heard raised voices.

"She's dangerous, Temur. Why in Qadan's name are you marrying her?" Amslan.

Lien froze. Though she didn't want to get caught listening, she wanted to hear the answer.

"She could be an asset. She understands the Bonamese and can help us negotiate to get our land back."

What land?

"She tried to kill you."

"The emperor tried to kill her, which makes her a potential ally."

"It was probably his way of getting you to trust her."

"Then why use dragon's fire?" Temur sighed. "Her honour will not allow her to break her promises and despite her haughty demeanour I think she is naive."

Lien frowned. She wasn't haughty or naive.

Amslan scoffed. "What you see is her smooth, untanned skin and her wide brown eyes. Don't let her pretty looks blind you, brother."

"You're right. Her innocence may be a ploy which is why I need you to keep reminding me." He paused. "But if there's a chance she can negotiate a peace between our countries, I have to take it. Too many of our people are going missing, and too much of our land is being taken over."

What was he talking about? The Rhoran were causing the issues, not the Bonamese.

"I hope you're right, brother," Amslan said. "I need to go. Erdene will have dinner ready."

Lien moved away, heading to the training grounds to find Mongke. It was good to know the khan wasn't as trusting as he'd appeared.

When she returned to Temur's tent, she knocked on the door.

Temur opened it, his body filling the frame.

"Bolormaa asked me to tell you dinner is ready."

He smiled. "My *bayar*. How was your day?"

"It was educational," she answered as he took her hand, and they walked together to Bolormaa's tent.

His habit of holding her hand was one she could get used to. No. That wasn't right. She didn't like it, she had to pretend she did.

"What have you learnt?"

Remembering his comment, she told him the truth. "I have learnt I do not know as much about the world as I thought. Bolormaa has been patient with me and has shown me how to embroider in your way and how to cook." She needed him to trust her.

"Did you cook the meal we'll eat?"

She nodded.

"I can't wait to taste it."

It would be edible since Bolormaa had done most of the work. They entered the tent to find Bolormaa had already dished up and she and Mongke were waiting for them.

They took their places and Bolormaa told the men about their day. "Tomorrow I'll teach Lien how to felt."

"She will also require defence training," Temur said.

Lien twitched. What did he mean? He knew she was an assassin.

"She needs to learn more about the tribe's ways before she learns how to protect herself," Bolormaa protested.

"I won't have my wife unable to defend herself," Temur said. "She can join the morning classes tomorrow."

No. She couldn't show them her skills. Not without betraying the emperor.

How was she going to pretend to be defenceless?

Lien forced a smile. "I look forward to it."

Chapter 6

Lien woke as the first light of the day filtered through the top of the yurt. Though her back still pained her, it was time to continue her training.

After getting out of bed, she stretched and dressed, careful to keep silent. A guard was never on her door when she left the yurt, but that didn't mean there wasn't one during the night.

Taking her time, she worked through her ritual patterns. She would not dishonour Master Ying by forgetting what he had taught her.

The training had the additional benefit of centring her mind and focusing on the now. She pushed aside all thoughts and concentrated on the movements, her muscles stretching and singing in pleasure. This had always been her favourite time of day—alone, in her private palace, with no servants around, and she could be herself, do what she wanted. It had never lasted long enough and she would have to climb back into bed and pretend to still be asleep before the servants arrived.

With her training completed, she ventured outside with Kew. She wanted to observe the Rhoran morning routine.

The cool air held the faint smell of smoke. She held the door open for Kew and contentment, warmth and safety emanated from her dragon.

Lien glanced down at her. *What?*

Images of home, rightness, happiness.

What was wrong with her dragon? Why was she so happy? *They are barbarians.*

Kew turned orange. No.

She frowned. *The imperial palace is where we should be.*

Kew snorted and turned black. A chill ran down Lien's spine and she checked her surroundings. No guards, no danger, only a few children laughing as they carried their younger siblings on their backs, an older woman sitting on the front step of a yurt calling out greetings and Sukh making his way through the camp to the horses. It was peaceful.

Where is the danger?

An image of the palace. Lien shook her head. Kew was usually right but perhaps the change in location had messed with her senses.

"Kew! Come play with us," Shuren called.

With a happy prance, Kew trotted off. Lien stared. Kew probably liked it here because there were so many children to play with, but Lien couldn't let down her guard.

"Lien, I was just coming to wake you."

She turned to Erdene. "I woke early today."

"You must come for breakfast. Mother and I have been discussing your schedule." Erdene took her by the arm and walked towards Bolormaa's tent.

"My schedule?"

"Yes, we have so much to teach you. You will be our Tribal Mother and therefore you need to understand every aspect of our society."

"Tribal Mother?"

"Each tribe has a Tribal Father and Tribal Mother. These people are the leaders of the tribe and act as mother and father to us all. Temur is Tribal Father as he is khan and you will become the mother when you marry him."

She didn't know how to be a mother. "What does it entail?"

"People will call upon you to settle disputes, discuss spiritual matters with Solongo, and advise on marriage matches."

Similar to the level of responsibility the empress had back in the palace and a huge responsibility. She could direct the tribe, control what happened.

Maybe this was why the emperor had betrothed her to the khan. Maybe he too wanted the conflict to end, but could not admit it without appearing weak.

Inside the tent, Bolormaa waited with breakfast prepared. No Temur. Lien's muscles relaxed. As they ate, Bolormaa outlined their day; first was a session with Solongo to learn about the Rhoran spiritual beliefs, and then someone would teach her how to light a fire for cooking.

"This afternoon Sukh will resume your horse-riding lessons and then Amslan will take the weapons lesson."

Weapons. That would be tricky. Neither Temur nor Amslan knew how good she was. "The Rhoran are fierce warriors. Why do I need to learn weapons?"

Erdene smiled at her. "Basic weapons training is essential in case our warriors are away from camp. You also need to learn how to shoot a bow and arrow so you can hunt."

They expected her to kill her own food? Lien bit back a grimace. "Very well."

After they finished eating, Erdene accompanied her to the spiritual tent. It was cosy. Intricate embroidery hung on the walls depicting deities in all their glory, and piles of cushions were scattered over the floor.

Solongo stood in front of each wall hanging and told

Lien about the God or Goddess they represented. The main one was Qadan, God of Life, responsible for birth, deaths and marriages.

"We also honour our ancestors, those that have come before us," Solongo said. "Each family has a particular day significant to them, and we celebrate all our ancestors on the longest day of the year."

Lien frowned. That was similar to what the Bonamese did. "What about the Great Khan?" The story of the Great Khan who had united all the Rhoran tribes and brought peace to the land was legendary even in Bonam. She'd overheard Master Ying and Kun discussing it during a training session. It was rumoured the khan had been buried with untold riches and an object of great power.

Solongo smiled. "We celebrate the Great Khan in summer, when all the tribes gather for the great hunt. We pay the Great Khan homage and thanks as a united group, as should be the way."

"Where is he buried?"

"No one knows. A few of his most loyal followers took his body and laid him to rest where he would be undisturbed."

The Bonamese wouldn't treat an important figure with such disrespect. He should have a monument. Though she didn't know where they would erect it. "In Bonam the stories of the Great Khan focus on the riches he is buried with."

Solongo walked her to the door. "As with most legends, it has been exaggerated over the years. From all reports, the khan didn't care for material wealth, only for uniting the nation and ending the relentless fighting."

A noble person. Lien inclined her head. "Thank you for your time." She followed Bolormaa to the horse yard where three children waited. "These are some of Sukh's children," Bolormaa said. "Shuren, Jochi and Nekhii." She indicated little Shuren and her two brothers. "Take Lien to your mother when you're done," Bolormaa said and left her with them.

Lien smiled at Shuren. "What are we doing?"

"Collecting horse dung for the fire." She held a scoop in her hand.

Lien glanced at the eldest boy who was perhaps fourteen years of age for confirmation.

"The dung needs to be dry," Nekhii explained. "Else it won't burn."

"Sometimes by the time we collect it, it's already dry enough," Jochi said. He held a large leather hide in his hand. "But most of the time we put it on the hide to dry out."

She watched as they examined the manure and scooped it into the hide.

Nearby one horse defecated and Lien scrunched her nose.

"We don't collect the fresh stuff," Shuren told her. "In summer, it's best to let it dry a couple of days in the field first." She passed Lien the scoop.

Good to know.

Lien examined the dung and with Nekhii's guidance she chose lumps to add to the collection. It didn't smell as bad as she'd feared, more like dried grass. None of the children was the least bit bothered. It was part of life and the way they contributed to the tribe's wellbeing. It was smart not to rely on only a few.

Shuren and Jochi, who was only a couple of years older than his sister, argued over the best pieces and the best way to teach Lien, with Nekhii stepping in to stop things from getting too heated.

Their relationship was sweet.

"We're done." Shuren grabbed Lien's hand. "Now Mother will teach you how to light a fire."

Lien followed her to their tent to discover Odval was their mother. Geriel and another girl, perhaps sixteen years in age were also inside.

"Welcome, Lien." Odval held her arms out in the traditional greeting and Lien responded in kind. "These are my oldest daughters, Geriel and Checheg. How was your lesson?"

"Enlightening," Lien replied.

Odval smiled. "Good. Let me show you how we use the dung to light our fires." She drew Lien into the tent to the central fire. The dung was dry and crumbled in Odval's hands. She built a little box out of the pieces, with one side open and then lit it, blowing on the embers until it caught alight. The smoke smelled like a grass fire. "Now you try." She smothered the fire and gestured Lien closer.

Lien smothered her grimace as she knelt by the fire and reached for the dung. It wasn't as disgusting as she'd thought it would be. After two false starts, she had the fire burning.

She grinned. She'd done it. Day by day she learnt new skills which would help her survive.

"Time to make lunch," Odval declared.

Lien got to her feet. She couldn't wait. In the palace only her training had ever challenged her whereas here, everything was new and different.

Her stomach squirmed. But that didn't mean she enjoyed living here more than the palace.

The palace had many advantages.

She just needed to remember what they were.

After lunch, Sukh handed her a saddle and she accompanied him to the horse pens. She scanned the horses and picked out Batu. A little thrill went through her.

"Put the saddle over the fence for the moment." He handed her a bridle. "Let's fetch Batu."

The leather was smooth in her hands. She followed the short man over to where Batu grazed and Sukh greeted the horse with a pat and a low murmur.

Suddenly the horse whinnied and reared back, its eyes wide. Lien leapt away from her hoofs as other horses scattered. Lien whirled around. Kew raced towards her, pleasure radiating from her.

Lien hurried to intercept. *Stop.*

The dragon did as she asked, her confusion clear.

You're scaring the horses. She turned to find Sukh had Batu under control. "I'm sorry. I'll ask Kew to stay away."

"You can communicate with her?" Sukh asked.

Lien nodded.

"Well maybe we can come to an understanding," Sukh said. He murmured something to Batu and then said to Lien, "Bring Kew over."

She gestured to Kew and together they walked to the horse. Batu snorted and tossed her head, but stayed where she was.

"Does Kew hunt?" Sukh asked.

"No. She's always been fed." To Kew she sent the thought, *The horses are friends, not for eating.*

Kew nodded.

Sukh squatted down. "Can I touch her?"

"Yes."

Kew let him stroke her and Batu lowered her head to sniff at her. Kew butted the horse's head with her nose and Sukh smiled. "I think they'll be friends." He stood. "But now we need to continue with your lesson. You put the bridle on like this." Sukh showed Lien how to put the bit between Batu's teeth and slip the leather over her ears. "Now you try."

She followed his instructions, stroking Batu's nose as she slipped it on and tied it.

"Good. Bring her over to the fence." He walked away.

She could do this. Holding the bridle under the horse's chin, she made a clicking noise like Sukh did and pulled Batu towards the fence. The horse followed her.

Sukh nodded his approval. "You're a fast learner. That's good. Tie her to the fence and we'll put on the saddle."

She circled the reins around the wood, tying them loosely.

Sukh put the saddle on his horse and cinched it. "You've got to be careful. The horses like to bloat their stomachs which means you must tighten the saddle again before you get on." He grinned. "Otherwise you'll slide straight off the other side."

It was impossible not to smile back at him. His grin was so wide and cheeky and full of humour.

When she'd successfully saddled Batu, Sukh told her to mount. "We'll go for a ride today."

Her stomach clenched. Did he mean out on the steppes? What if she got lost? Though Kew would find her. *Stay here while I ride.*

He helped her onto Batu and then mounted his own horse. "This way."

One child nearby opened and shut the gates for them and they rode out over the steppes. The low yellow grass rustled under the horses' hooves. The whole horizon was full of small undulating hills.

"How do you navigate when there are no markers to take reference from?"

"There are markers if you know where to look," Sukh replied with a chuckle.

Not to her eye. "It's all so vast. I wouldn't know Bonam existed if I hadn't come from there."

"Your people make themselves known, but we shouldn't see any of them this far from the border."

What did he mean? "How far are we?"

"A few days ride."

Which could be anywhere between thirty leagues or two hundred leagues depending on how fast they rode. Not helpful.

Sukh pushed his horse into a trot and Lien followed suit, unable to talk while she concentrated on keeping a steady rhythm and not bouncing out of the saddle. By the time he pulled his horse to a stop, her thighs ached. She glanced over her shoulder to see how far they'd come and her heart jumped. The camp had disappeared. They hadn't ridden very far. "Where's the camp?"

"Over that rise." Sukh pointed. "The steppes are deceptively hilly and you could lose your way if you came out alone."

She believed him. "How do I find my way back?"

"You need to learn to recognise the different shapes of the land." He beckoned her closer. "What shape do you see there?"

She squinted. "It looks a little like the curve of a horse's back."

He nodded. "And the rise over there?"

"It's more round, like the Empress's favourite headdress."

Sukh chuckled. "You need to remember the shapes, always checking behind you to make sure they look the same when you get over. Then you will recognise the land and the way back."

Lien frowned. It was a lot to remember.

"I want you to canter now. It's much easier than trotting if you relax into it." He cantered around her before stopping. "Your turn."

She could do this. She kicked Batu into a canter. The motion was soothing, a pleasant roll and the ground rushed by underfoot. The breeze on Lien's face was fresh and as Sukh rode past her, she urged Batu faster to catch up. He glanced at her and grinned, kicking his horse into a gallop. Lien couldn't resist. She wanted to catch him.

Batu thundered over the ground, drawing even with Sukh and a laugh ripped from Lien's mouth. She stiffened, the sound so unfamiliar.

What was she doing? She shouldn't be enjoying herself. She should be learning how to navigate and learning about the tribe, not having fun riding a horse. She slowed Batu, her heart thudding.

Sukh swung around and returned to her. "Is everything all right?"

"I didn't want to tire Batu."

"Don't worry. She could run for days." He leaned over and patted Batu's rump. "That was some impressive riding for someone who's never ridden."

Lien flushed. "I got carried away."

"It's hard not to when you embrace the freedom of the horse."

He was right. It was a freedom she'd never known. At the palace her every moment was monitored, her words watched.

Sukh glanced at the sun. "We should head back. I've got to get you to camp for weapon lessons with Amslan." He smiled at her. "Let's test what you've learnt. You can lead the way."

Oh, no. She'd not paid any attention to her

surroundings as she'd galloped after Sukh. She'd forgotten everything he'd taught her in the thrill of the moment. How could she have been so foolish?

Determined not to admit her mistake, she turned Batu and rode back in the direction they'd come. Maybe their hoof prints in the dirt would lead her the right way. But scanning the ground in front of her didn't reveal any discernible differences in the earth. She swallowed. Sukh gazed off to the side unconcerned.

He would know the way back if she failed.

The rise in front of her was on an angle, kind of pointed at one end. As good a place to start as any.

Lien scanned the land, hoping for something which would spark a memory, but though the rises differed from one another, they didn't appear familiar. The sun was still high in the sky and its heat burnt the top of her head, causing drops of sweat to trickle between her breasts. She had brought nothing to drink. Hadn't thought to. She should do so in future.

After a good space of time had elapsed, she conceded defeat. "Are we anywhere near camp?"

"I wondered how long it would take you to ask." He chuckled. "It's this way." He turned his horse ninety degrees.

Lien followed. "How could you keep track while we were riding so fast?"

"This land is my home, child. I recognise every hill and hollow. In time you will learn it too."

In time. Did she have time? She needed to get back to the palace, tell the emperor everything she had learnt, resolve the conflict between their countries. The twist of loss in her gut was unwelcome. She wouldn't be allowed to ride there, but only because it wasn't proper for a princess to be on a horse.

After they'd arrived back at camp and she'd taken

care of Batu, Sukh took Lien across the camp to the training ground. Several large targets were set up at a distance from the yurts and a group of teenagers and young adults waited.

Geriel left the group and ran to them. "Father, how was your ride?" She grinned at him, the same cheeky smile.

"Enjoyable. Lien is learning fast."

"That's good." Geriel took Lien's hand. "You can partner me if you'd like."

Lien let Geriel drag her over to the group, nodding a farewell to Sukh. If the emperor had taken a Rhoran wife, Yu and the empress would have left her floundering and forbidden any of the other women in her circle from approaching.

Amslan strode out in front of the group holding a bow and arrow. "We'll start with archery." He scanned the group and then smirked when he noticed Lien.

He wouldn't make it easy on her. And she had to pretend she had no skill with any of the weapons. An imperial princess did not need to fight.

She listened to his clear, concise instructions and then took the bow and arrow he handed her. "You're aiming for the target, not any people." His words were only loud enough for her.

She ignored him and waited for the others to take aim before following suit.

"Hold the bow like this and draw the arrow back," Amslan continued his instruction.

Lien held the bow loosely in her hand and set the arrow as Amslan had shown. She drew the arrow back, conscious Amslan observed her.

"Aim," he called.

She took aim at the target, a fur stretched across a frame.

"Fire."

Using her speed, she loosened the tension on the bow before releasing it so the arrow flew only a short distance before landing in the dirt. All the other students' arrows landed on target. She frowned and asked Amslan, "What did I do wrong?"

One boy laughed, but stopped when Amslan glared at him.

"More tension on the bow," Amslan said and ordered them to take aim again.

She sighted the large target, almost impossible to miss. Still she couldn't show them what she could do. She needed to keep her skills a secret, needed to make them believe she was helpless.

Again when he gave the command to release, she relaxed her hold too quickly for him to notice and the arrow flew a little further, but still hit the ground.

"Don't worry, Lien," Geriel said. "I took ages to get it right, didn't I, Amslan?"

He nodded.

It was sweet of Geriel to be encouraging. She held the bow with a competence of someone who'd done it many times before and she'd hit the bullseye each time. She would have been an asset to the emperor's bodyguard.

They worked through their quiver of arrows and with the last arrow, Amslan stood behind her, helping Lien draw out the string.

His whole body tensed and he murmured in her ear, "I know you can do this."

At the last moment before she released the string, she moved the bow so the arrow flew to the side, missing the target by about a foot.

Intense pleasure filled Lien at Amslan's frustrated growl. It made the whole charade more bearable.

He glared at her. "Let's practise with the sabres."

This would be more difficult. She couldn't block the attacks of her partner if she wanted to keep up her pretence. She turned to Geriel.

"Lien, you can spar with me," Amslan said.

Lien forced a smile. "You should teach not spar."

"I can teach by example, and Temur wants his betrothed to protect herself."

Did Temur want someone to beat her? "I would appreciate your help."

"Put up your guard."

Lien watched what the others did. She'd never used a sabre but she had practised with swords.

"Attack!"

Lien made a wide, clumsy swing with the sabre, opening herself up for attack and as she did, Amslan dodged her attempt and rapped her hard in the side with his blunted sabre. She bent over, gasping. So that's how it would be.

She gingerly straightened. "I left myself open, didn't I?"

He nodded and smiled. "You should keep your movements small and quick."

Lien bristled. He was enjoying this. She couldn't let her anger goad her into giving herself away.

"Like this?" She made her movement smaller, but still slow and didn't block his counter-attack which hit her other side. She winced in pain.

Amslan smirked. "That's better, but you need to change direction in an instant to block. You need to be much faster."

Lien pushed down her temper. The only person who could beat her in one on one combat was Master Ying. This man couldn't. Still she had an image to uphold. "Could you show me how to block again?"

"Give me your best shot."

It was a dare Lien refused to take. She kept her attack small and only slightly faster than her previous one, bracing herself for the impact. Amslan's sabre blocked hers and the vibrations rattled through it, numbing her arm so she dropped the weapon as he followed with a stab to her stomach. Her breath rushed out of her and she crumpled to the ground, making her expression distressed.

"Amslan!" Geriel hurried to her side.

"She's winded." He knelt next to her with a show of concern. "You must learn to protect yourself, Princess. Perhaps we should have private sessions."

That was the last thing she needed. "What a kind offer, Amslan." She sucked in more air and sat up. "Unfortunately all my time is taken up preparing for the wedding and learning about the tribe. Perhaps after I am married I will have time for private lessons." She wouldn't be able to walk if Amslan insisted.

"I'll discuss it with Temur."

Would he agree? "Thank you for your concern." She got to her feet with Geriel's help. "Are we finished for the day?"

"Yes."

"Then I will see you tomorrow." She bid the others farewell and walked back to her tent. As she shut the door behind her, she clutched her sides and slid to the ground, her whole torso aching.

Amslan really was a barbarian.

~*~

A few minutes later someone knocked on the door. Lien forced herself to stand, took a couple of deep breaths against the pain and brushed down her caftan. She needed to pretend all was well. Opening the door, she found Temur standing there with a bowl of water, some bags of herbs and a cloth in his hand.

Lien stepped back.

"Amslan tells me he trained with you today." Temur moved forward into the tent and Lien had no choice but to let him in. "I thought you might need healing." He set the items on the table.

What?

"Come and sit on the table, my *bayar*, and let me tend to you."

Lien stared at him. At the imperial palace, women tended the men, not the other way around.

He continued to watch her.

His kindness and courtesy made it difficult to remember he could be the enemy. The emperor had wanted him dead. She ignored the way her heart fluttered when he met her gaze. It must be a response to the potential danger he presented.

She walked over and lowered herself to sit on the table.

"Where did he hit you?" Temur asked as he rinsed the cloth in the water and squeezed it out, sprinkling herbal oil on to it.

"My ribs."

"Lift your top and let me see."

Blood rushed to her face. She would do no such thing. It wasn't proper.

His warm and soothing chuckle distracted her as he unwound her sash.

She grabbed his hand, stopping him from lifting the fabric.

"My *bayar*, we are to be wed. There is nothing to be shy about." His eyes held hers, capturing her and she released his hand.

She shouldn't trust him like this. She had to

remember her mission was unclear and until she returned to the palace, she should keep her distance from him.

He lifted her caftan and swore, gently running his hands over her stomach and sides.

Lien shivered. His touch made her insides dance. She blinked and pushed his hands away.

"I am sorry he has hurt you, my *bayar*. I will have words to him over this," he growled.

Purpling bruises covered her midsection.

Temur took the cloth and softly pressed it against the bruises. The cold soothed and she closed her eyes.

"Is keeping your skills a secret worth this pain?"

Lien's eyes flew open, shock rushing through her.

"You must be able to defend yourself. You're an assassin." His hands moved across her stomach, sending warmth to her toes.

She needed to ignore her body's reaction. It was purely physical. "Then why make me take these lessons?"

"The tribe expects it. You are learning our ways and it would be strange if you didn't."

She was tired of these games. The Rhoran weren't so honourable. They had killed her parents. "You say they are defensive lessons, but the Rhoran attack as well."

Temur shook his head. "Only when attacked first."

"That's not true! Your people attacked my family unprovoked. They slaughtered my parents and my brother while they were travelling to Chungson."

Temur glanced at her, eyes wide. "When?"

"Eighteen years ago."

He frowned. "We were at peace with Bonam then. I remember the first war between our countries because I'd just turned eleven and wanted to fight. That was seventeen years ago."

"Perhaps that's what started the war."

"I will ask Father about it. I'm sorry about your family. You must have been young." The sympathy in his eyes cooled her anger.

"I was five." So many times she'd wished she hadn't been sick and been forced to stay at home, instead of going to Chungson with her family. She hissed as he pressed too hard on one bruise.

"I'm sorry." His thumb caressed the spot.

Lien didn't dare move. Sensations flashed through her body, running up and down before pooling low in her torso. How could he make her feel like this? It should repulse her. He was a barbarian, he was her enemy—he was her betrothed. Was this the way husband and wife should behave?

Temur continued to wash her bruises and she refused to meet his gaze. Her confusion would be easy to see.

He sighed. "Let's get dinner." He moved away to clean up and Lien retied her sash.

She was cold now without his touch, but that was a good thing. After she'd told the emperor what she knew, he wouldn't need her to marry the khan. She couldn't get attached to Temur or the tribe.

Her heart was heavy as Temur took her hand and led her out of the tent.

The sooner she got back to the palace, the better.

~*~

It was a quarter moon before Sukh allowed Lien to ride out on the steppes by herself. He was confident she would find her way home again and it was the first time she'd been by herself since she'd arrived. She lifted her gaze to the sky as she cantered, the wind rushing past her. Laughter bubbled inside her and she released it with joy. This was the perfect way to end a day.

She froze.

No. That wasn't right. It couldn't be.

She couldn't be happy here.

She slowed Batu to a walk.

The past quarter moon had been a lot nicer than she'd expected. She enjoyed learning new things and each day had added to her knowledge: she could dismantle and erect a yurt, she could make a bow and fletch an arrow—though she would need practice to be any good at it—she'd learnt how to make and repair a bridle and each day she'd made a different dish for dinner.

She felt useful, part of the community in a way she never had at the palace.

Lien grimaced. That was blasphemous.

The emperor needed her loyalty, she had to educate him so the conflict ended and no one else died. She frowned.

Why didn't he know what the Rhoran were like? He was God's representative. Why hadn't he asked God for guidance?

Perhaps that's not the way it worked.

It shocked her how misinformed the emperor and Master Ying were. Almost everything they'd told her about the Rhoran was untrue. The Rhoran weren't unintelligent and they weren't barbarians, they just had a different way of living to the Bonamese.

Guilt punched her stomach hard. How could she even dare to question the emperor—to believe he was wrong?

She crested a small rise. In the gully, a lone figure rode slumped over the front of his horse. She tensed, checking the surroundings, but no one else was around. The rider appeared injured, but it could be a ruse. Lien drew her sabre and moved to intercept him.

As she rode closer, his clothing identified him as Rhoran, but he didn't stir as she rode up beside him.

Protruding from his back was an arrow, the red fletchings identifying it as one of the Bonamese Imperial Army.

She tensed, expecting riders to crest the hill in front of her.

Her heart pounding, she reached over to shake him.

No response.

His pulse was slow, barely there. She had to get him back to camp.

Why did he have a Bonamese arrow in his back? He could be a spy, a threat to the emperor. Perhaps she shouldn't help him.

No, she couldn't leave him here like this. He might have family in camp, someone she'd sewn with, or chatted to. She could never face them again if she did nothing.

Dismounting from Batu, she then mounted behind the man, being careful not to disturb the arrow. She kicked his horse into a canter, holding Batu's reins in one hand and her other arm around the man so he didn't fall.

Where had this man been to be attacked by the Bonamese? The question made her nauseous.

As she rode into camp she called to the first person she saw, "Get Temur and a healer." She slid off the horse as others came running.

"What happened?" Temur was by her side.

"I found him unconscious, slumped over his horse. No one else was around."

Several men lifted the man off the horse and carried him into the healer's tent.

"I don't know who he is."

Temur's eyes flashed. "I sent Chinua to notify the other tribes of our wedding. When he didn't return we assumed he would travel with one group."

His anger was palpable in his stiff posture, his hard stare.

Did he blame her?

If he was telling the truth, Chinua had no reason to be anywhere near the Bonamese border.

A couple of the gathered crowd glared at her, their suspicion clear. The arrow was Bonamese and Lien was Bonamese.

They no longer trusted her—if they ever had. Master Ying was right about enemies pretending to be friends. The generosity and sincerity *had* been a show.

And she'd fallen for it, like the fool she was. "I will take care of the horses."

Temur nodded and headed for the healer's yurt. As Lien gathered the reins and led the horses back to the herd, people whispered and stared.

Kew trotted up to her and rubbed against her leg.

She had one friend here. She would take her and go, leave the steppes forever and return to the palace where she belonged. Where she was an imperial princess and expected to behave as such. Where servants did all of her bidding and no one expected her to learn new things.

The pang was painful.

No, she didn't want to be a part of the tribe. She wanted to help the emperor.

She unsaddled both horses and brushed Chinua's horse which was lathered in sweat. Where was her loyalty to her people?

But who were her people now?

The emperor had given her away like she was a bolt of silk without the slightest explanation.

But the Rhoran were now suspicious of her.

Confused thoughts battered her mind. She had to get away. After she turned Chinua's horse back into the herd, she swung up on Batu's back.

Stay here, she ordered Kew.

Kicking her horse into motion, she let Batu have her head.

They flew over the steppes together, going faster than Lien had gone before. She held on as Sukh had taught her, letting the speed wash her mind clear. They rode hard for some time before Batu slowed.

Lien directed Batu up the small rise before she dismounted, rotating in a full circle to ensure she was alone. Batu's breath was heavy and she'd worked up a lather of sweat.

"Sorry, lady." Lien stroked her nose and gathered up some sparse vegetation to wipe her down. "I didn't mean to run you so hard."

Batu pushed her head into Lien's shoulder and then grazed on the grass.

Lien paced.

She'd been so busy learning about the Rhoran that she'd lost sight of her mission.

But what was her true mission?

As far as the Rhoran were concerned, she was Temur's betrothed.

In the Bonamese culture, when a woman married, she moved into her husband's house and became part of his family. While she could still visit her siblings and parents, they were no longer considered part of her family. To the emperor and the rest of the Bonamese, when she married Temur she would no longer be an imperial princess. She would be Rhoran.

Is that what the emperor wanted? Or had it been an excuse for her to get close enough to kill him?

She had no idea.

The emperor was enigmatic at the best of times.

If the emperor got to know Temur, she was sure he would like him. They needed to spend time together, discuss issues openly without fear.

The breeze blew loose strands of her hair across her face and she pushed them back.

But what about Temur's claim the emperor had tried to kill her?

It couldn't be true. She was loyal and had trained hard to be the best fighter in the bodyguard. She was family. The emperor didn't want her dead.

Before her attack, Temur had moved her and the man she'd come to know didn't strike her as the type to use a woman as a shield. Temur was more honourable.

Wasn't he?

So why had Li Ping attacked her?

Her stomach churned.

The only way to get answers was to return to the palace. She'd told Bolormaa she wanted to collect some of her things before she married. Now she had to make it happen.

Batu snorted and nudged her shoulder.

Lien blinked. The sun was low in the sky. She had been out here for too long. Time to return to camp, to discover the truth and move forward. She mounted Batu and set off.

Chapter 7

It was almost dark when Lien arrived back at the herd, where both Kew and Sukh waited for her.

"I wondered where you'd got to." Sukh held on to Batu's bridle and waited for Lien to dismount.

"I went for a ride." Lien retrieved the brushes from the box, while Kew wrapped herself around her ankles, her unhappiness clear.

I'm sorry. I had to get away. She ran a hand over Kew before turning back to Batu.

Sukh rested his hand on her shoulder. "It must have been distressing for you to find Chinua. I hope you're feeling better now."

Her chest squeezed. "Thank you." A sweet man. He and his family had all been so kind to her and Geriel was fast becoming her friend. If this was an act, then she was happy to be fooled.

"I'll take care of Batu." Sukh took the brushes from her. "Temur asked to see you when you returned."

Lien's stomach clenched. Would he tell her she was no longer welcome? "Thank you." She gave Batu a final pat and set off towards Temur's tent with Kew trotting next to her.

As she went through the camp she passed a group of men chatting. They stopped speaking, their gazes following her.

Kew snorted.

Lien's stomach churned, but she lifted her head high as she continued walking. This was more how she'd expected to be treated from the beginning. It should not surprise her or hurt as much as it did.

She smiled at two women who had taught her to fletch and their answering smiles were more cautious.

She swallowed the lump in her throat. Show no emotion, be calm. She pictured the faces of her family.

Taking a breath, she knocked on the door to Temur's yurt. Light spilled out as Amslan opened the door and behind him sat the old warriors around the table, their faces grim. She was interrupting some kind of war council. "Temur asked to see me."

"How nice of you to rejoin us." Amslan barred her way. "You should come back later."

"Amslan, let her in," Temur called. "She might be able to help."

Bracing herself, Lien entered and stood at the edge of the room, unsure where she should go. Kew was her default brown colour, unconcerned. Lien scanned the steely stares of the men until she reached Temur at the head of the table. "How is Chinua?"

"He's recovering thanks to Amslan's work." Temur gestured for her to sit at the end of the table.

Amslan? What had he done?

The weight of her sabre at her side comforted her. Sitting, she asked, "Has he said why he was shot?"

"He was shot because he's Rhoran," Amslan growled. "He was shot because he found some Bonamese on our land and they wanted no witnesses to what they were doing."

Lien ignored his animosity. He had a right to be upset. "And what were they doing?"

"Searching for something," Temur cut in. "Can you tell us what?"

She had no idea. "The emperor is building a wall along the border."

The men around the table laughed and Temur asked, "Do you know why?"

She hesitated. She wanted to win their trust back and it wasn't a secret. "The emperor hoped it would stop the raids."

A burst of derisive laughter, this time from Amslan.

"Let me tell you the truth," Temur said. "This wall your uncle is building is several leagues inside Rhoran borders, capturing most of the little fertile land we have. He is using any Rhoran he captures and Bonamese political prisoners to build it. No walls will keep us out if we want to attack Bonam." Temur's glare pierced through her defences.

His restrained anger was magnificent, the coldness in his eyes, the tension in his muscles. He would be a formidable enemy. She didn't doubt he believed what he said. Even if he was wrong.

"But the men Chinua found were further inside our territory and quite a distance from the wall," he continued.

She bowed her head. "I don't know what they are doing. I'm sorry." This was her chance. "Perhaps you could ask the emperor yourself," she said. "I would like to return to the palace to gather things I left behind. You could come with me." She held her breath.

"Perhaps," Temur said. He gestured for her to go, so like the emperor dismissing someone.

Lien sucked in a sharp breath as she bowed. He was very angry. Worry swirled in her stomach as she left the tent, with Kew alongside her. She was used to the animosity from Amslan but Temur and the other men concerned her. She'd thought they'd accepted her. If they distrusted her, they wouldn't allow her to return to the palace.

And she desperately needed to.

Lien entered her tent where she found Erdene waiting for her.

"I wanted to check how you are. It must have been a shock to find Chinua."

Her words mirrored Sukh's. Did they believe her so weak? "It was." Motioning for Erdene to sit, she said, "Tell me, was he badly injured?" She took a cushion at the table opposite the woman.

"He lost so much blood and the wound got infected on his journey back here. If Amslan wasn't such a good healer, Chinua would have died."

Lien frowned. "Amslan is a healer?"

"He's our best."

No one had ever mentioned it. "Where did the attack happen?"

Erdene hesitated. "You should ask Temur."

"Temur is busy and you know as much as he." Amslan would have confided in her.

Sighing, Erdene said, "He was returning to camp when he noticed people in the distance. Thinking they must be Rhoran, he rode over to invite them to the wedding and discovered they were Bonamese."

"How many?"

"Too many for him to take on by himself. They chased him, but he escaped."

It had to be a lot. Single Rhoran men had attacked parties of ten before.

"Our people are upset," Erdene continued. "They want to blame someone and you remind them of our enemy. Try not to let their animosity bother you. It won't last long."

Lien frowned. "Will Temur lose the tribe's respect and the role of khan if he marries me?"

"No. The khan may marry who he chooses, but there may be people who don't appreciate him choosing a Bonamese wife."

"He had little choice."

Erdene raised her eyebrows. "There is always a choice."

She was right.

"Do you not wish to marry him?"

Lien pressed her lips together considering her answer. "I would prefer not to cause problems for Temur. Amslan is very outspoken against me. I'm uncertain how your election of a khan works, but surely Amslan can become khan?"

Erdene laughed. "Amslan doesn't want to rule. He's Temur's best friend. He just doesn't trust any Bonamese. His parents are missing and presumed captured by your people. He is worried about them. I'm surprised Temur hasn't told him to keep his dislike to himself—at least in front of the others. I'll have a word to him."

That explained things. "Thank you."

Erdene stood. "If there's nothing else I can do for you I will go. You should sleep, you've had a busy day."

Lien nodded. "Goodnight."

After Erdene left, Lien cleaned up and climbed into bed, Kew curling up around her feet.

Should she press the point about returning to the palace? She needed answers, but she couldn't afford for Temur to suspect her motives.

She would broach the subject again tomorrow.

And hope for the best.

~*~

Lien woke, instantly alert, her heart pounding. In the darkness she made out the shape of a person bending over her. Were they here to kill her? Did they blame her for Chinua's injury? As the person leaned closer, she grabbed their throat. "Who are you?"

"It's Amslan." His voice strained. "You shouldn't be able to move so fast."

She kept her hand steady. She couldn't let her guard down. "What do you want?"

Amslan shifted, breaking from her hold. "Temur requested your attendance questioning our prisoners."

Prisoners? She sat up. Had they caught the Bonamese who had trespassed? She wanted to know why they were there as much as the Rhoran did. "Wait outside, while I get dressed."

Amslan hesitated, then walked out of the tent.

When the door clicked shut, she got out of bed and dressed. She almost tripped over Kew lying on the floor. "Thank you for the warning."

Kew opened an eye, the white showing against the darkness in the tent. She closed it again unperturbed. Did that mean she didn't consider Amslan a threat? Could Kew be tricked? Or more alarmingly, could Amslan be trusted?

You can come with me, tell me if the men are speaking the truth.

Kew groaned and got to her feet.

As they exited the yurt, Amslan spun around, his posture stiff.

"This way." He led her through the camp to a tent on the outskirts where two guards stood outside. The guards nodded at Amslan as he went in. Kew glanced at them as she walked past, a wariness to her step. These men didn't like Lien.

Lien scanned the tent. Several Rhoran warriors sat around a table eating and drinking. Temur looked up and said in Bonamese, "Princess Lien, perhaps you will get better results questioning the prisoners."

At her name the two Bonamese straightened their stance. They were naked from the waist up, covered in dirt and blood, with bruises over their torsos. Their hands were tied above their heads to a pole which ran along the roof line, their torsos stretched long and their knees bowed. Exhaustion and defeat lined their faces.

Though their pants were grubby, there was no mistaking their red colour.

Lien's skin flashed hot. These were no ordinary soldiers. They were from Prince Kun's imperial guard.

They shouldn't be so far from the imperial palace.

The man on the left tried to fall to his knees but his bonds held him in place. He kept his head lowered, while the other man glared at her.

Insolence. Her chest squeezed.

These men knew the protocols. They knew how to respond when faced with the imperial family. Something was very wrong here. Walking closer to the prisoners she asked Temur, "What answers do you want?"

Temur switched to Rhoran. "I want to know why they are on my land."

She addressed the man with his head lowered first. "There is no need to kneel as you are restrained."

"You are not Bonamese. You are Rhoran scum." The man on the right spat at her feet.

She froze. Never had a Bonamese treated her with such disrespect. Temur backhanded the man. "Do not insult my betrothed."

The soldier gaped at him before lowering his head. "My apologies, State Princess. I thought you had already married."

Had Kun told him to treat her this way, or was it the man's own prejudices showing? She folded her arms, kept her gaze serene while her insides swirled. "Why has First Prince Kun sent you to Rhora?"

The man who had tried to kneel hesitated before saying, "We cannot tell you, State Princess."

"Even in these lands you must still obey imperial commands and I command you to tell me why you are here."

"We were scouting areas for the new wall," the man who spat at her said, moving ever so slightly as if trying to loosen his bonds.

Kew walked past his feet and puffed out fire. The man yelled and jumped to avoid the flames.

"You are lying," Lien said. "The punishment for lying to a member of the imperial family is beheading." She wouldn't carry out the threat, but she wanted to instil fear into them.

The man paled. Turning her back on the prisoners to give them time to sweat, she almost collided with Temur who strode past her.

Thunk.

One prisoner yelled as the smell of blood filled the air.

She flinched, the blood draining from her face. No. He couldn't have. She gritted her teeth as bile rose in her throat. She couldn't react, couldn't let her disgust show. Couldn't show the Rhoran warriors or the prisoner how much the beheading affected her.

Kew wound around her ankles and Lien breathed shallowly, the smell making her dizzy.

"Amslan, take the princess outside while we clean up," Temur said.

She inclined her head at the order and Amslan held

her arm, guiding her out of the tent so he was between her and the scene behind. She gripped him as her legs threatened to collapse under her. No. Sheer willpower had her strengthening her stance and letting go. Show no weakness.

As they got outside Lien gulped in fresh breaths of air, hoping he wouldn't notice.

Amslan led her away from the guards. "Sit down, before you faint." He pushed her gently to the ground.

She didn't fight him, sinking to her knees and lowering her head. She swallowed to clear the lump in her throat and when she spoke, her voice was calm. "I did not expect Temur to behead the man."

"That's obvious." Amslan squatted down next to her. "How can you be an assassin if you nearly faint at a beheading? Or is this another one of your acts?"

She didn't answer him. She couldn't tell him the truth.

The silence stretched, long and uncomfortable.

Finally Temur came out and knelt down next to her. "Are you all right, my *bayar*?" He took her hand and caressed it.

She wanted to snatch it back—he had just killed a man in cold blood—but she understood why he had. He had to show he was serious about getting answers. The remaining prisoner may be more willing to talk. "I did not mean for you to kill him."

"He needed to pay for his disrespect to you."

That wasn't the main reason he'd done it, but she pretended to believe him. "Of course." She hesitated. "Do you want me to return and ask more questions?"

"If you are up to it," Temur said.

Lien would do what he required of her. "Yes."

Temur stood and helped her up. "I appreciate your help. I know it is late, but we need to prepare in case an attack is imminent." He ran his hands down her arms. "Shall we go?"

They had removed the body and placed some furs over the ground where the prisoner had stood. The remaining Bonamese had blood spatter on his face and kept his head lowered, his whole posture defeated.

He believed he would die. With nothing to bargain with, would he talk? "Why were you in Rhoran territory?"

The man met her eyes briefly before staring at the floor. "We came looking for you, State Princess."

Her skin prickled. Why would Kun search for her?

Temur translated for the men who didn't speak Bonamese and the Rhoran murmured.

"Do you have a message for me?"

"No, State Princess." He swallowed. "First Prince Kun ordered us to find and kill you to preserve your honour from having to marry one of these barbarians." He sneered at the Rhoran.

Shock rippled through her. Kun had always been kind to her during training. Did he care so much he wanted to protect her? She kept her tone even as she asked, "The emperor himself gave me to the khan. Why would the First Prince presume to overrule him?"

"I don't know, your Highness."

Kew turned an emerald green and circled around Lien. It was the truth.

"Were you not concerned the emperor would discover what you had done and punish you?"

The soldier's eyes widened. "No. If the barbarians cared enough to tell him it would be our word against theirs. Everyone knows the barbarians are liars."

Temur's mouth drew into a tight line, his eyes cold. "That will do. You may return to your bed."

Lien hesitated. She was wide awake and had more

questions. But it wasn't her place. "Shall I leave Kew here? She will turn green if the man is telling the truth." And Lien might get a sense of what they discussed from her dragon.

Temur nodded. "Thank you."

Lien knelt in front of Kew. *Stay here and help Temur, please.*

Kew blew warm air in her face and nodded.

Thank you. She rose. "I will see you in the morning."

"Amslan, accompany the princess back to her tent," Temur said.

She wanted to be alone. "It is not necessary." Lien left, not waiting for Amslan. She needed time to process the information. Intrigue amongst the emperor's children wasn't uncommon but she had no claim to the throne, no reason to be targeted unless it was because of her failure. Had Kun known what she had been ordered to do and wanted to punish her?

The despair was a heavy lump in her stomach. She blinked back tears and forced herself to take long, steadying breaths. She gazed up at the clear night sky, the stars bright. If only her parents were here to guide her, to tell her what she had done wrong.

Amslan fell into step beside her. She wanted to order him to leave her, but her orders meant nothing here. Instead she didn't acknowledge him. They walked in silence before he said, "I don't trust you."

Lien didn't bother looking at him. "I know."

"You're one of our enemy and you're keeping secrets."

"You may believe that if you wish."

He grabbed her arm, forcing her to stop and face him. "I do." His grip tightened and the animosity came off him in waves before he let go. "You're not who you seem. You were shocked when Temur killed the soldier."

"Yes." There was no point denying it. He was an intelligent man. Lien continued towards her tent and as she reached for the door handle he said, "If you do anything to harm Temur or Erdene, I will kill you."

She expected nothing less. Inclining her head, she said, "Temur said much the same thing." She shut the door behind her.

Amslan swore and his footsteps faded away.

Lien closed her eyes. No one had ever felt that passionately about her, no one would kill someone if she was harmed. She shouldn't envy Erdene but she did.

Moving over to the table, she sank onto the cushions.

The smell of blood hung in the air like a phantom and in the silence, the thunk of the beheading echoed in her ears. She could visualise it, imagine the blood spatter, the head flying off, the pool of blood spurting from his neck.

She pulled a bowl closer and dry retched into it. Bile rose, the acrid taste filling her mouth and she spat it out. On and on she heaved until she was empty. Tears ran down her face, not for the man who'd died but for what he represented.

Kun wanted her dead.

Was it because she had failed in her mission to kill Temur?

Or had he been behind the initial attack on her as Temur had suggested?

Was he carrying out orders from the emperor?

Wiping her face with a cloth, she crawled to bed and curled into a tight ball. Tears welled in her eyes again. She had been so *sure* of her place, so certain she was the best person to protect the emperor. But she was wrong.

Temur was still alive and she was in the Rhoran camp clueless as to what she had to do.

She was useless. Worthless.

A failure.

She sobbed until sleep finally rescued her.

~*~

"Good morning, Lien. It's time to get up."

Lien pried her eyes apart, squinting at the bright light from the lantern Erdene had lit on the table. It was still night. Had she just fallen asleep? Wiping the sleep from her eyes, she sat, her head muggy, her eyes heavy. "What time is it?"

Kew climbed onto the bed and bumped her head against Lien's.

Lien closed her eyes as her dragon sent her images. The prisoners, the beheading, Kun wanting her dead. Her chest tightened. Kew followed the images with an overwhelming feeling of love. Someone still cared for her.

"Just before dawn." The smile on Erdene's face faded. "Are you all right? You look awful."

Lien grimaced. "Could you get me some water?"

"Yes, of course."

The pounding in her head made it hard to focus. She swallowed, her throat raw. "Why are you waking me so early?"

"You're leaving for the imperial palace this morning to collect your things."

Her skin prickled. She was going back? What else had Temur learnt while questioning the prisoner?

Erdene handed her a cup of water. "Here you go."

"Thank you." Lien drank it slowly. "Who is coming with me?"

"A few warriors. Temur wants to go via the

borderland to check the wall, so he and Amslan are going and Sukh will be there as well."

Lien rose and dressed, her mind racing. If she went back to the palace, would Kun try to kill her again? She had to ensure they travelled under the emissary flag to be safe, until she spoke with him. Then she could talk to the emperor and Master Ying and tell them what she'd learnt.

They would be pleased with her and the conflict between Rhora and Bonam would be over. Then the emperor would resolve the issue of her betrothal to the khan.

Lien followed Erdene towards Temur's yurt. Inside he and Amslan ate breakfast.

Temur smiled at Lien. "My *bayar*, has Erdene told you the good news? You can return to the palace to pick up your things."

Lien knelt at the table. "Yes, she has. Thank you for this opportunity." Amslan stared at her. "It will be wonderful to visit my family." Only it wasn't true. She wanted to speak to Kun and the emperor, but the palace itself held no appeal.

"We will leave as soon as you've eaten," Temur said. "It is a long journey, but Sukh has assured me you will be fine on Batu."

"I will enjoy it." It was the arrival at the palace that concerned her. What kind of welcome would she receive?

He stood. "Amslan and I will check the preparations. Please meet us at the horses within the hour."

She inclined her head.

Erdene sat next to her as the men left the tent. "I have a bag you can take for your clothes. I'll bring it to your tent when we return. What items did you want to gather at the palace?"

"Some of my mother's jewellery," Lien said. "And a few fragrances which may be useful, but most of my clothing is not appropriate." She smiled. "I can not imagine riding wearing my gowns."

"No, things are different here," Erdene agreed.

But she was becoming accustomed to them. And that was part of the problem. She enjoyed learning new things, enjoyed riding across the steppes, and talking to people as she worked, even enjoyed watching the children play. How would she adjust to palace life if the emperor wanted her back?

And what would she do if he ordered her to kill Temur? Or ordered her death?

After last night, returning to the palace no longer held the appeal it once did, but she would do as she was bid.

Just like the perfect imperial princess.

Chapter 8

The sun had risen above the horizon as Lien left her tent, Kew by her side. In the horse yard, ten male warriors packed supplies and prepared their mounts, taking extra horses to travel faster. Lien saddled and bridled Batu. She was the only female going, something the Bonamese would consider unseemly.

Kew trotted next to her, exuding displeasure about the journey.

You stay here. You can't keep up.

Kew snorted, blowing smoke out of her nose. Batu shied away and Lien held tight to her bridle to stop her from running.

"What's wrong?" Sukh hurried over.

"Kew wants to come with me."

Sukh crouched down to Kew. "You need to stay here. We'll be travelling too fast for you."

Kew turned her head away.

Sukh sighed and stood. "We'll start out at a canter and it will stop her from following."

The dragon coughed.

"I don't think it will work."

"Mount up, everyone," Temur called.

Having Kew with them would be a comfort and would also enable Lien to tell whether anyone was lying to her, but she couldn't say that to Temur. She had to pretend this trip was about getting her things back.

"Lien, is there a problem?" Temur asked.

"Kew wants to come with us."

Temur pursed his lips and asked Sukh, "Could she ride a horse?"

Lien blinked. Why would he let her come? Unless he wanted to use Kew's skills. Was there more to this trip?

"Maybe." Sukh was quiet a long moment and then dismounted. "Batu's willing. I'll hold her head while you both get on."

How did he know what Batu wanted?

Lien communicated the option to Kew who grunted. *You ride Batu, or you'll stay here.*

Kew blew out smoke but flapped her small wings to hover above Batu and Lien guided her on to the horse's back behind the saddle.

Kew dug her claws in and Batu skittered sideways.

"Settle," Sukh soothed.

After a few minutes both animals settled and Lien mounted. "Thank you, Sukh."

"My pleasure." He remounted and Temur gave the command to leave the camp.

Halfway through the third day of their journey, Temur rode up next to Lien. "Come with me." He and a few of the warriors broke off from the party and headed east.

Lien trotted after him, Kew grumbling at the jolting movement. Both dragon and horse had accommodated to each other well, with Kew walking when the party walked, and riding Batu when they went any faster.

As they crested a rise, the infamous wall stretched

out across the steppes. The structure loomed two and a half times the height of the Hall of Clarity and about fifteen yards wide. So many workers digging, and hauling stone and bricks. Hot and dusty work.

"You need to witness the construction," Temur said when she joined him.

One worker captured her attention. From the distance he appeared small and emaciated, his actions slow and exhausted. He dug his shovel in, but it skimmed across the ground and the man stumbled and fell. He needed food and rest. Where was a supervisor?

She scanned the people and spotted a man dressed in a blue uniform approaching the prone body.

He would help.

The supervisor shouted, prodded the body with the toe of his shoe and then whipped it several times, the crack carrying across the land to Lien.

Her breath caught in her throat. The man needed help not punishment. The body didn't move although the supervisor whipped him a couple more times.

She gaped. How dare he! The supervisor needed to be stopped, *he* needed to be whipped.

She dug her heels into Batu's sides and the horse responded, bursting into a canter.

"Lien!" Temur called.

She ignored him. She would discover this man's name and report him to the emperor.

Temur galloped up alongside her, using his horse to turn Batu, and grabbed the reins to pull the horse to a halt. "Wait!"

She glared at him. "What are you doing? That man must be stopped."

"And how are you going to stop him?" Temur demanded. "If you charge towards the wall in Rhoran clothing, they will think you're attacking and shoot you.

Do you want to die?"

Lien glanced over at the shouts of alarm and the guards forming a line of defence. They wouldn't hit her, but they might hit Batu or Kew. He was right. "Then we walk over."

He shook his head. "It's too dangerous and too late." He nodded towards the wall.

The supervisor motioned to two other workers who picked up the body and threw it on to the sand and stone construction of the wall. Seconds later dirt covered it.

Lien blinked, unable to comprehend. They had just buried the man in the wall.

Even if he had died of exhaustion, it was no way to treat the deceased. They required ceremonies and the soul had to be released. She pressed a hand against her stomach. "This isn't right."

"No, it's not. But the emperor doesn't care."

She glanced at him. "He can't know about this."

Temur raised his eyebrows.

She wouldn't believe it. The emperor got reports from all over the empire, but perhaps the supervisors didn't include the deaths of workers. The emperor wouldn't be this callous, this cruel.

"Let's go back." As she approached the group, Amslan said, "It's lovely how the Bonamese treat their people."

Lien had no words. For once she agreed with him. How could the emperor boast about the efficient and successful wall building when his people were being worked to death?

"We must catch up with the others," Temur said.

With the image of the man being buried replaying in her mind, she followed. Suddenly returning to the palace was essential. She needed to tell the emperor the truth, to explain his men were lying to him about the Rhoran and the wall, and who knew what else. He needed to be informed.

He wasn't a monster.

~*~

It was nearing midday the next day when they approached the imperial city, its red walls contrasting against the lush countryside. The horses' hooves clopped against the paved brick road and the tall trees in the surrounding forest shaded them all. Not long now and they would move out of the trees and onto the plain which surrounded the city, making any sneak attack from an enemy impossible. Kew trotted alongside Batu, occasionally darting off into the trees and then back again. The red in the distance was a jewel, a statement, protection against all those outside its barriers.

Lien would go straight to the emperor, tell him all she had learnt. The image of the man dying at the wall haunted her as did her confusion. The emperor was supposed to be omniscient and if that was true, then he had to know about the way the builders were treated.

Sukh carried the white flag of emissary, granting them safe passage. The guards on the walls watched their approach, but word would have already reached the palace of a Rhoran group riding towards the city.

"Almost there," Temur said as he fell back to walk with her.

She nodded.

"How are you feeling?"

"It is a little strange to see the city again. It's so red."

He laughed. "It is. Like a fatal wound on an animal."

She flinched as he kicked his horse into a trot.

A thick twang reached her ears. Instinctively she twisted as an arrow flew towards her. She gasped, brought her arm up to deflect it. The white feather fletching brushed along the back of her arm before the head buried deep into her back. Pain shot through her and she slumped forward, grunting. "Arrow!"

Around her the Rhoran warriors yelled and formed a barrier around Temur. She gasped and tasted blood as it dribbled from her mouth. The pain was hot fire deep in her chest.

Only the secret bodyguard used arrows with white fletching.

Had the archer been aiming for Temur?

Her body grew heavy and each breath was like breathing underwater.

"Amslan! Heal her," Temur yelled as he grabbed Batu's reins and the group rode out of the trees on to the field.

Batu's gait was too jerky, too much. Each step was pure torture and she couldn't hold on. Her strength drained away, her head dizzy.

She bent over Batu's neck, tried to cling to her mane, but her fingers wouldn't grip. She slid to the right.

Amslan leapt on behind her, swearing as he did so. He stopped her slide. "Hold on. This will hurt." He ripped out the arrow and ice-cold agony shattered her skin.

Then his hands covered the wound and heat replaced the cold. Fierce licks of fire darted over her skin like lightning.

She squeezed her eyes closed, gritted her teeth.

"Stay with me," Amslan growled.

She didn't want to. The pain was too much. Somewhere in the distance Kew bellowed in rage.

"Kew." Was she hurt?

"She's in the forest chasing your attacker," Amslan said, his voice strained.

The fierce fire melded into warmth. Did the pain disappear just before death?

"Amslan?" Temur called.

"It's done." His arms wrapped around her, securing her against him and he nudged Batu closer to Temur.

Why was he being kind?

Lien opened her eyes. They were halfway between the forest and the city gates, all the warriors still alert but their weapons now sheathed.

"Are you all right, Lien?" Temur asked.

She touched her side. Her dress was damp with blood, but there was no pain. No wound at all.

She frowned. How could that be?

"Temur, she has the gift."

Every muscle in her body froze. How did he know about the gift? She shifted, trying to move away from him, but he held her firmly in place.

Temur looked at her and then back at Amslan. "Really?"

Amslan nodded.

"What form does it take?"

"I can't tell."

Form? What did he mean? This was a dangerous conversation. "How am I healed?"

Temur frowned. "Amslan is a healer."

"He used no medicine, no tonics, what magic is this?"

"It is the gift. Amslan can heal, Sukh can communicate with horses. Do you know what we're talking about?"

Lien hesitated. The gift was the Bonamese's biggest secret. She had sworn a vow to the emperor never to reveal it to another person, but had also promised never to lie to Temur. They couldn't possibly be talking about the same thing. She'd never heard of anyone healing like Amslan had. "No."

Her stomach swirled and she prodded where the arrow had pierced her skin.

Nothing. No bruising, no blood, no pain.

How did it work?

How many others could heal in the same way?

"Temur, we need to keep moving," Chinua called. "Forward or back?"

"Visitor protocol states we will be safe once we're inside the palace. Will the emperor honour that?" Temur asked Lien.

She hesitated. The last time the Rhoran had been there, the emperor had planned to kill them. "Possibly." They'd been shot at while riding under the emissary flag. A worm of doubt crept into her mind. "I will talk to him immediately on arrival."

Temur studied her for a long moment. "Forward."

Before Amslan moved to his own horse he murmured, "If you betray us, I will kill you."

She should have told Temur about her suspicions, that the emperor was ignorant, but saying such a thing was blasphemy.

Kew ran across the flat field, and relief filled Lien.

Her dragon projected images at her. A lone archer, wearing the red of Kun's guard. Kew burning his leg, but him riding away. She frowned. Kun again. She needed to talk to him too.

"Let's go." Temur kicked his horse forward and Lien fell in behind him.

Would the palace bring any answers?

~*~

The east gate of the imperial palace towered far above them. At the top, archers patrolled the walkway ever vigilant and at the base a ten-yard wide moat surrounded the whole complex. It was a fortress, a pinnacle of engineering and the place Lien had once called home. As they crossed the bridge, two guards stepped out to block the entrance, hands resting on their swords.

"What is your purpose at the imperial palace, barbarian?" one of them demanded.

"We accompany Khan Temur and State Princess Lien," Amslan said. "The princess wishes to collect her personal belongings."

Lien shifted in the saddle. She did not look the same as when she'd left, not in the Rhoran style of dress, with her hair braided and sitting astride a horse, her skin darker from spending so much time in the sun. Would they recognise her? These guards wouldn't, but the ministers inside would. She allowed the guard to catch her eye before lowering her head in the proper manner. Kew trotted to the front of the group. At least her dragon was recognisable.

"State Princess." The guard bowed low. "We were not expecting you. Please allow us some time to prepare."

"Perhaps we could wait in the courtyard so I may dismount from this animal." It wasn't a question.

"Of course. This way."

The guard led them into the courtyard before allowing them to dismount.

The term courtyard, like most of the Bonamese culture, was an understatement. The area which made up the public section of the imperial palace was five hundred yards wide and almost one thousand yards long. A wide stream meandered from the scholars' quarters on the western side, around to the eastern side near the servants' quarters, before disappearing under the wall which separated the public area from the emperor's private area. Only three bridges spanned the stream, all in front of the Hall of Clarity which stood in the centre of the courtyard. Though the pavilions had small gardens around them, not a leaf or blade of grass dared be out of place. The hedges were trimmed and the trees had been shaped to be pleasing to the eye. There was nothing natural, nothing earthy about the place. People had made their stamp on the environment.

Where there was no grass, bricks and tiles covered the ground and absorbed the heat so it was a few degrees warmer inside the palace than outside it. At the corners of the buildings hung incense sticks and the sweet smoke was harsh to her nose. She hadn't missed it.

Lien should feel a sense of home-coming being so close to the emperor, but everything felt a little manufactured, a little unnatural.

Two officials stood in the Peace Pavilion, deep in discussion and behind them several people moved in and out of the temple. Government officers hurried around the library and the Office of Ministers in the distance, with the large rectangular building of the Office of Internal Scrutiny looming to her right.

Guards from the barracks located inside the palace's thick external walls emerged and surrounded them.

Was this common policy?

Beside her, Amslan tensed.

"Relax," Lien whispered. "It would be bad etiquette for them to attack." In public at least.

Amslan grunted.

Her skin prickled. She needed to speak to the

emperor, before this turned into an incident which would ruin his honour. She spoke to the guard assigned to them. "Send someone to fetch Prime Minister Cong."

"All of the ministers are in session, State Princess."

"That wasn't a request," she snapped, putting enough bite in her tone to have him standing to attention.

"Yes, State Princess." He called an order and one guard hurried away.

A trickle of sweat ran down Lien's back. The sun was viciously hot today and the dark paving trapped the warmth at her feet. No one had offered them a drink, or even a simple parasol. She wasn't certain how the Rhoran were normally treated, but this was no way to treat a State Princess. Doubt continued to spread over Lien's skin. She yearned to order they fetch Master Ying, but she wasn't meant to know him.

When the guard returned, he didn't have the Prime Minister with him, but Minister Fai, one of the lowest level government ministers.

A further insult.

"State Princess, I apologise for the delay." He bowed low. "We were in session and did not hear about your arrival until now."

Lien inclined her head.

"The emperor cannot meet with you until this evening. He has guests from Chungson. If he had known you were coming…" The chastisement was clear.

Lien said nothing. She didn't have to explain her actions to anyone but the emperor. But at least with the Chungson delegation here, the Rhoran should be safe. No one would dare breach the emissary treaty with outside witnesses. Her whole body relaxed.

"I'll arrange accommodation for your men in the barracks and you may stay in the women's quarters."

It would enable her to speak to her master and gather her things.

"Is this how you treat a Khan?" Temur asked, nudging his horse forward. "I expect the same courtesy you show your other guests and my betrothed will stay with me."

It would be harder to get answers with Temur around, but she couldn't tell him that. She would make do.

Minister Fai blanched and bowed. "Apologies. I thought these men were merely guards. I will arrange something else." He turned to go.

"We will take care of our horses while you do," Temur said. "Where can we stable them?"

A frown flittered across Fai's face and he called to a guard. "Show them to the stable."

Kew slunk back from where she had been exploring, her colour dull.

What's wrong?

An image of Master Ying floated into her mind. Kew had never left Lien alone with her master and often blew smoke at him. She'd never forgiven him for the one time he'd trodden on her tail.

Kew nodded towards the Office of Internal Scrutiny. Master Ying stood at one door. He was watching proceedings, analysing whether the Rhoran were a threat. If she couldn't get an audience with the emperor, Master Ying could clarify her orders.

His hands moved in a blur, too fast for anyone without the gift to see.

Meet me at the Peace Pavilion tonight at midnight.

Why the delay? *Someone attacked us just outside the palace.*

I have dealt with it.

What did he mean? She wanted to ask more questions but he moved away before she could.

Her heart thudded. She would have to sneak out of their accommodation. But she should have her own room. It shouldn't be too difficult.

"Lien, are you coming?" Temur asked.

She glanced at him. All the others followed the guard to the stables. "Of course." She gritted her teeth. Out on the steppes taking care of Batu was expected, but here… her face heated with shame. Aside from Master Ying, no one else she knew would see her, but word would spread that the State Princess had returned dressed like a barbarian and been forced to work.

She could not let the humiliation show.

Once in the shaded confines of the stable, she focused on unsaddling Batu and brushing her. She would miss her horse if the emperor annulled her betrothal and she had to stay here.

Minister Fai returned and his jaw dropped as he saw Lien brushing the horse. She ignored his reaction and put down the brush. "Is our accommodation ready?"

He shut his mouth and nodded. "If you would like to follow me."

Temur stepped next to her, took her hand and the rest of the warriors fell into position around them. It was a clear defensive movement, an implication the palace was not safe, which the emperor could consider rude.

Fai didn't say a word. He led them over one of the ornate wooden bridges which spanned the stream, past the huge Hall of Clarity and the Harmony Pavilion to the western gate. The library's roof shimmered in the sunlight and they walked along its verandah. She'd never been this close to the building, having had to rely on servants to bring her books Master Ying deemed appropriate for her to read. He had never allowed her to browse its shelves and read its knowledge.

The minister stopped at a door to a small building close to the western wall of the imperial palace. Why were they here? Most guests stayed close to the Hall of Clarity in a place of honour. He unlocked the door and lit a lantern. Then he smiled and gestured them inside.

Amslan went in first, hand on his sabre and scanning the area before he motioned them to follow.

Dusty stale air wafted out of the room as Lien waited for her turn to enter. She'd never heard of guest quarters here. As she entered, Chinua lit another lantern which illuminated the room with shocking clarity.

Whatever it's original purpose, the quarters hadn't been used in a long time. A layer of dust covered the long wooden table, muddy footprints lined the grimy floor, and the faded divans were in a style popular when Lien's grandmother had been alive. A long corridor led off the room and Chinua walked down it.

The emperor wouldn't agree to her staying here. It wasn't even fit for servants. Still she couldn't bring it up with Fai. Show no emotion. She had to remember that now she was back in the palace. Never let them know your true feelings.

She turned to the minister. "We will take our meal here. Ask a servant to bring it after they come to dress the beds and clean this room." She paused to let him acknowledge her request. "I expect them here within the quarter hour." She turned away and he left.

"Welcoming, aren't they?" Amslan wandered around the room and drew his finger through the dust on the table.

Lien said nothing. So far nothing was as she expected. No welcome, no delight in her return, no basic etiquette in her greeting. But the emperor hadn't known she was coming.

Temur touched her arm. "Go nowhere without at least two of us with you," he said. "I don't believe it is safe for you here. We will get what we came for and leave tomorrow."

Had he come for something other than her things? She still didn't know what the prisoner had told him.

Chinua had lit more lanterns down the corridor and she followed the light. How much room did they have? Chinua grinned at her. "It's not as nice as home, but it'll do."

Three translucent sliding doors partitioned the rooms from the corridor. Each room contained three mismatched beds—not enough for them all—and the same level of dust as the main room. Solid brick lined the back wall, but the side walls were timber. At the end of the corridor was a storage cupboard full of servants' clothing.

She would speak to the emperor about this. Disgusted, she shut the door and returned to the main room as someone knocked on the door. Amslan let two servants in, who cowered under his stare.

The man was terrifying them.

"Don't mind him." She hurried forward. "He won't hurt you."

The women turned to her and their eyes widened. They bowed their heads.

"State Princess, it is an honour."

"Thank you." She didn't have the patience for protocol today. "We need the rooms cleaned."

"Yes, State Princess." They answered in unison and raised their heads. One girl, she couldn't have been more than fifteen, gasped at the state of the room. She dropped to her knees in a low kowtow. "Apologies

State Princess. This room is not fit for your presence."

The other girl followed, kowtowing and apologising.

How tiresome. "I do not blame you for the dust," Lien told them. "We will wait outside until you are finished."

"Thank you, State Princess."

"Good idea," Temur said. "Why don't you show us around your home, Lien? We have seen little of it before."

They had as many misconceptions about the Bonamese as the emperor had about them. She could take this opportunity to educate them. "Of course."

Once outside she stopped to let her eyes adjust to the bright sunlight. Their rooms hadn't even had windows. Kew stayed next to her, clinging close in a way she hadn't done since she'd left the palace.

"Which way first?" Temur asked.

She needed to focus. "This building in front of us is the library."

"What's its purpose?" Sukh asked, falling into step beside her.

Lien blinked. Didn't he know? "It houses many books. We gather our knowledge here so we may learn and remember."

"Ah, that makes sense."

"What's the hut over there?" Chinua pointed.

Hut? There were no huts in the imperial palace. She followed his gaze and swallowed a smile. "It's a contemplation pavilion. People go there to think."

"You need a separate place to think?" one warrior asked. "Don't you do it in your head like the rest of us?"

"People in the pavilions are not allowed to be disturbed. It's a place of peace and serenity."

"Huh." He curled his lip.

How else could she explain? "It is similar to the feeling you get when riding across the steppes, the wind in your face and your concerns forgotten for the moment." She blinked. How could she compare such a simple activity with something as intricate as meditation?

He nodded. "Ah."

But she was more confused than ever. Their cultures were so different. Could she bridge the gap between them? Continuing to walk along the paved path, she turned away from the Gate of Heavenly Virtue and instead pointed out the Hall of Clarity.

"What's through the big gate?" Amslan asked.

"It leads to the emperor's private quarters where only the emperor's family is allowed."

"Is that where you lived?" Sukh asked.

She nodded. "I lived in one of the small palaces inside."

"There are multiple palaces?" Chinua asked. "How big is this place?"

"Big enough for the emperor, his wives and children." And all their associated servants.

"But you're not his child."

"No, but my father was his brother."

The gates were wide open with guards on either side. A palanquin moved past with an entourage of guards and servants. Fen. Lien didn't want her cousin to see her like this. Fen glanced towards her and then said something to the servant nearby. The servant bowed and hurried through the gates towards Lien.

Sukh stepped a half pace in front of Lien and Chinua moved next to her.

Pleasure washed through her. They wanted to protect her.

The servant stopped two yards away and bowed low.

"Speak," Lien ordered.

"First Princess Fen sends her warmest greeting and invites you to join her for tea in the Jasmine Palace."

Oh, no. She didn't want to be stuck with Fen for hours. She needed to be available for the emperor, needed to educate the Rhoran. "Please thank the Princess most kindly for the invitation, however I am showing my betrothed around the palace."

"Nonsense, Lien," Temur said. "You must join your cousin. I would love to meet more of your family."

The servant's eyes widened, but she didn't speak.

Lien should have warned Temur about her cousin. "We would be honoured to join her." Perhaps this was an opportunity to teach Temur about Bonamese customs.

As they all walked over, Fen's mouth dropped open and the guards on the gate tensed.

"Please tell First Princess Fen that my betrothed would like to meet her," Lien told the servant. Fen should adjust her invitation to have tea in one of the public halls, rather than allow the Rhoran into the private area. Lien waited at the base of the steps until the servant delivered the message and Fen nodded her acquiescence, gesturing Lien forward.

Fen should know better. The emperor would not be pleased. Had the empress not taught Fen these basic rules?

Lien climbed the stairs. Would she see Kun, or was he with the emperor? When she reached her cousin, she bowed. "First Princess, thank you for your invitation."

"I was most pleased when I heard you had returned," she said.

News had spread fast to the women's quarters. "Permit me to introduce you to my betrothed, the Khan Temur of the Rhoran."

Temur stepped up beside Lien and bowed low. "A pleasure, First Princess."

Fen glanced at Lien as if not sure what to do. Lien inclined her head and mouthed, *Thank you.*

"Thank you, Khan," Fen replied. "You have many men with you today."

"Only a few, First Princess," Temur replied with a smile. "This is a social visit, but we must keep up appearances, mustn't we?"

"Of course." She turned to Lien. "Let us go to my palace."

They walked down the paved corridors Lien had travelled many times in the past. The walls of the individual palaces were so familiar and yet they brought no comfort, no sense of loss.

"Where did you live, Lien?" Sukh asked her.

"The Lotus Palace."

"Father has given it to his latest concubine," Fen said.

So there would be no visiting it. But here was the opportunity she needed. "Do you know where my things are? I would like to collect my mother's jewellery."

"I shall find out for you." Fen flicked her wrist as she ordered one of her servants to search.

As they continued to walk, Amslan grumbled, "Why is there so much brick?"

"It keeps the palace protected," Lien said. "The emperor has lovely gardens though."

"Shall we drink tea in the cherry tree garden?" Fen asked.

"That would be delightful." Lien had forgotten how hot the palace became in summer.

"Set up the tea." Another wrist flick and another servant ran to do Fen's bidding. Had Lien been like that? Perhaps not as she had never had the same number of servants as Fen. But now it seemed a little odd to send someone to do something she could do herself.

Had she changed so much in so little time?

They crossed a small ornately carved wooden bridge over the stream and entered the emperor's lush private gardens. Only family were allowed here—and their retinues.

The gardens brought an immediate relief from the heat radiating off the buildings. Lien inhaled, appreciating the sweet scent of jasmine and the shade from the nearby Maidenhair tree.

The tree had always symbolised escape to her. She could disappear into the garden, away from any expectations and obligations. When she'd been much younger, she'd hidden from her carers by climbing into its branches while they searched for her. She blinked. She'd forgotten the urge she'd had to get away, and the unseemly way she'd behaved.

They continued to wander, so incredibly slowly that Lien longed to stride ahead. But Fen wore a silk gown and balanced on high heels, so she could not go faster—nor was it ladylike to do so.

Eventually they reached a small clearing which contained a round table with three chairs around it. On top of the table sat an exquisitely decorated teapot with three matching cups. Fen sat and motioned for Lien and Temur to do the same.

Fen's retinue moved away to a respectful distance while the Rhoran spread themselves around the table in defensive positions. Lien frowned. Only seven men— there should be nine.

Her heart rate increased as she counted again. Definitely seven. Where were Berke and Chinua? If someone found them wandering by themselves they would be killed.

As a servant poured the tea, she caught Temur's eye and then looked at each guard. He frowned.

He didn't understand.

Kew pranced around the clearing, happy snorts of smoke puffing out of her nose.

Lien let out a sigh. *Kew, two men are missing. Can you find them and bring them back?*

"Shall we make a toast?"

Fen's voice had Lien blinking. "Of course." She lifted the delicate tea cup and inhaled the steam. "Jasmine, my favourite."

"How lucky," Fen said. "We didn't get to spend enough time together when you were here."

"No, we didn't." With the five-year age gap and Lien spending most of her time training it meant she didn't know her cousin well. Kew chased a butterfly across the garden, dancing around it as it fluttered from flower to flower. Lien smiled. "Kew likes butterflies."

Fen giggled. "I've missed her."

She tuned into her dragon. *Kew, the men.*

Images came back. Searching.

What were they looking for?

Temur appeared unconcerned, but he must know two of his men were missing. What was he up to?

Fen lifted her cup. "To reuniting family."

Temur touched Lien's hand before she could drink. He smiled at Fen. "It is a Rhoran tradition that the host or hostess drinks first."

It wasn't a tradition Lien had been taught. In fact she was certain the guest had the privilege of eating or drinking before the host.

Fen's smile was forced. "How quaint." She sipped from her cup. "Don't let your tea go cold."

Lien lifted the cup and Temur slapped her arm. The cup flew out of her hand, tea spilling down her top and the cup crashing onto the ground breaking into a dozen pieces. Her mouth dropped open as she stared at him, her face hot. China was expensive.

"I'm so sorry. I saw a bee." He stood, knocking the table and his own cup crashed to the ground. Normally he wasn't this uncoordinated. He pulled her to her feet, brushing down her top and murmured, "The tea is poisoned."

What? "Fen drank it," she hissed.

Fen ordered a servant to clean up the mess.

"There are two chambers in the pot. I've seen it before."

Her chest squeezed. She wanted to deny it, but Master Ying had once shown her such a teapot. The poison could be emptied into the teapot after the first cup had been poured. But Fen hadn't poured the tea. Was her servant working for Kun?

"I am fine." She gently pushed Temur away. To Fen she said, "I am so sorry about your beautiful cups." She picked up the teapot and poured Fen more tea, feeling around the top and discovered the button. "Please drink and settle your nerves." The servant who prepared the tea would stop her.

Fen shook her head. "I am fine… but your clothes are wet. You should change."

Kew returned, sniffing around the table near the spilled tea and her scales turned black. Something was definitely wrong with the tea.

"Don't drink from the ground, Kew," Fen said.

Lien's mind whirred. Could Fen know about the poison? She was close to her brother, Kun. Lien stepped back. "You are right, I must change. I hope we will see each other again before I leave."

"Certainly. I'll send a note when we find your belongings."

"Thank you." Kew stood close to Lien, guarding her.

It truly wasn't safe here. Who was Kun's target—her or Temur?

"My guards will accompany you back to the gate," Fen said.

They still needed to find the missing Rhoran. Lien walked next to Temur. "Where are Berke and Chinua?"

He glanced at her. "I don't know."

He needed to understand how serious this was. She kept her voice low. "If someone discovers them in the emperor's private grounds, they will be executed."

Temur scowled.

Kew, find Berke and Chinua.

Kew shook her head, her worry clear.

Temur and Amslan can guard me. We can't leave the garden without them.

Kew snorted and ran off.

A messenger ran up to the group and bowed to Lien. "The emperor will grant you an audience in an hour at the Hall of Clarity."

She froze. The Hall of Clarity was for official state business. It wasn't where the emperor met with family and friends. Was she no longer either? "I am honoured."

The messenger bowed and departed.

Kew trotted out from the trees with Berke and Chinua. The tension in Lien's chest didn't lessen.

Was Kun acting on the emperor's orders? He wouldn't dare commit such a breach of etiquette without the emperor's knowledge.

Suddenly she wasn't so keen to see her uncle again.

Chapter 9

Once inside their quarters, Lien went straight to her bag and took out her red silk gown. She'd repaired the hole and cleaned the blood from it when she'd been at camp to prepare for her return. She needed to present the image of a princess to the emperor.

"Our clothes not good enough for you?" Amslan asked.

Not for the emperor. She turned her back on him. "Temur, may I have a word?" When he nodded she went down the corridor to the end room. "What is going on here?"

He lowered his voice. "Keep your voice down. These walls have ears."

The brickwork appeared solid enough to her, but she wouldn't discount the possibility. Master Ying had taught her to be wary.

"What were Chinua and Berke looking for?" she murmured.

"Do you believe now the emperor wants you dead?"

She hesitated. "I believe it's my cousin, Kun." She hoped it was.

He sighed, his exasperation clear. "I don't

understand your blind dedication," Temur said. "You've been stabbed, shot and almost poisoned. What will it take to make you see?" He left the room.

Lien stared after him. He could have been the target of all those attacks, and he'd avoided answering her question.

Was she being naive?

Her hands shook and the gown rustled. Quickly she changed and brushed out her hair. No time to put it up in the intricate styles of the palace. She had to settle for a braid twisted into a bun, pleased she had learnt how during her time with the Rhoran.

When she was ready, she took a deep breath and returned to the main room where the Rhoran sat chatting. Temur looked at her. "You look lovely, my *bayar*."

Heat infused her cheeks. "Thank you. I am ready."

They all stood. The warriors would defend Temur, but it would solve all of their problems if she died at the palace. Her skin prickled.

Kew bumped her ankle. She would always have her dragon.

In the foyer to the hall, Prime Minister Cong greeted Temur and then turned to her. "State Princess, how lovely to see you. The emperor is finishing business and then he will be ready for your audience. Wait here." He left before Lien could say anything, leaving them standing in the corridor.

Lien stared after him. Cong should have led them to one of the small private side rooms and given them refreshments, instead of leaving them here like commoners. Had the emperor told him to treat her this way? Maybe the emperor did want her dead. Her hands grew clammy.

"I don't like this," Amslan said.

Neither did she.

"Stay alert," Temur ordered.

"State Princess Lien." The male voice was low so no one could overhear.

The young man had a pleasant face with his dark hair cut short in the latest fashion. His clothes were of good quality and he held himself with a confidence that spoke of being sure of his position in life. Several guards stood two paces behind him. He wasn't anyone she recognised.

He bowed. "I am so pleased to meet you. When I heard you were to be wedded to the Khan I was going to send you a message." He acknowledged Temur with a nod and then glanced around.

Who was this person? "I do not believe we have met."

"Forgive me, Princess. My name is Anming, Lord of Chungson."

Chungson was a neighbouring state, now a vassal of Bonam. This man must be one of the visiting guests Minister Fai had told her about.

"I am pleased to meet you," Lien said. "Are you here to deliver the annual tribute?"

The man scowled. "Yes, but I am not here to talk about politics." He lowered his voice further. "I have a message from your brother."

Her brother? Impossible. Who did this man think he was? "My brother is dead." Her voice was as flat as her heart.

"No, he has been a guest at our palace since he was a boy." Anming blinked. "But you didn't know." He took two steps back. "I'm sorry, I thought you had allies here."

The blood drained from Lien's face so fast she swayed. Her brother was alive?

Temur grabbed her arm to steady her, wrapping an arm around her waist and Lien drew on his strength. Her mind whirled with questions, but it couldn't be true. It was nothing but a cruel trick, designed to give her hope. No one would keep that information from her. "Does the emperor know?"

"No!" Anming hissed. "Who do you think tried to kill him in the first place?"

She stepped back, shock spearing through her. "I don't understand."

Anming looked around and then said, "We cannot discuss this here. When do you leave?"

"Tomorrow," Temur said.

"I will send word with a meeting time." He hurried away.

Lien's head spun. But nothing made sense. The term guest was often used as a euphemism for hostage, but Chungson was now a state of Bonam. There was no reason for them to have Bao as a hostage, no reason the emperor would allow it.

"Lien, Cong is approaching," Temur murmured, squeezing her arm.

She blinked and focused. She wanted to ask Cong, wanted to tell the entire world her brother was still alive, but if Anming was right about the emperor...

Prime Minister Cong smiled at her. "The Emperor will see you now."

"Thank you." She needed to focus on this task first. Discover if the emperor wanted her dead or if he was ignorant. And if it was the latter, then perhaps there could be peace between the two countries.

"You need to leave your weapons here," Cong said to Temur.

Temur's smile was lethal. "After what happened the last time we were in the hall, I believe it prudent to hold on to them."

Cong bristled. "You can not be armed in the emperor's presence!"

"We will keep our distance."

"Absolutely not."

Lien could protect herself and she didn't want to endanger Temur. She placed a hand on his arm. "I will go in alone."

"It is not safe for you."

Cong coughed in outrage.

A warmth spread through her body at Temur's concern. "I have Kew and Prime Minister Cong will guarantee my safety."

Cong nodded. "Certainly."

Temur looked at her for a long moment. "Amslan, you and Chinua go with her."

The men handed Temur their sabres and followed her into the hall.

It was full of onlookers, whispering as she approached the throne where the emperor sat, his yellow silk gown flowing on to the floor and his expression stony. His dragon sat by his side as if picking up his displeasure, the colour of his scales a dull red. He perked up seeing Kew by Lien's side, but neither dragon moved to greet the other.

"The Rhoran Khan's betrothed, Lien," Prime Minister Cong announced.

She flinched. He had stripped her title.

Lien's pulse thudded as she knelt and kowtowed in front of the emperor. He was angry. Were there archers lining up to shoot her as she knelt? She waited silently as the time dragged out. Only commoners were made to bow for so long. Not even the Rhoran had kowtowed in front of the emperor. She squeezed her eyes shut. She used to be the emperor's favourite. Did he not care for her anymore? Despair threatened to overwhelm her.

Kew radiated love next to her but it wasn't enough.

The memory of being stabbed flashed into her mind, the colour of the emperor's dragon, the satisfaction he'd projected from the emperor as she'd fought for life. Maybe all those attempts *had* been on her life not Temur's. Her hope, her naivety, her heart shattered while she knelt, her head pressed into the cold wooden floor. She was not welcome here.

"Rise and state your business."

Lien kept her eyes lowered, fixed on the wooden parquetry beneath her feet. "I wish to collect my personal belongings, Heavenly Majesty."

"Why has it taken you so long to return?"

"I was injured and have only now recovered enough to make the journey." The back of her neck itched. Everyone stared at her, she was exposed and vulnerable. Then Amslan coughed behind her. How ironic that his presence brought her comfort. She wasn't alone.

"What do you wish to take?"

"My mother's jewellery and a few trinkets which have sentimental value."

The silence was long.

"I divided your things amongst the women. You may try to find what you need."

He had given away her possessions and was making her gather them like a servant. Tears pricked her eyes but she blinked them back. She wouldn't show him how much it hurt. She had lost her family again.

Prime Minister Cong gestured for her to follow him. No. Not yet. She needed answers before she left, but she couldn't ask them here, in front of everyone.

"Heavenly Majesty, may I speak to you privately

before I leave?"

Silence. She didn't dare look up to see his expression. Her fingers ached with the effort not to clench them into fists.

"If time permits."

Cong gestured to her again and this time she followed him, her posture straight as she left the room.

Once out of the hall she walked straight past Temur and the others waiting for her and stepped outside into the dusk. Gardeners scooped the leaves from the stream in front of her, keeping up the appearance of perfection, hiding the ugliness underneath. The palace was a pretty facade. With her head held high, she walked back to the guest quarters.

From behind her, Temur asked, "How did it go?"

She couldn't hear Amslan's answer, but the truth was, it was worse than she'd ever imagined.

The emperor, her uncle, one of her few remaining family members, had abandoned her. He didn't care what happened to her. She was dead to him.

Her chest squeezed so hard it was difficult to breathe. She needed to be alone, she needed to grieve.

Walking into their quarters, she headed straight to her room. As she slid the door shut, Temur placed a hand out to stop her. No, she couldn't deal with him right now. "Leave me," she ordered, the pent-up despair and anger clear in her voice.

He hesitated before stepping back. "I am here if you need me, my *bayar*."

The gentle thud of the door meeting the wall caused all her barriers to crumble. Tears flooded down her face, blurring her vision as she almost tripped over her long gown. Why was she even wearing this stupid thing? She was no longer Bonamese, not according to the emperor. She pulled and tugged at the restrictive fabric, fighting to get it off. It was impractical, decorative, stupid. It boiled all her worth down to her appearance.

She was more than that.

Finally freeing herself, she flung it on to the floor and pulled on the caftan and pants of the Rhoran. This was better, comfortable, practical, useful.

And that made her cry even harder. She sank onto the bed and curled into a ball.

Her ties to the Bonamese had been severed this day.

Her family no longer wanted her. She had no purpose. She was nothing. Had everything been a lie?

Kew scratched at the door and then it rumbled open. She tucked her head into her arms so no one could see her cry.

Kew's cold scaly head butted hers. She was all Lien had. The only good thing to come out of the palace. Glancing up, she spotted Sukh in the doorway.

"Oh, child." He slid the door behind him and walked over, pulling her into his arms. "Why do you cry so?"

She couldn't speak. His kindness made her sob harder and she wrapped her arms around him, crying into his chest.

"Hush, child.

Why had she received more comfort from the Rhoran than she ever had from her own people, her own family? He rubbed her back as if she was a child and Lien envied Geriel for having a father like this. She had precious few memories of her father, such as sitting on his knee while he spoke with his dragon, Manalin.

Her tears lessened and the tightness in her chest and throat eased.

"What happened to make you so upset?" Sukh asked when she raised her head.

She wiped her face on her sleeve and took a long breath in. Should she tell him the truth? She glanced at the walls, remembering they had ears. "Will you walk with me?" She could keep Sukh safe if someone attacked her outside.

"Of course."

Lien walked into the main room with her head held high, Kew by her side. It was of no matter if these men had heard her weeping. "Sukh and I are going for a walk."

Temur got to his feet. "I will come with you."

Sukh shook his head. "We have things to discuss."

He frowned. "It is not safe."

"Chinua and Berke can follow us at a distance," Sukh said. It was not up for discussion. No one would dare challenge the emperor that way. If they did, they wouldn't be at the palace long.

Temur nodded and Berke and Chinua followed them into the warm night air.

Outside the confines of the four walls, Lien felt exposed, as if at any moment an arrow would fly her way. "Let's go to the Harmony Pavilion." It would offer protection against attack.

"Why are you so upset?"

How should she start? The Rhoran had such a different society. How could she explain her grief? She cleared her throat. "All my life they taught me the emperor is the embodiment of God on Earth. I was told to be grateful he took me in when my parents died, to worship him for his goodness, that he could do no wrong."

Sukh strangled back a laugh.

She couldn't be angry. "It might seem funny to you, but I knew nothing else. My parents and brother died when I was five and I remember little of my time with them."

And now her brother might still be alive. Hope filled her, washing away some sorrow, but it would crush her if Anming had lied.

"Did no one talk to you about them?"

She shook her head. "It was as if they never existed. Occasionally I would run into my brother's best friend, Jie and he would speak of my brother."

"That is no way to honour your dead."

"No, it's not." But she'd been too young to know better.

"Today the emperor treated me like a commoner, with less respect than he showed Temur when he last came. I have angered him, and am no longer worthy in his eyes."

Sukh put a hand on her shoulder. "You feel you've lost your family again."

She nodded. Though Sukh had acted more like a father to her in the past half moon than the emperor ever had. She walked up the steps of the pavilion and settled on one of the polished wooden benches inside. Berke and Chinua took up positions at either entrance and Sukh settled on the bench beside her.

Dare she voice her greatest concern?

"I fear Temur may be right. I fear the emperor may want me dead."

"All signs point towards it," Sukh agreed. "Three attempts are hard to ignore."

"I thought they were meant for Temur," she said.

"Then the assassins need better training."

His words were like a dagger to her chest and she gasped. How could she have been so blind? Ying had trained her, had trained all the secret bodyguard, and the emperor's main bodyguard. Anyone he trained had excellent accuracy. The arrow *was* meant for her. If

Amslan didn't have the gift of healing, she would be dead.

She closed her eyes against the fresh wave of grief.

"Why would he want to kill you?" Sukh asked.

"I do not know." She had done everything he'd ever asked of her—except kill Temur. But she didn't want Sukh to know what the emperor had ordered her to do.

She shouldn't meet with Ying tonight. He would succeed where others had failed. He would kill her—unless she could convince him she had more value alive than dead.

Perhaps that was the solution.

She could tell Ying how wrong they were about the Rhoran and she'd be more use to them alive, in the Rhoran camp, a liaison between the two countries.

She remembered the situation at the wall.

No, the emperor had to know the truth. He wanted to wipe out the Rhoran.

So she needed to persuade Ying she would make the perfect spy for the Bonamese, help him defeat them from the inside. He wouldn't realise she was lying until much later when she was back in Rhoran territory.

The idea was so shocking, so rebellious and yet felt so right.

The emperor had constantly lied to her: about her brother, about the wall, about her mission. Temur had been upfront and honest at all times. He had given her a place to stay despite not trusting her, not wanting to be stuck with her.

She had been far more content riding across the steppes than she had ever been in the confines of the palace.

But could she convince Ying she was telling the truth? She would have to give him some information of value in order for him to believe her. But what?

"Child, we should return to our quarters. It is safer for you there."

She began to walk back to the rooms. "Sukh, what is the real reason Temur has returned here?"

Sukh pursed his lips. "You need to ask him."

So there was a real reason.

She smiled. The emperor had made a mistake. He was arrogant and childish to treat her the way he had. If he had been smart, he would have welcomed her back, made her feel like she was at home, so she doubted what the Rhoran had told her and doubted her own suspicions. He was a fool.

She would help Temur achieve his purpose.

And show the emperor how wrong he was to dismiss her.

~*~

When Lien opened the door to their quarters, she walked directly to Temur. "May I have a word in private?"

Temur followed her outside. No other buildings were nearby, and the guard walkway was high enough above them their words shouldn't carry. He caressed her arm. "Are you feeling any better?"

"Yes, thank you. The emperor's reaction took me by surprise."

"I tried to warn you."

"I know." She would no longer be so blind. "My experience with the emperor was not the same as yours, and the man I thought he was would never hurt me." She gave a wry smile. "I thought the conflict between our countries was a simple misunderstanding. I thought after I'd told the emperor what I'd discovered, everything would be resolved."

"We have tried," Temur said. "What did you want to

speak about? We should not stay too long in the open like this."

"I want to offer my assistance."

"With what?"

"With the reason you returned to the palace." She didn't wait for him to deny it. "Chinua and Berke wouldn't have disappeared today without your order, and my knowledge of the palace may be of some help."

"Why the sudden interest?"

"I find I don't much care for the idea the emperor wants me dead."

Temur chuckled. "Neither do I, but I do not require your help at this stage."

She hesitated. It went against everything she had been taught to break a vow but the emperor had broken much more sacred agreements. "My gift is speed."

His eyebrows raised.

"I can't demonstrate here, but once we're inside… If there is anywhere you need to go, I can move faster."

"I would like to see this, but after we have left the palace."

He didn't trust her. The pang in her heart was sharp. Still so naive. He wouldn't trust her, just because she'd changed her mind. She needed to prove herself to him.

"All right." Should she tell him about her meeting with Ying? He might not understand. If she could think of a way out of the midnight meeting, she would use it, but not turning up could prove she no longer trusted the emperor—and that would be very dangerous for all.

She followed Temur back inside.

She had to meet Ying.

And hope she survived the night.

~*~

The rumble of the sliding door woke Lien. She must have drifted off while waiting for the others to fall asleep. Someone stood in the doorway, the light from the main room casting them in shadow. "Who's there?"

"It's Sukh, child. It's my turn to take guard duty."

She'd been sharing a room with Sukh and Chinua because there weren't enough beds. "Leave the door open." She needed to leave now, needed to meet with Ying, but it would be tricky to sneak out of their quarters. Temur had ordered they guard the main door from intruders.

"If you wish."

She would wait until Berke came into the room and fell asleep before leaving. Otherwise someone would notice her missing.

She lay still pretending to be asleep, waiting for Berke to return. She kept waiting. Perhaps Berke had gone to sleep on the divan in the main room. She was just about to move when Chinua crept out of the room, tapping softly on all the doors as he went past.

What was going on?

She peered out the doorway as Temur and Amslan came out of the adjoining rooms. After a quiet discussion, the main door opened and four men left.

Where were they going?

Her heart rate increased. Ying was out there tonight. If he saw them, it would be catastrophic. She needed to distract him and find out what the Rhoran were doing.

She centred herself and then ran. Sukh sat at the table, but she didn't stop. Instead she flung open the door and was through. She sped across to the verandah of the library where the lanterns had already been extinguished. She crouched and scanned the surroundings. The Rhoran warriors made their way towards the Gate of Heavenly Virtue.

They would get themselves killed.

A guard called out and Lien froze until she distinguished his words. He spoke to the next guard on shift. This was the worst possible time for the Rhoran to be out. Too many eyes, two sets of guards who could catch them.

What were they thinking?

She had to stop them.

Waiting until the Rhoran had paused behind the far corner of the library, she raced over, placing her hand over Temur's mouth. "Don't shout."

He jolted and swung around to face her. "Where did you come from?"

Amslan swore under his breath.

She crouched low, indicating they should do the same. "The shift change has begun. Wait until it's finished."

"How did you get past Sukh?" Temur demanded, his voice low.

"It doesn't matter." She had to make him understand it was too dangerous to be out.

"Is he still alive?"

She gasped as if he'd punched her in the stomach. "Yes." She hissed. "I told you my gift is speed. He didn't see me."

She didn't have time to explain, but she would demonstrate. "I have to meet my old assassin master and he will kill you all if he finds you. Give me time to ensure he goes back inside and then I will help you with whatever you're doing."

"We don't have time for this," Amslan said.

"You don't have time not to." She couldn't read Temur's eyes in the darkness. "Please." She didn't wait for his response. Instead she raced across the ground to the Hall of Clarity and keeping to the shadows, continued to the Peace Pavilion. Ying had chosen the pavilion as a test for her. It was on the other side of the courtyard and she could use little to hide her passage.

She scanned her surroundings. A flash of movement towards the pavilion. He was there. Quickly she joined him. She fisted her hand and crossed her arm over her body. "Master." Her breathing was even, but her heart raced. She needed to convince him to spare her life.

"Why is the khan still alive?" he asked, his voice low.

So she was supposed to kill him. "I thought the betrothal superseded those orders, but I wanted to confirm, hence the reason I returned."

"Tell me your news."

Lien stood to attention, her back straight, arms by her side as she gave her report. Her heart thudded so hard in her chest it was almost audible. She had to be convincing. "By the time I regained consciousness I was in the Rhoran camp. It took many days until I healed."

Ying said nothing.

If she acted like a good soldier, she couldn't question the stabbing. "While I was there, I learnt many things about the Rhoran, and I became concerned the emperor's information was incorrect."

"Are you questioning what I taught you?"

She hesitated. "I heard the Rhoran were savages who treated their woman as slaves, but I saw no evidence of that in the camp. I thought the information the emperor had been given had been twisted and maybe the emperor intended me to correct it."

"What else did you learn?"

"They believe in many gods, but their way of honouring their ancestors is not dissimilar to ours."

"Did they tell you about the Great Khan?" he asked quickly.

Did he believe the rumours? "Yes. They celebrate him in summer when all the tribes get together for the great hunt."

"Where is he buried?"

"No one knows. It is said his most loyal followers took him away and buried him. The spiritual leader said the stories of his wealth are exaggerated."

"What else?"

Something in his tone put Lien on edge. Her shoulder blades itched but she didn't move. "They each specialise in one aspect of their livelihood and their craftspeople are talented." Though Ying wouldn't care, she still had to try to change his opinion and end the conflict.

"Do you have any information which the emperor may find useful?" His disdain was clear.

She wasn't fooling him. She had gathered so much information and now she would never divulge it. Still she had a role to play. "There is truth in them being filthy and never bathing." She allowed disgust to tinge her tone before glancing at Ying, as if uncertain. "Master Ying, if I may ask a question of my own?"

He nodded.

"Have I displeased the emperor?" She paused. "He did not appear happy."

"The khan is still alive. You have failed your mission, is that not reason enough?"

"Of course." Lien bowed her head again. The animosity came off Ying in waves. She was out of her depth. If he killed her now, she couldn't protect the Rhoran. She had to give him something which would prevent him killing them all.

There was one thing… no, she didn't know enough details. But it would definitely make Ying hesitate before attacking them.

Temur had never said it was a secret and it was all she had. She prayed to her parents she was doing the right thing and said, "There is one thing the emperor should know about the Rhoran."

"Go on."

"I discovered the Rhoran also have the Gift."

A slight tension in Ying's shoulders was the only sign of his reaction. "How many?"

"Every family," she lied.

"That is interesting." He was silent. If he assumed they were all fast, all warriors, then he would not attack them. "I will speak to the emperor and send you a message in the morning. Do not leave until you receive it." Without a word of farewell he raced to the main hall and then slowed, strolling out from the verandah and towards the Gate of Heavenly Virtue.

If Temur hadn't listened to her this would be catastrophic.

She waited for an outcry, a clash of metal. Silence.

When Ying was out of sight, she moved back to the library.

Temur swore as she crouched down next to him.

"Thank you for waiting."

"What happened?" he demanded.

"I needed my old master to believe I was still faithful to the emperor. He has gone to speak with him now."

"She's lying," Amslan hissed.

She ignored him. "You need to be careful. If he catches you, he'll kill you all. Where are you going?"

Temur was silent for a long moment. "We have information some of our people are being kept prisoner here. We want to free them."

There were no prisons in the palace. "Where?"

"There's a room in the wall of the emperor's garden."

So that's what Berke and Chinua had been looking for. "You found it?"

Berke nodded. "About halfway along. We didn't get inside."

She could prove herself. "Let me check. I'll be faster." She evaded Temur's grasp and sped out across the space between the pavilion and the gate. She moved at speed, only Ying or one of the other women of the secret bodyguard could see her.

The night was quiet, and dark with no moon in the sky.

Racing across the bridge into the garden, she stopped next to the large maidenhair tree. She needed to be careful not to use all her power. If she used too much, too quickly it would drain from her.

As she slipped through the garden, her ears strained for sounds. Nothing aside from the rustle of the gentle breeze through the leaves.

She found the door, in the middle of the wall, between the two main watch towers. Trees surrounded it, probably to hide its existence from any guards stationed on the walls. No windows to peer through and no way of knowing what was on the other side. Once through the door she had to render any guards in the building unconscious immediately.

She scanned her surroundings, checking the walls for guards, the garden for movement. All was still. Then out of the corner of her eye something moved. She turned ever so slowly as a man walked through the gardens towards the door.

Ying.

Her stomach clenched as he entered the room. She didn't move for several minutes after the door closed, her skin tight and her whole body alert. She'd been a second from giving herself away. If Ying had seen her she would be dead.

Lien gradually relaxed her muscles. What were her options? She couldn't go inside while Ying was there.

But she also couldn't tell Temur of the delay in case Ying left while she was gone. She had to stay, had to ensure Ying had left before she went in. She crouched down to wait.

Time ticked by and her legs cramped, her body grew stiff. She shifted, stretching out her legs and noticed a dark figure creeping towards the door. Her heart beat faster. It had to be one of the Rhoran.

Her leg cramped as she stood and she winced. He was getting closer, but she couldn't put weight on her leg, couldn't stop him.

She picked up a stone and threw it, hitting him in the back. He stopped, whirled around.

The blood in her legs warmed up and she ran across to him.

Amslan.

"What are you doing?" she whispered. "Ying is inside."

"Says you," he sneered. "I'm surprised you're even here. I expected you to be long gone. You won't stop me going in there."

She could stop him, but if he was unconscious he would be vulnerable. "I would have gone in if it was safe."

"I don't believe you. You want us to fail."

The door opened and Lien yanked Amslan behind a tree, clamping her hand over his mouth. She froze and Amslan did the same.

She held her breath as her former master walked back through the garden. When he was gone, she removed her hand from Amslan's mouth. "I'll go first and tell you when it's safe."

He nodded.

So this is what it took to subdue Amslan.

Taking a couple of quiet breaths to settle her nerves, she then ran across to the door, opened it, slid in and closed it in a blink of an eye. Two guards looked towards her and she spun, racing across to one and then the other, knocking them unconscious with sharp blows to the neck. They wouldn't be out for long.

A long central table occupied the bulk of the room, with bench seats on both sides. Two lamps illuminated the text on the books lying open on the table, and the teapot and cups. The walls contained shelves full of books and incense burned in one corner, giving off a spicy scent. It looked like a research room, but there was one other door.

Lien picked up the lantern and moved over, listening. Quiet. She cracked open the door.

An empty and cold room. The bright light highlighted weapons and torture devices lining the walls. She cringed. This had to be the place.

The door on the opposite side of the room was closed, and keys hung on the wall. She unlocked it, leaving the lantern behind so it didn't silhouette her. Cautiously she opened it and the most putrid smell wafted out, a combination of faeces, sweat and rotten reeds. She gagged and her eyes watered. To one side someone moaned.

How could Ying leave the prisoners like this? Why hadn't he ordered the room cleaned? She retrieved the lantern and held it in front of her as she walked into the cramped dark space. Three limp bodies lay across the floor, covered in a mixture of reeds, blood and excrement. Lien wanted to shut her eyes at the horror.

One body moved, opened its eyes and squinted

toward the light. He was Rhoran. He tried to speak but no words formed.

"Don't be afraid. Khan Temur sent me." They needed Amslan. She hurried to the main door as Amslan crept inside dressed as a Bonamese servant in black clothes and a cone-shaped hat. He hadn't waited for her. She shook her head.

"That way." She pointed.

He ignored her and went over to the guards, holding something up to their noses.

"What's that?"

"Something which will keep them unconscious for a couple of hours," he said. "They won't remember anything when they wake."

Impressive. She wanted to ask more, but now wasn't the time. She sniffed at the liquid in the jug on the table. It didn't smell so she tasted it. Water.

She followed Amslan into the room and he swore. "Mother, Father." He dropped down next to the woman.

These were his parents? No wonder he was in such a rush. She poured the glass of water and handed it to Amslan's father. His grip around the cup was loose and his other hand was swollen to twice the size so she held the cup to his lips and helped him to sip it.

His first words were, "You're Bonamese."

Lien nodded. "My name is Lien. I am Temur's betrothed. We will get you out of here." A fierce determination swept through her. No one should be treated this way.

Another body stirred, a man. "We've told you all we know about the gift. Please don't hurt us any more."

Nausea rose in Lien's stomach as she examined their wounds. Many were still bleeding—fresh injuries. She'd caused this by telling Ying about the gift. She never should have said anything.

"Cheren, you will be safe," Amslan said, looking at the man. His hands were on his mother's leg and his face strained. He must be healing her.

"What are your injuries?" Lien asked.

Amslan's father said, "We each have a broken leg. The bones in my hand are shattered and Arigh's arm is broken. Cheren has broken ribs." He took another sip of water. "We have countless bruises and cuts over our bodies. The sores are getting infected."

Lien couldn't stand the exhaustion on their faces. How strong was Amslan's healing? None of them were in any state to move and their smell would alert anyone within ten yards. "How often do the guards change? How often do they come in?"

He shook his head. "It's dark in here. We don't know when it's day or night. The guards come and go but there are only four and the bastard in charge— Ying."

Ying had tortured these people himself. How had she ever thought him honourable, a person to emulate?

Why had she ever respected him?

She wouldn't make that mistake again.

Chapter 10

"Why did he capture you?" Lien asked.

"He wants to know where the treasure of the Great Khan is buried," Arigh said.

Amslan growled. "He's torturing our people because of fairy-tales and legends?"

"He heard an artefact was buried with the khan, one that grants any who touches it the gift."

She froze, goosebumps spiking her skin. If Ying got it, he would be unstoppable. "Is it true?"

"No." Amslan glared at her, before taking his hands off his mother's leg. "Can you move it?"

She nodded. "Thank you."

He placed his hands over her arm.

"Wait." Lien stopped him. "Heal everyone's legs first," she said. "Arigh can walk out with a broken arm." If his gift was like hers, using too much would tire him, and they didn't have a lot of time.

"She's right. I'll be fine," Arigh said.

Lien checked the guards were still unconscious.

"How long will it take?" she asked Amslan when she returned.

"Maybe an hour. Their internal injuries need healing

too."

"And what's your plan to sneak them out of here?" How had he got past the guards on the gate in the first place?

He nodded towards a bag he'd been carrying with him. Inside were the servant garments which had been in the cupboard in their quarters and some dried meat. She handed the food to the prisoners. Cheren's hand shook as he took the food. They were all so weak.

"Can they walk the distance?"

"If it gets us out of this place we will," Amslan's father growled, so like his son.

"All right. You need to change." She stood and used her foot to clear away the straw and muck and then helped Arigh to her feet. The woman clutched Lien's arm with one hand, her grip pathetically weak. They would be in trouble if someone caught them.

Lien helped her undress, wincing at the bruises and infected sores she had all over her body. Lien used the water to wash some muck off Arigh's skin before helping her into the servant clothes. Nothing could be done about the knotted mess of her hair, but the hat would hide most of it. She would be presentable from a distance and in the dark.

"Amslan has finished with Yeke," Arigh said.

Her husband clambered to his feet, swaying a little. His movements were slow and full of pain as he stripped, using the inside of the clothes to wipe away the grime and then tossing them on the straw. He shrugged off Lien's attempt to help.

"Are the others coming?" Lien asked.

"No, they're waiting for you." Amslan glanced up. "You should do your speed thing and tell them what's going on."

"Which way are you taking them?"

"The servants' gate."

She wouldn't ask what he'd done to the guards inside. "It would be better if they went one at a time. A group of servants at this time of night will draw attention from the guards on the watch towers."

He frowned. "Really?"

"Yes. Most of the palace is asleep."

"I'll go first," Yeke said, straightening his stance and wincing.

"I'll show you the way."

"Wait." Amslan stared at Lien as he stood and rested his hands on his father for a moment. Yeke sighed. "Thank you, son. Now finish healing Cheren."

"If he dies, you die," Amslan said to Lien.

Arigh gasped but Lien nodded. Taking the empty water jug and cup, she placed them back on the outside table and then led Yeke outside. Once he was safely under a tree, she checked the surrounding garden for people but it was empty. "This way."

At the edge of the garden she pointed to the wall. "The door over there is the servants' entrance. You can walk straight through to the other side of the wall. I will check for guards before you get there."

Yeke nodded.

"When you're in the main palace area, head left. There's a building next to the west gate which is our quarters."

"All right."

She waited to make sure he got over the bridge without being seen and then sped back to where she'd left Temur.

He swore. "Where have you been?"

"Ying went to visit the prisoners," she said. "We had to wait until he left. Amslan is in there healing them at the moment. Yeke is on his way back. He'll be coming through the servants' entrance soon."

"How many prisoners?" Temur asked.

"Three; Yeke, Arigh and Cheren. They're badly injured. Amslan will not have the energy to heal all their wounds. They will still be weak."

"At least they're alive," Temur said, relief in his tone.

"We can help them," Berke said.

Lien shook her head. "It will draw attention. A guard might investigate if he thinks something is wrong. You should return to the quarters before you're caught."

Temur looked at her. "We'll wait until Yeke comes out."

He didn't believe her. The realisation was like a stab to her gut. Well she would prove him wrong. "All right."

She ran to the servants' gate and slipped inside. One guard sat at the table, his eyes closed, head lolling backwards. Unconscious. But there should be more than one guard. She opened a trunk and her stomach clenched. A body had been shoved inside, folded up in an unnatural position. She lowered the lid as the door to the private palace opened.

Yeke.

She breathed a sigh of relief. "Temur is on the other side."

His face was pale and his steps slow. She sniffed at the teapot on the table and poured cold tea into a cup. "Drink this."

Yeke sank onto a chair and panted. "It was further than I thought."

"Not far to go now. Head for the pavilion over there." She pointed in the general direction. "Temur is waiting. He and the others can help."

He nodded. "Arigh will need assistance."

"I'll go to her as soon as you leave."

He stood. "See you there." After he closed the door behind him she waited for any cries of alarm, and when they didn't come, she raced back to the prison.

Cheren was on his feet, dressed as a servant, while Amslan continued to heal his mother, his face strained.

"We need to go," Lien said. "It will be light soon."

Amslan nodded. Lien gathered the clothing and stuffed it back in the bag Amslan had brought.

"Why did you do that?"

"No point showing them the prisoners are wearing different clothes." She scanned the straw and muck for any other clue who had freed the prisoners and then locked the door behind her. She hung the key back on the hook. "With any luck they won't realise they're missing until we leave."

Amslan smiled. "Good idea."

A positive sentiment from Amslan. That was a first. Lien checked the main room, placing the lantern where she'd found it and then followed them into the garden. Arigh crossed the bridge first after getting the directions from Amslan. Lien scanned the shadows of the buildings for any sign someone was watching. Arigh stumbled and fell, her cry loud in the night.

Amslan moved forward and Lien grabbed his arm. "Wait. You can't be seen."

He struggled against her, but Lien held on and then Arigh picked herself up. Amslan went still. Arigh's steps were small, slow. She would not make the full distance. She was too exhausted.

"I'll get her," Cheren said.

"No." Lien scanned the surroundings. No one had been alerted by the cry. "Let me. I can carry her back." The woman was nothing but skin and bones. Lien had never carried anyone at speed before, but she had little choice. She needed to get Arigh to safety before they discovered her.

"Go," Amslan ordered.

She ran, her footsteps quiet on the pavement. As she reached Arigh, she heard a rattle of metal. Guard.

The nearest building was yards away. There was no time. "Quiet now." She swept Arigh up in her arms and ran towards the shadows of the wall.

Arigh grunted but fell silent.

In the shelter of the building Lien put Arigh down. There had to be a less awkward way to run with her. Footsteps grew closer and Lien moved in front of Arigh, bracing herself.

The guard wore black and carried a bow and arrow as well as a sword strapped to his waist. He moved past them, heading towards the stream.

Lien prayed Cheren hadn't left yet.

When the guard was far enough away, she murmured, "Climb on my back." She squatted down. The children had carried each other this way in the camp, arms around the carrier's neck, legs wrapped around their waist. Arigh climbed on.

The guard faced away from them. He wouldn't see her if she used her speed—no one would unless Ying was still around. And that would cause a whole lot of other problems. She couldn't explain away rescuing a Rhoran prisoner.

"Ready?"

"Yes."

Sprinting as fast as she could, Lien headed for the main gate, keeping close to the shadows cast by the buildings. She paused before crossing the open distance between the closest building and the gate. She would go straight to the sleeping quarters.

She adjusted her hold on Arigh, and ran, darting

across the clear pavement, through the open gates and towards their quarters.

She pulled to a stop outside, threw open the door and hurried inside.

Sukh leapt to his feet as Arigh groaned. "Lien?" he hissed. Then his eyes widened. "Arigh?"

Lien lowered Arigh into a seat. "She needs food and rest," she murmured. "The others are on their way here too." She poured two glasses of tea from the pot on the table and gave one to Arigh. Her own head spun as her heart rate slowed. They'd made it without being spotted.

But the night wasn't over.

"What's that smell?" Sukh asked.

"Me," Arigh said.

Lien slid the bag off her shoulder. "And their old clothes. We should dispose of them."

"We'll figure it out."

"I need to check the others," she said. "Arigh can have my bed."

"Thank you, child," Sukh said.

Her body tingled. He trusted her.

At the door she scanned the area. Two figures made their way towards her and from their build, she was sure it was Yeke and one of the Rhoran. That left Cheren and Amslan.

She raced to the pavilion where Temur waited. "I carried Arigh to the quarters."

"Can't you give some warning before you appear like that?" Chinua grumbled. "You've taken several lives off me tonight." He scowled.

"Sorry." She froze and checked the sky. Definitely lighter. "You need to get back to the quarters. There will be another guard change soon and the servants will get up. When they discover the body in the guardhouse, there will be an uproar."

She hadn't considered that. What would the emperor do? Would he acknowledge the loss of his prisoners, or pretend it hadn't happened?

"I'll wait here in case Cheren needs help," Chinua said. "You go back."

Temur nodded.

At that moment Cheren walked out of the servants' entrance. Lien sighed.

Only Amslan to go and as much as she didn't like the man, it would cause too many problems if someone caught him. She waited next to Chinua while Cheren made his way slowly towards their quarters. He wasn't struggling.

Still no sign of Amslan. What was taking him so long?

"Are you coming back?" Chinua whispered.

"What about Amslan?"

"He can take care of himself."

She couldn't leave him there. "I'll wait."

As Chinua left, someone exited the servants' gate and hurried towards the Office of Internal Scrutiny. It wasn't Amslan.

What should she do? If she searched for Amslan she risked running into Ying again.

The sky lightened in the east and the buildings around her took on a more definite shape. A couple of early birds whistled their morning greeting to the sun. Colours lightened from black, to grey, to a faint blush of red, before deepening.

She would need to move soon.

She glanced over her shoulder at the Office of Internal Scrutiny and her heart stopped.

Ying strode in front of a contingent of guards heading for the servants' entrance. She had to distract him. Shuffling around the pavilion she stood and climbed its steps. Never had she felt more like a target. She sat on the bench where she'd spoken with Sukh not so long ago and folded her hands in her lap.

Would Ying notice her?

Her shoulders tense, she kept her head lowered, but her eyes on the gate. It opened when Ying was still halfway across the courtyard.

Amslan. She'd recognise his cocky walk anywhere.

She coughed delicately and the sound carried across the morning. All she needed was to get Ying's attention on her, not the man crossing the pavement towards the guest quarters. If Amslan had noticed the guards coming towards him, he made no sign of it.

Lien waited, keeping her posture as serene as possible as she tracked his movement.

"State Princess Lien, what are you doing out here alone?"

Inwardly she flinched as she turned to Ying who stood with two guards behind him. "I've taken to waking early while out on the steppes," she replied. "And wanted to take time in contemplation, before we return."

His hands moved in a silent language. *Do you know about the missing guard in the gatehouse?* Aloud he said, "Does the khan treat his betrothed so callously that she is left without protection?"

Lien shook her head in answer to both questions. "I must confess he does not know I left."

"You should return at once." *Find out what you can and report to me.*

Lien stood. "Of course."

She made her way down the stairs and back towards the quarters. She didn't dare look back, but he was watching her. And she wasn't sure he believed her lies.

~*~

Lien reached the quarters just after Amslan. She shut the door behind her and leaned against it, the tension leaving her body. Except for the prisoners, all the Rhoran were in the main room, eating the food they'd brought with them.

They still had to get out of the palace without being caught.

Her head whirled and her eyelids fluttered closed. She needed a few hours sleep.

Sukh brought her some meat and a mug of tea. "Eat, child. You must be tired."

"Thank you." She took it and sat at the table next to Chinua.

The warriors chatted like it was any normal morning. Did they have their plan to get the prisoners out already in place? Would they tell her?

Temur leaned over to her. "Why don't you go to sleep?"

"What time are we leaving today?" she asked.

"As soon as you get your belongings."

She blinked. They should leave as soon as possible, before someone discovered the prisoners were missing. She didn't want to be responsible for them getting caught. "We can leave now. I can go without my things."

Temur frowned. "They are your last connection to your parents."

Her heart twisted. "But they are just things." She would manage with her memories of them and if Bao was indeed alive, it would be better than any trinket. She needed to speak to Anming again...

Her brain was too tired to think properly.

"Go to sleep, my *bayar*. You look dead on your feet." He helped her to stand and led her to the far room which was empty.

The prisoners must be asleep in one of the other rooms.

"I will go into the women's quarters when I wake," she said. "Hopefully I'll find my items and we can leave."

"Don't worry about that now," he said. "Go to sleep. Thank you for your help last night." He smiled and slid the door shut behind him.

~*~

The rumble of the door opening woke Lien and she lifted her head, blinking to clear her eyes. She'd only just fallen asleep. Temur stood in the entrance, his expression grim.

What was wrong? "Is it time to go?"

He shook his head. "The emperor wants to see you. Alone."

Fear gripped her. They must have discovered the prisoners were missing. "What time is it?"

"Just past eight."

So she'd had a few hours sleep. Not as much as she needed. She got up, smoothed down her caftan.

"Wear this." He placed a dark green caftan and pants on the bed, shaking out the top, and then slid his hand into a hidden pocket, drawing out a knife and handing it to her. Arming her before she went into the emperor's presence.

Her eyes widened. The knife was well built, solid, but light. She slid it back into the pocket and nodded. "I'll change."

He left her and she dressed. What did the emperor want?

The other bedrooms were empty as she walked past, but only five men sat in the main room.

Where were the others? No, the less she knew, the better.

"The messenger is waiting for you outside." Temur leaned in, kissing both her cheeks and whispered, "Be very careful."

She nodded, her heart racing, not from fear but from the genuine concern in his eyes. Did he really care what happened to her? Perhaps her actions last night had proven to him she was on his side.

Kew joined her as she opened the door. The servant bowed. "This way please."

Lien followed her across to the Hall of Clarity, but rather than being taken into the large hall, she was led to one of the small receiving rooms where they held meetings with dignitaries.

It was too late to be shown common courtesy. She had chosen her path and she wouldn't be deterred from it.

Inside, the emperor sat behind a long table adorned in a rich red satin cloth with a pot of tea on top. He wore his formal yellow gown again and a thick musky scent hung in the air from the incense sticks burning in the corner. To his right stood Ying.

Neither was smiling.

Lien's heart clenched and she longed to reach for the knives in her pockets.

"Leave us," the emperor commanded and the servant bowed and hurried out.

Lien kowtowed, every sense tuned to Kew for danger.

"Stand," the emperor said.

She climbed to her feet. No one spoke. Kew stood next to her silent and still. How had she ever mistaken the emperor's attention for affection? He didn't care for her. He never had.

After a long wait the emperor gestured to Ying.

"A guard was murdered last night," Ying said.

Lien kept her face an impassive mask. She would not show any emotion. "It grieves me to hear it."

"The Rhoran are responsible. Why did you not stop them?"

"I am sorry, Master. I heard nothing last night. They were all in their beds when I left to meet you." She would stick to the truth, or as close to it as she could.

"Those sliding doors make a lot of noise."

"Perhaps they left while I was with you."

Ying frowned. "How did you get out without them hearing?"

"During the shift change. The Rhoran are a suspicious group and they kept two guards in the main room all night. When my roommate went to take his turn, I slipped out."

"You shared a room with them?"

"There were not enough beds for me to have a room to myself, and the Rhoran do not understand the intricacies of a man sharing a room with an unmarried woman." She allowed a little tremor of distress to go through her. Better they believe she was disgusted by the Rhoran still.

"You did not hear them return?"

"No, Master." She paused. Though she didn't want to put Anming in the path of the emperor's displeasure she said, "Are there not other guests in the palace? Could one of them be responsible?"

"Unlikely," Ying replied. "You were awake early this morning."

She nodded. "The Rhoran are early risers and noisy with it. I wanted to take time for contemplation. I believe they are planning to leave today."

"What about the things you came for?"

"I hope Fen will have found them for me," she said. "Temur is keen to return to the steppes and will not wait. He only agreed to bring me here because he was touring the border."

The emperor finally spoke. "Fen wishes to take you to Jung Li's Dumpling House for tea. She will return your belongings then."

Relief filled her. They could leave soon. Lien bowed. "Thank you, Heavenly Majesty."

"The next time I see you, I expect you to have fulfilled your mission." He waved his hand in dismissal and Lien backed out of the room.

Did either of them believe her?

Leaving immediately would arouse suspicion, but perhaps they could leave from Jung Li's.

When she arrived at the quarters, Sukh and Berke were back.

"Good morning, child. Did you sleep well?" Sukh asked.

"Very well, thank you," she lied. "My cousin Fen has invited me to take tea with her at Jung Li's. She will return my things then." If people were listening, she needed to be as enthusiastic as possible.

"Where is Jung Li's?" Temur asked.

"On the edge of the city, near the river. It's near the gate we came through on our way here."

"Then we shall come with you and leave when you have finished."

Lien's shoulders relaxed and she smiled. They were returning to Rhora.

Fen called for Lien mid morning. Amslan, Kew and Sukh stayed with her while the rest went to saddle their horses.

A two-person palanquin sat just inside the western

gate, its blue curtained sides hiding who was inside.

"Ready, child?" Sukh asked.

Lien nodded. Perhaps as soon as they were out of view of the palace, Temur could order them to leave.

She walked over to the palanquin and a servant pulled back the curtain to reveal Fen inside, her pink satin gown pressed to perfection and her hair styled in a beautiful decorative twist. She looked the perfect princess but she'd known there had been poison in the tea.

"Cousin." Fen smiled. "Shall we go?"

"Certainly," Lien said. "Did you find my things?"

Fen tapped a box next to her. "All here."

"Let me carry it for you," Sukh said from behind Lien.

A tiny frown creased Fen's forehead. "That won't be necessary. Lien needs to look through it."

"We insist, Princess," Amslan said. "It is far too bulky and ugly a box to ride with such beauty."

Lien blinked at his charm. She never would have expected it. She lowered her voice. "I find it safer not to argue with them."

Fen gestured for them to take the box. It was small enough to carry with both hands, leaving the carrier vulnerable to attack. Sukh and Amslan solved the problem by each taking one of the wrought iron handles and carrying it between them.

"Let's go," Fen said.

Across the courtyard the other Rhoran entered the stables. Lien climbed into the palanquin. "The khan asked me to wait for him." Kew tried to climb up too, but Fen held out a hand to stop her. "Kew can walk, and the Rhoran will catch up. They're on horses." She gave the order to leave.

The curtain shut. Amslan wouldn't be happy, but

Lien wasn't either. "I must apologise again for the incident yesterday," she said. "My betrothed is very clumsy."

"It is of no matter." Fen waved her hand, almost hitting Lien.

Careful. "How have you been, Fen?"

"Very well. Mother has spoken about finding me a suitable match."

Like Lien, Fen would have no say over who she married. "Has she mentioned any names?"

"There is a Lord Anming from Chungson," she said. "He is here at the moment for other business. And there is a duke from the Laksung province."

"Do you have a preference?"

"I will do as my mother and father bid."

She had no choice.

Outside the palanquin, people called to one another, and the scents of baked wares and flowers wafted in. Lien longed to pull back the curtain and check where they were going. They could be taken anywhere but at least Kew, Amslan and Sukh were close by.

"What is it like, living with the barbarians?"

Lien brought her attention back to her cousin. She needed to continue her pretence. "They live in tents," she said. "There is dust and dirt everywhere and they don't bathe."

"They don't bathe?" Fen pulled a face.

Lien nodded. "I haven't been clean since I left."

"How do you stand it?"

"We must do as the emperor bids us," Lien said.

"Are there many in your camp?"

"At times it appears like an endless sea of yurts," she said. "Other days it feels like I have seen everyone in camp too many times." Everything she said could be repeated to the emperor, but she would give him no real information. "I had to learn to ride astride a horse," Lien continued. "They are great big dirty creatures."

"How hideous. At least you have Kew. I was most concerned when she disappeared and I am happy she reached you."

A light clunk and the palanquin stopped swaying.

"We have arrived, First Princess Fen," a voice announced from outside.

Fen smiled. "How lovely."

The curtains lifted and Sukh held out his hand to help Lien out. She scanned the area. Temur and the others were astride their horses, and in front of her was the dumpling house.

"Lien, we must go down to the river before we eat. It is horridly hot today," Fen called.

Across from Jung Li's was a small gap between the bamboo hedge and a path which led to the river. She had always been forbidden to go down there as anyone could hide behind the hedge—it wasn't safe for a princess.

"I do not think it wise."

"Nonsense." Fen waved her hand at Lien. "We have all my guards and your Rhoran to protect us."

Stories of Fen's reaction when she didn't get her own way were epic and Lien didn't want her to throw a temper tantrum. "Of course."

Her fingers twitched towards her knives but she resisted the urge.

She followed her cousin down the path and into the clearing, Sukh and Amslan on either side of her. As they cleared the bushes, she sighed in relief. It was empty.

Hedges ran in a neat row all around the clearing, with only two breaks in it—the one she'd walked through and another upriver. The river flowed fast here which would make crossing it difficult, and on the opposite bank grew thick bushes preventing a person from climbing out the other side. The square area reminded her of the horses' pens. It was private and the noise of the city didn't permeate.

Her shoulder blades twitched.

She wanted to mount Batu and get out of here. "Fen, I am hungry," Lien said. "Could we go now?"

Fen turned and smiled. A movement in the corner of Lien's eye made her twist. The red-clad soldiers of Kun's imperial guard strode through the gap upriver and spread out, their hands on their swords.

Her heart leapt.

It was a trap.

Chapter 11

Lien tensed, ready for anything but she merely said, "Are Kun's guards here to protect us as well?"

Fen laughed. "You can drop the act, cousin. We know you stole the emperor's prisoners."

Fen wasn't part of the secret bodyguard. She wasn't involved in state matters at all and shouldn't have a clue about the prisoners.

Around her the Rhoran drew their bows and arrows and moved in around Temur. He narrowed his eyes, waiting for her response, his own arrow pointing at her.

She flinched. He thought she had betrayed him. "What are you talking about? Come, let's go to Jung Li's."

Fen shifted and attacked, her strike lightning—no, gifted—fast.

Lien blocked and punched her in the face, reacting on instinct. Fen slumped to the ground unconscious and Kun's guard parted, letting Ying through.

Her stomach roiled. She could beat any man—except for Ying.

He glanced at Fen and then back at Lien. "That

answers my remaining question about your loyalty."

She had to bluff, otherwise they wouldn't get out of here alive.

Heart pounding, she bowed to him. "Master, I am confused. Why did Fen attack me?"

To her right Amslan swore and swung his bow and arrow towards her. She was caught in the middle; if one side didn't kill her, the other would. How had it come to this?

"These games are not honourable," Ying said.

Nor were the lies they had told her. She clenched the knives in her pockets.

Amslan drew back his bow. She would die, but she would save the Rhoran first.

"Temur, run!"

Amslan released the arrow and Lien moved fast, dodging it and striking at Ying. He stepped back and countered with a sharp punch towards her stomach which she only just deflected. Pain shot through her arm at the impact.

War cries filled the air and Kew bellowed, but Lien only had time for Ying. He fought fast and she moved backwards towards the river, away from the rest of the fighting, defending herself. She had no opportunity to attack Ying or to retrieve her knives, but the Rhoran clothes made it easier for her to move. She focused as he had taught her, dodging and anticipating his every move.

She had to keep him occupied long enough for Temur to defeat Kun's men. If she failed they would all be slaughtered. She had to give them the opportunity to escape.

Ying's foot hit her hard in the thigh and she went down, rolling away on the soft mud and on to her feet, ignoring the throbbing pain, and blocked the next kick directed at her midsection.

She breathed evenly and continued to block almost rhythmically.

Bless the ancestors. It *was* a rhythm. He was leading her through one of her patterns—toying with her.

The realisation must have shown in her eyes because he smiled, slow and devil-like. True fear strangled the breath from her body and fine sweat prickled the hairs on her arm.

Ying stopped. "You learnt nothing of what I taught you."

Not true. He wanted her to feel worthless. She gasped, but didn't dare take her eyes off him to find out how the others fared. She would die here today, but she would die fighting. Her fingers curled towards the handles of the knives, but before she grabbed them he attacked, swiftly, viciously. Each punch carried his full weight behind it and pain bloomed from every place he made contact. Blow after blow hit her as if she was a stuffed sandbag they had used in practice. He was punishing her.

Fending off the blows, she continued backing away. She had to time this perfectly.

She slipped on the muddy bank and fell, arching her back to narrowly miss a foot to the face. She rolled and Ying's foot came down on her arm. He grinned and applied more pressure to break the bone.

This was her chance.

She flicked her free arm and the knife slid into her hand. She slashed at his hamstring, piercing his skin before he jumped back. He swore as she leapt to her feet, blades in both her hands.

Ying paused. He had taught her where the main arteries were, and how to cause the most harm. She could do significant damage and it was her only advantage.

Panting and aching, she didn't blink. They stared into each other's eyes waiting for the next move. His were deep black pits of disdain.

Her whole body grew heavy. It couldn't take much more punishment. She had to end this.

She attacked, desperate but focused, aiming only where she could do the most damage; the neck, the eyes, the groin. He blocked her first attack, but wasn't fast enough to block her second strike to his neck.

He was slowing down too.

A thin trickle of blood seeped from the wound. Not deep enough to hurt.

Fury flashed across his face, the first show of real emotion. She was getting to him. She blocked his counter-attack and slashed towards his face but he was no longer there. As she swung around, his foot caught her side and she stumbled, the wind almost knocked out of her. He followed with a turning kick and she let it hit her, capturing it with her arms and slicing across his achilles tendon with her knife.

He roared with pain and wrenched his leg away. She had to follow it up but she had no more strength left.

Kew flashed an image into her mind of Lien face first on the ground. The most likely outcome, but she didn't want Kew to witness it.

Leave.

Ying frowned at her.

Kew moved behind Ying. What was she doing?

Awareness flashed in Ying's eyes. He knew something was behind him. She had to attack now, before he hurt Kew. She threw a flurry of punches, which he blocked systematically. It was no use. He was stronger than her.

Kew burst into her mind, an insistent image of her

falling to the ground. All at once she understood. Lien flung herself on to the mud, as a kick connected and her ribs cracked. Fire scorched the area where she had just stood.

But Ying was gone.

Lien scrambled to her feet, her chest screaming, and whirled around, preparing for the attack.

Bodies of Kun's guard littered the ground and the Rhoran sat atop their horses staring at her with a mixture of disbelief and awe on their faces.

"Is he gone?" Temur asked.

"I don't know." If Ying returned she wouldn't be able to stop him. "We have to go."

She stumbled forward, grabbing on to Batu's saddle for support. She had to mount, had to get out of here.

Kew growled as the pain crashed down around Lien and dragged her under.

~*~

Lien jerked awake, agony searing through her, and she blinked in the darkness.

"It's all right. You're safe for now." Temur adjusted his grip on her. He hugged her from behind, no not a hug, holding her in place, so she didn't fall off his horse.

Intense pain filled her. The fight. Ying. Her pulse spiked. "How far?" she croaked.

"Quite a distance from the city." He passed her a water bag. "We haven't stopped in case Ying sends people after us. We won't reach the steppes until midday."

Good, but they needed to remain vigilant. If Ying caught up with them… "How are the others?" Had anyone been injured?

"In a better state than you."

There was more she needed to ask, to remember, but pain fogged her mind.

"Amslan," Temur called.

The dark shadow of a rider moved next to them.

"She needs healing. Have you recovered?"

"Yes."

Temur halted his horse and slid off, holding Lien in place so she didn't fall. His absence left a coldness behind her. Amslan switched from his horse to Temur's, his hands rough.

"This will hurt," he said.

More than it already did? Impossible.

Searing lightning heat hit her and she lost consciousness.

~*~

When Lien woke again it was daylight and Kew was curled up next to her on the hard grassy ground of the steppes. Kew blew smoke over her as she struggled to move, a sharp pain in her ribs making her hiss. Ying had broken her ribs. Why hadn't Amslan healed them? Blinking against the harsh sunlight, she took in her surroundings. The Rhoran sat in a circle eating, their horses picketed nearby. She counted them, needing to make certain everyone was there.

No. Two were missing and Arigh sobbed in Amslan's arms.

"She's awake." Chinua's voice above her—her guard. The pinch in her heart pained her as much as the rest of her body. She shut her eyes briefly.

Amslan shifted his mother to Sukh and rose with Temur.

Their expressions were grim, which she expected from Amslan, but she'd never seen Temur's eyes so flat, so hard, so angry. "How are you feeling?"

In danger. She needed to be upright, ready to defend herself. Sitting up, she breathed through the throbbing pain in her whole midsection. Shuffling her legs to a more comfortable position made her groan. "I hurt."

"I can't believe you're still alive." Amslan grumbled. His face was pale making the dark rings around his eyes stand out even more. He had healed some of her injuries on the journey—though it didn't feel like it. It was past time she acknowledged him and his skills. "You saved me, again."

He nodded, his lips tight together.

"Thank you."

"You set us up." His whole body tensed and Kew rose, putting herself between Lien and Amslan. She growled.

"You lured us to the river to have us slaughtered."

"No!"

"You told Ying about the gift, didn't you?"

Lien glanced at Temur. "It was the only way to prevent Ying from killing us. If he thought you all had the same gift as me, he wouldn't attack us."

"Stop him from killing you maybe. He discovered each gift was different as soon as he questioned my family."

"I didn't know about the prisoners."

How could he believe she'd planned this? She'd almost been beaten to death, had fought harder than she ever had before to save their lives. If she hadn't been there, Ying would have killed them all before they'd blinked. But if she hadn't been there, they wouldn't have been at Jung Li's. They should have left first thing that morning.

Temur handed her some food and she bit into the dried meat, her jaw aching from the chewing motion. She forced herself to swallow.

Behind them the rest of the Rhoran were silent. She was no longer one of them, no longer welcome. Her throat ached. She met Temur's cold gaze. "I was attempting to get us out of the palace alive." The men towered over her so she shifted to get to her feet.

"You shouldn't move." Temur put a hand on her arm, stopping her.

They didn't want her to stand.

Couldn't they tell how much pain she was in? She wasn't a threat to them.

"Leading us straight into a trap hurts your argument." Amslan scoffed. "Is Fen like you?"

Fen. She'd forgotten all about her cousin. "She didn't train with me. I had no idea she was fast. Her attack caught me by surprise."

"You lied to me about the gift," Temur said. "Why should I believe you now when you've proven you don't keep your promises?"

Guilt flooded her. "I didn't think my gift was the same. As far as I knew, the gift could only make you fast." Even she heard the excuse in her voice. "If I was on the emperor's side, you would all be dead. Ying and I could have killed all of you in seconds."

"If you hadn't fooled Temur, if we hadn't waited for your belongings, my father would still be alive." The anguish was clear in Amslan's voice.

Shock speared her system. "Yeke is dead?" She glanced at Temur.

He nodded. "They left before us and were ambushed away from the city."

Tears sprang to her eyes. He'd been in no state to fight.

"Don't you dare cry for him." Amslan's punch connected with her jaw and threw her back on to the ground. Kew roared and let out a stream of flames which forced Amslan backwards. Lien's body screamed, but she pushed herself back to a seated position.

"We must keep moving." Temur called for everyone to mount up.

He didn't admonish his friend. She was more an outsider now than when she'd first arrived. But she wouldn't be a burden, no matter how much her body ached, and she wouldn't be left behind.

She crawled to her knees and then, using Kew as a brace, she forced herself to her feet, stumbling until her legs strengthened. Shuffling across to Batu, she stared at the stirrups. How on earth could she mount with her ribs aching so?

"Let me help, child," Sukh said. "Everyone is upset now, but things will settle when we get back to camp."

She turned to him, blinking back tears of gratitude. Placing her foot in his cupped hand, she let him boost her up, hissing in pain, and nudged Batu towards the camp.

~*~

The journey was long and tortuous. Using breathing exercises and centring her mind, Lien attempted to visualise her family and block out the incessant throb of her whole body, but any misstep by Batu sent pain coursing through her. Not even the thought Bao might be alive was enough to keep the pain at bay.

They rode well into the night on the second day and woke early the next morning. Lien sat on the edge of the group, forcing down food, until the pain in her jaw became unbearable. She put it aside and took quiet, slow breaths.

"For Qadan's sake, child, you're still in pain," Arigh said next to her. "Let me get Amslan to examine you."

"I do not believe it wise." Why was this woman

being kind to her? "Do you not think I caused your husband's death too?"

Tears welled in Arigh's eyes. "No. You did what you could. Amslan is upset but in time he will realise we couldn't have escaped without your help."

"Thank you."

"I should thank you. I am sitting here on the steppes, in my homeland because of you."

It wasn't enough. "I wish I had saved Yeke."

"Me too." Tears glistened in Arigh's eyes. "Let me call Amslan over. It is not right for you to suffer so."

Her empathy made no sense. Lien deserved to suffer. "Wait." She didn't want to draw attention to herself. "Amslan is not well himself. He exhausted himself healing everyone."

"It takes energy to heal, but Amslan is young and recovering quickly."

"I cannot allow him to heal me," she said. "I will survive until we reach camp." She deserved this pain, this punishment for ever believing the emperor's lies.

"Camp is another few days ride from here."

A few more days! It would be hell, but she wouldn't risk Amslan's health no matter how badly he treated her.

"Temur, tell this stubborn child to let Amslan heal her," Arigh called.

The whole group turned to Lien. She straightened her spine. Temur walked over and examined Lien.

She met his dark gaze.

He hesitated.

"I am fine." She ignored the twinges in her jaw.

Kew snorted and lightly bumped Lien's side.

She gasped as pain shot through her skin, making her sweat.

"I can see that," Temur said dryly. He called Amslan

over. "Your mother wishes for you to heal Lien."

"It is unnecessary," Lien said.

Amslan was silent for a moment as he examined his mother and then her. "She will survive the journey home."

Lien wanted to laugh at his grim tone. "I can keep up."

"Let's mount then," Temur ordered.

She'd broken her promise and destroyed any trust he'd had in her. No longer would he hold her hand, or touch her unconsciously. No point wishing the old Temur back.

He was the cold man she'd expected of him back in the beginning.

As she rode out behind the party, a tear escaped and ran down her cheek.

Every morning brought new pains and intensified old ones. Meditating to block out any feeling rarely worked. When Sukh rode back one day to report the camp was just ahead Lien slumped forward in relief, and then immediately straightened at the pain.

The whole tribe gathered to greet them and to hear the news, laughing and cheering when they saw Arigh and Cheren. Lien kept to the back, and after Kew jumped down, she slid off Batu and unsaddled her horse. She didn't belong here.

Sukh put a hand over hers and she jolted at his presence. "I will take care of her. Go find your tent and I'll send Geriel to you."

Her throat closed at his kindness. She nodded and moved around the crowd towards the yurts. Geriel caught up with her.

"My Qadan! What happened to you?" She stared at Lien, horrified.

What must she look like? Her body was still one huge purpling bruise so her face must be too. "I had a fight."

"I'll say. Come with me." Geriel took her arm and led her towards Lien's tent.

Relief swept through her when she stepped through the door and her gaze went to her bed. Something soft and warm. She lay down, grimacing at the pain and then exhaustion swallowed her.

~*~

Movement on her bed awoke Lien. Temur sat there, his expression grim. How long had she slept?

"Good morning, Lien." His tone was much kinder than it had been since the palace.

She blinked at him, her brain struggling to wake up, her body still aching. She must have slept all night.

"How are you today?"

Lien shifted to a seated position and the now familiar pain throbbed through her. "Sore." She could admit it now they were back in camp. Now she wouldn't be a burden.

He nodded. "The healers will concentrate on you today. They examined the others last night and all just need more food to get their energy levels back to normal."

"I'm pleased to hear it."

He studied her. "I believe you are."

Lien wasn't sure what to make of him. He had changed during the journey—could she trust him?

"Erdene brought you something to eat." He lifted a tray from the floor and placed it on her lap, taking the lid off the bowl. The smells wafting from it made her mouth water. Picking up a spoon, she tasted the broth and sighed with pleasure as it slid down her throat.

"I would like to thank you for rescuing members of my tribe."

Lien paused before sipping the next spoonful. He said *my* tribe, not our tribe. If he no longer considered her part of his tribe, would their marriage be cancelled? He hardly needed to worry about the emperor's wrath anymore—the emperor had attacked first. "You do not blame me for Yeke's death?"

He hesitated, then ignored the question. "Did you know Fen's plan?"

She shook her head. "No. I thought we were going to Jung Li's." She hesitated. "What happened to her?"

"We tied her up and left her there."

"Oh." How dangerous would it be for her cousin? Ying must have returned for her.

"She sent you into a trap and yet you are worried about her?" Temur's voice was incredulous.

"She is a child of her upbringing," Lien said. "She has been taught the emperor knows best in all things and with no one to tell her differently, how is she to know?"

"You continue to surprise me."

She couldn't read his expression. She hated this distance between them. "Temur, I am truly sorry for what happened. If I'd been more alert, if I hadn't put so much faith in the emperor's honour, none of this would have happened. If I'd known Fen had the gift I would have told you to leave without me."

"I thought you needed our protection."

She winced. "I'm sorry. I should have told you about my gift earlier."

"Why didn't you?"

She needed to tell him everything. "I didn't trust you. Like Fen they had always taught me the emperor is the highest power and going against his orders was unthinkable. But he'd ordered me to kill you, and then to marry you and I didn't know which order to follow."

"So you returned to the palace to get clarification." His tone was hard.

She shook her head. "No. I'd been taught the Rhoran were barbarians, but after I arrived here, I discovered otherwise. I thought the emperor was misinformed and I wanted to educate him. I wanted to put an end to the conflict between our people." She paused. "I didn't want to believe what you said about the emperor, but then I saw the truth with my own eyes."

"You gave us the opportunity to rescue our people."

It was something.

"How long have you been training?"

"Every day since they discovered my gift at eleven."

"Ying was your master. How many other students are there?"

"Two who I know of, but Fen wasn't one. There might be more."

"We couldn't see you and Ying when you fought, only sounds and dirt moving."

She'd told him she was fast. "I had to keep him occupied long enough for you to escape. If he'd defeated me, he would have killed you." She paused. "I told you to run."

"It wasn't possible." He took the empty tray from her hands and placed it on the table. "I'll send Geriel and the healers." He gestured to something behind her and walked out.

She turned, met Amslan's gaze. He had a bow and arrow pointing straight at her heart. Her pulse thudded.

He would kill her now.

Slowly, his gaze still on hers, he relaxed the bow and replaced the arrow in his quiver. He followed Temur out of the yurt.

Chapter 12

Lien didn't move until the door clicked shut behind Amslan and then her whole body slumped in shock.

Amslan had been there all along, behind her with the arrow ready to fire if Temur had given the word.

If she'd made the slightest wrong move, she'd be dead.

She sucked in air as nausea swirled around her stomach like a dust storm. It hadn't even occurred to her to check the rest of the yurt for people. She'd trusted too much.

All hope of being accepted into the tribe vanished.

She'd fought for them until she nearly died and *now* they didn't trust her. Was she a prisoner? No, Temur wouldn't have left her untied if she was. So what did he want from her? Should she escape before he made up his mind? She could navigate the steppes now and ride for days, even injured as she was.

But she didn't want to leave.

More than ever she wanted the comfort and community she'd found while she'd been here. She wanted the freedom of being a woman in Rhora, she wanted to learn everything about survival and the tribe, she wanted to make friends with Erdene and Geriel.

Had her naivety ruined that forever? She should have paid more attention to Kew's dislike of Ying, questioned it.

Where was Kew? If her dragon had sensed what Temur had been planning with Amslan, she wouldn't have allowed them inside, would have been there to protect her.

Had someone harmed her?

She swung her legs off the bed and pain swamped her. Lien breathed through it. She could do this. She had to get up, find Kew.

The door opened and Lien tensed until Geriel walked in carrying bowls and cloths.

"Where's Kew?" Lien tried to stand, but her legs wouldn't support her weight. She fell back on to the bed.

"She's gone with the children to collect dung for the fire." Geriel hurried over. "Lie down. I will heal you."

Ointments and herbs would not do much to fix the battering her body had taken. But Temur would be in no hurry to have her back at her full strength.

"Thank you." She lay on her back, still ready to defend herself if she needed to.

"I'm not as strong as Amslan, but I'll do what I can." Geriel rubbed her hands together to warm them.

"Do you have the same gift?"

Geriel nodded. "It appeared late with me. I was sixteen and had already begun training as a healer so it made sense to continue."

"How does it work?"

"It's a connection, a focus," Geriel said. "I can feel some pain and know how it needs to be fixed. Then I visualise fixing it." She shrugged. "I don't quite understand it, and it takes all of my energy. Amslan keeps trying to help me, but I must be a slow learner."

Lien smiled. "I used to meditate for ten minutes before I used my gift. The same meditation each time and it pulled my focus in, prepared my body. Now I simply think of the meditation and it prepares me."

"Your gift is fighting?"

"No, speed." What had the other warriors told the tribe about what they'd seen? "I could teach you the meditation if you'd like."

Geriel smiled. "That would be great. Thank you." She slid her hands under Lien's top and rested them on her stomach. She gasped. "You must be in agony." Her tone held sympathy. "I'll fix your ribs first."

Lien met her eyes, saw the compassion in them. "Thank you."

The searing pain of healing hit her and then blackness claimed her.

When Lien woke, she was alone. She shifted to a seated position. The sharp pain in her ribs was gone, as was the tenderness in her stomach. Something moved below her and she swung to defend herself, heart thumping, but it was Kew getting to her feet.

She scanned the room. On the table was a tray of food. When was the last time she ate? Her jaw still ached, but she needed to keep her strength up.

She stroked Kew, and the tension in her body released. Slowly she stood and made her way over to the table. Every step was agony, but she could do it. Would do it.

Kneeling down on the cushions with some difficulty, she then reached for a piece of cheese. It would be soft enough for her jaw to handle.

Temur still didn't trust her. If he had, he would have had Geriel or Amslan heal all her aches and pains.

She was such a fool.

So ridiculously naive to believe the emperor didn't know what was going on.

Temur wouldn't marry her now. She'd been in such a good position; to have a home, status and marry a man who had been kind to her and she'd thrown it all away.

The cold, silent Temur could do anything.

She sighed, ate a piece of meat and then handed some to Kew. Kew sniffed and snorted, but Lien paid her no mind.

She should travel to Chungson, find out whether her brother was alive. It made no sense to trust Anming, a complete stranger, no sense that Bao was alive, even if all her prayers had asked for it. It could be a trick to lure her away from the Rhoran to kill her.

But if it wasn't…

If Bao was alive, they could build a new life together.

She yawned.

Her head drooped, so heavy it was hard to hold up. Giving in to temptation, she leaned over, resting her head on her arms on the table. She shouldn't be sleepy, she'd just woken up.

Kew growled, but Lien's mind wouldn't focus, as if she had no control.

Almost as if she'd been drugged.

Lien woke in the dark, stretching in her bed, enjoying the way the muscles in her back felt.

Something was odd about that. Kew jumped onto the bed and came right up to her face, sending images into her mind.

She had fallen asleep and then Sukh had put her into bed and Geriel had done more healing on her.

No, she hadn't fallen asleep. Someone had drugged her.

Lien's chest tightened. It hadn't even occurred to her to check the food. Foolish. Would she ever learn?

She needed fresh air. *Kew, let's go.*

Lien flung open the door and almost crashed into Sukh who stood outside.

"How are you, Lien?" He fell into step with her.

So, they were guarding her now.

"I wish to be alone." The camp was quiet and it was close to midnight.

"Temur is worried about your injuries. He doesn't want you to push yourself too hard."

Lien stopped and stared at him. "We both know that is a lie."

Sukh said nothing.

"No one trusts me now they understand my capabilities." She continued walking towards the horses.

"That's not true."

"No? Then why did they drug me?"

Sukh puffed out a breath. "Where are you going?"

"I need to clear my head." She whistled for Batu. She wanted to leave this place and never return.

"I can't let you leave, Lien." Sukh touched her arm.

She whirled on him. "Do you really think you can stop me?"

He released his grip. "No. I only ask and hope you will listen."

Damn him. Lien couldn't refuse. Not after his kindness. He was the only one who wasn't suspicious of her.

She wanted to yell and scream, but she would never cause a scene. She sank to the ground, her body shaking, tears rolling down her face. Squeezing her eyes shut, she tried to stop them but it was no use. They would not be stopped. As Kew climbed into her lap, she gave herself over to them and sobbed.

Sukh sat next to her and put his arm around her. "It will turn out all right, child."

Lien rested her head on his shoulder, taking the comfort he offered while it lasted.

Some time later Lien calmed herself. What had she done?

She'd broken down in front of this man, shown her weakness to him. She might as well have given him a knife and exposed her throat. Pushing away from him, she stood. "I apologise for my outburst."

"Child, I have three daughters. I am used to it."

Her heart clenched. She was sure Geriel had never sobbed over him like she had.

"Are you ready to go back to your tent?" Sukh got to his feet.

What choice did she have? "Yes." The urge to flee was gone now.

They walked through the dark, but out of the corner of her eye, Lien saw movement. She tensed as she made out the shapes of two people. "You're not the only person guarding me, are you, Sukh?"

He hesitated. "No."

More people had seen her breakdown, had witnessed her weakness. She resisted the urge to speed across to her tent, to show them they couldn't stop her. It wouldn't help them trust her.

Lien continued, stopping outside her door. "Thank you, Sukh. For everything you have done, for all of your help."

"You remind me of Odval." She heard the smile in his voice. "Ours was an arranged marriage and she was not happy to move tribes, to live with me. She took time to trust, to settle in to our ways."

"But she didn't have to earn the tribe's trust."

"Of course she did. But not everyone almost gets their tribe members killed."

Lien pressed her lips together.

"It will take time, but for what it's worth, you have mine."

Tears pricked her eyes, but the lump in her throat made it impossible to speak. She nodded to him and escaped into her yurt.

Lying down on the bed, exhaustion swamped her. Kew curled up next to her.

Was Sukh right? Did she need to wait this out, show they could trust her, teach them everything she knew about the Bonamese?

Or was she being far too naive again?

~*~

In the morning, Lien rose and ran through her patterns, pushing through the residual pain. She needed to warm up, be flexible and ready to defend herself if required. No one had told her what to do, so she would act as if everything was normal. Kew stayed with her as she headed to Temur's tent for breakfast, her stomach jittering as she knocked on the door, uncertain what her welcome would be.

Temur opened the door. "You look better." He gestured for her to come inside where his family already sat at the table.

"I apologise for being late."

"We thought you might need your sleep after what you've been through." Bolormaa gave Lien a warm smile and indicated she should sit.

At least one person here didn't show her disdain. Mongke and Amslan watched her with varying levels of suspicion and she couldn't read Erdene's expression. She took her place at the table and ate as the conversation flowed around her.

"Perhaps you'd feel up to some embroidery today, child," Bolormaa said.

"That sounds wonderful," Lien answered, surprised by her desire to do something normal.

Temur interrupted. "I thought Lien could show us the skills she's kept hidden." His tone was mild.

Tension sprang to her muscles. What did Temur want of her? "If you would like me to, my khan."

"She's not fully recovered," Bolormaa protested. "Let her rest today."

Bolormaa's defence warmed her, relaxed the tension in her body. "Thank you for your concern, Bolormaa. I am capable of demonstrating."

Bolormaa frowned at her and then at her son. "Temur, I must protest."

"If Lien is happy, then so am I."

There would be no further concern about her wellbeing.

Bolormaa opened her mouth and then closed it again with a snort of unhappiness.

As the others left to get ready for the day, Lien asked, "What would you like me to demonstrate?"

"Everything." His voice carried little emotion and he looked past her as if something on the opposite wall interested him. "I'm sure you know different techniques we can learn."

She wanted to demand he look at her. "Very well. Where is this demonstration going to take place?"

"In the training area."

When he said nothing else, Lien asked, "Shall I go there now?"

"Yes. Amslan will be there."

He didn't even glance at her as she left the tent. Strange how she'd grown used to the attentive Temur who had called her his joy. It was foolish to miss it now.

She walked through the camp towards the training area. A few people greeted her, but many turned away as she walked past. She held her head high, shoulders back and greeted everyone by name. She would not cower.

Only Amslan was in the training area setting up the targets. As soon as people found out about the demonstration, there would be a crowd.

"Would you like help?" she asked.

He glared at her. "Your help isn't needed anywhere."

Kew growled, but Lien paid the animosity no mind. It hadn't changed and it was almost comforting in a way. Taking one of the lighter targets, she set it up some distance away before returning to get another one.

Amslan glowered. "Where are you going to stand to hit that?"

"Over there." She pointed in the opposite direction.

He grunted. He didn't believe she'd do it. Well, the purpose of the exercise was to show them what she could do. Lien wouldn't leave anything out. She wanted them to understand exactly how dangerous she was so there could be no more misunderstandings. She wouldn't lie to them any longer. And if they didn't trust her now, they definitely wouldn't afterwards.

By the time they'd set up the area, the whole camp had gathered. Everyone's eyes were on her as Temur walked out into the middle of the field and stood next to her.

"Lien has agreed to show us her fighting abilities," he said. "They are more advanced than she revealed to us." Voices murmured as he stepped back into the crowd with Amslan.

Here she was the centre of attention, an easy target should anyone wish it. Well so be it. "My gift is speed. I move faster than most and it gives me a tremendous advantage." She indicated the target about a hundred yards away. "How fast do you think I can reach that target?"

She waited and one child called out, "Ten seconds."

"Will you count for me then?"

The child nodded. "Go!"

Lien sped to the target and stopped. It took a second for all heads in the crowd to turn to her and the collective gasp was audible from where she stood. The child yelled, "One second!"

Lien jogged back to the crowd. "I was taught to focus on speed and hone my skill until I was as fast as I could be. But speed alone won't help if you need to stop someone." She picked up a quiver of arrows and a bow. "I had to practise every day with a bow and arrow until I hit the centre of the target every time."

This time she didn't use her speed. She aimed and fired at each target, moving in a circle until they each had three arrows sticking out of the bull's eye.

"That was slow," Shuren complained.

Lien smiled. "That was so you could see. Would you like me to do it faster?"

The assembled children cried, "Yes!" She didn't dare check Temur's reaction. Instead she retrieved the arrows from the targets, struggling with the last deeply embedded ones. Sukh came to help her.

"Thank you."

She demonstrated her speed with the bow and arrow and then continued her demonstration with her knives, throwing them at the targets. When she finished she scanned the silent crowd, noting the disbelief, fear and awe on their faces. At least now they understood she wasn't someone to mess with. Perhaps it would grant her a measure of safety.

"There may be times when I have no weapon at hand and my body must become a weapon. I learnt patterns which taught me how to block and make counter attacks." She showed them one of her more complex patterns, breathing evenly and keeping the moves slow and fluid.

When Lien finished, Geriel said, "It's like you're dancing. Can that actually stop an attack?"

"Yes. Would anyone like to attack me?"

The crowd murmured. Bolormaa stepped forward. "I don't want someone to hurt you, child."

Lien smiled. "I do not believe it will be an issue."

A few people laughed.

She surveyed the tribe. "I promise not to use my speed."

"I will." Geriel stepped forward and flashed her a smile. Another ally.

Odval brought a hand up to her mouth and Lien said, "I will not hurt Geriel."

Geriel attacked then, throwing a punch at Lien's face. Lien twisted, blocking with an upward swipe of her arm, and then swept Geriel's legs from under her and lowered her to the ground. "Good idea to try the element of surprise."

Geriel gaped at her before laughing. "Did you use your speed?"

Lien held out a hand to help her up. "No, I didn't."

Dusting herself off, Geriel returned to the crowd. "Who's next?"

A few of the younger men had a go and were efficiently disabled. As Lien lowered the last man to the ground, the crowd cheered. Perhaps she was winning them over.

"You've got double practice this afternoon, Kushi." Chinua laughed as Kushi got to his feet and rejoined the group.

Who would be next? So far none of those who stepped forward had been the elite fighters of the tribe.

"I'll go." Amslan.

This would be a real test. She would have to be careful with him. He'd been analysing her moves, assessing any weak spots. Any good warrior would have done the same before initiating a fight.

Nerves raced over her skin as he approached and she bowed to give him the respect he deserved.

He struck at her head, but she was ready for it. She twisted so it brushed her side, a dull pain, but one she could ignore. Unlike the others he wanted to hurt her and would use all his ability.

She respected that.

Careful not to use her gift, she blocked and turned, anticipating his next move.

He feinted left and then attacked with his right fist.

She blocked his punch with a kick and followed it up with a side kick to his stomach, which knocked him back a step. Elation flooded Lien as he glared at her. If he wouldn't play nice, she didn't need to.

His next attack was fierce, a flurry of punches and strikes designed as much to confuse as they were to hurt. Lien stepped back a few paces, side-stepped and aimed a kick to the back of his knee, which made him fall to the ground.

She moved away to allow him to get up.

The crowd was silent, watching intently.

Amslan was one of their best fighters. If she beat him, especially not using her powers, there would be great dishonour.

But if she let him win, there would be some who would understand what she'd done and the result would be the same.

Amslan's next attack captured her attention. One punch landed, numbing her right arm, so she countered with a kick. He dodged and threw a punch at her face, then her stomach.

Damn, he'd been holding back.

His attacks came thick and fast and Lien focused on her breathing, blocking and then attacking. One punch landed against his hard stomach, bringing her close enough to smell his sweat. She spun away, narrowly missing his counter-attack.

Temur walked towards them. "Enough."

Lien stopped, but Amslan didn't. His fist hurtled towards her with the full weight of his body behind it.

Her jaw exploded in pain as she fell to the ground.

Chapter 13

Face throbbing and mouth full of dust, Lien pushed herself to a seated position, spitting out the dirt and wiping her face with the front of her shirt. The whole tribe was silent.

Temur offered her a hand and she studied his face before she took it, allowing him to help her to her feet. The crowd cheered.

Amslan breathed heavily, but his eyes showed a reluctant respect. It would do for now. She touched her aching jaw and asked Temur, "Is there anything else you would like me to demonstrate?"

"We've seen enough for today." He addressed the crowd. "It's time for the midday meal." Without a further word to her, he walked away with Amslan.

Lien watched him go, a lump in her throat. She had a long way to go. He would no longer come to her tent with the offer to heal her.

Geriel jogged up. "Are you all right?"

A warmth spread through Lien at her concern. "I will be fine."

She took Lien's hand. "Come on, you're bleeding. You need to get cleaned up." As they walked to the healer's tent, she said, "Can you teach me to fight like that?"

Lien would love to give back to the tribe, to teach them, but she didn't want to overstep her boundaries. "I'll ask Temur if I may."

Geriel grinned. "You were amazing. If Temur hadn't stopped the fight, you would have beaten Amslan."

"Amslan is a good fighter."

"Yes, but you're better." Inside the tent, Geriel cleaned Lien's split lip. "I should thank you. You're giving me plenty of opportunity to practise healing."

The smile hurt, but then Geriel placed her hand over Lien's jaw and a few minutes later the pain was gone. "It is I who should thank you."

Geriel grinned. "Come on. You can eat with us. Maybe this afternoon you can show me that meditation?"

"Of course." Lien's steps slowed as she approached Temur's tent. "I should talk to Temur now," she told Geriel.

"All right. Do you want me to wait for you?"

"No, thank you."

"Come by the tent when you're done." Geriel waved and walked off.

Lien had one family who was there for her. But Bao was also somewhere out there. Maybe. She had to find out for sure.

Stomach churning, Lien knocked and entered Temur's tent, finding him alone inside, sitting at the table, some food in front of him. She hesitated in the doorway, waiting for him to greet her and when he didn't, she asked, "Was the demonstration suitable?"

He was silent, his face unreadable.

Lien returned his gaze, unease making her stomach churn faster.

"You could have escaped at any time after you'd been healed." He said it with no emotion.

She nodded and closed the door behind her. "I could have left the camp, but I didn't know the way home."

"And you wanted to spy on my tribe?" The faintest hint of anger touched his voice.

"No… not entirely." Would he believe her if she explained? "The emperor gave me to you, and an imperial princess does not defy the emperor. At first I learnt as much as possible in case the emperor asked me, but it sat uneasy with me."

His face was hard.

How could he understand the turmoil she'd been through when he'd grown up in such a loving family? "I spent my whole life believing the emperor was the embodiment of God on earth. That kind of upbringing is not something which can be swept away in an instant. I didn't believe my family wanted me dead, and I thought if I gave the emperor the information he wanted, he would love me." She needed to keep the emotion out of her tone, otherwise he would think she was trying to manipulate him.

His expression grew even colder.

She hurried on. "But life with the Rhoran was so very different from anything I had experienced—so much warmer, freer and challenging." Her voice caught and a flicker of empathy flashed in his eyes. Perhaps being emotional was the answer. The Rhoran were far more honest in their emotions than the Bonamese. "I'd been taught the Rhoran were barbarians, that they'd killed my parents and were a threat to the Bonamese, but I saw none of that. I began to enjoy myself."

"But you still went to the palace believing you would betray your promises to me?"

"No! I really thought the emperor had been misinformed and when I told him the truth, it would stop the conflict between us." So incredibly naïve and self-absorbed. "I wanted peace, I wanted to stop anyone else losing loved ones."

His expression didn't change.

Suddenly the only thing she wanted in this world was to stay with the Rhoran. "Temur, you have seen what I can do. If I was going to kill you and your people, I would have done it by the river with Ying. The emperor has betrayed me, I do not want to return."

"You could destroy my people."

"Yes." Why should he let her stay when there was a risk she would turn on them? "If you would prefer, I will leave, go to Chungson and discover the truth about my brother." She hesitated and then inhaled deeply and removed her knives from her belt, handing them to him handle first. "Or if you truly believe I will harm the tribe, then you should kill me now." She knelt and closed her eyes, her heart thumping hard in her chest. If he tried to kill her, she would leave.

The minutes dragged on, but Lien didn't move. She stayed kneeling, back straight, head bowed, eyes closed, every sense tuned to him, waiting for him to act. Outside people called out to each other, unaware of the life and death situation occurring so close to them.

After an eternity, Temur said, "Stand up."

Relief coursed through her veins, her whole body light, as she opened her eyes and stood.

"Why did you not kill me at the palace when we first met?"

Part of her power came from his belief she was a killer assassin. If he knew she'd never killed anyone, it might lessen his respect. But she needed to tell him some truth. "It was your compassion," she said. "You knew I didn't want to marry you, but you could not refuse. I hesitated and Li Ping did not."

He handed back her knives. "Solongo says the Gods still bless our union. We will marry in a half moon." He walked out of the tent.

Lien let out a long breath and sank down on to the cushions next to the table, her legs too weak to hold her. She could stay. Her gaze caught the closed door. But Temur was unhappy about their marriage. Was it wrong of her to want to stay, to make him marry her when he didn't want to?

She would get a home out of the arrangement, but what did he get? An inconvenience.

She admired Temur and didn't want to hurt him.

She'd never been so confused. Life had at least been simpler at the palace. She'd been told how to think, how to act and what to do. Here she had no idea.

And she didn't want to make the wrong choice.

With no appetite for food, she returned to her own tent.

A half moon.

That was all the time she had to figure out how to make Temur trust her again.

~*~

In the morning, Lien rose at dawn and dressed. Temur had agreed for her to teach Geriel and early morning was the best time for both. It was still dim, the sun peeking over the horizon and the yurts around her were just getting some colour. She rubbed her hands together to warm them as she walked through camp.

When she arrived at the training ground, she found two dozen women around her own age waiting for her. Geriel grinned at her. "They heard about the lessons, and wanted to join in. That's all right, isn't it?"

Lien nodded, a thrill going down her spine. Temur had given her permission to teach whoever wanted to learn, but she hadn't thought many would want to be taught by her. "Line up in four rows," she ordered. She'd start with basic attacks and blocks, warming them up. Lien demonstrated and then walked up and down the rows making corrections. The women learnt quicker than the Bonamese women had.

Satisfied they had grasped the basics, she taught them a couple of kicks.

"This is weird," Geriel said as she did a front kick, and then overbalanced and with a shriek, landed hard on her buttocks. As the others laughed, Lien helped Geriel to her feet.

"Balance is as important in hand-to-hand combat as it is on a horse," she said. "If you overbalance you may end up in a vulnerable position, unable to recover fast enough to defend yourself from the next attack. I want you all to stand on one leg."

As they found their centre, she checked if the rest of the camp was waking. She jolted. How long had Temur been watching? She walked over, nerves bubbling to the surface.

"How are they going?" he asked.

"They learn quickly," she said. "Though some moves are foreign to them." She called to the women to change legs.

"I imagine your numbers will increase tomorrow." Temur gestured to some early risers who watched the training session.

"Does that please you?"

"You have things to teach us." He glanced at the women. "I'll leave you to your lessons." He walked away.

Lien let out her breath. He was marginally warmer towards her today. She gave the women leave to rest and explained the dynamics of the next kick.

When she called the lesson to an end, Geriel moaned. "I was just getting the hang of it."

"Continue practising in your own time," Lien said. "Through repetition we learn the movements and can increase our speed."

"Could we have another lesson this evening?" one girl asked.

Lien smiled at their enthusiasm. The Bonamese women had never enjoyed learning. "Of course. Before or after dinner?"

"After," Geriel said. "Most of us have to help prepare the food."

"All right. I will see you then." A lightness entered her body as the women left. Perhaps this could be her contribution to the tribe.

Mid-afternoon Lien attended a training lesson run by Chinua. They started with archery practice. Chinua walked over to her. "You don't need me to tell you what to do." He laughed. "Why don't you help me correct the others?"

A warm glow filled her. He respected her skills enough to acknowledge them. She placed her bow back in the rack and moved over to a student at the end of the line.

After watching the first few shots, she said, "Your elbow is too low."

He scowled at her. Unperturbed, she moved closer. "Take position." When he did, she lifted his elbow further. "Now breathe out as you release the arrow."

Still frowning, he took the shot and hit the bull's eye.

He grinned, his earlier surliness gone. "Thanks."

"You're welcome." She moved on to the next student.

They worked for half an hour on archery before switching to wrestling. With no idea what to do, Lien watched the pairs wrestle while Chinua explained the moves to her. After the opponent was on the ground, it took little time to disable them.

"We don't wrestle a lot in combat," Chinua said. "Our preference is fighting from horseback or with a sabre, but as a last resort wrestling works." He grinned. "We generally hold contests with the other tribes. People love to watch it."

She understood why. It was fascinating to see the mechanics of the fight, the manoeuvring into position.

"All right." Chinua turned to her. "Time to learn. I want you to punch me."

"Are you sure?"

He chuckled. "Yeah, just don't use your speed."

Lien got into position and threw a punch, not too fast so she could see what he was doing. He blocked, stepping into her and then using his hip, he threw her over the side of his body on to the ground. He followed up by pinning her and faking a couple of punches.

Her side ached from hitting the ground and she was effectively trapped against him. Lien huffed and then grinned as he got up and offered her his hand. "Show me how."

After Lien learnt the throwing technique, it was time for sabre practice. Chinua showed them different attacks, both on the ground and on horseback. She lined up across from her opponent, Kushi and when Chinua gave the command, she kicked Batu into a canter. Kushi came closer, his horse almost next to hers. She reached out, deflecting the first attack, but overbalanced and he caught her under the ribs with his next strike and her breath left her.

Manoeuvring away from him, she gasped until she could breathe properly. "Well done." She had a lot to learn.

Kushi frowned. "You could have beaten me with your speed."

Maybe. "If I don't learn the correct technique I will be of no use should someone with the same gift attack me, or if I am too exhausted to use it."

"I hadn't thought of that."

They returned to their positions and ran through the exercise again. This time Lien didn't even deflect the first attack and her ribs ached. "Can we stop a moment?" Chinua showed the correct method to one of the other pairs.

He moved from the waist up, keeping his lower body straight and balanced. Anticipating the strike, he twisted, blocking the blade much like she would deflect a punch and then changed direction in an instant, slicing across his opponent's chest.

So that's how it worked. "Shall we try again?"

"Yes," Kushi said, a slight frown on his face.

This time Lien copied Chinua's example and Kushi grunted as her attack hit him in the ribs. She grinned. Turning Batu, she asked, "Are you all right?"

Kushi nodded.

Not long after, Chinua called a halt to the practice and announced they would go through axe work tomorrow. Another weapon she wasn't familiar with. She couldn't wait.

Lien rode Batu over to the grooming area and unsaddled her.

"How did you pick it up so fast?" Kushi asked as he unsaddled his horse next to her. The question held no suspicion, just curiosity.

"Chinua's block is much like my martial arts, so I applied those skills."

He raised his eyebrows. "My sister attended your lesson this morning," he said. "She's excited by what she learnt."

She beamed. "I am pleased."

He hesitated. "Are you only teaching women?"

It never occurred to her the men might want to learn. Bonamese men would never take lessons in warfare from a woman, even if they had known of her skill. "I will teach anyone who wants to learn."

"What time is your evening lesson?"

"After dinner."

He nodded. "I might see you then."

The Rhoran culture was a constant surprise to her.

Lien continued brushing Batu, a smile on her face.

~*~

Lien's classes grew. In only a few days she had to run four classes a day as tribes arrived for the wedding and the big hunt which would take place afterwards. Her students were a mixture of men, women and children of all ages, from warriors to healers and artisans. Some of her students taught her a few things too, applying Rhoran thinking to Bonamese techniques to take her by surprise. Chinua was particularly good at using grapples and throws to stop her attacks. She tweaked her lessons to incorporate Rhoran improvements. Any variations could give her an advantage should she ever come up against Ying again.

Aside from her training, she learnt more about the responsibilities of a Rhoran wife and tribal mother.

Women from the different tribes gathered daily to catch up on news and teach her while they embroidered or worked on other tasks.

A quarter moon after she returned from the palace, Solongo invited her to the spiritual tent. "Sit, please." The spiritual advisor indicated the cushions by the table and then handed her a cup of tea.

"What are you going to teach me today?" Lien asked.

"Teaching isn't why I called you here." Solongo sat next to her, her expression a little concerned.

Lien waited for her to continue.

"Bolormaa told you about certain customs regarding the wedding?"

"Yes."

"The most difficult one is to have Temur retrieve you from your family. No one wants you returning to the palace." Solongo smiled. "As such, Odval and Sukh have offered to adopt you. I understand Sukh has been giving you daily riding lessons and you've spent time with Odval and her children."

Lien nodded as her mind whirled. Sukh and Odval *wanted* to adopt her. They already had five children of their own.

"The Gods believe this would be a good match," Solongo continued. "But you can choose not to."

"What happens if I'm adopted?"

"We hold a simple ceremony, here in the spiritual tent and I will teach you the words to say. From then on, you will be part of Sukh and Odval's family and have the same responsibilities as their children—to obey them, support them and take care of them when they are old. You will also be required to guide your brothers and sisters, especially as you will be the eldest child."

Parents and siblings—all she ever wanted. "I would be honoured to be adopted by them."

Solongo smiled. "Wonderful. I'll send word to them and we'll do the ceremony this afternoon. You will need to prepare a small gift. Perhaps Bolormaa has some sweet curds you can give them."

"I'll ask her."

"Good. Now let me tell you about the ceremony."

~*~

Later that afternoon, Lien carried a bowl of sweet curds to the spiritual tent. Her stomach swirled with nerves as she stepped inside and found Solongo and one of the other spiritual advisors there.

Solongo smiled. "Put the gift on the table. The others won't be long."

As Lien did so, the door opened and Temur walked in. Her muscles tensed. She'd barely seen him over the past few days and had taken to eating with Sukh's family.

"Temur, I'm glad you could make it," Solongo said, walking over to him. "You can be our witness. Sit over here." She led him to a seat on the opposite side of the tent.

He looked at Lien, but before she could speak to him, her new family arrived.

"Lien! I'm so excited I could burst." Geriel rushed up and squeezed her. "I've always wanted an older sister."

Lien's chest tightened. "I have always wanted a sister too."

"You're getting three." Shuren slipped her hand into Lien's. "Plus two brothers." She scowled at Jochi and Nekhii.

Lien laughed. "My brother was my favourite person

in the world."

"How about now?" Checeg asked.

Lien hesitated. "I thought he died many years ago, but when I returned to the palace I spoke with someone who said he was still alive. I hope to find out the truth after I am married." She didn't look at Temur.

Geriel wrapped an arm around her shoulder. "We'll help. You don't have to do it alone."

Tears pricked her eyes and she blinked.

"We should begin the ceremony," Solongo said.

Lien picked up the bowl of sweet curds and stood in front of Solongo, between Sukh and Odval, as the spiritual advisor spoke.

"We call on Qadan to witness as we unite Lien with her new family."

Behind her Shuren and Jochi whispered and Temur stood to the side , his eyes on her.

"Sukh and Odval, you wish to accept this child as one of your own, and you promise to nurture her, support her and care for her from this day on?"

"Yes." Sukh and Odval spoke together.

"Lien, you wish to accept these two as your parents and you promise to obey them, support them and care for them from this day on?"

"Yes." The words came out as a whisper, her throat too tight for anything else. She swallowed hard and then repeated louder, "Yes."

Solongo gestured for the children to come forward. "Geriel, Checeg, Nekhii, Jochi and Shuren, you wish to accept Lien as your new sibling, and you promise to support and nurture her from this day on?"

"Yes," they said as one and then Shuren added, "Yes, yes, yes." She giggled.

"Lien, you wish to accept these five as your new siblings and you promise to teach, guide and support them from this day on?"

Lien smiled. "Yes." She glanced at Shuren. "With pleasure." The little girl beamed at her.

"Please swap your token gifts as symbols of this acceptance."

Lien handed Odval the bowl of curds and then turned to Sukh and took the leather riding whip he gave her. "Thank you."

"Under Qadan's guidance, I now proclaim you one family."

Geriel's hollering made Lien wince, but she hugged her new family, emotions whirling around inside her. As she stepped back she said, "Thank you." She cleared her throat. "I have been without family for such a long time and the fact you all want me..." She paused, blinking and swallowing again so she could finish the words. "It means more than I can express."

"Child, there is no need to thank us," Odval said. "You have been part of our family since you first lit a fire in our hearth."

Sukh nodded. "And speaking of which, let's go eat."

Lien's gaze caught Temur's and he smiled at her.

Her breath caught. The first smile he'd given her since she'd returned. Perhaps finally she'd done something right.

"Come on, Lien." Jochi tugged on her hand. "I'm hungry."

Lien laughed and joined her family.

After dinner Lien watched her family prepare for bed. Geriel and Checheg placed several large mattresses on the floor in the sleeping section of the yurt and Shuren and Jochi kissed their parents goodnight and lay down.

Lien frowned. "Do you all sleep there?" There would barely be any room to move when all the children went to bed.

"It's cosy," Geriel said, "and warm in winter."

Having a tent to herself was a luxury. Though now she had a family to consider. "Do you want to sleep in my yurt?" she asked Geriel. "There's a little more room."

"Yes, please." Geriel grinned as she glanced at Odval. "That's all right, isn't it, Mother?"

Odval nodded. "As long as Lien is happy. Why don't you two go now? Checheg and Nekhii can clean up tonight."

"Aww," Nekhii said.

"Why can't I sleep there too?" Checheg asked.

"Because I said so," Odval said.

"I can help with the dishes," Lien said. She didn't want to be a bother on her first day.

"No need, child." Sukh walked her to the door. "It's been a big day for you."

Geriel grabbed her hand. "Come on, before they change their mind." She tugged Lien out of the tent and sighed in the cool evening air. "Today is the greatest day ever. I've got a new sister and a night away from the family."

Lien frowned. "Don't you ever sleep in other yurts?"

"There's no point. I can't talk privately with friends when their parents are the other side of the curtain."

Lien hadn't considered that. "You can sleep in my tent until the wedding if you want."

"Yes! It's too bad it's next quarter moon."

The wedding. Had she proven something to Temur today? Did he trust her a little more? Could their relationship improve until they returned to how things had been?

As they entered the yurt, Lien said, "Can I get you a drink?"

"No, I'm fine." Geriel left her shoes by the door and then sat on the bed. "Now we're alone, I want to know how you feel about marrying Temur."

Lien stepped back. "Ahh…"

Geriel patted the bed. "Come on. This is important sister talk."

The knock on the door had Lien sighing in relief. When she opened it, her heart jumped. "Temur."

He smiled. "I wanted to check how you're feeling," he said. "The ceremony can be draining for some."

Lien ran a hand over her arm. "I am well. I shared dinner with my family and Geriel is staying with me tonight."

"Go away, Temur," Geriel called. "We're having woman talk."

Heat rushed to Lien's cheeks as Temur grinned.

"In that case, I'll leave you to it. I am pleased you are well."

He walked away and Lien stared after him.

This was more like the man he'd been when she'd first arrived.

"You've just answered my question," Geriel said.

Lien closed the door. "What?"

"You were staring after Temur with a smile on your face." Geriel winked. "I'd say that means you're happy about marrying him."

Lien joined her on the bed. "He was not happy when we returned from the palace and I thought I had ruined everything."

"Temur cares for us all," she said. "He thought he'd brought a deadly threat into the camp."

"How do you know?"

"I heard Mother and Father talking one night. Father knew you would never hurt us, but he said Temur needed to understand it for himself."

Perhaps now he did. Lien hesitated. She had questions about the wedding that she'd been too embarrassed to ask. Maybe Geriel could help. "Do you know anything about the wedding night?"

Geriel's eyes widened. "You mean after the ceremony?"

She nodded.

"Didn't they talk about it at the palace?"

"Not openly." She hadn't listened to Yu's discussions during training because she didn't want to know what she did with the emperor. But one of Lien's duties was to provide Temur with children, and she'd avoided thinking about what that entailed.

"You should talk to Mother," Geriel said. "But from what I've heard, men often like to take control of the situation. So I guess you just follow where he leads."

Lien's stomach churned. "What if I do something wrong?"

Geriel frowned. "I don't think you can. Follow your instincts, but don't be too eager in case he believes you're more experienced than you are."

Follow but don't be too eager. She could do that.

"I think Mother and Father will look for a match for me at the wedding." Geriel grimaced. "They consider twenty-two past time, but I wanted to find a love match."

"There's no one you like?"

She shrugged. "Not really, and I'm not ready to marry. I want to experience the world more before I settle down." She sat straighter. "Maybe I could come with you when you go to Chungson."

Lien liked the idea of her sister coming with her. "I'll talk to Temur and our parents about it."

"Thank you." She clutched Lien's hand.

Lien smiled at her. "Any time, little sister."

The next day Lien was wandering through the camp thinking about the wedding when she heard Shuren call, "Temur! Temur!" She glanced over to find a crying Shuren tugging on Temur's hand not far away. She'd been so preoccupied she hadn't noticed either of them.

"What is it, Shuren?" Temur knelt down to her height.

"Saran won't play with me. You need to make her!"

His lips twitched in a smile. "Why doesn't she want to play with you?"

"Because she's mean!"

"Then why do you want to play with her?"

"She's my best friend. She said she'd go riding with me."

"Perhaps you can go riding with someone else," he suggested.

Shuren pouted and then brightened. "Will you go riding with me, Tribal Father?"

Temur didn't hesitate. "Of course. Tell your mother where we're going and I'll meet you at the horses."

"Thank you!" Shuren threw her arms around Temur, hugging him.

Lien's chest tightened. How could she have ever thought the Rhoran were barbarians? No one at the imperial palace would have paid the slightest bit of notice to the request of a six-year-old—she knew from experience. But Temur was so kind to take time out of his day to make Shuren happy. Suddenly Lien wanted to speak to Temur, to acknowledge his good deed, and perhaps speak of their future together. She hurried over.

"Temur."

His smile faltered as he turned. "Lien. Have you finished your embroidery for this morning?"

"Yes." She wasn't sure how to express herself. "Thank you for riding with Shuren. She seemed upset."

This time his smile was genuine. "I imagine by the time I get to the horses, both Shuren and Saran will be waiting to ride with me."

"And you'll still go?" There would be no need if the girls were friends again.

"Of course. I gave my word." He frowned. "I would not disappoint a little girl so."

That wasn't what she meant. "No, I–"

"Temur, hurry up!" Shuren yelled.

He chuckled. "If you excuse me, I must meet Shuren."

Lien's shoulders slumped as he walked away. She'd lost her opportunity.

Next time she'd be better prepared.

~*~

A few days later, Lien packed her few belongings into a bag. Today she would travel with her family to the new camp to allow them to carry out the wedding traditions. She wouldn't see Temur again until he arrived at the camp to claim her as his bride.

She rubbed the bumps on her skin.

Her nerves tempted her to call Kew and ride south, go to Chungson, find her brother and not deal with marrying Temur. But she wouldn't run even though she hadn't discussed their marriage with him. She'd been so busy teaching or spending time with her new family and when she'd seen Temur they had never been alone.

To think she'd been revolted by the idea of marrying a barbarian and now all she wanted was for him to show her the affection he had before, the affection he showed the rest of the camp.

Geriel entered the tent without knocking and

Erdene was with her. "We're ready to go."

"Have you packed?" Erdene asked.

Lien picked up her bag and followed them outside.

"I can't believe my baby brother's about to get married." Erdene's face lit up with excitement and a little sadness. "He will look so handsome in his wedding outfit." She turned to Lien. "I'm sure you will be just as beautiful."

Kew joined her and they walked over to the horses where her family waited for her. Odval hugged Lien. "You must be so excited. Come on, we must leave so the camp can start preparations."

This was it. When Lien returned, it would be for the marriage ceremony. Temur was nowhere in sight. She ignored the ache in her heart. This was her duty. If she'd ruined what they'd had, she would make do. All her life she'd known she would have no choice over who she would marry.

Lien mounted Batu as warriors from all the tribes joined them. "Why so many?" she asked Sukh.

"The emperor may still retaliate. Temur wants you protected."

She didn't need protection, but perhaps it was a symbolic gesture. She checked her knives in her belt. "Which way?"

Sukh gestured and they set off at a trot so Kew could keep up.

An hour later they reached the new camp, a sea of white tents so no one could claim Lien came from one particular tribe. Lien rubbed down Batu and then followed Sukh's family to the central cooking fire for the midday meal. They sat and drank tea, discussing the latest news with the others gathered there. Lien recognised many from her training sessions, but couldn't keep up with all the names mentioned. Her head spun. She wanted time to herself, but she wouldn't be allowed to go riding alone.

Odval turned to her. "It is tradition to show our daughter the bridal gifts we are bestowing on her husband so she understands how much she means to us."

Lien blinked. She'd assumed there wouldn't be a bridal dowry—she didn't want Sukh and Odval disadvantaged for adopting her. "Are bridal gifts necessary?"

Odval frowned. "Of course." She linked her arm through Lien's. "They're this way."

Geriel and her siblings followed as Odval led Lien to a large tent. Sukh opened the door and motioned for her to enter. As she stepped over the threshold her mouth dropped open. The tent was full.

Some items were from the emperor's tribute—bolts of silk, bags of rice and an assortment of other things. As she scanned, she noticed a small pile of gifts to one side. What caught her eye was a pair of the most exquisitely decorated saddles. She walked closer and knelt down, rubbing her hand over the decoration— one had a stallion on it and the other had a dragon like Kew.

Lien glanced at Sukh. "These are amazing."

Sukh smiled. "Our gift to you both."

"Did you make them?"

"Yes, we both did."

"Thank you." She gave in to her urge to hug him, not sure who she surprised most, herself or him.

Jochi piped up, "I made you these." He picked up a pair of carved wooden statues of a stallion and a dragon.

"And I made you this." Checheg pulled out an

embroidered wall hanging of a Bonamese princess next to a Rhoran Khan.

Her chest tightened and her eyes filled, blurring her vision. She couldn't breathe. It was the kindest thing anyone had ever done for her. She had to get out of here, had to find some air. "Thank you," she whispered. The door was so far away.

"Would you like to go for a ride?" Sukh asked.

She nodded and hurried out of the tent. Squeezing her eyes shut, she wiped at the tears and took a deep breath. Kew circled around her.

I am fine. Stay here while I go riding.

Kew puffed out smoke and fell back with the children.

Sukh called for the warriors to join them, but they kept a respectful distance as Lien mounted Batu.

Sukh glanced at her. "Ready to go?"

"Yes." Together they kicked their horses into a gallop. As the wind rushed by her, she let the tears fall.

No matter what happened with Temur she would have Sukh and his family. They had welcomed her, made her feel part of them, in a way she hadn't felt since her own family had died. It soothed an ache in her which had been there for so long, she hadn't realised she'd had it.

As her tears lessened, Lien slowed Batu, wiping the remaining tears from her eyes.

Sukh pulled his horse alongside Batu and spoke. "As your father it is my duty to ensure you will not bring dishonour to your family. The biggest dishonour you could bring to us is to be a poor horsewoman and to mistreat your horse." He smiled. "That is not a problem. You ride like you were born on one." He paused. "Though we are not blood, I believe the spirits of my ancestors must flow through you."

Lien stared at him, momentarily lost for words. "I am honoured." Trite, but there were no words to convey how much it meant to her.

"You will become mother to our people and that is an honour to us. Your mother will speak to you about what you need to do. We are pleased you have joined our family."

Lien had lost so much when her family had died and Sukh was proud to claim her as one of his. "Thank you for accepting me." She hesitated. "After what happened at the palace, I thought I had lost everyone's trust."

"Not everyone had been riding with you regularly," Sukh said. "You drop your guard when you're on Batu and I saw your true self. I know you didn't mean to trap us."

The lump in her throat returned. She was so very lucky. She would never be able to thank him properly. They rode over a small rise and words became the least of her worries.

At the bottom of the rise were a dozen elite Bonamese soldiers.

Chapter 14

Sukh grabbed the reins of her horse and whirled them around so fast Lien almost lost her seat. He shouted a warning to the warriors and kicked his horse into a gallop, pulling Batu with him.

No. They shouldn't be running. "Sukh, we have to help."

Behind her, the Bonamese roared a battle cry and an arrow whizzed past, landing on the ground ahead. Too close. The Rhoran were outnumbered.

Sukh growled. "I must protect you."

No. Temur wouldn't care if she was injured, but she wouldn't forgive herself if the warriors were killed when she could protect them. She withdrew her knives, guiding Batu with her knees, and glanced back at the battle.

Her heart leapt. The hill hid it from her.

Lien and Sukh galloped across the steppes, away from the camp and the fighting. Sukh checked behind them and then slowed the horses. "We'll wait here for the others to catch up." He kept Batu's reins in his hand and she longed to rip them out and return to the battle.

The Bonamese were deep in Rhoran territory. Did they want to disrupt the wedding? Or did they want to kill her?

Lien kept her gaze glued to where they had come from, waiting for the Rhoran to appear, waiting to confirm they were all alive. She rubbed Batu's neck, crooning as the horse's shoulders heaved with the exertion. A few minutes later a Rhoran rider came into view. Another soon joined him and they gestured to Sukh.

"It's safe." He nudged his horse back the way they had come.

Lien followed, counting the warriors as they appeared. She let out a sigh of relief. All were there.

As they joined the group, she took stock of their wounds. One man was bleeding from a gash on his head and another held his side where an arrow protruded. A few others had cuts but nothing serious. She didn't need to ask about the Bonamese. No prisoners meant they had all been killed.

Now on high alert, the warriors formed a tight circle around Sukh and Lien and they returned to camp.

A warrior rode ahead to speak to the sentry and raise an alarm. Half the camp was waiting for them when they arrived.

"Lien, are you hurt?" Odval clutched Lien's arm as she dismounted. Warmth filled Lien at the concern in Odval's eyes. "No, but I need to check those who were." She pulled her arm away.

"Of course." Odval went to greet her husband.

A groan captured Lien's attention as the man who had been shot was helped from his horse. His face wan, two warriors carried him into a nearby tent. Lien followed.

"It's not too bad," Geriel announced as she

examined the wound. "He's wearing silk."

Moving closer Lien saw the warrior wore an undershirt made from silk. Geriel teased the fabric from around the arrow, allowing it to come out easily.

"The silk isn't damaged," Lien said.

Geriel looked up. "No. It's so tightly woven it doesn't break and makes it easier to remove the arrow."

That explained why she'd never noticed any of the Rhoran wearing the fabric. They used it for practical not decorative purposes.

As Geriel continued working on the man, Lien checked the other warriors patching themselves up. She went to each man and thanked him for protecting her.

One man grinned at her. "We would die to protect our mother."

A lump lodged in Lien's throat. They treated her as if she was already married, welcomed her into their tribe.

As she exited the yurt, she almost ran into Odval. "Sorry."

Odval gripped her hands. "If you are satisfied the warriors are fine, we need to speak."

"Yes, of course." Lien followed her back to their tent where she sat at the table across from Odval.

"A mother and her daughter would normally have this discussion when the daughter is with child, but you will become the tribe's mother and so we must have it now." Odval poured drinks.

Lien shifted, suddenly unsure.

"To be a mother you must learn to be many things: you must be patient, you must be kind, and you must be strong. Sometimes you have to be strict and punish your children, but it is always for the good of the family." She handed Lien a cup. "Never show favouritism and always listen to both sides of the story before making a decision. Some children are sent to test you and you must be fair."

Lien drank slowly.

"Always make time for your children and listen to their worries even if they appear insignificant to you." Odval took a sip of her drink.

"Is Bolormaa upset about losing her position?" Lien had worried about it, but it hadn't seemed prudent to ask. Any Bonamese with an equivalent title would have fought to keep it.

Odval laughed. "She is relieved. It is a difficult job and it is an advantage to have youth on your side."

Unease brushed Lien. The thought of being Temur's wife was frightening enough, and now she would be a tribal leader—their mother. She had so little idea about what to do, had never had a role model.

Odval patted her knee. "Don't worry so. Bolormaa and I will be here to help. We are your mothers and it is our job to be here for you."

Lien's chest swelled even as her shoulders relaxed. She had family now, ones who would protect her.

"Now, it is time to prepare dinner." Odval rose and Lien followed her out of the tent.

After dinner, Lien escaped the chatter by the fire with the excuse she had to check on Batu and Kew. She needed time to herself, to let her thoughts flow. Kew lay near where Batu grazed, soaking up the last of the day's sun.

Lien knelt next to her, stroking her scaly skin, and closed her eyes, breathing deeply. Batu nuzzled her face and Lien rubbed the horse's velvety chin. Here she could relax, here she could focus.

Tomorrow would change her life. She would be Rhoran and all final ties to the Bonamese would be severed. Her only worry now was how her brother would treat her when he found out. She had no way of knowing what kind of man her funny and kind brother had grown up to be.

She would have to find out. After she married and the conflict with the emperor had settled, she would ask Temur's permission to visit Chungson.

Her attention turned towards Temur.

She wanted what her parents had had, love and laughter in their marriage. She remembered evenings, when they were all alone and they would play together as a family. They had loved one another deeply, she was certain.

Perhaps one day she would have that—if not with Temur, at least with any children they had. No matter what happened with him, she would do her best for her family, she wouldn't let her children ever feel unloved. And maybe she and Temur would learn to love one another. She opened her eyes, and darkness had fallen. Time to go.

Standing, she called to Kew and together they returned to the tent.

~*~

Lien woke early. She lay there for a moment, allowing her eyes to adjust to the dim light and breathing slowly to calm the nerves in her stomach. It didn't help. Today was her wedding day.

She crept out of the tent, careful not to wake any of her new family. A few minutes running through her patterns and centring herself would calm the maelstrom inside. Greeting the warriors guarding the camp, she walked out on to the steppes away from the tents. The sun peeked above the horizon bringing a soft glow to the land. She inhaled the cool air and began; block, counter, block, attack. The rhythm soothed her and her body flowed with the moves, changing from one pattern to the next without pause.

By the time she finished, she was calm. Turning back towards the camp, she faltered. Sukh and the warriors were watching her. How long had they been there? Her cheeks warmed, but she held her head high as she walked towards them.

"That was beautiful, child," Sukh said.

"Thank you."

The warriors didn't say a word, but respect shone in their eyes.

Sukh accompanied her back to their tent where Odval and the children were having breakfast. There was so much chatter and noise, laughter and teasing. Lien smiled as she took her seat between Shuren and Geriel.

"It will be Geriel's turn to marry next," Checheg said. "If anyone will have her. You should look for options while the tribes are together, Mother."

Geriel elbowed her sister. "I need to finish my healer training before I marry."

"I'm never getting married," Shuren announced. "Boys are silly."

Lien smothered a smile. She couldn't imagine ever declaring such a thing at the palace. Not that she'd had much chance to talk. Meals were a time for silence, especially from the children.

"Your opinion may change." Odval shared a glance with Sukh. "Mine did."

After breakfast, Sukh and his sons left the tent to allow Odval and her daughters to fuss around Lien. She washed with water and then dressed in an undergarment of silk.

"I've never been to a wedding before." Shuren

danced from foot to foot, unable to sit still.

"The ceremony is boring," Checheg told her. "But the party afterwards is fun."

"This will be my first wedding too," Lien told Shuren.

"Really?" Odval asked as she braided Lien's hair.

"Kun is the oldest of the emperor's children and he has yet to take a wife."

Geriel tugged Lien's hand closer and cleaned her nails. "So you have no comparison." She dabbed scent on Lien's wrists and neck. Lien hadn't been this pampered since she'd been at the palace.

"No, but I daresay it will be a lot more joyful than a Bonamese wedding."

"Why is that?" Checheg asked.

"The Bonamese are taught it is a sign of an uncontrolled mind to show emotion."

Geriel laughed. "They must think us crazy then."

"Yes," Lien said.

Odval fetched Lien's bright red silk dress which had been hanging up and helped her into it. The heavy weight settled around her and was added to when she put on the embroidered emerald green sleeveless jacket. Mounting Batu while wearing this would be difficult.

She perched awkwardly on the table while the others got ready. As they finished the final touches, Jochi ran in. "They're coming!"

Lien swallowed hard. This was it. The beginning of the next stage of her life. Her hand trembled as she handed her mother's silver necklace to Geriel who clasped it around Lien's neck. The butterflies fluttering in Lien's stomach morphed into swallows, dipping and diving when Odval placed the cylindrical hat on her head to finish the outfit.

Jochi grinned. "You look pretty."

"Thank you."

Sukh entered followed by Nekhii. "They're here."

Lien stood, brushing the front of her jacket and Kew, now a matching shade of red, stood next to her, every bit the regal and distinguished dragon.

Horses snorted outside the tent and voices murmured. Lien unclenched her hands and her head spun as the nerves fought a vicious war in her stomach. She hadn't been this nervous when she was ordered to kill Temur.

Kew butted her leg and puffed out a breath and Geriel squeezed her hand. No matter what happened, she wasn't alone. A calm stole over her.

At the knock on the door, both Sukh and Odval went to answer it. Temur walked in and Lien's eyes widened. Magnificent. The fit of his rich red jacket accentuated his muscular frame, broadening his shoulders, and the embroidered felt crown he wore gave him authority. For the first time, his hair was neatly plaited. He looked every bit a powerful ruler for the Rhoran.

Her body warmed.

He would be her husband in a few short hours. They would begin a life together.

Her eyes met his, and instead of the disinterest she expected, she saw approval. She flushed, glancing at Amslan next to him. Even he wasn't scowling at her. Would they both be nice to her on her wedding day?

Temur spoke, low but confident. "I have come here today to request the gift of your daughter, Lien, to be my wife." He kept his gaze on Sukh and Odval.

"It is our pleasure to gift her to you and welcome you into our family," Sukh said as Odval offered Temur a cup full of milk.

Temur took the cup with both hands and drained it

slowly before giving it back to Odval.

Odval led Lien forward. "The creation of our love is now yours." She presented Lien to Temur and Temur tucked Lien's arm snuggly under his. His grip comforted her and he smelled divine, fresh, yet spicy, his body warm.

"I thank you for the honour." He led Lien out of the tent to where Batu and his own horse stood resplendent in their ornate saddles and bridles. She gasped at the sight behind the horses—a whole contingent of mounted warriors dressed in their full leather armour with sabres at their belts, and bows and arrows at their backs. They were breathtaking, formidable.

At the front of the warriors, Chinua winked at her, and some tension left her body.

Temur squeezed her hand and she flinched, turning her gaze back to him. His eyes were full of concern. She smiled. "They are magnificent."

"Indeed." He smiled back and some of her fear faded as he helped her to mount her horse. She settled her dress around her and they rode towards the main camp with the warriors in formation around them and Kew trotting at Batu's heels. Lien waved to her family who would follow a short distance behind.

She rode so close to Temur she could have reached out and touched him, but they didn't speak. She had no clue what to say to him. At least his posture was relaxed and some of the tension between them was gone. Finally.

At the camp, everyone was dressed in their finest, a sea of faces waiting for them, and they cheered as Temur and Lien circled the camp three times. Finally they stopped in front of Bolormaa and Mongke's tent.

She needed to remember what to do.

"Permit me to introduce you to my bride, Lien,"

Temur said.

"It is our pleasure to welcome you into our family," Mongke said as Bolormaa handed Lien a cup of milk to drink.

Lien took it in both hands and like Temur, she drank it slowly before handing it back. "I thank you for accepting me into your family." The words never felt so true, and her chest swelled, making it hard to breathe. She had two families now—Odval and Sukh, and Temur's family. She hugged them both and then with Temur she walked over to where Solongo and the rest of the Rhoran waited around a raised platform.

"May the Gods and Goddesses bless this marriage as we celebrate the union of our tribal father and mother." Solongo tied their hands together with silk and placed them in a bowl of water, adding oils and herbs and murmuring a blessing.

Temur raised his voice. "I pledge to honour and protect Lien through all of my days."

Her turn. "I pledge to honour and protect Temur through all of my days." The words resonated around her, binding her to this man.

Lifting their hands out of the water, Solongo said, "May their union be happy and bountiful."

The tribe repeated the words as Temur and Lien, hands still tied, turned to face them.

It was done.

She was married and no longer an imperial princess. The people standing before her were her people now.

The nerves melted away as she spotted Shuren doing a celebratory dance at the front. She had a new family now. Lien smiled as she walked with Temur into his tent and sat on one of the two chairs next to each other. It was time for the gifts. Every family would offer something to help them build their new life together. With their hands still tied together, she and Temur would have to work together to accept the gifts, learning from the outset how to be one.

Bolormaa and Mongke came first and gave them a thick, carved staff and a bowl of sweet curds. Temur took the staff and helped her hold the bowl. "As our tribal parents, sometimes you will need to coerce and sometimes you need to be strict." Bolormaa kissed Lien on both cheeks.

Sukh and Odval came next, presenting the saddles. Lien reached for them only to have one hand not move, tied to Temur as it was. She stopped pulling as he reached out and her arm jerked forward.

He winced. "Sorry."

This would take practice.

Erdene and Amslan followed, Erdene beaming with happiness and even Amslan showed cheer. Their gift was a healing potion which Temur received. "Just in case she tries to poison you," Amslan murmured.

Temur laughed, but Lien wasn't sure Amslan was joking. "You're very kind."

The long procession of people and gifts seemed never ending. Each gift had been carefully considered and related to the individual's gift or speciality. Cheren, the tribe's best fletcher, presented Lien with an exquisite bow and quiver of arrows. "You know what to do with these."

She glanced at Temur, their hands reaching for the quiver at the same time, working together. Hope sparked in her belly.

When the procession ended, the sun was low in the sky and Lien's stomach rumbled. Finally alone in the tent with Temur, she wanted nothing more than to untie herself and have a moment to herself to process everything. The tribe had been so very generous and they had everything they needed to start a home, but she needed quiet.

"Come, my *bayar*." Temur helped her stand. "It is time for us to eat."

The endearment was so sweet after so much time without it. Her heart jumped. Maybe, just maybe, things would be all right.

She followed him outside to the communal fire and they sat on some furs, still tied together. The next tradition would be for them to feed each other, such an oddly intimate process. It reminded her of the day she'd woken up in the camp and had demanded Temur eat first. It seemed so long ago.

Bolormaa presented them with the first dish of horse head soup. Temur dipped the spoon in and held it to her lips. She opened her mouth, allowing him to feed her. The soup slid down her throat, warm and meaty and her eyes met his as she swallowed. They were dark but no longer full of contempt. No, it was more like desire. She choked. Was he looking forward to the wedding night?

Her heart fluttered. She took the spoon to get his portion, and unable to resist, she watched him as he took what she offered, his eyes not leaving hers. Her body heated. Gods, she didn't know what to do, how to feel about the pleasant sensation swirling around her skin.

She should have asked Odval and Bolormaa more about the wedding night. She should be better prepared.

She inhaled and his scent tickled her nose, soothing her.

All would be well. She could trust him.

The feast lasted long into the night. After dinner,

someone played a stringed instrument and voices joined in to sing. People clapped and children danced, Kew joining in and prancing around.

The joy was infectious and Lien tapped her hand against her thigh. She loved the energy of Rhoran celebrations.

"Come." Before she blinked, Temur tugged her to her feet. "Let's dance."

The crowd roared their approval.

"I don't know how." Panic squeezed her chest. It was so fast, so active, she had no idea what to do.

"Trust me." He clasped their tied hands, and his other arm swept around her waist and then he spun her and it was all she could do to hold on.

"Relax, my *bayar*, I won't let you go," he murmured. In that moment she found her rhythm and allowed him to lead. The world reduced to the beat and Temur, his arms, his gaze. He spun her faster than before and she laughed, the joy rising from her and out her mouth.

He slowed, stopped as the music did and brushed a loose hair from her face. "That's the first time I've heard you laugh. It's beautiful. I'd like to hear it more often."

She couldn't speak. The intensity of his gaze had stolen her words.

"Let me get you a drink." He gestured to someone and then pulled her back to the furs.

As it grew late, the songs changed to slower, more rhythmic tunes and fatigue swept over her. She closed her eyes, resting against Temur's shoulder.

He chuckled. "It's time we went to bed."

Suddenly awake, she sat up straight and flushed hot. She was sleeping with Temur tonight.

"It's all right, my *bayar*. I won't hurt you." He stood and pulled her to her feet. The crowd grew quiet as if on command. "My wife and I would like to thank you for the kindness you have shown to us, and for all of your well-wishes. It is however, time for us to sleep."

"And other things," someone called.

Lien's face flushed, glad of the dark. Temur clasped her hand as they walked to his tent, the whole tribe behind them, singing. She could get used to the nice Temur, the man who cared for her.

Temur opened the door, the light from a lamp spilling out. Together they walked over the threshold as the tribe finished the wedding song and cheered.

The clunk of the door shutting behind them was final. They were alone. Just the two of them, in their tent, with a bed behind the curtain—a bed she would share with her new husband.

Temur tugged her closer, pulling her body against his. He was so firm, so warm, so masculine. Gazing up at him, his eyes transfixed her as he lowered his head, his mouth finally meeting hers.

Lips warm and gentle caressed hers, nudging them slowly open with his tongue as he took her deeper. All thoughts drifted out of her head as a delicious light-headed feeling replaced them, and then the tingling sensation moved languorously lower, infusing her with heat as it slid down to her belly.

So this was what it was like to be properly kissed.

He pulled away and she stopped the small moan of protest. She should be reserved, in case he believed her experienced.

Still moving slowly, he untied their hands, letting the silk slide over her wrist before dropping it to the floor.

Her skin was so sensitive, and she wanted more.

Temur drew her across the room towards the bed and she resisted slightly so he wouldn't think her too forward. A slight frown flitted across his face.

Had she done too much?

Reaching up he removed her headpiece and placed it on the table. His own crown soon joined it. Tugging her closer to him, he undid the buttons on her jacket, showering small kisses over her face as he did so.

How could she feel so much at once? Every nerve ending in her body danced. She wanted to respond to him, to unbutton his jacket, but what if she did something wrong?

Her jacket slid to the floor, and the lack of weight made her feel almost naked. But soon she would be. She stood still, uncertain, as Temur caressed her back, kissing her again so deeply she forgot to think. His hand moved further, pulling her dress up and slipping under it until his fingertips brushed her breasts.

Fire shot down to her core, and she gasped, stepping back from the shock, her eyes wide. No one had told her it would be so intense. She wanted more, but she hesitated.

Temur spun away, a curse muttered under his breath. He grabbed the furs from the bed and threw them on the floor before whirling to face her.

"You needn't be so terrified." He stepped forward and his expression, one of frustration and anger made her step back. He swore again. "I won't force myself upon you. I'm not a barbarian."

He extinguished the lamp, plunging them into darkness. As her eyes adjusted, he lay down on the floor. Was she meant to join him there? She took a small step forward. How could she tell him she wasn't afraid? That she wanted him to continue?

"Get into bed," he growled. "I won't attack you in the night. You have my word."

Unable to find the right words, she lay on the bed, still fully dressed. Her body protested at the lack of attention and she clung to the sensations. Was this how husband and wife were meant to feel?

Could this be a test to prove she wasn't experienced and she should wait for him to continue?

No, it was more likely she'd messed the whole thing up.

~*~

The next morning Lien woke as the door clicked shut. She sat up, glancing around the empty yurt.

Temur was gone.

Without saying a single word to her.

Her gaze caught the food on the table and she remembered the last tradition she had to fulfil. A new bride was confined to her tent for three days after the wedding and when she reemerged, it symbolised her rebirth into the tribe.

Temur wasn't allowed to speak to her this morning.

Stuck, alone, for three days.

A blessing. It gave her time to figure out what had gone wrong last night, time to work out what to say to Temur.

She sat at the table, picking at the food as last night played over and over again in her head.

She groaned. If only she could talk to Odval or Erdene, someone who had experienced a wedding night, and they could tell her what she'd done wrong.

But no. She had three more days of solitude and only her confused thoughts for company.

To clear her mind, she trained, running through all her patterns, practising kicks and blocks until her breath came in gasps and she dropped to the bed in exhaustion.

And still she was no closer to an answer.

Someone had left her embroidery on the table, so

she picked it up, but with no one to talk to, her mind wandered.

She'd done something last night to make Temur not want to consummate the marriage. A half moon ago she would have been relieved, but now, being rejected by her husband after he'd made her feel so sensual hurt. Was she so repulsive he couldn't bear to take her?

But he'd kissed her sweetly and she'd wanted more.

Perhaps her inexperience was tiresome for him.

Or maybe it wasn't her mistake.

She paused. Perhaps Temur couldn't do what he was supposed to. Perhaps he had blamed her for his own inadequacies.

The idea sat more comfortably with her and she examined it, going through the whole event again. There'd been whispers back at the imperial court about men who were unable to perform. At the time she'd believed the women were cruel to discuss it with others, but now she was glad they had, otherwise it would have never occurred to her.

Finding the first moment of peace she'd had since she'd woken, she closed her eyes and stilled her mind.

In the evening, a knock on the door signalled her meal was ready. Lien had to retrieve it quickly to ensure no one saw her. As she ate, she considered Bolormaa and Odval's advice.

"As soon as you emerge, you will be the tribal mother," Bolormaa had warned. "And with all the tribes gathered, there will be many people who will want you to solve their problems."

Odval had nodded. "You should spend your three days conserving your strength."

But Lien was no longer used to being idle.

When she finished eating, she prowled around the

tent. She'd not paid attention to it before, but this was now hers. Someone had moved her clothes and scent bottles there before the wedding. She hesitated in front of the two chests in the tent. Perhaps the contents would tell her something about her husband. She pushed aside her guilt and opened the first chest.

Empty.

She moved to the next one.

Also empty.

Had Temur emptied them before the ceremony, or were they used to store items when the camp packed up and moved?

Voices occasionally carried into the tent and two people stopped outside to discuss the upcoming hunt. Geriel had explained the significance of the event. All the tribes took part and herded wild animals to a predetermined place to kill them. It enabled them to replenish their meat supplies in preparation for the winter and was a chance to practise their battle skills.

She hoped it would take place while she was in here. She didn't want to kill anything.

When darkness fell, Lien climbed into bed. Maybe she could sleep away the hours.

But no, Temur's scent surrounded her. How could she sleep with the reminder of the previous night?

With the uncertainty of what was to come.

She tossed and turned and it was the early hours of the morning before she finally fell asleep.

An argument outside the door woke Lien. She opened her eyes, blinking to clear them and adjust to the sunlight streaming in the top of the tent. The tent was warm and it had to be nearly midday.

"I'm going in to confirm she's still there," Amslan said.

"You will not!" Erdene protested. "Just because she hasn't eaten her breakfast does not mean she has disappeared."

"I don't trust her."

"That is something *you* need to sort out," Erdene snarled. "I will not have you breaking this tradition because of your trust issues. She is our tribal mother and she deserves your respect."

"She may be injured."

"Then we'll send Kew in. She'll tell us if Lien is injured."

Amslan growled in frustration and Lien smiled. She must have slept through breakfast. She didn't dare answer because she wasn't allowed to indicate her presence in the tent—the empty meal trays notwithstanding.

"Get the dragon."

"No. You fetch Kew while I wait here." Erdene wouldn't budge.

The stomp of footsteps faded and then came a knock.

"I'm turning my back," Erdene called.

Lien grinned and opened the door, picking up the tray. Erdene wiggled her fingers at her, but otherwise showed no response to the door opening and then closing.

Lien swallowed her laughter. Erdene trusted her.

She settled at the table. Her stomach rumbled, but her head was musty from sleeping so late. She would train after she'd eaten to clear her mind.

"Here's Kew. Open the door so she can go in." Amslan was back.

"There is no need. Lien has retrieved her lunch tray."

A pause. "Are you sure?"

"Amslan, don't question my integrity," Erdene snapped. "You need to stop being so suspicious. Help organise the hunt."

"Would you like to join me?" His tone was conciliatory. Maybe he had a soft side.

"No. I believe I will protect my sister's honour, in case others are not so trusting."

"You're staying here?" Amslan asked.

"If that's what it takes. You may fetch me a seat."

Warmth spread through her. Erdene was claiming her as a sister, and cared enough to stand up to her husband to protect Lien's honour.

After she finished eating, she placed the tray outside the tent. Erdene sat primly on her seat, embroidering. Lien wished she could invite her in to talk, but instead she let Kew inside and shut the door. Embroidery would at least keep her hands busy. She picked up the small picture she'd begun for Odval and Sukh to show her appreciation for their support.

Kew sniffed around the tent and then made herself comfortable on the bed, content to rest.

It was nearing dinner when there were loud voices outside the tent again.

"Amslan tells me you've been here since midday," Temur said.

Lien stopped sewing. Would he mention their wedding night?

"I felt it necessary to protect my sister's honour," Erdene answered.

"Why don't you get yourself something to eat and I will stand guard for a while?"

A long pause before Erdene said, "No. I don't think so."

"Why not? You must be hungry."

"Temur, I have known you since you were born. I

know when you're not telling me something. Lien must not be disturbed."

"She's my wife," Temur growled.

"And she still has another day of solitude. Shall I send for Solongo?"

"I need to discuss something with her."

Lien's heart jumped.

"You'll get the chance in another day."

Lien wanted to open the door, but it could be a test of her obedience.

"Geriel, will you please get Lien and myself some dinner?" Erdene called.

"Sure."

Temur lowered his voice. "Erdene, your loyalty is misguided."

"She's my sister and your wife, how is that misguided?"

A pause. "Because she tried to kill me."

Chapter 15

The blood drained from Lien's face. Why would he tell Erdene now?

Erdene gasped. "What?"

Temur cursed. "I shouldn't have said anything."

"Maybe not, but now you have to explain." Her tone was hard.

"When the emperor betrothed her to me, she was meant to kill me."

"You're still alive."

"Someone attacked her first."

Erdene laughed. "We've both seen how fast she is. If she'd wanted to kill you, you'd be dead." She hummed in consideration. "And since then she's rescued my in-laws, saved you from an ambush, and taught the tribe everything she knows about the Bonamese." A pause. "If you still considered her a threat, you wouldn't have married her."

Lien sighed as relief filled her. Erdene hadn't turned against her.

"I need to speak with her," Temur insisted.

"No. She will be allowed to honour our traditions," Erdene said. "Go away, brother. You may return after two nights."

Lien waited for his response, but he was silent. Why did Temur and Amslan want to see her? Was it only because they didn't trust her to stay there?

"Here you go, Erdene. Shall I leave Lien's tray at the door?" Geriel had returned.

"Yes, please."

"Why are you sitting here?" she asked.

"My husband and brother seek to interrupt Lien's solitude."

Geriel gasped. "But why?"

"I don't know, but I will stay here until she is reborn."

"You don't need to do this on your own," Geriel said. "I'll take a shift and others will too. Why don't you take your dinner and find others to help? I'll stand guard."

"Do you believe you can stand up to the khan, Geriel?" Erdene asked.

"To protect my sister's honour I will." Geriel's voice was fierce.

Lien closed her eyes, blinking away the tears. She had gained two sisters willing to stand up for her, to protect her. It was more than she'd ever hoped for.

"Then I will go. Knock on the door to tell Lien her dinner is here and then turn your back so she can retrieve it."

At the knock Lien smiled. For the first time since she had arrived at the Rhoran camp, she felt at home.

Lien awoke the next morning energised and eager to start the day. She would enjoy her last day of solitude. After training, she picked up her embroidery. A group of women had gathered outside and were chatting. Lien could imagine them all sitting in a circle, embroidering or mending as they spoke. She moved her cushions closer to the door so she could listen.

Her picture had only just begun to take shape. She

would never finish it by tomorrow at this rate.

But perhaps her speed would help. She'd never tried to sew quickly before. Using her speed, she embroidered a line of simple stitches. Not pretty, but she could improve.

After a dozen attempts, she could do a row of simple stitches in seconds.

She grinned.

Outside, no one spoke of why they were there, but towards midday, Bolormaa called out, "You still have one more night until you may see her, son. A husband must learn patience."

The women chuckled and continued their conversation.

Lien's heart squeezed. Temur still wanted to visit her. What would he say to her tomorrow? What should she say to him?

They needed to talk, clarify what happened, figure out how to live with each other.

And they still had to consummate their marriage.

The next morning she freshened and dressed, her stomach a bundle of nerves at seeing Temur again and taking on the tribal motherhood, such a mantle of responsibility.

Outside people murmured as they gathered. When Solongo spoke, Lien brushed down her tunic and faced the door as she'd been instructed. Both her mothers, Odval and Bolormaa would accompany her out and present her to Temur. Then they would hold a ceremony to officially pass the tribal motherhood from Bolormaa to Lien.

When the door opened, Bolormaa and Odval walked in. Both smiled as they approached and hugged her.

It felt so good to have their arms around her, to be

welcomed and supported by them. Whatever happened, she would have these women to help her.

Each took one of her hands and led her to the threshold. They stepped over and turned back to Lien.

"Child, welcome to this world," they said.

Lien stepped out and the crowd burst into cheers and applause. Her gaze fell on Temur in front of her. She couldn't read his expression—he wasn't smiling, but nor did he look as grim as he had in the past. She smiled at him and then acknowledged the rest of the crowd, ignoring the swirl in her stomach.

Solongo stepped forward and the crowd hushed. "Today is an auspicious day. We farewell and thank our tribal mother, Bolormaa, as we welcome our new mother, Lien. Let us journey together to the fire." Solongo led the procession through the camp to the communal fire. Lien walked next to Bolormaa, aware Temur's eyes were on her as he walked behind them.

"Relax, child," Bolormaa whispered. "Odval and I will support and guide you." She took Lien's hand and squeezed it.

A lump formed in her throat. "Thank you."

The ceremony was short. Solongo said a few words, Bolormaa handed Temur an ancient baby blanket which Temur then handed to Lien. "Nurture our tribe as you will our children." His expression was intense.

Children. What would it be like to see Temur hold their baby? The vision came to her mind with great clarity and she smiled, taking the blanket. "I will nurture, protect and care for you as you are a part of me." Her chest swelled with emotion. These were her people now, and though not all of them had accepted her, she would fight to the death to protect them. As she scanned the crowd she recognised people from her own tribe such as Arigh and Chinua and those from other tribes whom she had yet to meet. She would need to learn their names and take care to listen to all.

"To our mother," Bolormaa said.

"To our mother," the crowd chanted back.

She now held one of the most powerful positions in Rhoran society. She should be pleased, not terrified she might mess it up.

Temur held up a hand for silence. "It is time to hunt."

The tribe roared and dispersed, some heading for the horses, others rounding up children so they didn't get underfoot.

The hunt was now?

"Are you joining the hunt?" Bolormaa asked.

"Yes," Temur answered for her. "She'll ride with me."

Dread filled her. She didn't want to kill. Before Lien could respond, Checheg ran up to her. "Mother, you must help me." She clasped Lien's hand.

Lien glanced around for Odval and Bolormaa smiled at her. Oh, Checheg was referring to her new role. "What is wrong?"

"Father won't let me go. You must tell him to let me."

Sukh walked towards them so Lien waited until he arrived before speaking. "Tell me, what are the rules of this hunt?" She directed the question at Sukh.

"Only adults are allowed," he said. "Checheg has not yet reached adulthood and is ineligible to attend."

"But I was given adult responsibilities for the wedding," Checheg protested.

"Which was a privilege, not a right," Sukh admonished.

Checheg's eyes pleaded Lien.

Temur and Bolormaa were both silent behind her.

This was her first test. "Tell me, why are you in such a rush to kill?"

Checheg gaped at her. "I'm not. I want to ride."

Lien turned to Sukh. "Are all hunters expected to kill the prey?"

"Yes. It is a great dishonour if someone lets an animal escape."

Lien gazed at Checheg. "Do you still wish to ride?"

Checheg hesitated. "No, Mother."

"Then stay and help Odval take care of the children."

Checheg walked away, a slump to her shoulders. If only Lien could trade places with her.

"Thank you, Mother." Sukh smiled at her.

Lien inclined her head and he left.

"Well done, child." Bolormaa hugged her. "You handled that perfectly."

She frowned. "If I had wanted to let Checheg go, could I have overruled Sukh's wishes?"

"Of course. You are tribal Mother," Temur said.

Temur had to trust her to give her such power. "What do I need to do now?"

"You need to change for a start. Come to the tent and I'll explain." He strode off without waiting for her.

She would be alone with her husband again. Maybe he would tell her what had been so urgent. She followed him into the tent, her pulse racing.

He faced her, his expression unreadable. "Put riding clothes on."

Was there a right way to raise the topic of their wedding night? She took what she needed out of her trunk as Temur paced, his eyes on her. He wouldn't give her privacy to undress. She swallowed. He was her husband.

Unwinding her belt, she asked, "Do all the adults

take part in the hunt?"

"Some always stay at the camp with the children, but most enjoy it. Each year they take turns to go."

"The women as well?"

"Rhoran women must be capable of surviving without their men."

Lien turned away as she slid her tunic off, the air dancing over her bare skin, before she replaced it with another one. She faked nonchalance as she slid off her pants. "What animals are we hunting?"

"Whatever we find out there."

He was back to the terse Temur—his kindness hadn't lasted. Disappointment filled her as she tugged on her pants and tied the belt. "Are there other rules?" She turned to find his back to her. "I am ready."

He glanced at her. "Follow my lead and kill any animals that come near you." He hesitated, opened his mouth to say something else and then shook his head and left the tent.

Lien let out a breath. Perhaps he didn't know how to raise the topic either or wanted to focus on the hunt. She grabbed her new bow and arrows and hurried after him. "Shouldn't we leave some animals alive so they can breed?"

He nodded. "We do, but you must set an example for the tribe."

Being the mother of the tribe had its disadvantages.

They arrived at the horses and Lien whistled Batu to her. Kew trotted up. *You must stay here,* Lien told her. *You won't keep up and it could be dangerous.*

Kew grumbled.

You need to keep the camp safe for me.

Kew flushed multiple colours and nodded.

Thank you. Lien nudged Batu into a trot after Temur.

The large group of riders, men and women, young

and old took her breath away. Some wore armour, others content in their normal clothes, but all had weapons strapped to them. They rode as one wave, and from time to time groups broke off and headed in a different direction with no discussion.

"Are we forming a circle?"

Temur nodded. "We surround the animals and then herd them towards the valley."

Her muscles tensed but she kicked Batu into a canter to keep up with the others. She hadn't been to this part of the steppes. As they crested a hill a dry riverbed was below them. The slopes of the banks were steep and it would be difficult for any animal to get out.

As if on cue, a horn wailed, and the Rhoran shouted. The grunts and squeals of animals filled the air. The riders around her kicked their horses into a gallop as more Rhoran poured over the crest in front of her, driving frantic deer, wild pigs and elk before them.

It would be a slaughter.

"Lien!" Temur commanded.

She kicked Batu into a gallop to avoid getting in the way, and drew her bow. The Rhoran moved in a rhythm of their own, riding fearlessly, at one with their mounts. The sight of so many animals being killed made her stomach twist. She didn't want to take part in this, even if it was important to the survival of the tribe. How Amslan and Temur would laugh if they realised she'd never killed a living thing.

Suddenly a wild boar broke away from the group and headed straight for her. Her pulse throbbed in her head as she sighted down her arrow, meeting its terror-filled eyes. She didn't want to, but Temur's voice in her head said she must set an example. She closed her eyes and released the arrow.

The boar squealed.

Lien opened her eyes. It was on the ground in front of her, struggling to get back to his feet, squealing in terror. She hadn't killed it. She notched two more arrows and let them fly into its heart.

The boar stilled.

She stared down at the animal as blood seeped out of the wounds and its open eyes stared blankly back at her. Dead.

A shout nearby had her tearing her eyes away. It was over. Animals lay dead all around her and already some Rhoran butchered them, preparing the meat for transport.

So much death.

So much blood.

Lien's stomach rolled as she slid off Batu and vomited. Her stomach heaved and tears blurred her vision. She didn't have the stomach for this. No wonder the emperor had wanted to get rid of her. She was useless as an assassin.

"Lien?" Temur called.

Wiping her mouth on her sleeve, she said, "Yes?"

He dismounted and took the few steps toward her, ignoring the dead animal. "Are you not well?"

"I am fine." She pressed a hand to her stomach as it threatened to prove her wrong.

He frowned. "No, you're not."

She breathed deeply and the scent of blood filled her nose. She clenched her teeth and swallowed hard. "Of course I am. See, I killed my first boar." She waved a hand in the general direction of the animal.

Temur's eyes widened. "Is this your first kill?"

She opened her mouth to deny it, then remembered her promise. "Yes."

He swore. "Why didn't you say something?"

"You didn't ask."

"Damn it. Sit down before you fall down." He pushed her gently to the ground, ensuring she was well away from the animal and then settled next to her, with his arms around her. He sighed. "I am sorry, my *bayar*."

His gentle tone weakened her. She couldn't allow it to. She pushed him away. "I am not certain you are."

He raised an eyebrow.

"One day you are kind, and the next you are rude and distant. I don't know where I stand, I don't know what I may confide in you." She stood, her legs a little unsteady. "When you have decided whether you will trust me, please tell me."

As he opened his mouth to speak three short, sharp horn blasts filled the air. His face paled. "The camp is under attack."

The reaction was instantaneous. Lien gaped as the Rhoran left the animals and mounted their horses, galloping towards the camp. She leapt onto Batu, settling low against her neck, urging her faster and faster. There were mostly children at the camp—and her family and Kew. Bolormaa, Odval, Erdene and Checheg flashed through her mind. She had convinced Checheg to stay behind.

She had to save them.

An attack on the camp could only mean the Bonamese. Had those they'd encountered before the wedding only been a scouting party?

The ride was endless, hill after hill before finally the camp came into view. Tents blazed and the clang of weapons was clear. She whipped the bow from her back and notched an arrow. The first Bonamese had his arm raised to strike Checheg. Lien didn't hesitate. The arrow flew fast and true, striking him in the chest, killing him instantly. The next held a group of children cornered near a wagon. He fell as Lien's arrow hit him and the children ran.

So many Bonamese, a sea of black. But she couldn't think, couldn't feel. Had to act.

She used her speed to release arrow after arrow until she had none left.

Grabbing her knives from her belt, she leapt off Batu and joined the fray. Bolormaa brandished her sabre at one of the imperial soldiers. He blocked and disarmed her. No. He wouldn't kill her mother.

In a blur Lien was behind him and her knife slid along his throat before he lowered his sword. Blood spurted over Bolormaa, and she flinched, but swept up her sabre and with a quick, "Thanks," she turned back to the fight.

Lien kept moving. Her people depended on her. She couldn't focus on the deaths, not if she wanted to ensure none of them were her own family. She picked up a quiver of arrows dropped by one of the Bonamese and fired them in quick succession. No one she aimed at survived.

She let her training take over. Attack, block, attack, spinning like a whirlwind through the camp, leaving death in her wake.

"Help!" The cry came from a group of children desperately trying to hold off three Bonamese. She raced over and killed the soldiers, leaving the children gaping at her. They needed to be protected. She scanned the camp and found a group of smaller children huddled behind one tent. "Join them."

"We can fight," an older boy protested.

"You will protect the younger children," Lien told him. With some yurts burning, it was too dangerous to have the children hide inside. They might be trapped. "Gather up as many as you can and head north."

The boy nodded and ordered the children to follow

him.

Kew raced over to her.

Lead the children to them, Lien told her. *Then get them out of here*. She caught sight of Kushi and some of his friends struggling with the Bonamese. She tightened her grip on her knives and sped to them.

Pockets of fighting were everywhere. There had to be a thousand Bonamese, but now the hunters were back, the numbers were in the Rhoran's favour. And they were angry.

Lien leapt over dead bodies as she rushed from fight to fight with no idea of how much time had passed.

Then a loud horn broke the air. The sound of retreat. She killed the man in front of her as she glanced around to take stock. Temur and Amslan fought side by side with some soldiers who weren't backing down. A third man approached, swinging his sword towards Temur.

Temur stumbled, going down on one knee.

The Bonamese soldier smiled.

Her heart in her throat, Lien ran.

Chapter 16

Temur was going to die.

Lien leapt forward, her gaze locked on the enemy's sword arm as it descended towards her husband. With a crash, her sabre blocked the blow, the momentum carrying her and the soldier away from Temur. The soldier cried out and clutched his arm, his sword falling to the ground. He turned towards her, his eyes wide and defiant. Lien froze as his face sparked recognition. He'd received a military award at the palace and she had pinned the medal to his tunic.

His mouth dropped open.

She had to act. He'd been about to kill Temur. Swinging her sabre, she slit his throat. All life left his eyes, replaced by the glassiness of death.

Her stomach convulsed as she turned away from the horror. Temur stabbed the soldier who'd come at him from the side and Amslan killed the man he fought.

The remaining Bonamese fled, and she pivoted, checking her surroundings, gasping for breath. Some Rhoran chased the invaders, while others turned their attention to the tent fires, beating them out before they set the whole camp alight. Still more gathered the children and searched for loved ones.

"Thank you, my *bayar*." Temur strode over to her. "Are you all right?"

Blood covered her hands, warm and sticky. She scrubbed her hands on her tunic, blocking memories before they crippled her. She nodded.

"We need to help the injured," Temur said, concern clear on his face.

"Of course." And find her family, confirm they were alive. She moved through the camp, helping those she could and calling for assistance when required. Checeg, Shuren and their brothers were with Kew, and Geriel and Odval helped the injured.

Smoke and death intertwined, the smell making Lien nauseous, but she didn't stop.

Bolormaa and Mongke directed the efforts to stop the fires, and Sukh rounded up the horses which had got loose in the battle. The only person she hadn't seen was Erdene.

Where was she?

The camp was huge, and people were everywhere. She was probably helping somewhere.

A low moan caught her attention behind one yurt. Sliding her knives into her hands, she twisted and her heart stopped. Erdene lay there, hands clutching her stomach, her hands and shirt red with blood. Dropping to her knees, Lien yelled, "Amslan!" She lifted Erdene's hands away, saw bits of her insides that should never be seen. Fear leaped to Lien's throat. She jumped up and grabbed the nearest person. "Help Erdene." She needed Amslan. He was the only one who could save her. But where in Qadan's name was he? She raced through the camp searching, her exhaustion making it hard to go as fast as she needed to. Finally she found him at the far end tying off a bandage on someone who'd been stabbed.

"Amslan." She dragged him to his feet.

"What?" He turned, annoyed.

"It's Erdene."

Fear crossed his face. "Where?"

Lien pointed. He was too heavy for her to carry, so she had to run at his pace, so incredibly slowly, while her sister lay dying. When they arrived Amslan pushed the man helping Erdene out of the way and placed his hands on her wound. He swore. "Lien, hold her hand."

Lien held it, murmuring to her. "Hold on, sister. You need to hold on."

As Amslan began the healing, Erdene screamed once and fell unconscious.

Sweat poured down his face, the strain and concentration clear. Lien didn't dare interrupt him. The man who was there said, "I'll fetch help." He ran off.

Lien closed her eyes, praying for Erdene. How many others were fighting to survive? How many of her people had been killed today?

The emperor needed to pay. How dare he invade Rhora like this? How dare he attack an undefended camp? Anger sizzled over her skin. He'd gone too far this time.

Amslan gasped and slumped against Lien. She opened her eyes. Had he used too much of his gift? His face was pale, and he panted. Erdene's eyes fluttered open for a second and then closed.

"Is she going to be all right?"

He nodded, tears streaming down his face. "I'll take her to the healers' tent."

Dark rings were already forming around his eyes. "You need to have yourself checked while you're there." She helped him to his feet.

His glare made her smile. "We can't afford to have

you unwell, Amslan," she said. "There are others who need your skills."

The man returned with another healer. Between the two of them, they carried Erdene to the healers' tent with Amslan stumbling behind.

Lien didn't have the luxury of joining them. She had to help others.

Dirt, blood and death were everywhere. Her mind reeled at the senselessness, wanting to block it out, pretend she wasn't witnessing the grief, the pain and the fear. She had to be strong. She had duties to carry out.

Though it was almost as if there was nothing for her to do. The older children gathered the younger children together, counting them and organising searches for any who were missing. A group of women beat out the tent fires while the healers and young adults helped the injured. The warriors walked around the camp ensuring any Bonamese left behind were dead, or taking them aside to be questioned.

"Muunokhoi, can you return to the hunt to finish butchering the animals?" Temur was bloodied and covered in dirt, but he was alive. Relief soothed some of her anger.

Muunokhoi nodded.

Temur noticed her and called out, "Have you seen Erdene?"

She walked over. "Amslan has taken her to the healers' tent. She is alive. He healed her."

Concern crossed his face. "I'll drop by when I get a chance." He hesitated and then said, "I'm glad you are well."

"Thank you. And I you."

He smiled briefly before someone called his name.

She needed to continue her rounds, continue to help her people.

They would talk later.

~*~

It was late in the day before the camp returned to a semblance of normalcy. Lien struggled to put one foot in front of the other as she made her way back to the healers' tent. She was beyond exhausted. Using so much of her gift had sapped her energy. Geriel had pressed food into her hand earlier, but Lien couldn't swallow any of it. Her stomach was as uneasy as her soul and the thought of food was more than she could take. Each body she passed was a reminder of the lives she'd taken. She didn't even know how many. The way she'd switched off her revulsion and killed terrified her.

The bodies of the dead Bonamese had been collected and taken away over the steppes and left to the animals, with no honour and no ceremony. It hurt to think they would not meet their ancestors in heaven. They had been following orders, but had known the risks of going into battle with the Rhoran.

And she'd had to protect her people.

The injured had now been helped, the butchered animals from the hunt had been transported back to the camp and the Rhoran who had died had been taken to the spiritual tent to prepare for the burial service.

Those she'd killed would never again breathe the fresh air of the steppes, would never laugh at a joke, would never hug a loved one, would never experience the joys of watching their children grow.

She squeezed her eyes shut.

"Lien." Temur stopped in front of her. "We're discussing the attack now. Would you like to join us?"

It was the last thing she wanted to do. It would hurt too much to know how many people had been killed or injured, how much damage had been done to the camp, but it was important for her to go as tribal mother. "Yes."

He led her to his tent where representatives of all the tribes gathered. They joined the circle, sitting cross-legged.

"Bolormaa, will you tell us what happened?" Temur asked his mother.

Bolormaa moved to the centre of the circle. "Some time after you left, Checheg went for a ride. She spotted the Bonamese army heading our way and raced back to warn us." Bolormaa nodded towards Sukh. "They mustn't have seen her as we had time to send a rider to call you and gather our defences." She sighed. "They had only just attacked when you arrived back. We were very lucky."

An understatement. If Checheg hadn't spotted them, the whole camp could have died, they'd been so outnumbered. Today could have ended very differently. Thank Qadan she'd told Checheg to stay.

"About a dozen yurts have been destroyed by fire," Bolormaa continued, "but those families have shelter for the night." She returned to her seat and Temur called on Amslan. "How many injured?"

Amslan swayed a little as he stood, his face even paler than before. "One hundred, only a dozen seriously. Another twenty dead."

She'd expected more, especially considering the numbers of dead Bonamese she'd seen being loaded onto wagons, but even twenty was too many.

"Do the healers need our assistance with anything?"

"I'd appreciate some people to tend the injured during the night. The healers need to rest."

"I'll arrange it."

Amslan sat and at Temur's gesture one of the senior tribesmen from another tribe stood.

"Was the hunt salvaged?" Temur asked.

Muunokhoi nodded. "We saved most of the meat. Wolves took some of the kill, but we have enough to divide amongst the tribes."

Finally Temur asked Chinua to stand.

"What of the Bonamese?"

"Five hundred dead."

Gasps went around the room and Lien's mouth dropped open. The Rhoran were great warriors but twenty dead versus five hundred was unbelievable.

"Those who were injured killed themselves rather than being taken for questioning," Chinua continued.

Temur held up a hand to quiet the murmuring. "Are you sure we killed so many?"

Chinua glanced at Lien and hesitated.

Lien's skin tightened. She wanted to slap her hands over her ears to block his next words.

"Most had their throats slit."

She clenched her teeth, swallowing the bile as all heads pivoted towards her. She refused to meet anyone's eyes even as her pulse beat in her head. She was the only one who could get close enough to slit their throats.

"How many?" Amslan asked the question Lien didn't want answered.

"Over half."

Her mind screamed at her, and her stomach swirled like wind through the grass, but only the slightest twitch on her face betrayed her inner turmoil. She visualised her family, their smiles and laughter to keep calm. Suddenly she was grateful for her time in the palace which had taught her not to show her true emotions.

"Lien saved us today," Chinua said.

Was it right she had to take one man's life, in order to save another's? The Bonamese *had* attacked the camp. It was unprovoked. They had to understand some of them would die.

Nausea rose in her stomach. She'd been given a gift and she'd used it to kill hundreds. There was no justification. Blocking out what the others were saying, she stared ahead and concentrated on her breathing.

The face of the last soldier she'd killed floated through her mind. He'd been older than her, but still young. He might have had a family who cared for him, parents who would grieve.

She squeezed her eyes shut, hoping to block his face out, but it came back stronger.

A hand touched her shoulder, and her eyes flew open. The tent was empty aside from Temur who watched her with concern on his face.

"Where?" How had everyone left without her noticing?

"It's all right, my *bayar*. The meeting is over. You can let go now."

She gritted her teeth to resist his kindness. The misery welled up inside her, battering her defences. Her body shook and her teeth chattered as big fat tears fell out of her eyes like a waterfall. She blinked, trying to stop it, but she couldn't control any of it.

Temur gathered her into his arms and held her, murmuring nonsense.

And all her walls crumbled down.

She wept until she had nothing left inside. Utterly exhausted, she couldn't have moved even if it meant saving her own life. And all the while, Temur held her.

Someone knocked on the door.

Lien buried her head into Temur's shoulder. "No." She couldn't let anyone see her like this.

"They're bringing you food." Temur called, "Come in."

A scaly head nudged at her shoulder. Kew had entered with whoever had brought food.

Amslan.

She gazed at him, too exhausted to hide her face. Let him think what he would about her breakdown.

"I've brought you some soup, Mother." His smile was gentle as he placed it on a nearby table.

Lien stared at him. Where was his barely restrained disgust, his mocking smile at her distress?

"You need to eat and then you need rest. Erdene asked me to tell you if you don't eat, she'll come over and make you, and she shouldn't be out of bed."

"Erdene is all right?" Relief swamped Lien.

Amslan nodded. "I got to her in time." He paused. "Thank you." He left the tent.

Temur chuckled as he shifted her in his arms and picked her up, carrying her to the table. "You needn't be so shocked, my *bayar*. Amslan is a good man."

His arms cocooned her, offering her comfort.

"To others." She gazed at the soup in front of her and her stomach protested. "You need to ensure he gets his rest. He's exhausted."

Temur took her hand and kissed her knuckles. "Arigh and Mother will see to him," he said. "I need to make sure you eat. We don't want Erdene getting out of bed."

Lien reluctantly picked up the spoon and dipped it into the bowl. The broth contained meat and the smell reminded her of all the death. She dropped the spoon and pushed away from the table, dry retching. "I can't." She tried to stand, but her legs wouldn't support her.

"Lien, you must eat. You need the energy."

"Please don't make me. I can't… not after I've killed so many." Her voice choked and her stomach heaved. No tears came though. She was dry.

Temur swore, picked her up and carried her to the bed. "If you won't eat, you need to sleep." He laid her on the bed.

Kew jumped up and licked Lien's face, blowing smoke on her.

Temur moved away and Lien reached for him. "Please, don't leave yet." She couldn't bear to be alone with her thoughts.

He hesitated and then lay down next to her, drawing her close to him. "I won't leave you, my *bayar.*"

She drew comfort from him and exhaustion pulled her down into sleep.

~*~

Lien awoke with a start, sweating and shaking. The remnants of her dream attacked her—the soldier's face—the shock and recognition before his life drained away.

"I'm here, Lien." Temur moved the curtain aside and sat on the bed. "Bad dream?" He handed her a drink.

Relief filled her. He was there. She nodded, taking the cup with shaky hands. She took a small sip, forcing herself to swallow. Her stomach still swirled, uncertain how to react.

Daylight shone through the open crown in the roof, and voices murmured on the other side of the curtain.

"Amslan and Chinua are giving me updates," Temur explained. "Amslan wants to ensure you eat something."

Her throat closed over.

"He's brought broth. You need to eat it." He stroked the loose hairs of her fringe back from her face.

The thought of eating made her nauseous, but

without the energy she would be useless to her people. She had to try. She nodded.

"Amslan, bring the food."

Amslan appeared around the curtain carrying a tray. His face was still pale and his eyes sunken.

Lien frowned at him. "How much have you eaten?" She balanced the tray on her lap.

"Enough," he said.

She doubted it. "I will only eat if you do." He was their best healer and he needed to be healthy, especially if they hunted down the remaining Bonamese army.

"Don't be ridiculous," Amslan growled.

She crossed her arms. "As tribal Mother you will do as I ask."

Temur grinned. "You'd better do what she says, Amslan. I think she means it and I would like my wife to eat something."

His support surprised her.

Chinua appeared at the curtain holding a bowl. "Here you go, Amslan." He winked at Lien.

Temur gestured for him to sit at the end of the bed.

Lien waited until Amslan took his first spoonful. Now she had to eat. She'd promised.

Cautiously she sipped a small spoonful. It slid down her throat, its taste bland, before settling in her stomach. She waited for a reaction, but it stayed put. After checking Amslan was still eating, she took another small sip.

The silence was deafening and Temur's gaze made her uncomfortable. She couldn't read him. "What is happening today?"

"We will hold another tribal council and ask if yesterday's attack has changed some minds," Temur said.

She frowned. "What do you mean?"

Temur smiled. "While you were isolated, we had a series of meetings to discuss whether we should search for the Great Khan's burial site. Most believe it is either a myth, or if they believe it is true, that we shouldn't disturb it. However we think the Bonamese you discovered before the wedding were searching for it."

Lien nodded. "The emperor wants more men with the gift. Only Ying has it. If he had an army of those with the gift, he would be unstoppable."

"You must explain this to the tribal leaders." Temur's mouth set in a grim line.

It made no sense. "Why can you not command them to do as you say? You are khan."

"On a matter such as this it is a tribal decision and our spiritual advisors such as Solongo have more influence. They understand how the ancestors may react to such a disturbance and how it will affect the tribe."

Amslan put aside his empty bowl. "If it pleases you, Mother, I will check on those who are injured."

Lien's mouth dropped open. He was asking her permission? "Of course."

After he left, Lien said to Temur, "Perhaps a healer should check Amslan to make sure he hasn't injured his head."

Chinua and Temur both laughed.

"Mother, not only did you save our tribe, but you saved his wife," Chinua said. "He is indebted to you and you have earned his respect."

Respect. A glow spread through her chest.

"Chinua, you have not yet reported on what the scouts discovered," Temur said.

"They tracked the remaining Bonamese across the steppe far to the south east before stopping to rest. Their horses won't keep up such a pace today." He paused. "There are seven hundred men, but we can defeat them."

It made no sense. "If they had wanted to destroy us, the emperor would have sent more soldiers," she said. "The Rhoran ruthlessness is legendary." She smiled to soften her words. "All know you will not let such an attack go without retaliation."

"Of course not!" Chinua said.

Something tickled the back of her mind. She took another sip of broth, needing the energy to sift through her foggy brain. "Could they be a decoy?" she asked. "A group designed to distract you?" Attacking while the Rhoran were at their strongest was stupidity at its finest.

And Ying wasn't stupid.

Chapter 17

Temur frowned. "Why do you think that?"

She hesitated. "It makes little sense for them to attack us when everyone is gathered together, and then not to use their whole army." It was suicide. "Maybe we should send scouts west just in case."

"And leave those who attacked us go free?" Chinua growled. "They must be punished."

She held up a hand to calm him. "I agree. But we could afford to send a couple of people to check the surrounding areas. Especially when the Bonamese won't expect it. What better punishment than to thwart their real plan?"

Temur was silent for a moment. "Chinua, ask Solongo to change the tribal council to tomorrow after the funerals and send scouts west."

Temur hadn't dismissed her theory. Pleasure hummed over her skin as Chinua left the tent.

Suddenly they were alone again and she stiffened.

"You appear much better today, my *bayar*."

His kindness helped to ease some of her tension. She nodded.

Temur hesitated and then sat at the foot of the bed,

a deep frown on his face. "Can you explain something to me, Lien?"

He called her by her name. Lien's stomach clenched.

He stood and paced the room. "When we first met, you had been ordered to kill me."

She nodded.

"Had you had any other orders before these?"

"No."

"So your first mission was to kill me." He shook his head in disbelief. "Initially I didn't believe you had any real skills. Then after we returned to the palace I realised how wrong I was. You could have decimated my tribe."

It explained why he'd been so cold to her. "You were upset you had put the tribe at risk."

He nodded. "And now you've just saved my people." He frowned. "I've changed my opinion of you so many times. I don't know where you fit." His eyes searched hers for an answer.

"I have changed my opinion of the Rhoran too. And I was not honest in the beginning."

"But are you being honest now?"

"Yes."

"I hope so." After a long look, he took her empty bowl and moved to leave the tent.

She needed to fix this. "Temur, wait."

He turned back to her.

She opened her mouth, and then closed it again, not sure how to say what she wanted to say.

"What is it?"

Taking a deep breath, she said, "I want to talk to you about our wedding night." Her face heated as his expression showed no emotion. She swallowed. If she wanted their relationship to improve, she had to try too. "I didn't find what you—we—did repulsive. The intensity surprised me. I didn't mean to make you feel rejected. I am not experienced in those ways." Her skin glowed and she looked at the ground, unable to look him in the eye.

Temur stepped forward, squatted down to her height and tilted her chin up so she was looking at him. "I am relieved, my *bayar*. I didn't want to force you, and afterwards, I realised I might have misread the situation. Erdene wouldn't allow me to see you so I could explain."

Hope filled her. "I am not used to being open with my emotions, but I will try with you."

He brushed his thumb over her cheek, his smile sweet. "I would like that, my *bayar*. And I will be honest with you." He kissed her gently on the mouth. "I must see to the tribe."

Lien nodded, and after he left, she sighed. Showing her vulnerability could only help their relationship. She stood, her legs weak and shaky and stumbled over to the table, where she sat with Kew beside her. The battle yesterday had been brutal, but the heavy exhaustion cloaking her might also relate to using her gift so much.

She picked at the food Amslan had left her. Getting her strength back was a priority. Her tribe needed her more than she needed sleep. She had to review the battle strategy Ying had taught her, had to figure out what his true plan was. But every way she assessed it, she kept coming back to the Great Khan's treasure. The hope the Bonamese could subjugate the Rhoran for good would be a big enough incentive for the emperor to invade Rhora. It was the last country bordering Bonam that he hadn't conquered.

As she left the tent with Kew, she paused. The air still smelled smoky and the ground was churned up from all the fighting. Blood spatter covered some of the yurt walls.

"Child, how are you feeling?" Odval hurried over with Bolormaa and hugged her.

"I am well," Lien said.

"Nonsense." Bolormaa snorted. "Any fool can see you are exhausted. Have you eaten today?"

Her heart warmed at their concern. "Yes, Mother. I ate with Amslan."

"Good. He needs energy as well."

"Where are you headed?" Odval asked.

"I would like to visit the healers' tent."

"We will join you," Bolormaa said.

Many of the signs of the previous day's battle were already gone. The burnt homes had been disassembled and their owners had salvaged what they could. Now the women and children were beating wool to make the felt needed to remake their homes.

"The tribe is quick to recover," she commented.

"It is not our way to dwell on the past," Odval said. "Out here on the steppes we must be prepared for anything and if our tribe is fractured we are vulnerable."

"In a few days you wouldn't guess someone had attacked us," Bolormaa continued. "We cannot show our enemies we are weak."

The Rhoran were so formidable.

The journey through the camp was slow. Word had spread and everyone wanted to thank Lien for what she had done yesterday. More than a few expressed their concern about her wellbeing.

Though the horror of slaughtering hundreds of people hung over her, she responded to her people's comments and compliments with as much grace as she could. She would mourn the lives lost on both sides in private.

They arrived at the large healers' tent full of the injured. Some sat on their beds and talked with each other, while others lay still or moaning.

"Erdene is over here," Bolormaa said.

"I will be there shortly." She couldn't ignore the other injured. It wouldn't be right. The first patient was Cheren, the man she'd rescued from the imperial palace. His arm was bandaged and he had a nasty lump on his head.

Grinning at her, he said, "Thank you for saving me again."

Lien frowned.

"The scum who gave me this," he indicated the lump on his head, "was about to finish me off when he spouted blood from his neck and fell to the ground dead. I'm assuming it was you."

She let out a breath. She had no recollection of Cheren. "How is your head?"

"There's nothing wrong with me," he moaned. "They want to keep me here because of the lump. It's driving me mad. I should be helping to plan the retaliation."

She wouldn't mention there might not be one. "The healers are well trained. You must be patient. Perhaps they will let you fletch arrows while you're here."

Cheren brightened. "Good idea." He called to a healer and Lien moved to the next patient.

She took almost an hour to reach Erdene. Her face was pale, but she was alert, and the smile she gave Lien lightened her worry. Bolormaa moved aside so Lien could kneel next to her.

"How are you feeling?" Lien asked.

"Like I've been stabbed in the stomach." Erdene laughed carefully, her hand on her side.

It was music to Lien's ears. "Is Amslan happy with

your progress?"

She scowled. "He's been fussing and he's in a worse state than I am. You need to make him rest, before he causes himself some damage."

Amslan was across the room, giving one patient more healing. His face strained. He was overdoing it. "I will have a word with him."

"Make sure I'm watching when you do." Erdene grinned.

"How long until you can leave?"

"This evening," she said. "I only need rest and Amslan wants to monitor me. I'll be fine in a couple of days." She yawned.

"I'll leave you to rest now."

"Don't forget to speak to Amslan."

Lien nodded. She left Bolormaa and Odval saying their goodbyes and went over to where Amslan was speaking to Cheren.

Amslan inclined his head. "Mother." His eyes were still shadowed and his skin had a grey tinge to it. She needed to help him.

"Come with me." She picked up cheese from the nearby table and led him to an empty bed. "Lie down."

He scowled. "I'm busy."

She gave him the cheese. "Eat. No one will die if you don't heal them. You need to take care of yourself." Would he obey her? "I want you to rest for the remainder of the day, unless Temur has need of you."

His glare was fierce. "My people need me."

She nodded. "They need you whole and healthy. You're no use to us if you collapse. Lie down."

He glanced over to Erdene who nodded her head in agreement. With a muttered curse he lay down.

"Geriel!"

Her sister looked up from where she was changing a dressing. Her eyes weren't as shadowed. Maybe she hadn't been using her gift as much.

"Amslan is to rest today. He is not allowed up, unless he needs to relieve himself." She paused. "If you need more help or he gets up, send someone to fetch me."

Geriel nodded. "Yes, Mother."

She waited for a second for Amslan to protest again and when he didn't, she walked outside, taking a deep breath. He had listened to her. Maybe this could work.

Kew trotted up next to her.

What have you been up to?

Kew nodded towards the camp fire where children gathered, mending items.

How are they? For some children it would have been the first time they had experienced a battle.

Kew's response was calming.

"The children understand battles are a part of life," Odval said. "Though the reality has shocked some, like my Shuren. I must check her." She left.

"There's Temur." Bolormaa walked towards her son.

Lien's skin tingled. He'd been talking to one child and now straightened, his own face showing signs of fatigue.

"How is my sister?" he asked.

"She tires easily, but Amslan is happy," Bolormaa told him.

"And Amslan?"

"He is resting in the healers' tent," Lien said.

"Good." Temur held her hand. "The tribe is organising the funerals for tomorrow. As tribal Mother you are expected to visit each bereaved family and offer them comfort."

Her body tensed. In Bonamese society showing grief was a sign your emotions ruled you. The Rhoran wouldn't be so subdued and she had no idea how to handle their reactions.

"I can join you if you would like," Bolormaa offered.

Lien hesitated. "Please, if it is not against protocol." Hopefully Bolormaa's familiar face would help, and no one would blame Lien for the attack.

Temur nodded his assent.

With her hands clammy, Lien followed Bolormaa to the first family.

"Bataar was the father to five children," Bolormaa told her. "His wife is Tegus. He was stabbed through the chest."

Lien cringed. "How old are his children?"

"The oldest is eighteen and the youngest is five."

What could she say to Tegus? She still had young children to support and it would be difficult without her husband.

Bolormaa knocked and entered a tent. Inside it was dim, the flap over the tent's centre closed. A figure sat on a bed, her head in her hands while a young woman, someone Lien recognised from her training sessions, comforted her. Sitting on the floor below them were four children, all watching their mother, waiting.

The sorrow was palpable and Lien hesitated, resisting the urge to leave.

"Our tribal Mother is here," the young woman told her mother.

Tegus looked up, her eyes puffy. Then she focused on Bolormaa and wailed, "Bataar is dead. My husband is dead." She rocked back and forth with tears streaming down her face.

Lien froze. What was she supposed to do?

The smaller children on the floor burst out crying

and her ears stung with their high-pitched wails.

Bolormaa hugged Tegus and the young woman slipped off the bed and gathered one of the wailing children in her arms.

Lien had never witnessed so much suffering, so much emotion. Bolormaa gestured to the children on the floor. Of course. She could comfort them, though they might not want it from a stranger. Sitting cross-legged she placed her hand on the back of the little boy who couldn't be over five. He climbed into her lap, throwing his chubby arms around her neck, sobbing into her chest.

Her heart broke. She cuddled him, rocking him back and forth, murmuring to him. Things would have been so different if she'd had someone to hold her when her parents had died. She slid her arm around the older girl next to her and she leaned in, crying. Nothing she could do would take away their grief.

Eventually the sobs lessened and the wails quieted. Bolormaa whispered something to Tegus and stood, moving over to the table to get a cloth and something to drink. She returned to the widow and washed her face with the cloth as if she was a child and then gave her the drink. She passed the cloth to the oldest daughter who wiped her own face and those of her siblings next to her before passing the cloth to Lien.

"It is time for you to eat." Bolormaa pulled the woman to her feet.

"I cannot! My Bataar is dead. I am alone."

"Nonsense," Bolormaa said firmly and marched the woman to the table. "You have your children and Bataar is with his god. There is no other place he should be."

Lien's mouth dropped open. That was a little unkind.

Tegas brushed her hair from her face and sat. "You are right. He is in a better place." She sniffed back more tears. "Children, join me. We will eat to celebrate your father's journey to Qadan's side."

The switch made Lien blink, but the children reacted swiftly, standing up and joining her. At Bolormaa's gesture, Lien rose and together they said their farewells.

Outside the tent Bolormaa sighed and rubbed her face. "Not all families will be as hard," she assured Lien and took her hand.

Some of her tension released, though her head ached.

"Let's go to the next one."

She was exhausted from that single display of grief. How would she get through the others?

After visiting all the families, Bolormaa had taken one look at Lien and sent her back to the tent to rest. Lien hadn't argued. She'd never seen so many tears, felt so much grief, thick and palpable in the air. Only a couple of families remained stoic and shed no tears, and Lien worried for them. Perhaps they would grieve in private.

She entered Temur's tent and found him inside. He glanced up and then frowned and strode over to her. "You need to rest." He slid his arm around her waist and led her over to their bed. With deft fingers he undid her belt and then hesitated.

Lien's face heated. "I can manage."

He nodded, turning his back and Lien undressed and slid under the covers. "Don't let me sleep too long," she said. "I still need to check the funeral details."

He sat on the bed. "Everything is taken care of. You should sleep as long as you can. It will be another long day tomorrow." He kissed her forehead. "I will take care of everything for you."

Her heart squeezed and she swallowed hard. "Thank you."

Temur brushed her hair off her face and then stood. "Sleep now, my *bayar*."

His kind tone lulled her and sleep pulled her under.

~*~

The next day the funeral rites began at dawn. The sun's rays hovered at the horizon as Lien walked across the camp with Temur by her side, her hand in his. It was still, only a quiet murmuring of voices as each tribe gathered their deceased, and laid them ceremoniously on top of a cart. Lien mounted Batu, but the spiritual leaders led the procession, followed by the deceased and their families, and then she and Temur led the rest of the tribes. Though not part of a normal funeral, warriors surrounded the group, fully armed and ready for any attack. Lien carried a quiver of arrows and her bow on her back.

By the time they reached the sacred place where the graves had been dug the day before, the sun was well over the horizon. The graves were wide and deep, big enough for the dead, their horses and any possessions they were taking into the afterlife.

Solongo lit a fire in the centre to cleanse the surrounds. Lien scanned the mourners, noting the tears running down Tegus's face, and her children gathered around her. This was only the beginning for them. They would have to learn how to live without Bataar, continue making adjustments to their everyday life.

Her attention was drawn to the graves as each horse was led over, made to lie down, and killed with a direct strike to its heart. Lien flinched and Temur slipped his hand into hers, squeezing it gently. She didn't look at him, but his touch soothed her. This was the Rhoran way. They then lay the deceased on top of the horse and family members brought mementos, things they might need in the afterlife—a bow and arrow or a sabre for a warrior, a spindle for an embroiderer. Each loved one stopped by the grave, said a few words and then walked around it three times before moving to the fire and running their hands through the smoke to cleanse themselves.

Lien stared at the fire, the orange flames and white smoke swirling in patterns, the heat not enough to burn her face from this distance. She ached too much to focus on the graves. She grieved for those who died, but the Bonamese she had killed would get no such ceremony. Their spirits would be caged inside their bodies and their families could not say their goodbyes.

Kew walked forward, her bearing erect, her colour a rich green.

Lien took a small step forward, uncertain what she was doing. Temur tugged her back as Kew approached each grave and blew flames and smoke over the bodies. Temur nodded in approval.

She let out a deep breath. Somehow her dragon knew what to do.

When the ceremony was complete, the graves were covered with dirt and the procession made their way back to camp. Each tribe retreated to their own camp to hold a midday feast and to talk about the deceased, sharing stories and memories to honour their lives.

Lien attended the meal for Tegus's husband, but said little. She closed her eyes against the tears.

"Are you all right, my *bayar*?" Temur asked.

Her heart was so heavy in her chest, weighing her down with sorrow. "I am weary."

He squeezed her hand. "An hour more and you may go without causing offence."

She tried to eat the food someone had placed in front of her. She was used to pretending everything was fine.

Finally Tegus and her children departed to hold vigil in their tent in case Bataar's spirit got lost and tried to return. It was their duty to prevent him from entering the tent and to show him the way to the afterlife.

Now she could leave. Temur spoke with Solongo, so Lien stood and headed back to Temur's tent. She needed to grieve in private for both peoples.

Needed to acknowledge the Bonamese dead.

Even if she'd killed most of them.

~*~

At dusk Lien left the tent. She had fallen asleep, drained by the past few days, but at least now she had enough energy to attend the tribal council.

She walked into the gathering hut and over to her husband. Solongo and the other spiritual leaders were there as well as tribal elders and leaders both men and women. As she knelt next to Temur, his eyes searched hers. "How are you feeling?"

"I am rested." She couldn't tell him how heartbroken she was.

He nodded, but the concern didn't leave his face.

When the final attendees arrived, Temur spoke. "The Bonamese have invaded our land and attacked us, unprovoked. Rhoran tradition tells us we must not let this insult go unanswered."

People murmured in agreement and Temur held up a hand. "However, we now have someone who can give us an insight into why the Bonamese have done this. We would be wise to listen to what she has to say." He indicated for Lien to speak.

Lien swallowed hard as all eyes turned to her. This

was the first time they had asked her opinion in public, the first time it had been respected. "The Bonamese have always been wary of the Rhoran. They could not beat us in battle so therefore gift us tribute acknowledging our prowess. They know they cannot stop us. When they invade our lands, they ride understanding they are unlikely to ever see their home again, for the Rhoran leave no man standing."

The group nodded and smiled.

"For this reason the attack on the camp makes no sense. If it was retaliation for rescuing a few prisoners they would have been wise to wait until after the tribal gathering."

"The Bonamese aren't known for being sensible," Solongo said.

Lien blinked. "The Bonamese expect us to chase the attackers and yet according to our scouts, they rest within striking distance. This is a terrible tactic and not one a senior Bonamese officer would make."

"Then why have they done it?"

She hesitated. Was it right to voice her opinion when she could be wrong? Temur nodded at her. "I believe the soldiers are a diversion and they want us to attack them. They may have more men waiting to attack the camp, or they want to keep us occupied while they slip past unnoticed."

A few people murmured and Muunokhoi spoke. "That's a lot of guessing, with no evidence. We cannot let this attack go unpunished on speculation." He glared at her.

He was right to be suspicious.

"Chinua has sent scouts across the steppes to find any other Bonamese parties," Temur said.

"What would they want on our lands?" someone asked.

"The artefact of the Great Khan," Temur said.

"It's a myth," one of the spiritual advisors said.

"That may be true," Lien responded. "But as long as the emperor believes it, he will search for it. He believes it will bestow the gift on men so he can form unstoppable armies."

Solongo frowned. "Do none of your men have the gift?"

"Only Ying, as far as I know."

"Surely some gifted women have had sons as well as daughters," Solongo said.

Lien hesitated. "What do you mean?"

"The gift is passed down, mother to child, though not all children receive it."

Lien sat back. How had no one realised it was a trait passed down? The Bonamese didn't know a lot about it, and the emperor wouldn't believe something so special could come from women. It was by chance that anyone had noticed she had the gift when she'd raced Kew across the gardens and won. Xue couldn't ever be told, for if he knew, the women would become baby producers and nothing else. She shuddered.

"Xue doesn't know," she said. "If he found out, it would take years for any offspring to be old enough for his purpose. The artefact is the only way for Xue to reap the benefits."

Solongo nodded. "Of course."

"It doesn't matter, they're still chasing a myth," Muunokhoi argued.

"You think we should allow them to trespass on our land, kill our animals and attack our camps because they are mistaken?" Temur asked, his voice low.

"No. We need to stop them, *if* what you are supposing is true."

Chinua entered and directed his words to Temur.

"The scouts have returned."

"What do they report?"

"There is a large contingent of Bonamese soldiers to the west of here. They are heading towards Lake Tolui and the mountains to the north-west. The soldiers who attacked us have not moved from the place they camped last night."

Next to her, Solongo gasped, her eyes widening and she glanced at the man next to her.

"How many men?" Temur asked.

"Too many to count," Chinua said. "Thousands."

Sending so many soldiers away from Bonam would leave the country vulnerable against invasion. The emperor really wanted the artefact.

Temur scanned the people in the tent. "Do we allow this insult to go unpunished?"

"No," Muunokhoi said. "But we need to also address the party which attacked us, lest they try again."

"Then let us discuss what to do," Temur said.

It was late before they had agreed on a plan.

Lien followed Temur out of the gathering tent, bidding everyone goodnight. The fatigue sleep had chased away was now creeping back. As they returned to their tent, Temur asked, "What do you think of our plans?"

She couldn't prevent more bloodshed. Xue needed to be stopped. "They are well thought out. My only concern is if Ying is there, they may defeat us."

Temur frowned. "There must be a way to neutralise his speed."

She'd never considered it. "You are right." Perhaps Solongo knew of something. Which reminded her. "I believe there must be something important near Lake Tolui."

"Why?"

"Solongo was shocked when Chinua mentioned it. Could the Great Khan be buried there?"

"It is possible." He scratched his chin. "I will ask her about it." He stopped outside their tent, took her hands in his. "How are you feeling, my *bayar*?" His eyes searched hers.

"I am tired."

"And in your soul?"

She closed her eyes. "It too is tired. I prefer not to think of it."

"I cannot promise you won't have to kill again. You are too valuable to be left out of a fight." He wasn't happy about it.

"I will do my duty."

"I thank you for it." He drew her close against him wrapping his arms around her so she was cocooned by him. She relaxed into him.

After a moment he smiled down at her. "I must find Solongo and ask her what is at the lake."

Lien hesitated. "May I come?"

"Of course."

The camp was quiet at this late hour. Only those who had been involved in the council were still out, some discussing the plan. They knocked on Solongo's door and she invited them in and offered them a drink as they sat at the table.

"Thank you for asking Kew to breathe over the graves. The families are honoured a dragon would cleanse their loved ones."

"It was Kew's idea," Lien said. "She understood what was needed."

As Solongo poured their drinks, Temur said, "What are the Bonamese heading towards?"

Solongo raised an eyebrow. "Didn't Chinua say it

was Lake Tolui?"

Temur nodded. "But what is there?"

"You should ask the Danil tribe. It is their area." She sipped her tea.

"You were shocked when you heard where the Bonamese army was," Lien said.

"I was simply amazed they'd travelled so far on to the steppes without us noticing."

Temur pursed his lips. "If there's a chance the artefact of the Great Khan isn't a myth, we can't risk the Bonamese getting it."

"The story has been told for generations," Solongo said. "Who knows what is truth and what is myth?"

Something in her manner, a slight twitch in her shoulders made Lien say, "You do."

Chapter 18

Solongo stared at her, a flash of concern on her face.

Lien was certain she was right. "As the chief spiritual adviser for all the Rhoran tribes," she continued, "it would be your duty to maintain the secret and ensure no one disturbs the peace of the Great Khan."

Silence.

"Is Lien correct?" Temur asked.

Solongo opened her mouth and then closed it.

"I can leave." Her Bonamese heritage may be a problem.

Solongo shook her head. "That won't be necessary." She sighed. "You're right, but I won't tell you where the tomb is."

Temur rocked back on his heels. "Does the artefact exist?"

"An artefact of significance was buried with the Great Khan, but its purpose or powers has been forgotten. Our ancestors did not want the truth known."

Temur was silent for a moment. "We have to assume the myths are true. We can't afford to let the Bonamese find the item. Is there anything you can tell us which may help?"

"I will discuss the matter with the Gods." She turned away, the conversation over.

Temur scowled before saying, "Thank you." He gestured for Lien to rise and they left.

"Does this change our plans?" Lien asked.

He shook his head. "No. We need to deal with the party which attacked the camp first. And the rest of the tribe can prepare for the bigger battle."

She hated the idea of Ying getting closer to the artefact while they stayed still, but they needed to prepare properly.

As they neared their yurt, Lien's footsteps slowed. They hadn't consummated their marriage yet and the uncertainty niggled at her.

She followed Temur inside and he moved over to the bed, undoing his belt and then removing his tunic. The candlelight flickered off his strong muscled chest and attraction stirred.

Her hands hovered over her belt, then she unwound it, folding it until she clasped it in her hand. She placed it in her wooden chest, her caftan loose against her. Temur's eyes were on her but she couldn't meet them.

She tidied the bottles on the table and then finally looked at her husband.

Temur walked towards her. "Would you like to sleep now?"

Her face heated and she shook her head. "I would like to..." How did she say it?

He smiled. "Would you like me to continue what we started on our wedding night?"

His gaze captured her and all she could do was nod.

He pulled her close, running a hand up her back until he cupped her face, and ever so slowly he lowered his head and his lips met hers.

~*~

Movement next to Lien woke her. It was still dark, but someone was in her tent. Her heart raced.

"Go back to sleep, my *bayar*," Temur said.

She unclenched her fist. Of course, it was Temur. "Is it time?"

"Yes. I'll be back by the end of the day. You're in charge while I'm gone."

Her stomach churned. Anything could happen in the battle and she didn't want to lose her husband. She wanted to tell him to be careful, but it was bad luck to voice such concerns to anyone going into battle. As he opened the door to leave, she couldn't stay silent. "Safe journey."

"Thank you, my *bayar*." The door thudded shut, too final a sound.

Lien lay in bed as images from the previous battle assaulted her, the memory of the sword slicing down towards Temur so clear. In her mind this time she didn't make it, and the glazed expression of the soldier she'd killed became Temur's.

She forced away the image and rose. Perhaps she should have gone, if only to protect her husband. Pacing across the room in the dark she stubbed her toe on the table. The pain broke through her looped obsessing and she exhaled. This was ridiculous. Temur and the Rhoran were experienced warriors. They knew the land better than the Bonamese and were attacking before dawn so they would have all the advantages. There was no reason to worry.

She sighed.

Lighting the lantern, she gave herself a moment to adjust to the brightness. With another battle looming ahead, one Ying might take part in, it was essential she find a way to neutralise his speed. Otherwise he would decimate them.

The Rhoran had many techniques which differed from the Bonamese. One had to stop Ying.

She just needed to find it.

~*~

The morning dawned unusually overcast and cold. Lien refused to see it as an omen. The battle would be well under way by now, but she couldn't obsess about its progress. Instead she kept her pace measured as she headed for the training ground. She would show her students the new pattern she'd created. It would keep them all busy.

Geriel was already at the training ground when Lien arrived. "You're here early."

The woman shrugged. "I couldn't sleep after Father left."

Lien nodded. "They'll be back by dark." And hopefully would have few losses. But until then, they both needed a distraction. "I have been working on some new patterns, incorporating some Rhoran moves. Would you like to see?"

Geriel grinned. "Yes, please."

As others joined them, she taught them the new patterns. Some caught on quickly, but others couldn't focus. Erdene swore as she tripped and fell. "This is stupid." Her colour was much better and she had recovered well from her wound. "I feel so useless."

She wasn't talking about the training. The pattern wasn't a good enough distraction.

Clapping her hands to get their attention, Lien said, "I have a challenge."

The teenagers' faces lit up.

"We need to neutralise my speed. My old master, Ying is faster than me and if we cannot figure out how to stop him, we may lose battles in the future." Most of the people here were young, too young to go into battle, but they would have heard how many she'd killed. "Does anyone have any suggestions?"

"We shoot you," someone yelled. When the whole group turned to face the boy, he grimaced and said, "I mean them."

"How do you aim at a target you cannot see?" Lien sped to the person next to him, taking her down to the ground.

The boy blinked. "That makes it difficult."

Geriel spoke. "We need to watch you in action," she said. "If we split into two groups, one can watch and the other can attack. Then we may spot a weakness."

"Good idea." Lien laid down the rules. "If I brush your throat, or throw you to the ground and poke you, you must play dead." The group nodded.

In less than a minute the whole group lay on the ground. "What did you see?"

"Nothing," Erdene said. "You weren't even a blur. It was like an invisible thing had knocked them all over."

Geriel shook her head. "That's not right. There are little dust clouds where she steps." She screwed up her face. "Can you do it again? I'd like to anticipate your move."

A faint tickle of hope entered Lien. "All right." She helped the teenagers to stand. "Ready?"

When they nodded, Lien blocked the first attack and 'killed' the person before going on the offensive, spinning and twisting until something hit her ankle and she stumbled, falling to the ground. Before she had the chance to get up, they surrounded her.

Huffing out a breath, she grinned. "What hit me?"

Geriel picked up the staff from the ground.

"Good work."

The woman shook her head. "No, it's not good enough. We were watching your steps carefully and timed it right. I was nearly too slow. In a real battle, none of us has time to stand around. We'd be killed where we stood."

"There's also the risk of hitting one of our own warriors," Erdene added.

"You are right." Lien got to her feet. "We need to improve this."

The two groups changed positions and those who had been the attackers became the observers. They worked through suggestions, discarding one after the other until the next group of students arrived for their lesson.

Lien gave them the same challenge and she worked through the groups until midday. They tried plenty of options but nothing that would work in a battle.

There had to be something. So many lives depended on it. Fatigue swept over her. She needed food and rest.

Bolormaa approached.

Her heart jumped. "Any word?"

"Nothing as yet," Bolormaa answered. "I doubt they'll send a messenger ahead. Not when they'll be home tonight."

Her calm confidence was reassuring.

"You've worn yourself out." She took Lien by the arm. "You need to eat before you cause yourself harm."

Lien dismissed her students and accompanied Bolormaa to her tent where they ate with Mongke and Erdene.

"A small issue has arisen," Mongke said when they had finished eating. His too casual tone had Lien instantly alert.

"What has happened?"

"Two of the tribes are getting restless," he said. "We have been gathered together for longer than usual and tempers are short."

"Which tribes?"

Bolormaa named them. "The Adhan live closest to the Bonamese border to the west, near the southern mountains. They are concerned the Bonamese will have damaged their land on their journey and want to leave to protect it. They were also the tribe most outspoken about Temur marrying you."

No one had mentioned it to her. "And what of the Danil?"

"They live in the area where the Bonamese are heading. They want to ensure every Rhoran is available to protect their land."

It made sense to be worried. "Where are they camped?"

Mongke grimaced. "Right next to each other which means they overhear comments. Tensions are high."

The Rhoran were an emotional people. If one tribe offended the other, they could cause real division no matter what Temur ordered. She would have to speak with them both, lest something happen before Temur returned. She said as much to Temur's parents.

They both nodded.

"Might I suggest you invite them to the gathering hut?" Bolormaa asked.

Lien rose. "Thank you for the food. I shall speak with the two tribes now."

Mongke rose as well. "Good luck, Mother."

Nerves tingled over her skin as she sent children with messages to the two tribal leaders, asking them to meet her in the gathering tent.

On the way she stopped at her tent to retrieve drinks. Others were inside the gathering hut, so she chose a table away from them.

Batzorig from the Danil tribe arrived first. A short man, with an easy grin, his dark hair flowed to his waist. He spotted Lien and strode over, smiling. "Mother, you wished to speak with me?"

"Yes, please sit." She indicated a seat and offered him a drink. "How is your family?"

"The Danil are well, Mother, though we worry about our land."

"Yes, I know. I wish to discuss this when Muunokhoi arrives."

Batzorig scowled. "The man thinks his land is in danger, but the Bonamese have only passed through. It is my land they will search, my land they will dig up."

Lien held up a hand. "Your concerns are valid, but we must have unity." The tent door opened and Muunokhoi stepped in. Tall and confident in his role as leader, he expected to be listened to when he spoke. He grimaced when he saw who was with Lien and then strode over.

"You called me?"

Lien ignored the lack of greeting and gestured for him to sit. "Thank you for coming, Muunokhoi. How is your family?" She poured him a drink.

"They are restless." He took the cup she offered.

"I understand you are both worried about the Bonamese. They do not comprehend the delicate balance between the people and their environment and do not take precautions to ensure the land survives into the next season."

Both men nodded.

"However," Lien continued, "the tribal council agreed on how to respond. You were both in attendance when the decision was made." She paused. "Our warriors will return this evening after defeating the men who attacked us. We will then begin the next phase."

"But they could ruin our land," Muunokhoi complained.

"They have already passed through your land and are on ours," Batzorig told him.

"More could come."

Muunokhoi was right. The Bonamese might send more men, though it was unlikely unless the group requested additional soldiers. And to do that, there would need to be messengers relaying reports to the emperor.

The emperor would be very annoyed if the messengers weren't getting through.

Lien held up a hand to pause the argument. "I have a solution."

Both men glared at her.

Hopefully Temur would agree with her decision. "Muunokhoi, when we ride to meet the Bonamese, you may take one hundred warriors to patrol the border."

Batzorig opened his mouth to protest, but Lien continued to speak. "You are to stop any messengers returning to Bonam. The emperor will expect regular updates and it will upset him if he does not get them."

Muunokhoi grinned. "I am happiest when the emperor is upset."

Good. She turned to Batzorig. "The rest of the Adhan warriors will join our army against the Bonamese. Are you happy with this arrangement?"

"Yes."

"Then I expect no more arguments between your tribes until after the Bonamese have left our lands."

"Agreed." Batzorig extended his hand to Muunokhoi.

Muunokhoi clasped it and they shook. "Agreed."

The men left and Lien sighed. It was a change to their plans, made without Temur's knowledge or agreement. Would he be upset with her, overrule her?

Would he even make it back to camp alive?

No. Don't think like that.

It was early afternoon and it could still be hours before they received any news. She returned the drinks to her tent and then wandered through camp. She didn't want to be alone now. All she would do was fret. Around her people prepared, some sharpening weapons, others packing provisions.

She moved towards the horses. It would be lovely to take Batu for a ride, but she was here to protect the tribe. She needed to set a good example.

She caught sight of Tegas milking her horse. Tegus placed the bucket to the side and stood from her kneeling position, patting the horse and giving it a light push to tell her she was finished. She paused when Lien walked up.

"How are you today?" Lien asked her.

Tegus indicated her bucket. "I am functioning."

"Is there anything I can do to help?"

"No. My eldest will help me churn the milk and the younger children are collecting dung for the fire. Temur ensured we have enough meat from the hunt."

"I am glad." Tegus still grieved but Lien couldn't alleviate her pain. "If you need further help, please tell me." She scanned the herd.

Batu trotted over and Lien took a brush from the supplies tent to groom her. Kew amused a group of children, changing her skin as they yelled out different colours. Lien smiled. Kew was so much happier here.

Satisfied with Batu's coat, she moved through the camp, speaking to people and helping where she could. And every time someone rode by, she checked whether it was Temur returning.

By mid-afternoon, everyone was getting restless. People snapped at each other and children bickered. She announced another training session and a large number of people attended, all wanting to attempt to neutralise her speed. As the sun hovered above the horizon, a young child ran up.

"The warriors are back!"

Her heart leapt. She didn't need to excuse herself as everyone moved in the direction the child had pointed.

Lien walked quickly, resisting the urge to run like the children. To run would suggest she'd had concerns about the success of the battle.

How she envied the children right now.

As word spread through the camp, many stopped what they were doing and joined the migration towards the warriors.

When Lien reached the horses' pens, the warriors were dismounting and the injured were being transported to the healers' tent. She scanned faces as she moved through the group, greeting some before moving on. Sukh was surrounded by his family and she approached him. "Father, I am pleased you have returned."

Sukh grinned. "As am I, daughter." Then he nodded towards the camp. "Temur's in the healers' tent."

She gasped as fear clutched her heart. Please don't let him be hurt. The image of a mortally wounded Temur flashed in front of her with awful clarity. No need for propriety now.

Without any further word she turned and ran.

Chapter 19

Lien paused outside the healers' tent and took a breath to calm herself before she walked in, scanning the occupants of the beds. A couple of dozen people were being tended, some with stab wounds, others with arrows sticking out of their body. Amslan healed one man whose face was so pale he didn't look Rhoran anymore and Geriel worked on another.

"Lien," Temur called.

Her gaze met his at the back of the tent, where a healer tended him. Relief flooded her, making her a little dizzy. He was alive, naked from the waist up and his pants were covered in dirt and blood, but the nasty gash in his left arm caught her attention. The healer was cleaning the wound which ran from the top of his shoulder to his elbow.

As she joined him, the healer applied a foul-smelling paste to his wound and Temur hissed. He grinned at her. "It stings."

The wound was deep and would require several stitches if a healer couldn't fix it. "Do you have any other injuries?"

"No. This is enough."

Amslan walked over, his eyes already shadowed and Temur waved him away. "There are others who need your help more."

As much as Lien wanted Temur healed, she agreed with him. Amslan had been using his gift almost constantly over the past few days and it was wearing him down.

The healer handed Temur a cup of litak and he gulped it down as the healer took up a needle and thread. This would hurt, but the hideous drink would numb some pain.

As the healer stitched, Temur closed his eyes and clenched his hand. Lien hesitated, but as he sucked in a deep breath she clasped his fist between her hands and rubbed it. Maybe she could distract him. "How did it go?"

He opened his eyes. "It was a success." He let out a whoosh of breath as the healer completed the first stitch of what would be many. "We attacked before dawn. The sentries they posted didn't have a chance to warn them, though they reacted quickly." His fist tightened in her hand as the second stitch was completed.

His pain hurt her. She could stitch much faster than this and surely it would hurt less. Stitching skin rather than fabric couldn't be that much harder. "Let me do it." She took the needle out of the healer's hand. "Help someone else."

"Have you ever done this before?" Temur asked.

Lien shook her head. "But it's just like embroidery isn't it?" She hoped.

Temur waved the healer away and Lien settled herself on the other side of him. She could do this. His wound wasn't bleeding much any more. Holding it closed with one hand, she asked, "What happened next?"

"By the time the sun was over the horizon we had killed half of the group."

As Temur described the battle, Lien stitched the wound together. The skin was thicker than fabric, but after a couple of stitches, she got the right angle and used her speed to finish.

"Done." Lien tied a knot in the last stitch and cut the remaining string.

Temur relaxed his jaw and stared at the wound. "That's amazing. It hardly hurt."

"I am glad." Lien wiped the wound clean and then took a bandage and wound it around his upper arm. "How many did we lose?"

Temur grimaced. "I don't know. Chinua collected the dead. We captured five Bonamese." He glanced around. "I need to go to the prisoners. Will you ask if anyone else needs stitches?" He grinned at her. "They will appreciate your gift."

His grin made her heart beat a little bit faster.

Pulling on his tunic, he continued, "And then visit the bereaved families?"

Lien nodded. "Of course."

She waited while he said a few words to Amslan and then left the tent. The tension she'd been carrying all day dissipated. Temur was safe.

"Lien, we could use you over here," Amslan called.

She rose and went to help her family.

~*~

It was well past dinner by the time she'd finished in the healers' tent and visited the families who had lost a warrior. Lien was drained of both emotion and energy, but she kept her expression calm as she walked through the camp, greeting people and making certain everything was as it should be.

A pulse at her mind made her stop. Kew was searching for her. She followed the feeling to the edge of the camp. Two warriors guarded a yurt and Kew was inside. This had to be where they were holding the prisoners, but why was she in there?

Lien greeted Batzorig. "I am needed inside."

He stepped aside to allow her in.

Her skin tingling, she stared at the sight which greeted her. The five prisoners stood stripped to the waist, their hands tied above their heads to a pole running across the roof and their torsos covered in welts and bruises. One of the Rhoran held a red-hot stick close to one of the prisoner's faces.

Nausea welled up in her. "Stop!" They couldn't torture these men. They'd already slaughtered most of the Bonamese.

Every face in the tent turned towards her and Kew raced over, pleasure emanating from her.

Temur tried to turn her back to the door. "Lien, you don't want to see this."

"You're right." She gestured to the bloodied Bonamese. "If we torture them, we are no better than them." The other Rhoran grumbled but her eyes were only for Temur. She had to convince him this was not the answer. "Like you, they have families, and have followed orders as they were trained."

He frowned at her.

"Remember how Arigh, Yeke and Cheren were treated? We cannot stoop to that level."

"We need answers," Chinua said.

"Are you getting any?"

Chinua shook his head.

Kew butted her legs and motioned to one of the Bonamese soldiers. She knew him.

Lien's muscles tensed. She walked over and he lifted his head, his face bloodied and swollen, but she'd recognise those eyes anywhere. Her chest clenched. "Jie?"

The man frowned. "Kixi?"

Lien blinked back tears at her childhood nickname and nodded as she gazed at the battered body of her brother's best friend.

"What are you doing here?"

"I am married to the khan." She turned away from his outraged stare and directed her words to Chinua. "Get me some things to clean his wounds." She wouldn't allow someone to torture him, couldn't bear for him to be killed.

One of the Rhoran swore. "He's our prisoner."

Chinua looked at Temur who nodded his assent.

As Chinua left the tent, Temur moved to her and lowered his voice. "We cannot let them go."

Her heart ached. Too much senseless violence and she'd already lost so much. She moved closer to him and murmured, "Please, give me some time to get answers. Perhaps we can solve this without death." She didn't care if it made her appear weak. She didn't care if the Rhoran thought it an affront to their people, or saw her as a traitor. Jie had been the only kind person in the palace after her family had died.

"Who is he?" Temur demanded, his voice low.

"My brother's best friend," Lien answered.

"You have tonight." Temur ordered the other men out of the tent.

Relief washed over her and she touched his arm. "Thank you."

"This is madness, Khan," one warrior growled.

Temur's response was too low to hear. She had to get answers or she'd lose their trust again.

Chinua arrived with the supplies and Lien took them and began bathing Jie's wounds. The other prisoners would have to wait.

"Why did they listen to you?" Jie asked.

"Women have a higher status amongst the Rhoran than amongst the Bonamese, and I am tribal Mother." She dabbed at the cuts on his face. "Are you the highest ranked officer here?" She needed to figure out how to save him.

He scowled. "Why do you ask?"

She smiled at his suspicion. "I would like to untie you all. An officer could issue orders not to attack me."

"Lien, that's not a good idea," Temur said behind her.

He was right, but she couldn't stand to have them all hanging there, their bodies bloodied and beaten. And even if they tried to attack her, she could defend herself.

"I am the commanding officer." He turned his head towards his men. "I order you not to attack State Princess Lien."

Lien shook her head. "I am no longer a princess. It would be best if you order them not to attack any Rhoran or try to escape."

Jie rephrased his order and the men acknowledged it. Lien moved to untie the ropes at his wrists, but Temur stopped her.

"He made no promise not to attack you," Temur said in Bonamese.

Did he not consider her Rhoran?

Jie scowled, but nodded. "I will not attack you, Lien or escape. You have my word."

Temur stood back and drew his sabre. "Just in case."

None of the men could harm her, but perhaps it was better to pretend she was helpless.

She helped Jie to the ground and gave him some meat from the table. Then together with Temur, she loosened the ties of the rest of the prisoners, and gave them supplies to clean their injuries.

"How long have you been here?" Jie asked, his voice low as she settled on the ground next to him.

"Almost two moons."

"Do they treat you well?"

Lien nodded. "Like one of their own."

"I am glad. I worried about you having no one after your family died."

Lien hesitated. She wanted to tell him Bao might not be dead, but she didn't dare. She didn't know where his loyalty lay. "I had the emperor."

"You were never a good liar, Kixi."

She blinked. What did he mean?

"I need to speak to the khan alone," Jie whispered.

Unease whispered over her skin. Something was different about Jie, but Kew appeared unperturbed. "What about?"

"It is something my soldiers cannot hear."

Whatever he tried, she could stop him. "I will ask." Walking over to Temur, she switched to speaking in Rhoran. "Jie wishes to speak to you alone."

"Who is he to you, Lien?" His eyes searched hers.

"He was the only person who was kind to me after my family died."

Temur nodded. "Then I will speak to him. He will need restraints if he is going outside."

She inclined her head. "Of course." The Rhoran would not like a Bonamese prisoner walking around.

She helped Jie to his feet, Temur by her side. "Come with me."

"Tie them back up and have some of your men guard them," Jie mumbled in Rhoran.

Temur called the guards in from outside and they retied the remaining prisoners.

Lien took a short rope from the floor. "You will need restraints."

He stood still while she restrained him.

Chinua approached Lien. "Mother, may we continue questioning the prisoners?"

Lien hesitated. Hopefully Jie could tell them everything, but it would be better if the other prisoners gave them some information. She glanced at her dragon. "Yes, but there is no need to torture them. Kew will turn green if they are telling the truth."

Kew flashed vivid green to show him.

He grinned. "That's useful."

With Temur leading Jie, they left the tent. She let her eyes adjust to the dark. Most people were in their tents, celebrating a successful battle and only a few walked through the camp.

"Don't speak," Temur warned Jie. "Keep your head down and move as fast as you can."

Jie nodded.

The less attention they had, the better.

Once inside their tent, Lien undid the ties at Jie's feet. As she reached to undo his hands, Temur placed a hand over hers.

"No, my *bayar*. There are weapons in this room and you are far too trusting. Jie may be a childhood friend, but he is also the commanding officer of the men who attacked and killed our people."

Jie settled on the floor. "Your husband is right to be concerned for your safety. You were always naïve and far too trusting." The bitterness in his tone made her blink.

"What do you mean?"

Jie hesitated, glanced at Temur. "I assume you have

no love for the emperor."

"No."

"Good." He turned back to Lien. "You always believed the emperor was a kind man. You did not understand he forced me to join the army because he wanted me killed."

She gaped at him.

"I am heir to my family's title and yet he still sent me away to one of the most beleaguered companies." He glanced at Temur. "The army building the wall."

"But why?"

"My friendship with you and Bao threatened him, he worried what I might tell you."

"About what?" Temur asked.

"About how Lien's family died."

She frowned. They were killed by Rhoran.

"My commanders couldn't ignore my success at getting the men to work and had to promote me. The emperor was not pleased when he recognised me on the day I became an officer."

Temur cleared his throat. "How about you get to the point?"

Jie scowled. "You need to understand my history if you are to trust me. He sent me next to patrol the desert border. It was a mistake because the whole company consisted of people who had displeased the emperor. There wasn't much for us to do out there except practise our skills and plan. He called me back specifically to lead the attack on this camp."

Which should have been a death sentence. It was pure luck Lien hadn't killed him herself. The blood drained from her head and she swayed.

Temur was by her side in an instant. "Are you all right, my *bayar*?"

She closed her eyes against the dizziness. "I could

have killed him."

Jie laughed. "I hardly think so."

Lien said nothing. It was too soon to tell him her secrets. She would be unwise to trust everything he said. Wishing she had brought Kew with her she asked, "Why did you attack the camp?"

"The emperor discovered the leaders from all Rhoran tribes would attend the khan's wedding. He thought it the perfect opportunity to kill them." Jie grimaced. "They told me the rest of the tribe members wouldn't be there and therefore it should be simple. He didn't risk his elite men though. The company was made up of soldiers who had done things the emperor disapproved of."

"I suspected the emperor would consider the wedding an opportunity, which is why we gathered en masse," Temur said. "After your attack failed, why didn't you return home?"

"My orders were to keep attacking until we succeeded."

"You must have been expecting retaliation," Temur said.

"We had nowhere to go. To return home would mean disobeying orders and we would be killed. To stay we had to face the Rhoran." He shrugged. "There was a slight chance we might survive another attack."

Xue did want him dead. "If the emperor treated the other prisoners poorly, why did you want to discuss this away from them?"

"They are not my men. Their loyalty may still be with the emperor. Most of my men are back in the desert."

That meant he had allies.

"Where does your loyalty lie?" Temur asked.

Jie glanced at Lien. "My loyalty has always been to

Bonam. It has suffered since the true emperor was murdered."

Lien gasped. Someone had been murdered? Xue was the only emperor she remembered.

"Who was the true emperor?" Temur asked.

"Why don't you tell him, Lien?"

She frowned. "I don't know what you're talking about."

"You do," Jie said. "The true emperor was your father."

Chapter 20

Shock pierced Lien, making her hot and then cold. She shook her head. "What are you talking about?"

He gripped her hand. "Don't you remember? We used to play in the garden and Bao would tell us all the things he would do when he was emperor."

She yanked her hand away as a memory surfaced. "Weren't they games?"

"No." Jie compressed his lips. "Your parents were emperor and empress. The whole country mourned when they died. The next in line for the throne was Xue."

Disbelief coursed through her. "How could I not know?"

"You were young and believed what they told you. Xue took you in to show how caring he was." Jie scowled. "He cared enough to ensure all the males were killed and no one was left to say it was murder."

Lien closed her eyes as fresh hurt battered her body. "You're saying Xue murdered my parents?" Temur wrapped his arm around her waist and his support soothed her.

"There is no proof, but my parents believed it." Jie

clenched his fists. "He killed our emperor and my best friend."

Her eyes flew open. If Bao wasn't dead, it meant he should be on the throne.

She exchanged a glance with Temur. Could she trust Jie with the truth?

Only Kew could tell her for sure.

"How did they die?" Temur asked.

"Officially they died after a raiding Rhoran party attacked them. In their rush to escape, they entered a flooded river and the palanquin tipped and they drowned, though they never recovered Bao's body. Everyone guarding them died and a farmer discovered their bodies."

She'd had no idea.

Her life had been a lie. The man who had killed her parents had raised her. Now Anming's words made perfect sense. If Bao was alive, the emperor would want him dead. She had to visit him, had to restore his place as emperor.

Had to defeat her uncle.

"It sounds like something Xue would do," Temur said. "Tell me, where is the imperial army now?"

Jie shook his head. "I'm not informed of their movements."

"Is there anything else you can tell us?" he asked.

"No. That is all."

"I'll take you back to the others, and we'll discuss what to do with you."

The Rhoran would want his death. As the commanding officer he had ordered the attack. But Lien didn't want him to die. There had been too much death and he was part of her childhood, one of the happy memories she had from the palace. And if he truly hated the emperor, he could be an ally.

Temur helped Jie to his feet and held him while Lien retied the restraints on his feet.

As she stood, Jie smiled at her. "I am not afraid to die, Kixi."

It may be true, but she didn't want to lose him. She couldn't speak past the lump in her throat as Temur led him out of the tent.

When Temur returned, Chinua and Amslan were with him, their faces grim.

"We have much to discuss," Temur said.

Lien poured them drinks, added food to the table and then sat.

"What did the prisoners tell you?" Temur asked Chinua.

Chinua frowned as he took cheese from the platter. "The soldiers don't know a lot. Lien's *friend* is their leader."

Lien said nothing.

"They formed the battalion after we visited the imperial palace and were told the wedding would weaken and distract the Rhoran."

Temur laughed. "They should have attacked on the wedding night then."

Chinua nodded. "I thought it strange as well."

"What did you find out from the officer?" Amslan asked.

Temur glanced at Lien. "Jie appears to have no love for the emperor," he said. "He believes Xue murdered the true emperor to take his place."

Chinua grunted. "Wouldn't surprise me. The Bonamese have no loyalty."

"The true emperor was Lien's father."

Chinua's mouth dropped open and he stared at Lien. "Shouldn't you have mentioned that?"

"I didn't know."

Amslan frowned. "Didn't the emissary say something about your brother when we were at the palace?"

She nodded, her chest still tight. "He said Bao was alive, and has been living with the Chungson since he was a boy."

"But wouldn't it make him the rightful emperor?" Chinua asked.

Temur nodded.

Now Jie had opened the door, snippets of memories flowed around her mind, blurry and indistinct. If only she could catch hold of one they would become clear. "I'll ask Kew if Jie is telling the truth."

"And if he is?" Amslan asked.

Temur hesitated. "After we remove the Bonamese from our land, we should visit Chungson."

"For what purpose?" Amslan said. "We don't involve ourselves in their politics."

"My wife's brother is there," Temur said. "He could be the ally we need."

"Or he could be worse than the current emperor." Chinua finished his drink.

Lien's heart squeezed. "He was kind as a boy," she said. "Though seeing our parents die might have changed him."

"Mother, we understand your attachment, but we need to be mindful of what is best for our people," Amslan said.

She wasn't used to his kindness yet. "This could be the best for our people."

Chinua stood, a scowl on his face. "Can we kill the prisoners now?"

"Jie could be an ally," Lien said. "He has men stationed in the desert who are loyal to Bonam and the true emperor."

Temur shook his head. "He cannot return to Bonam without being killed for failing his mission."

There had to be another option. Hope blossomed. "He could go to Chungson." She explained the agreement she had reached with Muunokhoi and Batzorig. "Some of Muunokhoi's men could take him to Chungson. My brother would trust Jie, and Jie could tell the Chungson about the lowered Bonam defences."

"The Chungson have lived peacefully next to Bonam for decades. Why would they risk war for us?" Temur asked.

Lien shook her head. Anming hadn't been happy about delivering the tribute, hadn't trusted the emperor. He'd been anxious about speaking to her. "I don't think they have any love for the emperor, but we need to ask Jie about their history."

"Even if your brother is alive, he may not be free to challenge Xue," Amslan said. "How old was he when he disappeared?"

"Ten."

"That's young," Amslan said. "The Chungson could have taught him anything."

Lien closed her eyes. He was right.

"First we need Kew to test Jie's honesty. Then we need to convince our people he should be allowed to live." It was no small thing. The Rhoran wanted vengeance, and Jie was the person in charge. Could she ask this of her people, for someone who she'd only known briefly in childhood?

"It's too much to ask." Chinua leaned forward. "We have suffered at the Bonamese hand, on his orders. He should be punished."

So many people would agree with him. "Does punishment have to be death?"

Chinua sat back, crossed his arms. "A life for a life is fair."

"But what if he can help bring down Xue? Surely that is worth something?" The desperation was clear in her voice. When would she learn not to hope?

"At the moment it's all guesswork, Mother." Chinua wasn't convinced.

"The other prisoners will have to die," Amslan said.

Temur nodded. "He's right, Lien."

Lien closed her eyes. "Let's test him then. Check if he's telling the truth."

Amslan stood. "Chinua and I will remove the other prisoners. Then you can talk to Jie again."

"Thank you." Temur accompanied both men to the door.

They meant to kill the others. There was nothing she could do about it. She should be distant and commanding, not allow her emotions to get in the way.

She met Temur's eyes. "I am sorry, my khan. I continue to cause you much trouble."

He walked over and pulled her to her feet, wrapping his arms around her. "You continue to bring new ideas to our people. Your mercy is not a weakness, it is a strength." He held her away so he could look at her. "I just don't know how many new ideas we will embrace."

He trusted her enough to give her a chance. That gave her hope. Lien leaned forward and kissed him. "Thank you."

Temur's eyes widened and then he smiled. "We should go."

They walked out and met Kew halfway across the campground. Amslan must have sent her away. Her dragon exuded satisfaction at recognising Jie.

You haven't saved him yet, Lien told her. *We need to test his honesty, and I need your help.*

Kew bumped Lien's leg, her confusion clear.

He may be lying about things he said. If he is loyal to the emperor, he could hurt my brother.

Kew had never met Bao, so she wouldn't have the same loyalty to him as she did to Jie.

Lien shook her head. She'd believed all the lies. It explained why they had removed all paintings of previous emperors. Xue had wanted no reminders of what he'd done.

"Let me go ahead, ensure they're ready for you both," Temur said.

She let him jog ahead. It had been a long and emotionally exhausting day. But Kew's presence by her side comforted her. Wafts of hearth fire smoke tickled her nose and laughter or cheers came from some yurts as she walked past. They were celebrating the victory, certain of their place in the world, knowing where they belonged. Had never been torn between two lives.

Kew rubbed herself against Lien and Lien squatted down to hug her. *I know you understand.*

"Lien, we're ready for you now." Temur walked towards them.

Lien stood, her heart beating faster.

They entered the tent. Jie sat at the table eating, while Amslan and Chinua stood guard, Chinua glaring at him. Empty ropes dangling from the rafters were all that was left of the other prisoners. Her stomach clenched.

"You've decided?" Jie asked.

"Not yet," Temur said. "Your next few answers will determine your fate."

They sat across from Jie, Kew by Lien's side.

He nodded.

"Are you loyal to the current emperor, Xue?" Temur asked.

"No."

Kew turned a bright green.

"Were you loyal to the past emperor, Huang?"

"Yes."

Kew stayed the same colour.

"Would you like the current emperor defeated?"

"Absolutely," Jie growled. "He needs to pay for what he did to the emperor, to Bao, to your people and so many vassal states."

Kew puffed smoke out of her nose in agreement and her skin went a deeper green.

Lien glanced at Temur. What now?

"Do you want to tell him what Anming said, my *bayar*?" Temur asked.

Her skin tingled. She had to trust him. "Lord Anming from Chungson said Bao is alive."

"What?" Jie's jaw dropped and he stared at her. "How can that be?"

"He only said Bao has been a guest of theirs since he was a boy. I did not have time to ask him anything further and I have not verified it myself."

"But, but… that means he's the rightful heir. He should be emperor."

Lien nodded.

"We would like you to travel to Chungson with some of our warriors, confirm if Bao is alive, and tell the Chungson lord the Bonamese army is in Rhora and the emperor's defences are low," Temur continued.

"They're here?" Jie asked.

"North-west of here," Temur told him.

"Why?"

"You don't need to know the reason."

A frown flittered across Jie's face. "What then?"

"Then we wait for answers. There must be a reason Bao hasn't claimed his throne. Is there something only the two of you would know to prove he is Bao? He will have changed since you last saw each other."

"I have many things I can ask him," Jie said.

"When we have defeated the army on our lands, we will contact you and Anming to discuss what we will do next."

"The Rhoran has never involved themselves in Bonamese politics. Why now?"

"The emperor tried to kill my wife multiple times," Temur said. "And he killed her parents. That is enough reason."

Lien's heart warmed though Temur's reasons weren't the only ones. Xue had stolen Rhoran land as well.

Jie smiled. "When do I leave?"

~*~

The next morning Temur called a tribal council. Lien stood by his side, hand in his, a united front, as he explained what they had learnt from Jie.

"It sounds like a trap," Muunokhoi said. "All we've got is the word of a man who attacked our camp and the whisperings of a lord too afraid to stand up for his people."

"If your brother is alive, why hasn't he confronted the emperor already?" Batzorig asked.

All good questions Lien couldn't answer.

"Muunokhoi will patrol the border anyway," Temur said. "It won't be difficult to take Jie with him and send a small contingent to Chungson. If they are both telling the truth, this could end the trouble we have with the Bonamese."

"Not before it causes us much more trouble," Mongke grumbled.

Lien blinked. For Temur's father to speak against

him meant the tribe wasn't happy. She needed to say something. "I understand your concerns," she said. "I do not know enough about the history of our people. Before Xue was emperor, what was our relationship like with Bonam?"

"Peaceful," Solongo answered.

"And how many of our people have gone missing or been captured since then?"

"Too many," Batzorig growled.

"Then perhaps the risk of trusting Jie and Anming is worth the potential benefits."

It took another hour of discussion before they agreed Muunokhoi would take Jie to Chungson.

Afterwards the camp prepared to leave, the warriors readying themselves for war, and the rest of the camp packing up to move further inland to the lake in the east. They were staying together to provide a better defence.

The army moved out at midday, a huge mass of bodies as each person rode with three spare horses. And they rode fast, Kew clinging to one of Lien's spare horses as they galloped in a single wave across the steppes. Lien understood why the Bonamese spoke in fearful hushed tones when they spoke about the Rhoran horde. They were impressive and terrifying.

On the second day, Muunokhoi brought Jie over to Lien to say goodbye.

"Aren't you coming with us?" Jie asked.

"No, I ride with the army."

"No! It's far too dangerous for you to go into battle."

His concern warmed her. "I will be fine, Jie."

"Do the Rhoran want you to die?"

Muunokhoi grunted, a slight smile on his face.

"Don't worry, they will take care of me." She smiled

at him. "May you travel without notice from others." If word got back to the emperor that Rhoran were seen in Chungson it could ruin everything. "And give my brother my love."

Jie scowled. "I will send word as soon as I can."

The small party left and Lien rejoined the army.

Late on the fourth day a scout brought news the Bonamese were only a day's ride away. Temur ordered the group to stop and rest.

In the distance the mountains soared, grey silhouettes on the horizon. When the leaders had gathered, Temur asked Batzorig to describe the land ahead of them.

"The land rises as we get closer to the mountains. We will enter the thick conifer forests about mid-afternoon tomorrow. There are many places for the enemy to hide and fighting will be more difficult amongst the trees, though we should be far enough away from the dragon breeding grounds for them to ignore us." Batzorig paused. "According to the scouts, the Bonamese army have camped on the edge of the forest. We can't hide our approach, so they will choose the battleground unless we lead them to our own choice." He took his sabre and drew in the soil. "The lake is in a small valley. Forest surrounds it on three sides, but the south side has open ground. If we lead them here we can trap them and the ground will give us the advantage."

"How will we do that?" Lien asked.

Batzorig grinned at her. "It wouldn't be honourable to ignore us, particularly if we send raiding parties."

The Bonamese would chase the Rhoran and find themselves trapped. Lien almost felt sorry for them.

Almost.

The next morning they rode at a slightly slower pace to rest their mounts. The dark shape of the forest appeared like a black hole and a shiver ran down her spine. But the plains in front of the forest were empty. Where were the Bonamese?

Temur sent scouts into the trees and the army stopped at a safe distance to prepare.

Lien's shoulders ached from tension. There would be a battle soon and she would need to kill more people to protect her family, her tribe. She ran a hand over the handle of her knives. How much blood would need to be spilled before the emperor had had his fill?

The sun dipped towards the horizon and still the scouts didn't return. Temur paced. "They should have returned by now."

No one said anything. The scouts were probably dead. Which meant the Bonamese could be anywhere.

"Set up camp and post sentries," Temur said. "We're far enough away to have warning if they attack tonight."

She wouldn't sleep. Not with the knowledge an attack could be imminent. Still she unpacked her bed and prepared both Temur and herself something to eat. She carried two bowls over to where Temur stood at the edge of the camp, looking towards the forest.

"Lien, Kew is heading for the forest." Amslan pointed.

Kew was quite a distance away trotting towards the trees.

Kew, what are you doing?

No response.

She gave her bowl to Temur. "I'll go after her."

"Don't get too close."

She nodded and jogged after her dragon. Kew had behaved well on the whole trip, keeping out of the way when camp was set up each night. The only time she'd been a problem was when she'd insisted on going with them.

Until now.

The light was fading as Lien caught up with Kew. *What are you up to?*

Kew's displeasure washed over her as she motioned to the trees and Lien recognised the action. The dragon recognised someone in there.

Who is it? The darkened trees were too close for her liking.

Images swam through her mind—Fen, Yu and Tai, all members of the secret bodyguard.

Her heart raced as fear turned her body cold. They were the reason the scouts hadn't made it back.

But why in Qadan's name were they there? Xue should have never let them leave the palace. They were supposed to be for his protection.

Was Xue with the army?

Lien gauged the distance to the trees. They were outside arrow range, but with the women's speed, it meant nothing. The camp was in real danger.

She needed to get out of here. *They are no longer friends.*

Kew's determination was clear. She wasn't happy Fen had attacked them.

You can't take them alone.

Kew snorted.

Let's go back. Lien turned towards the camp, gesturing Kew to follow her and sighed when Kew trotted over.

They needed to warn the others. Her shoulder blades itching, she continued at a steady pace, her ears straining for any sound behind her.

And then the patter of rapidly approaching footsteps reached her.

Chapter 21

Lien spun around as Tai sped towards her. *Kew, run!*

Her dragon let out a roar and a burst of flames. Lien ran to lure Tai away from her and Tai changed direction to follow Lien.

Her muscles strained as she ran, arms pumping, while her mind whirled. She needed to get some distance between her and the forest in case Fen and Yu attacked while Lien fought Tai. She'd need all the warning she could get.

Lien glanced behind. Tai was closer now.

"Lien, where are you?" Temur yelled.

Lien stopped, spun around, her knives in her hands. "Over here."

Tai halted only a few feet from her, gaze uncertain. She had knives too and wore Bonamese armour, her hair cut short, but she was still unmistakably female. How had Ying explained her presence?

"What are you doing here, Tai?"

Tai circled her, forcing Lien to have her back to the forest. Kew would warn her if the others came.

Tai glared. "We are here to defeat the Rhoran." She didn't even glance behind her at her enemy. She'd learnt

324

nothing in their classes.

And would pay the price.

The guards and many other warriors lined up at the edge of the camp, bows raised, arrows ready.

"Shouldn't you be playing your flute for the emperor?"

"He asked me personally to come." She stood taller, puffed out her chest. "He said I was to kill you for betraying him. I will become his favourite concubine."

What lies he spun. "Tai, you never defeated me in training." She couldn't let this drag on, not with the forest and the other women behind her. She had to disable Tai, stop her from hurting anyone.

The swoosh of arrows filled the air, racing towards Tai. They would kill her.

Lien tensed ready to run. "And what are Fen and Yu's orders?"

Tai opened her mouth to speak and the first arrow struck her, knocking her forward. A second followed and a third and Lien dodged as Tai fell forward on to the ground with a cry of pain.

Far in the distance, Fen screamed in rage.

The arrows stopped. Blood seeped out of the wounds on Tai's back. Lien checked her pulse. Nothing. Sorrow mixed with relief that she hadn't had to kill Tai. She scanned the forest, searching for movement.

It was still.

Kew hurried over, uncertainty exuding from her. *It's safe.* For now.

Temur ran to her. "Are you all right?"

Physically she was. "Yes." She ached for Tai. Such a waste. The emperor shouldn't have put these inexperienced women in harm's way. Lien had been the most battle ready of any of them and she'd stumbled at the first hurdle of killing Temur. The others had been more interested in gossipping than learning to fight.

Around her the men gathered up the useable arrows while Temur checked the body. "That's not Ying."

"No. Tai was with the secret bodyguard. Kew also recognised Fen and Yu in the forest." It had never occurred to her that Xue would send his daughter or any of the women into battle. They were supposed to be his secret, his guard, not fight in the army like any other soldier.

"How many women are there?"

"Three when I was in charge but that didn't include Fen." Even with their inexperience, they could do a lot of damage and Lien couldn't fight them all at once. Especially not if Ying was added into the equation. Her skin prickled. Her people were in real danger.

"Ying probably expected the women to slaughter us tonight."

So why send them now unless… "Ying can't be with them."

"Why do you say that?"

"Fen couldn't have been certain Kew had identified them. She lost the element of surprise attacking us now. Ying wouldn't have made that mistake."

"Perhaps he stayed behind to guard the emperor."

She shook her head. It didn't fit. "Unlikely. Someone needs to keep an eye on Fen and the others. Not many know what they can do."

"Why would the emperor risk his daughter this way?"

Anger burnt low in Lien's stomach. "Maybe he is punishing her for not defeating me at the palace." She scowled. "Besides, girls aren't worth much and he has plenty of daughters."

It would be worth the risk because the women could

potentially kill enough Rhoran to be of use.

"Will they attack tonight?" Temur took her hand.

"I don't know. Fen is angry. It might stop her thinking clearly or she might realise we will be ready for them. I will stand guard tonight." She was the only one who could see them coming.

Amslan approached. "What shall we do with the body?"

Temur looked at Lien.

She closed her eyes. Tai shouldn't be left out on the steppes to rot or be eaten by whatever animals came along. But the Rhoran couldn't risk going into the forest to gather firewood to burn the body. "We shall move her closer to the forest." Perhaps Fen would send someone to collect her.

The soldiers dumped the body about halfway between the camp and the forest. With Kew close to her ankles and Temur by her side, Lien walked back to camp. This was only the first skirmish in what could be a long and bloody fight. She couldn't afford to let her emotions get the better of her. She needed to be alert and ready for anything.

Lien sat with the sentries facing the forest as darkness fell and the crescent moon rose, giving them some light. The night made the forest appear even blacker. Geriel sat beside her. "How are you feeling, sister?"

Lien smiled. "Worried. Sad."

"Was the woman a friend of yours?"

"I trained with her, but she wasn't a friend. Yet her death saddens me."

"I'm sorry." Geriel hugged her. "Know her death has saved countless lives."

Geriel was right, but she wished Tai had surrendered instead.

"You need to eat something." Temur handed her a steaming bowl of soup.

"Thank you." The presence of the gifted women changed the whole dynamic of their battle plan. Each night since they'd left camp, she'd worked with the warriors to figure out how to combat Ying's speed and now she faced three fast enemies not one. She had to reduce the odds somehow.

Ying wouldn't be foolish enough to send them one at a time. She couldn't protect everyone. Maybe she needed to go on the offensive. Attack them before they were ready. But if she left the camp, it would be vulnerable.

She closed her eyes. Could she kill her cousin and the woman who had once been her friend? Fen had not hesitated in attacking, but Lien couldn't do the same. She was still weak.

Still letting her heart lead her instead of her head, even though Yu had never been a true friend.

But the thought of killing her filled Lien with dread.

~*~

Just after the sentry change around midnight, something crept out of the forest. Lien squinted, but the distance and the darkness made it impossible to see it clearly. It was low to the ground moving towards Tai's body.

"What do you think?" Chinua murmured.

"Moves like a wolverine," Batzorig said. "Probably looking for dinner."

Lien's stomach clenched.

Chinua touched her arm. "You can't scare it off. Temur's orders."

He was right, it would only put her in danger, but the idea of leaving Tai's body so carelessly, repulsed her. Was Fen watching? Did she care?

The wolverine stopped at Tai's body and Lien thanked the ancestors it was dark. She thought she heard the occasional crack of bone, but her ears could be playing tricks on her.

As the night dragged on, her eyes grew heavy. It had been a long day and a longer night. The men swapped shifts, but only she could warn them about the gifted women. Kew woke and stretched, nudging her and sending her images of Kew standing guard.

Can you see them coming?

Kew nodded, sent her a sense of awareness. Relief filled Lien. She could rest before the fight tomorrow.

"Kew will stand watch for a while," she told Berke.

He nodded. "Get some rest, Mother."

She returned to her bed, where she curled up and fell asleep.

"Lien, it's time to wake up." Temur shook her shoulder and she opened her eyes. The sun hovered on the horizon and the camp stirred. Kew trotted over, showed her the night had been quiet.

"Are we ready to leave?"

"Almost." He held out a bowl. "Eat and I'll pack up."

She stared at him a moment before taking the food. "Thank you." She moved away before he could tell how ridiculously happy it made her that he was taking care of her. After she had eaten, she joined him at the horses. The night before they had agreed to continue to the lake and draw the Bonamese out. With Kew at the back of the army and Lien at the front, they would be warned about any attack from Fen, Yu or Ying.

Lien scanned the forest for a sign of the women, but it was still. Not even birds flew amongst the branches.

She tightened her grip on Batu's reins and Batu side-stepped, snorting. Forcing herself to relax, she let out a deep breath. It was too quiet. The Bonamese army had to be somewhere. Ying was somewhere. What were they planning?

The emperor needn't have sent a whole army to get the artefact. If Ying had taken a small force it would have been far easier to sneak in unnoticed. So why the army? Did the emperor hope once they had recovered the artefact, he could use it straight away so the Rhoran had no time to prepare?

Shouts rang out behind her and Kew's frantic images filled Lien's head.

Yu.

Lien jerked Batu around and galloped towards the back of the group, her heart in her throat. When she arrived, twenty men were dead but there was no sign of the woman.

"What happened?" she asked the man next to her.

He shook his head. "Suddenly the men around me fell off their horses, their throats slit."

Lien turned to Kew. *Which way did she go?*

Kew nodded towards the forest.

Lien scanned the trees for movement.

Nothing.

More voices yelled, this time from the front of the army. *Temur.* Fear gripped her as she rode hard only to find more men dead and no sign of Yu or Fen.

Temur rode up beside her. "Can you see her?"

She shook her head. "She's playing with us." Fen and Yu could take turns to attack and Lien couldn't be in both places at once. She had to stop one and then focus on the other, but it was difficult with the army so spread out. "How much further to the lake?"

"At least another hour."

Lien dismounted and handed Batu's reins to Temur. He frowned.

"I'll be faster without her." She checked her knives and adjusted her bow and quiver, her stomach sick with nerves. "Keep Kew up the front with you." Her dragon might offer him some protection.

Temur hesitated and then nodded. "Be careful."

Was it concern on his face? Of course. If she failed the Rhoran would be slaughtered. Lien scoured the surroundings.

She had to stop Yu and Fen, but perhaps that didn't mean killing. She might convince them to surrender.

Movement at the back of the army—Yu sprinting out from the trees.

Lien ran, yelling, "Arrows!" The men reacted fast but not fast enough. Yu was on them, spinning and killing as she went.

Lien pushed herself harder as her people died in front of her. She couldn't risk using her bow and arrow in case she hit one of her own. "Disperse!" It was no use. Too many men close together for them to run. She snatched one of her knives from her belt, flinging it towards Yu. It missed, but got her attention.

Good.

Yu moved away from the army, still running at speed. She spun to face Lien and grinned. "Are you going to stop me?" Unlike Tai, she kept moving, not staying still long enough to be a target.

"If necessary." Lien withdrew her other knife. "But we don't need to fight, Yu. If you surrender I will ensure you are treated fairly."

"Aren't you going to join me? You always spoke about how we would defeat the barbarians together." Yu smiled.

The memory of those conversations made her sick.

"I was wrong. The Rhoran are good people. The emperor lied to us. He is not the man we thought he was."

They circled each other as they spoke.

"These barbarians have poisoned your mind," Yu hissed. "The emperor is our salvation."

Lien cringed. "Yu, please listen. I do not want to fight you. You were my friend."

Yu laughed. "You were useful to me," she corrected. "No Bonamese can be friends with the Rhoran." Yu attacked, slashing her knives towards Lien's face.

Lien weaved out of the way. She had to disarm Yu first. She tucked her knife back into her belt and focused on Yu's movements. They had sparred together often in the past. She feinted right and as Yu dodged, Lien changed direction, grabbing Yu's arm, and twisting her wrist so the knife dropped to the ground. Lien kicked the woman in the side, pushing her back, away from the fallen weapon.

Yu gritted her teeth and swapped her other knife to her right hand.

Behind Lien the Rhoran army murmured, but she didn't have time to check how close they were.

Yu prowled back and forth, keeping Lien between herself and the army as a shield. She tensed to attack, but Lien was quicker. She stepped into the strike, blocking it and capturing Yu's arm. Stamping on Yu's foot to distract her, Lien clutched her knife hand and twisted it then took the knife away.

The woman shrieked and punched Lien hard in the side.

Pain swept through her and she moved backwards to recover, but Yu followed. She attacked hard and fast, punching and kicking without pause, her face screwed up in fury. Lien defended herself, not wanting to kill her.

"You won't win." Lien counterattacked, landing two swift kicks to Yu's stomach.

Yu bent over, clutching her stomach and gasping for air. When she looked up, the determination in her eyes made Lien's blood run cold.

"I might not win, but I'll kill as many as I can before I die." She reached for something on the ground.

The knife Lien had thrown to distract her.

Fear raced through Lien's veins. Where was her army?

Sukh was so incredibly close, his bow raised, arrow in place, waiting for an opportunity to fire.

Yu straightened and lifted her arm to throw.

"No!" Lien lunged towards Yu, drawing her knife from her belt as she did so.

The knife left Yu's hand.

Heading straight for Lien's father.

Chapter 22

"Sukh, get down," Lien yelled. She flung her knife at Yu, but she was too late.

The blade hit Sukh in the chest with a sickening thunk. Horror filled her as Sukh's horse shied and Sukh fell. She raced to him, catching his body and protecting it as they both landed hard on the ground.

"Father!" Lien cried as Sukh clutched at the knife protruding from his chest just below his heart. "Get a healer! Get Amslan!" She put her hands over Sukh's, preventing him from withdrawing the knife. The blood was warm and thick on her hands. "Wait until a healer arrives." She pressed her hands over the wound and glanced up. Yu was on the ground, the knife protruding from her neck. Several Rhoran fired arrows at her prone body and she twitched and then fell still.

Yu was dead.

And Lien's reluctance to kill her may have killed her father.

Sukh's breath gurgled and blood seeped out of his mouth. No. Her heart lurched and she pressed harder around the wound. He couldn't die. She wouldn't let him. Geriel and Odval would never forgive her. She would never forgive herself.

Her weakness was for nothing. If she'd killed Yu immediately, Sukh wouldn't be dying. She had failed to protect her people, failed as tribal Mother. She was too soft. Tears streamed down her face.

"Move." Geriel pushed Lien away, placed her hands on her father's chest, her face pale. She mouthed the words to the meditation Lien had taught her as she closed her eyes.

Horror crossed her face and she gritted her teeth. "The blade pierced his heart. We need Amslan." Tears welled in her eyes. "I'm sorry, Father. It's more than I can fix."

The agony in Geriel's voice sliced through Lien. Where was Amslan?

He galloped up and slid off his horse, before bending over Sukh.

"It's his heart," Geriel said.

He placed his hands next to hers and then swore. "I need you to focus on the vessels," he told Geriel.

Lien moved back, out of the way, her muscles tight.

Sukh cried out in pain.

Tears blurred her vision.

"Lien, are there any others?" Chinua asked.

Turning, she scanned the area. All was still. If Fen had been smart, she would attack the front of the army now.

Maybe she didn't want to risk her own life.

"I see no one," she reported.

Sweat beaded on the healers' faces and Geriel's breaths came in gasps as tears ran unchecked down her face.

This was Lien's fault. She prayed Amslan and Geriel could heal Sukh.

"One more," Amslan muttered and Geriel nodded.

Lien gritted her teeth, kept her gaze on her father and the two healers. Around them the warriors formed a protective circle.

Suddenly Amslan and Geriel let out a combined sigh and both leaned back. Geriel slumped to the side, almost falling to the ground, but Lien caught her.

"How is he?" Lien directed the question at Amslan.

"He needs rest, but he will be fine." He glanced at Geriel. "She needs food and rest. It took a lot out of her." His gaze caught Chinua's. "Find her some food and keep her out of the battle to come."

"I'm fine." Geriel's protest was barely a whisper.

Lien squeezed her. "You are not."

Sukh opened his eyes and tears welled in her own. She wanted to fling her arms around him and hug him, but she didn't deserve to. "I'm so sorry, Father."

"Hush now, child."

"We should keep moving," Amslan said. "Your cousin is still around here somewhere."

She had no time for self pity. "You are right." Lien pushed aside her grief, wiped away her tears and got to her feet, helping Geriel to hers as Amslan helped Sukh. "Let's get to the lake."

~*~

The lake glistened below, the biggest body of water Lien had ever seen. It would take a strong swimmer to cross the expanse. The forest surrounded it on three sides, the trees almost at the shoreline, but from where she sat astride Batu, the ground sloped down until it became flat. A good-sized expanse from which to fight.

If they ever found the Bonamese.

Fen and Ying were still a threat, but the Rhoran could only wait so long, hoping to lure them out, before they'd have to go into the forest after them.

As they neared the lake, Solongo had become more insistent they hurry—but still wouldn't reveal where the khan was buried.

Warriors explored the shoreline, filling in holes and throwing larger rocks into the water so they wouldn't damage the horses during the battle.

Lien rubbed her aching neck. She was missing something, some reason why the Bonamese hid instead of fighting.

Temur nudged his horse closer to hers. "What is wrong, my *bayar*?"

"Stealth tactics are not like the Bonamese—not when the army is gathered. A show of force is required. I don't know why they're hiding.

"Could this be another diversion? Perhaps Ying has already gone after the artefact while we waste time on the army."

It made sense. But she couldn't follow him without leaving her people to face Fen alone. "I can't be in two places."

"So we must draw them out. It's time we went into the forest."

They would be more vulnerable there. She wouldn't easily see Fen attack. But perhaps she could use it to her advantage. "I will go." The words resonated a rightness.

"What?"

"If I go in, alone, I can find the army and dispose of Fen. Then our warriors can wait out the Bonamese, and I can go after Ying."

"You're assuming I'm correct about Ying going after the artefact by himself."

"Do you have a better idea?"

He grimaced. "No, but you're not going in alone."

Kew ran up to them, her colours changing. Lien

tensed. "Someone's coming."

Temur yelled a command and the warriors by the lake rode back up the hill.

The clanking and rattling of an army moving through the forest reached them first. Were they going to attack them here? The land heavily favoured the Rhoran, they had the higher ground.

The army emerged on the western shoreline, men dotted through the trees.

"Do they mean to launch a frontal assault?" Batzorig screwed up his face in bewilderment.

Where was Fen?

Lien picked out a general, his red lapels clear, and next to him was a small soldier. She almost kept scanning but the soldier flicked its wrists in a very Fen-like movement. "Fen's next to the general giving orders," she told them. "I can't see Ying."

The general shook his head and Fen stamped her foot.

"He doesn't want to do what she's suggested and disobeying an imperial order could get him killed."

"Let's hope he continues denying her then," Temur commented.

Lien continued to scan the shoreline for Ying.

"Can you goad her into attacking?" Amslan asked. "The quicker we kill her the better."

She flinched, then she remembered Sukh with the knife sticking out of his chest. Amslan was right. She couldn't give Fen the opportunity to hurt anyone. Straightening her spine, she nodded. "I can make her mad, but she needs to hear me."

Mongke handed her a conical shaped object. "Speak through here and your voice will carry."

Lien dismounted and took the object, then moved down the hill. She was too far away for an arrow to hit her, but she kept an eye out for Ying. The general said something to Fen but she ignored him, keeping her eyes on Lien.

Lien stopped and raised the cone to her mouth. "Yu is dead, Fen. You've killed both the women under your command. It is time you gave up and returned to the palace."

The general touched Fen's arm and she screeched at him, the words not clear.

"If you order your army to leave, we will let you go. No one else needs to die." She needed to draw Fen out, away from the other soldiers. If she got a little closer while Fen yelled at the general, she'd use her bow.

Fen drew her knives, holding one under the general's chin. She'd make no friends that way, but this was Lien's chance. Dropping the amplifier, Lien whipped her bow from her back. She fired, her arrow flying true, straight towards Fen.

A soldier yelled and threw himself in front of Fen, taking the arrow straight in the chest.

Fen spun, her body language shocked.

Lien notched another arrow and fired two in quick succession. This time Fen moved and the first arrow hit a soldier behind her, but the second hit its target and the general collapsed to the ground. Without him, the soldiers would have to listen to Fen. And Fen wouldn't make sensible decisions.

Several men crowded around the general as Lien moved out of retaliation range.

Fen yelled, horns bellowed and with a great shout, the army moved forward.

It had begun.

Lien ran back up the hill to where Temur and his men waited, mounted and ready. A mass of Bonamese bodies hurtled towards them but the Rhoran didn't move and Lien's eyes didn't waver from her cousin, standing on a rocky outcrop.

"Ready!" Temur commanded.

The warriors notched their arrows.

The enemy came within range.

"Fire!"

The sky blackened with arrows, whistling towards their targets. The front line of the Bonamese faltered. Lien had to wait until they went to hand-to-hand combat to attack Fen. She used her bow and arrows to kill the first twenty Bonamese to come within range.

Reaching for another quiver, she checked Fen's location.

Gone.

Lien jumped. *Where is she, Kew?*

Kew turned her head and Lien followed her gaze. Fen was close to the Rhoran frontline. *Hide somewhere safe.*

With the distance between the two armies rapidly closing, the Rhoran charged.

Lien sped ahead, moving towards Fen who veered to meet her. They couldn't fight here, in the middle of the battle, they'd be trampled. Lien headed for the shoreline and spun around, her knives in her hands.

Fen halted, her back to the battle. Up on the hill the Rhoran commanders directed the battle. Mongke noticed them and reached for his bow and arrow.

"You and these barbarians will die today," Fen hissed.

The hatred pinched Lien's heart. "You're wrong."

Mongke drew back his bow.

"An imperial princess is never wrong."

"You're on Rhoran lands now," Lien pointed out. "Your title means nothing."

The arrow arched through the air, falling directly

towards Fen. It wouldn't make it. They were too far away.

"It won't be Rhoran lands for long," Fen said. "When Father gets the artefact we will grind the Rhoran into the dirt and you will cease to exist."

So that was Xue's plan. How much more could she get Fen to tell her? "He doesn't know where it is."

"Yes, he does. Kun and Ying are on their way to get it now."

Damn. The army *was* a diversion. She had to go after them. There was no time to lose.

Fen launched herself at Lien, fists bunched, determination on her face.

Lien blocked the first two punches and countered with a kick which landed in Fen's stomach, pushing her back. Fen didn't have the skills to defeat her.

Behind Fen the clang of blades against shields was loud. Men yelled and grunted as they fought for their lives. The longer Lien spent fighting Fen, the less time she had to help her people.

Waiting for Fen's next punch, Lien blocked and grabbed Fen's arm, pulling her off balance and throwing Fen over her back. Following her cousin to the ground, Lien pinned her before Fen could blink.

"Get off me," Fen screamed, kicking her legs.

Lien checked to ensure no one was close enough to come to Fen's aid.

No one noticed.

"How many men did Ying take with him?"

Fen stared back at her, but didn't answer.

Lien held a knife against Fen's throat. "Tell me how many men Ying has with him or I will kill you."

Her eyes widened. "You wouldn't."

Lien hardened herself. Fen would turn on her the second she had the chance. "The only value you have is giving me the information I need." She shrugged in apology. "If you can't do that, there is no point in you being alive."

Fear made Fen's voice tremble. "Twelve I think."

An arrow flew so near to Lien she felt the air move. The battle was too close. She had to finish this. "I'm sorry, Fen. I can't risk you hurting my tribe." She gritted her teeth and in one swift movement, she slit her cousin's throat. Fen's eyes went wide and blood spurted out of her neck. She twitched once, then twice and was motionless.

Lien's chest squeezed so tight she couldn't breathe. She couldn't mourn now. She had to go after Ying.

But first she needed to tell Temur Fen was no longer a threat.

Lien scanned the battle and picked out her husband, fighting off two men. She sped towards him, drawing her sabre and dodging the large bodies of the horses from which the Rhoran fought.

Training took over. She blocked out the fact she was killing men and concentrated on protecting her people. It took her seconds to kill the two men attacking Temur. He gaped at her, just stopping the swing of his sabre in time. "Lien."

"Fen is dead and Ying has gone after the artefact."

She blocked a soldier's sword and killed him. "I'm going after him."

"You're not going by yourself," Temur growled.

Too many enemy soldiers around them. She killed another couple but more took their place. She didn't want to leave Temur vulnerable. "I'll be quicker alone."

"No," Temur said, killing another Bonamese.

Lien didn't bother arguing further. "Then get me some men."

<h1 style="text-align:center">Chapter 23</h1>

Lien fought her way back up the hill with Temur to where Mongke and the other older warriors directed the battle. Sukh sat nearby, his skin still pale, Geriel with him.

"Ying has gone after the artefact," Temur told his father. "I need ten men to go after him." Temur named the men he wanted, and with Mongke's help, they pinpointed them on the battlefield and Lien helped to extract them from the fighting.

Solongo ran up. "What's going on?"

"Ying and Kun have already left the army," Lien said.

Fear crossed the woman's face. "When?"

"I don't know. Maybe two days ago."

"We must go immediately," Solongo said.

Mongke nodded. "With the general dead they don't know who is in charge. If you need a diversion, we can retreat."

The Bonamese army would chase them and then be decimated. She ached over all the death, but her mission was Ying. "Let's go."

Sukh handed Batu's reins to Lien. "I'm going with

you."

Lien hesitated. Which group would he be safer with?

"Me too," Geriel said.

"No, Geriel," Temur said. "Your skills are needed with the army. Sukh can come with us."

Geriel scowled as Temur ordered, "Sound the retreat."

The man blew on a horn and then kicked his horse into a canter, leading the retreat away from the lake.

Batzorig motioned to Temur and Lien. "This way."

They followed him into the forest and away from the battle, riding hard until they were certain no one followed.

Riding under the canopy of the tall, bristly trees after spending so long on the steppes was like entering another world. Needle leaves cushioned the ground, muting the horses' tread. The trees blocked the sun, cooling the surroundings and the fresh, pine smell was a relief after the sweat and blood of battle.

Lien wiped her bloody hands on her tunic. The sorrow she'd been expecting wasn't there. She was numb. Lien had to think of her family; Temur and Sukh, Geriel and Erdene, Kew—

She gasped. Kew was hiding somewhere.

"What's wrong, Lien?" Temur asked.

"I've left Kew behind." Could Kew protect herself against the wolverines?

"She pinpointed your location in the middle of the steppes, the forest shouldn't cause her any difficulties."

He was right, but worry settled in the back of Lien's mind.

They circled the lake and Batzorig picked up a trail. "They're not hiding their passage."

"Are we sure it's them?" Amslan asked. "Would Fen have been in charge if Ying had stayed with the army until they attacked?"

"No," Lien answered. He wouldn't have let her make the mistakes she had.

"So which way do we go?" Temur directed the question at Solongo.

She clenched her hands, hesitated.

"Solongo, what is worse—a few of us knowing where the Great Khan is buried, or Ying getting that cursed artefact?" Temur demanded.

She grimaced and pointed north. "This way."

By dusk there had been no sign of Ying, and Lien's eyes were heavy. The ground sloped ever upwards and they would be in the mountains soon. As they entered a clearing at the base of the mountains, Batzorig said. "This is a good spot to camp for the night."

One side was a wall of rock and trees surrounded the rest. One less side they needed to guard.

"We should keep moving," Solongo insisted. "There's still a ways to go."

Batzorig shook his head. "It's too dangerous at night. We need to see where we're going, and if we light torches, we become a target for Ying."

"We may have gained ground by using the horses," Temur said. "Let's rest here while we eat. Then we can assess further."

Solongo scowled, but nodded.

If only they knew where Ying was. If he was behind them, they could be leading him straight to the tomb.

As they took care of the horses, Batzorig said, "We might see dragons flying overhead, but they should leave us alone."

Lien frowned. "The dragons fly here?" Kew couldn't manage more than a hover.

He nodded. "They have much bigger wings than

Kew. Hopefully we won't go too close to their breeding grounds because they're very protective."

"Where is it?" Temur asked.

Batzorig pointed. "We've never got close enough to see the babies because they won't let us anywhere near them." He examined the surroundings. "The ground will get steeper and rougher tomorrow. We may need to leave the horses behind."

"Will they be safe?" Lien asked.

"I can stay with them," Sukh said. He was still far too pale for her liking.

Anxiety was Lien's constant companion. It would keep him out of harm's way if Ying was ahead of them, not if he wasn't.

Temur nodded as they settled and passed around dinner.

It would be peaceful here if not for the ever-present concern Ying was out there somewhere. The shush of the wind through the trees provided a soothing background noise and the fresh scent of the trees revitalised Lien. When this was all over, she would ask Batzorig to show her all the forest's secrets.

As she reached for her drink flask a bellowing roar sent terror through her veins. Flames gushed towards her. She lunged to the side, pushing Temur out of the way, the heat from the fire far too close for comfort. Someone yelled in pain.

The place where they'd sat was engulfed in flames and four dragons flew past in formation and then up into the darkening sky. Bless the ancestors, she'd never seen such an impressive sight.

The other Rhoran scrambled to their feet, all checking the sky, waiting for another attack.

Chinua beat the flames out while Amslan helped the man who had been burnt.

"We must be close to their nesting grounds," Batzorig said. "But they're usually much further into the mountains.

Temur's sabre rasped as it left its scabbard.

Lien touched his arm. "Wait. They are only protecting their home."

"We can't sit here and let them burn us to death," Temur growled.

She'd never communicated with another dragon before, but she had to try. "Let me talk to them, show them we mean them no harm. I am fast enough to get out of the way if it does not work." The dragons appeared again through the trees and the others scurried behind the trunks, Chinua helping Amslan with the injured man.

Sending out her thoughts as she did with Kew, she said, *We are not here to harm you.*

No response. The dragons flew closer and the two in front opened their mouths. Flames flashed towards her and she darted out of the way.

Egg-stealer!

Lien clutched her head and winced as the words bellowed in her mind. So loud. So angry. But underneath it all was a lighter, familiar thread full of panic. Kew.

Where was she?

Temur strode over, pulled her hands away from her head. "What's happening?"

She breathed out as the pain receded and scanned the rockface where the dragons had landed. "Kew's somewhere nearby."

The little dragon raced into the clearing, keeping low and subservient. Images flashed through Lien's mind. "She's telling them we're friends and will not steal their eggs." She gasped and brought her fist up to her chest.

"What is it?" Temur asked.

Lien wanted to be sick. "Kew was stolen." Amslan had asked her where Kew's egg had come from. She should have realised.

Temur put his arm around her. "It was not your fault."

He was right, but she would make it up to Kew. "I can't understand the other dragons but Kew is projecting images of Ying. I guess she's explaining our mission."

The biggest dragon of the four turned to Lien, his scales dull and sandy brown, almost blending into the rock he sat on. A deep voice in Lien's head said, *You are as fast as the egg-stealer. I say you are one of them.*

His tone was full of authority. She bowed. "I am not. The man you speak of trained me, but I have learnt he is not a man to trust or respect," she spoke aloud and in her mind.

The dragon curled its lip. *Tell me how you would protect our eggs.*

Lien stepped back from the power in the command and Temur moved closer, placed his hand on her lower back to steady her.

"Can you hear what he's saying?" she asked.

He nodded, his eyes not leaving the dragons.

"We fight those who seek to steal from you. When we defeat them, we will stop them from coming to these lands."

Why have you not done so before?

"We did not know."

Your people have taken advantage of the reward we once gave them.

She frowned. "Forgive me, Great Dragon. I am ignorant of what reward you speak."

After the one you called Emperor Huang saved some of our

babies from harm, we sent one of our own to the imperial palace to teach you of dragon ways.

She jolted at her father's name and murmured. *"Manalin."*

The dragon nodded. *Yes.*

She had always believed Manalin was her father's dragon and had been killed at the same time as her father.

The dragon growled. *No one owns us.*

Lien had to fix this, had to right the wrongs Ying and Xue had done to them. She stepped away from Temur and knelt, bowing her head in deference. *"Forgive me, Great Dragon. I have recently learnt I am ignorant about much of my family's history. My father's brother raised me, he who ordered your babies to be stolen, and he told me the dragons gave each imperial child a dragon, to show their closeness to God."* As the dragon's rage grew in her head she kowtowed. *"I now know it was all lies."*

The dragon flapped its wings as if shaking off the anger and another memory surfaced. Kew had been growing bigger, getting used to her wings and knocking so many things over in her attempts to fly. One day she'd flown to the guards on the guard tower and when she'd landed, she'd crashed into a servant carrying a baby. The emperor had demanded Lien bind Kew's wings, had sat next to her as she did it. Lien had cried at Kew's discomfort, but afterwards the emperor and the empress had hugged her, had promised they would take care of her, had praised her. That one act of love had set her blind dedication to them. Horror flashed through her as the truth hit her. The emperor had made her bind Kew's wings so Kew couldn't fly away. Remorse choked her. She turned to her friend. *I am so sorry.*

Kew's forgiveness flooded her and she nuzzled

Lien's hand.

Calm determination settled over her. Xue would pay for all the atrocities he had caused. She faced the dragon. *"What would you have us do, to help you stop these thieves?"*

We need no help. We chased off a group not one day ago.

Ying and his party.

We know of the one you think, the dragon said. *The fast-as-wind-egg-stealer was not amongst the group. He, we would have killed.*

Perhaps it was the decoy group. "We believe the fast-as-wind-egg-stealer is in the area, searching for the tomb of the Great Khan."

He will not find it here.

Two of the dragons took off, flying over the mountains.

She had to convince the dragon to let them pass. "Ying seeks an artefact reputed to give all who touch it the gift to make them as fast as the wind. If more of them have this power, it will be difficult for you to stop them stealing your eggs."

The dragon growled. *Stop the group we chased away and we may let you pass to search for the one you call Ying.*

"Our priority needs to be Ying," Temur said.

Contempt from the dragon. *Prove yourself. Those whom you seek are in the forest towards the sunset, a short flight away.*

Both dragons flew away.

Lien stood. They had little choice. "If we help them, they may help us find Ying."

"How far is a short flight?" Amslan asked. "They could be anywhere."

Kew nudged Lien and sent her images.

"Kew can help us."

"We should attack at first light," Chinua said. "We can defeat them and then continue our search for Ying by the time the sun has risen."

Temur nodded. "Batzorig, go with Kew to scout. The rest of us will repair the camp."

Lien closed her eyes. They didn't have time to waste. "I will go with Batzorig."

Temur frowned. "That is not necessary."

She straightened her back. "It is. I can kill them all and be back here by midnight. We can go after Ying when I return."

He stepped closer, lowered his voice. "Are you sure?"

"Yes." Ying had to be stopped before he got the artefact.

He squeezed her hand. "Go then."

With Kew in the lead, Lien followed Batzorig into the trees. It was so much darker under the canopy, but her eyes adjusted. She moved silently, keeping close behind the Danil warrior.

After only an hour, Kew sent her a message to stop. Lien placed a hand on Batzorig's arm and crept forward.

Three sentries surrounded the group of sleeping men. They would need to die first. She slipped her knives into her hands. These deaths were necessary. She gritted her teeth and got to work.

The first sentry died, giving only a slight jerk as the blade sliced through his throat. She lowered him to the ground and went after the next one. The darkness was a shield, preventing her from seeing their faces, or the blood, but its warmth flowed on her hands. As the last sentry died, she moved to the prone, sleeping bodies of the remaining men. Most of them slept on their backs or curled on their sides. One soldier snored quietly in his sleep.

She needed to be fast. If one woke and warned the

others, Batzorig would be in danger.

Each kill took a notch out of her heart, but in less than a minute, they were all dead and the silence was absolute.

"It is done." Her voice was dull, wooden. She stood in the middle of the camp, centring her breath as Batzorig stepped out of the trees and inspected each of the men.

"Good job."

She didn't want praise for murder. She cringed, closing her eyes until Kew wound around her legs. Would the killing ever stop? Lien squatted down to hug her dragon, drawing from her strength. She had no time for pity. "Let's go." She strode out of the camp, away from the metallic smell of blood. Once again these men would have no funeral, their families would have no bodies to grieve over.

Batzorig caught up with her. "The wolves will feast well tonight."

Vomit rose in her mouth and she swallowed it down. She said nothing, but she took comfort from Kew's nearness as they returned to camp.

Temur was on sentry duty when they returned.

"It is done," she told him.

"Thank you, my *bayar*." He pulled her into his arms. "I wish I could protect you from this," he whispered. "I wish your gift was something else."

Tears welled in her eyes. "I wish that also."

Batzorig woke the others and they mounted.

"Ride with me," Temur said. "You can rest a while."

Relief filled her and she climbed up in front of him, his arms circling her.

Lulled by the horse's sway and Temur's warmth, she fell asleep.

Chapter 24

Lien's head ached when she woke the next morning. She was still nestled against Temur's chest, on his horse, and the warriors were spread out around them.

"How are you?" Temur murmured in her ear.

She shifted to look up at him. "I will be fine."

"Let's stop to eat," he called out and the warriors reined in their horses.

After he dismounted, Lien slid off and took the food Sukh handed her.

"Thank you, Father."

Amslan walked over, examined her. "You need to be at your best if you are to fight Ying." He touched her head and after a moment of heat, her headache was gone.

"Thank you." Her gaze met Temur's and his gentle smile almost undid her. All these men cared enough to look after her. She'd never felt so accepted. Her chest squeezed. "Any word from the dragons?"

"Nothing yet," Temur said.

"We're heading towards their breeding grounds," Batzorig said. "So they'll appear again."

Hopefully not to attack them.

After their brief stop Lien mounted Batu. It was slow going, with the horses picking their way over the sloping, rocky ground. Solongo led the way, urging her horse as fast as it would go. When it stumbled, Sukh took her reins. "Take it easy. She's going as fast as she can."

"They could be there by now," Solongo cried.

Lien's skin tightened. "Is this the most direct way to the tomb?"

Solongo hesitated. "It's the only way I know."

Kew growled and sent Lien an image of a dragon watching them.

"Do they want to speak with us?"

Kew shook her head.

A roar echoed through the mountains. Batu shied and it took a couple of moments before Lien got control of her. "What was that?"

"Dragon," Batzorig said.

Kew threw images at her. The brown dragon from the day before, an arrow through his chest. Flying to safety just over the ridge.

"Someone has shot a dragon." She turned to Kew. *Is it far? Can you lead us there?* They needed to help him.

Kew nodded.

"Amslan, can you heal animals?" She slid off Batu.

"Depends on the injury."

"Then come with me."

"Lien, wait." Temur grabbed her arm. "It's dangerous. Ying must be close by."

She hesitated. He was right, but they needed the dragon's help to find Ying. "His focus will be on the artefact." She hoped.

He released her, a deep frown on his face. "Go then. Be safe."

Following Kew, she and Amslan ascended into the

mountains. *Tell them Amslan may be able to help.*

She used both hands to scramble over the rocks.

At the top of the ridge, Kew indicated they should wait while she announced their presence. Lien sat on a boulder, panting, and scanned the surroundings. A few sparse trees, but it was mostly pale rock with the occasional tuft of green.

Amslan sat next to her. "What's happening?"

"Kew is telling them we are here." Down below Temur led the group further along the tree line. She tensed. She shouldn't have left them. If they encountered Ying before she returned, they would all die.

Kew sent her an image and she stood. "We can go down." The faster they helped the dragon, the quicker she could return to Temur.

Together they clambered down to where the dragon lay surrounded by three other dragons, one with his nose against the wound. The arrow stuck out of the dragon's chest, next to one of his wings.

Drop your flying sticks and come forward. The large green dragon across from her glanced up.

Lien lay her bow and quiver on the ground. Amslan did the same and they walked forward.

Riltien is gravely injured. The wound is not deep but the flying stick was poisoned. We must remove the stick quickly.

Lien grimaced. Poison. Again.

"It will hurt," Amslan warned. He stepped between the dragons and motioned for Lien to help him. "On the count of three."

Lien clutched the arrow and on Amslan's count she jerked back. The arrow came free. Riltien tensed but made no sound.

The poison is spreading too fast.

"What poison is it?" Amslan asked.

I am not sure.

"They used dragon's fire on Lien." He addressed the green dragon. "May I help?"

The dragon hesitated. *What do you do?*

"I have the gift of healing. I can mend injuries and disperse poisons."

Silence while the dragons communicated with each other.

Show me.

Amslan placed his hands over the wound and closed his eyes. His face was calm aside from a tiny tic above his right eye.

After several moments the green dragon said, *I understand. I will continue.*

Amslan stepped away and took a deep breath.

"How bad is it?" Lien asked.

"It spread far faster than it does in humans, but I've stopped it. The dragons can do the rest."

They moved away from the group to give them space and Kew joined them, climbing up on to the boulder to sit behind Lien and put her head on Lien's shoulder, pleasure and hope exuding from her.

"Why do you think wild dragons communicate with words whereas Kew only shows pictures and emotions?" Lien asked.

"I don't know," Amslan said.

Kew is still a baby and has not grown up with her kind. She has not learnt how to convert pictures to words. In the midst of the dragons, Riltien slowly got to his feet.

Lien grimaced. Kew had missed out on so much.

Thank you for saving me.

"We are sorry one of our enemy hurt you," Amslan said.

Riltien inclined his head. *Return to your group and I will send someone to lead you to him.*

Relief loosened Lien's muscles. "Thank you."

They climbed down the slope to where they had left their horses and then followed Temur's tracks until they caught up. Seeing him well made her smile.

"How did it go?" Temur asked.

"Amslan healed Riltien and the dragons will lead us to Ying."

"Good. There's been no trace of him."

A dragon landed in front of the group. His sandy brown scales were instantly recognisable and her heart twisted.

"Manalin." Memories flooded her in a tidal wave of emotion: sitting on her father's lap, listening to him discussing matters with Manalin; laughing in delight as Manalin flew above the palace in a display of aerobatics; Bao daring her to sneak up and touch the dragon while he slept. Tears pricked her eyes.

The dragon nodded to her. *Princess Lien, you have grown. I will guide you to the one who is faster than the wind.*

"It is good to see you, Manalin."

Temur stepped next to her. "Thank you. I am Temur, khan of the Rhoran. I appreciate your help in finding the one who causes both of us so much trouble."

Manalin inclined his head.

Next to Lien, Kew puffed up her chest and changed colours to match Manalin. The dragon didn't acknowledge her at all. He turned his back and walked forward.

Hurt radiated from Kew.

Lien sent her love and sympathy. Dragon society was a mystery to them both.

At midday Sukh called them to a halt. "The horses can't go any further."

"All right. Let's take only what we'll need," Temur

said. "How many people are with Ying?" he asked Manalin.

The same number as your group.

"Sukh, you can stay with the horses," he said.

Sukh nodded.

I will ask one of my kind to stay with you. He can protect you.

"Thank you," Sukh said and Lien relaxed.

"How far ahead are they?" Solongo asked.

Still some distance by the way you travel. I could reach them in little time were I to fly.

"We need to be prepared for an ambush," Batzorig warned.

Manalin snorted. *There is no need. Others watch their group and they will tell me if any leave.*

"I'm sorry, Manalin. I didn't know." Batzorig bowed his head.

There is much your kind do not know about us. Emperor Huang was the only one who showed any interest.

The mention of her father made Lien ache. "Manalin, will you tell me how you ended up at the imperial palace?"

Manalin was silent for a long moment. Finally he said, *The journey will take time and the story may teach you.*

Lien and Temur fell into step beside him.

We used to live in the mountains to the west of your imperial palace. Your father and some of his men had come to examine the plants which grew there. Huang wanted to discover if any could be used to cure your human ailments. He knew the area was our breeding ground and so he waited at the base of the mountains until Riltien went to find out what he wanted. He waited a long time. Manalin opened his mouth in a smile. *Eventually Riltien led his group to one of the low meadows so they could examine the plants. They were not allowed to explore further as there were nests close by.* Manalin paused. *Some prey had distracted the young dragon who should have been watching them.* He curled his lip. *One nest was attacked by a pack of wolves. The mother was badly injured while defending it. Huang heard the commotion and he and his men used their flying sticks to kill the wolves and save the nest. As a reward he asked to learn more about the dragons and so they sent me to the palace to teach him.*

"Were you with him the day he and my mother died?"

Manalin nodded. *I had left the palanquin to stretch my wings but returned when I sensed trouble. Your mother was frantic about your brother. I hid Bao from the one whom you call Ying, but could do nothing to save your parents.*

Lien's steps faltered, her breath gone. It was true. Ying had murdered her parents.

Temur put an arm around her. "Breathe, my *bayar*."

She gasped in air as anger simmered low in her stomach. "You know my brother escaped?"

I took him to Chungson. Your father had mentioned his concern about Xue's ambitions and asked me to take Bao to his neighbours should anything happen to him. And thus we repaid our debt to your father.

Lien was silent. Both Ying and Xue had to be stopped.

Temur squeezed her. "We'll make him pay for what he's done."

Some tension left her. She wasn't alone. She had her tribe and Temur.

The group has stopped. They are close to the tomb of the Great Khan and are preparing for something.

Lien's heartbeat accelerated. "How far away are they?"

If you travel faster, we could be there before the sun sinks below the mountain.

She squinted at the sun overhead.

"We must hurry." Solongo strode to the front of the

group. "They must not disturb the tomb. Could your brothers distract the group?" she asked Manalin.

I will discuss the matter with the others. Manalin continued to guide them but was silent.

Solongo increased her pace through the narrow paths and clambered over rocks. Lien and the rest of the warriors followed. The rocks were tough on her hands, scratching her palms but she didn't slow. They needed to get to Ying.

The dragons will make their wait uncomfortable, Manalin finally said.

It would give them a chance to catch up. The pass was completely shadowed by the time Manalin called a halt. *Rest here while I find out what is happening.*

Lien perched on a rock, taking the weight off her feet, and took the food Amslan passed her. Nerves prickled her stomach but she ate anyway.

They have built no defences. They hide amongst the rocks to prevent being burnt by the dragon's breath. The one you call Ying is not amongst them. The dragons do not know when he left, but they are searching for him now.

Solongo sucked in a breath.

Lien's stomach fluttered. This was her fight. "I will find him." And she would kill him or die trying. She turned to the spiritual leader. "You need to tell me everything about the khan's tomb and how to get there."

Solongo hesitated for only a second before nodding.

"You can't go on your own." Temur grabbed her arm, stopping her.

"I must." Inside she trembled. "Anyone who comes with me becomes a weapon Ying can use." She couldn't risk it. "You have your own battle. Kun is a vicious fighter. You must be careful."

"She's right, Temur," Amslan said.

"She can take care of herself." Chinua winked at her. "Take my spare arrows."

Lien clutched them. "Thank you."

Temur scowled but nodded.

Solongo drew her away from the others. "Trip wires line the narrow pass up to the top of the mountain," she said. "They're set at chest height to avoid animals springing them."

"What do they trigger?"

"Rock avalanches. I spoke to the Danil spiritual leader before I left and he checked them last month. They were still in place." She continued. "At the top is a meadow full of pits with sharp spikes at the bottom. You need to follow the trees to go through unscathed."

The traps should slow Ying down.

"Finally you'll pass through the breeding grounds and arrive at a cliff. There's a narrow path jutting out from the edge. The tomb is in a cave above the path."

"Thank you." Lien returned to the others. "I will be back as soon as I can."

"Make sure you are." Temur hugged her. "I need my wife back."

A lump lodged in her throat. She couldn't speak so she nodded and walked away.

Kew fell into step with her and Lien stopped. *You can't come with me, Kew.*

The dragon snorted.

She is right, little one. You must stay here, Manalin said.

Kew growled.

Lien squatted down. *I need you to protect Temur for me. Keep my family safe. Will you do that for me?*

Kew glanced at Manalin.

I will guide her from the sky, Manalin said.

Snorting, Kew sat next to Temur. He smiled and stroked her back.

The image gave her strength. "Shall we go?" Without looking back, she followed Manalin's instructions to sneak past the Bonamese and into the ravine.

The light was fading as she used both hands to scrabble up the sharp rocks. Not holding any of her weapons made her vulnerable, not only to Ying, but also to the wolves, leopards and wolverines which would be active as night fell.

Rocks tumbled down the path below her and she stopped. She was making far too much noise. Anyone in the vicinity would hear her.

Take the path to your left.

Though her eyes had adjusted to the dark, she could barely make out the slight deviation in the rock that was the path. She would have to go slowly here, to spot any cords stretched out. She withdrew her sabre and held it ahead of her, blade facing forward. If it cut any cord, it might stop the trap from springing.

The slope she was climbing levelled out and she moved faster.

Twang!

Lien leapt backwards as boulders thundered down the narrow path. Using her speed, she lunged for the steep slopes, and her momentum carried her out of their path. The boulders bounced and rattled, echoing down the mountain.

Hopefully Kun and his men would think it was Ying, and not come after her. She didn't need to fight two battles.

When silence fell again, she climbed down to the path and glanced up. High above her Manalin circled, keeping watch. She kept her sabre out, moving as fast as she dared, but encountered no more traps.

When the path split, she took the one that led higher

into the mountains. A few sparse trees dotted the trail, growing out of solid rock.

Something moves.

Lien crouched in a defensive stance, her eyes and ears straining. A faint scraping of bark alerted her an instant before a huge dark shape leapt down from the tree in front of her. She jumped back as the shape landed gracefully on the ground in front of her.

A leopard.

Chapter 25

The creature watched her, its body tense, its gaze unwavering. It would only take a small movement from her to make it attack. She didn't want to kill this magnificent creature.

They stared at each other for several long moments.

Leave her, Manalin said.

The leopard snarled and after a moment's pause climbed back up the tree.

"Thank you, Manalin." She kept her eye on the cat as she sped past it and further up the crevice.

You are welcome. The one who is faster than the wind is almost at the tomb.

Her pulse raced. "How far away am I?"

Still some distance. The egg-stealer is being slowed by traps.

She had to hurry. Traps wouldn't slow Ying down for long.

"Where is the meadow?"

At the top of this crevice.

She climbed faster, her thighs burning.

Near the top, she spotted another trap and ducked under the cord without setting it off. She examined the large meadow in front of her. Long grass, with the occasional dark shape of a tree—and pit traps. If she fell, she'd be dead. But she couldn't avoid it. The mountain rose in steep walls on two sides, impossible to climb.

She plotted her course, setting in her mind where each pit would be. It was tempting to use her speed, but she needed to conserve it for the fight. Instead, she jogged through the field, relying on Manalin to warn her if any predators lay in wait. Twice she stumbled on the uneven ground and was forced to slow. If she twisted her ankle, Ying had won.

A few yards from the end of the meadow the ground gave way beneath her. With a burst of speed she lunged forward, her feet slipping on the edge of the pit. Arms whirling she forced herself forward and her foot found solid ground. She ran to the rocks, arms pumping and then looked back.

She was through.

Not far to go and no time to rest. Ahead of her the mountain pass was shadowed and dotted with dark caves above her. Her skin prickled with tension. The dragons watched her. They didn't like her here. She picked up her pace, jogging as fast as she dared on the rough ground.

How did Ying get through? Lien asked Manalin.

He used his speed though he was burnt.

Good. If Ying was injured, it would give her a slight advantage.

She reached the end of the pass and the moon became visible. One side of the mountain fell away beneath her, a vertical drop straight down, and the other side soared upwards, an impossibly steep wall. The view took her breath away. Lake Tolui twinkled in the moonlight and the steppes stretched out to the horizon. In the far distance shone camp fires which must be the army.

She had no time to marvel at its beauty. She needed to stop Ying.

An extremely narrow ledge jutted out from the wall, no more than a foot wide in places. This was her path, but there were no gripping points, nothing to stop her from falling the hundreds of yards to the ground below.

He has entered the tomb.

Fear set her heart racing. The idea of Ying with the artefact terrified her more than falling.

Keeping her steps small and as light as possible, she shuffled forward, toeing the path to check it was still there before placing her foot down. In places the ledge had crumbled away and she had to stretch to reach the next solid part.

It was slow, far too slow, but she daren't use her speed. If she lost her balance, she would die.

She spotted a platform jutting out of the cliff. The tomb.

Her gaze fixed on her destination, she moved forward. The ledge shuddered underneath her and then broke away. She leapt forward, grappling at the rocky wall for purchase, the dirt digging under her nails, the rocks grazing her palms as she got a steady hold. She hugged the cliff, breathing hard to calm her rapid heartbeat, and winced as the rocks bounced off the cliff, echoing in the silence. She squeezed her eyes shut.

She'd lost her advantage. Ying knew someone was there. She had to be careful.

The platform jutted out about five yards above her and cast a shadow on the rock beneath it, making it difficult to see any handholds she could use. Somehow she had to climb the vertical face and get into the cave, without Ying attacking her.

She would have to trust her speed and balance as she never had before because there was no margin for error.

Where is he now?

I cannot look. He is armed with his flying stick and is waiting. Should I fly near, he will shoot me.

Just as Ying would shoot Lien the moment she appeared above the overhang. She needed a distraction.

Do you know what is inside the cave?

An image came to her mind. A large stone tomb in the middle of the cave surrounded by pieces of weaponry: bow and arrows, sabre, knives and most importantly a shield leaning against one wall. Towards the back of the cave a lot of things were scattered around. Not much room to manoeuvre.

If she could get to the shield, she had a chance of surviving long enough to fight. *Can you drop a rock on the ledge for me?* Lien visualised what she wanted Manalin to do.

Yes.

Her only option without harming Manalin. Lien centred herself, visualising the path up the cliff, and took a calming breath. *Now.*

She grabbed the nearest handhold and using her speed, pulled and pushed herself upwards to the overhang. As the rock hit the opposite side she pulled her body on to the overhang. Several arrows flew towards the ledge.

She flung herself towards the shield as Ying swung towards her and released an arrow. Lifting the shield, she prayed it hadn't rotted in the years it had been lying there.

The thud of arrows in quick succession jolted her arms but the wood held firm. Relief flooded her. She was in.

Now all she needed to do was defeat Ying.

She almost laughed.

"Lien, what a surprise." Ying chuckled. "I thought

the Rhoran would have killed you long ago."

Her pulse thudded in her head. Keep him talking and perhaps she'd figure out a way to kill him.

"The Rhoran saw value in my skills." The moonlight didn't penetrate far into the cave so she couldn't tell if the lumpy shapes in the back contained anything that would help her. At least the tomb was between her and Ying for the moment. She eased the bow off her back and leaned it against the wall.

"Until they realise you're too weak to kill. It's pathetic."

No, it was a strength, but this fight would end with one of them dead.

It had to be him.

She shifted and another arrow thudded into the shield, its tip penetrating at Lien's eye line. She needed to move fast, whatever she did. Ying had the definite advantage, but he wasn't attacking, which meant he was worried.

"Give up Lien. I don't have time to play with you today. I need to return to the army so they can destroy the Rhoran. At least the khan is already dead."

Her heart stopped. "He's not. Temur will defeat Kun and his warriors."

Ying laughed, full of mirth. "No he won't. I trained Kun personally. No one can defeat him."

His arrogance was breathtaking. "Did you train Fen too? Because she was easy to defeat." The words almost stuck in her throat and she closed her eyes briefly. Then her eyes flashed open. If Fen had the gift, Kun could too. Was that why Ying was so confident?

"She is still young. I will continue her training when we return."

"She is dead."

Ying's sharp gasp was music to her ears. "You killed

my daughter?"

His daughter? Her mouth dropped open.

"I will kill you for that alone. By the time Kun and I are done, the Rhoran will be a distant memory."

Temur.

Lien had left him and the others unprotected. Kun would kill them all if he had the gift.

Images of Temur flashed through her mind: his bright smile, his joyous laugh, the way he constantly touched her, brushing her arm or hand to show her he was there, that she was safe. He'd held her and comforted her while she'd grieved for those whose lives she'd taken. She loved him.

She froze.

Somewhere along the way she had fallen in love with her husband, the barbarian she had despised not so long ago.

And now he could be dead.

Sorrow threatened to swamp her until another thud in the top of the shield brought her attention back to the present. No time to indulge in her grief now. She had to kill Ying and then hunt Kun down and kill him too.

Before anyone else she loved died.

Ying had killed everyone she had ever cared about.

Anger exploded through her sorrow. He'd killed her parents and her husband, but she would not let him take her children.

She was tribal Mother.

Determination and confidence coalesced in her. Ying was no longer her master. He was the man who threatened her people's very existence. He would not defeat her.

She gripped one of her blades. Her hand darted out, as if to throw and an arrow thudded into the wall behind her. Dropping the shield, she threw her knife, its blade slicing through Ying's bow string and into his arm.

He roared, dropping the useless bow and his quiver of arrows as he extracted the knife from his arm.

She grabbed her bow and shot two arrows, but he was too fast. He darted out of the way and threw the blade back at her.

It whooshed past her ear and clunked into the wall behind her.

No time to pick it up. She kept shooting, keeping the stone tomb between them.

He moved out onto the platform where there was more space.

Only two arrows left and then she'd have no choice but hand-to-hand combat.

She sighted down the arrow. She needed to predict which way he would dodge.

Outside a dragon roared.

Ying spun and she let the arrows fly. The first hit him in the upper back and he stumbled forward, narrowing missing being hit with the second arrow.

Lien moved fast, clutching her last knife and racing forward. This was her chance.

She had to end it now.

As he whirled around, his face a picture of rage, she struck, aiming for his face and neck.

He dodged the attack, his speed almost unbelievable. She stumbled close to the edge of the overhang, her hands whirling to stop just in time. The forest was a long way down.

Ying yelled as he sliced his knife towards her. She blocked, the impact of the movement rattling her teeth, and she attacked, throwing punches and kicks as much to distract him from his surroundings as to hurt him.

She panted as her foot connected to his stomach. Ying gasped, but didn't pause as he kicked, sweeping her legs out from under her.

She hit the ground hard and his expression of satisfaction had her rolling away from the edge, towards the tomb, before she leapt to her feet again.

His face had more definition. The sun was rising.

Before she blinked, he was on her, fists flying, with no pause, as if he didn't have an arrow stuck in his back. Lien's next kick brushed his arm and he leapt back as if something had stung him.

His tunic was blackened where the dragons had burnt him. He was more vulnerable there.

She smiled.

He attacked and she defended, strike after strike. Her blade nicked his arm, but he ripped it out of her hand. Gone. Too far away to retrieve.

Ying staggered back and his face hardened.

Lien gasped, her sabre rasping as she retrieved it from her belt. Her last weapon. Her body ached, but she wouldn't give in to the pain.

"You would use that barbarian blade against me?" Ying yelled.

"I will use my people's weapons against you."

Ying attacked again, faster than lightning. He brushed her sabre out of the way as if it were a stick and kicked her hard in the chest.

Her ribs cracked and Lien flew backwards into the collection of objects surrounding the tomb. Pain ricocheted through her and her breath disappeared. No air.

Ying sneered. "Did you really think you could defeat me?" He walked forward.

She would die if she didn't get to her feet.

She swung her sabre towards him to keep him back

and the pain made her head spin. No. She blinked rapidly to focus.

Using the cave wall for support, she climbed to her feet, the muscles in her chest screaming at her not to move. She gritted her teeth, her gaze not wavering from him.

He attacked again, and she was too slow. He blocked the sabre, twisting it out of her hand, and her forearm broke with a crack. The sabre fell to the ground with a thud as she screamed, only the wall behind her stopping her from falling to the ground.

She would die.

"You are a mere female, tainted now with the barbarian stench. You will beg me to kill you before I am finished."

Fear lodged in her chest and she backed further into the cave. The dawn illuminated the possessions left with the Great Khan; a bolt of silk, bowls and tools, a table covered in embroidery, threads and bobbins, and a spear.

She was in the burial place of the greatest khan in Rhoran history. She would not surrender, she would not beg for mercy, she would not let a single groan cross her lips.

Her people's survival relied on her winning and making Ying pay for the devastation he had caused.

Cradling her broken arm to her chest, she stretched her other hand towards the spear, and clasped it. "Are you not concerned to be fighting in the resting place of the Great Khan?"

He laughed. "He is dead."

Lien shook her head as she adjusted her grip on the spear. "You are so woefully ignorant of our culture," she said. "I am the Tribal Mother. I am far more powerful than you could imagine."

Concern flitted across his face. "You talk nonsense."

She raised an eyebrow. "And yet you are here searching for the power I speak of." She had only one chance to fling the spear and she was too close to the wall. She stepped closer to him, gritting her teeth at the pain.

One more step. Her toe knocked a ceramic bowl on the ground in front of her. "I call upon the ancestors here in this sacred place to help and protect me."

She hooked the bowl with her foot and flung it at Ying's face. As he blocked it, she flung the spear, agony sweeping through her, causing her to let go too soon and crash into the table with embroidery on it.

He side-stepped the spear and grinned.

She clasped a heavy bone rod attached to some string. Would the string be rotten?

She swung the rod in a circle, faster and faster, a whirling distraction, and stared Ying down. "You will never defeat me or mine." Moving forward she kept the makeshift weapon in front of her. "The Rhoran are as fierce in death as they are in life." She motioned over his shoulder. Ying glanced behind and Lien attacked, throwing the rod, so the thread tied his hands together while she kicked him hard in the chest.

She sucked in air as Ying crashed into the cave wall.

She stumbled forward, her head spinning and her vision blurred.

He wrenched his hands free of the thread, face livid.

He was done playing. He would kill her now. She darted to the opposite side of the tomb, moving backwards. Then she was out of the cave, on the overhang. One false step and she'd fall to her death.

His fists pummelled her as if she was a punching bag. She lifted her one good arm the best she could, but it was no use. He kicked her square in the stomach and knocked her back, dangerously close to the edge. She bent in half, gasping for air, pain her constant companion.

"You'll never beat me," he snarled. "I taught you everything you know." He moved closer. Threw a punch.

Not everything. She twisted, and his fist ran along her side. He'd overbalanced, his armpit under her shoulder. She stood, using his momentum to throw him over her back in a wrestling move Chinua had taught her. Her ribs stabbed her from the inside. She fell to her knees.

Ying yelled.

Frantically she twisted, but the overhang was empty. She crawled to the edge. Ying fell, his arms flailing as if attempting to fly. She gasped as he hit the trees far below, impaled on the top branch.

Pain and relief suffocated her. Ying was dead. She had defeated him.

A noise next to her made her rip her eyes open again. Manalin landed on the overhang.

You are hurt.

"Yes."

One of my kind is coming to help.

"Thank you." Her head spun and the lure to close her eyes was strong. No. She couldn't give up. Kun could be on his way here right now.

Clenching her jaw, she tried to stand but pain twisted in her chest.

Stay there. Dhalin is here. The same green dragon who had healed Riltien landed on the overhang and hurried to her. She put her nose against Lien's ribs and Lien braced herself for more pain. Instead she felt a soft probing and her breathing became a little easier.

I have fixed your lung but I cannot fix your bones.

"Thank you." She would have to search the cave for something to brace her arm. Forcing herself to her feet, she swayed in agony. She could do this.

She stumbled into the cave. So many items.

A tray over with the other crockery. It might work. "Manalin, could you pick it up for me?"

He took the tray in his mouth and she reached for it and placed it on the tomb. She unwound her belt and then placed the tray under her broken arm. Her pulse thudded hard in her head.

"Hold this end." She gave him one end of her belt and he held it still while she wound it around her arm, securing it to the tray. She needed a sling as well. There was nothing she could do about her ribs.

She spotted her knives and sabre and with the dragons' help, she unravelled the bolt of silk until she found a section which wasn't rotten and cut a piece to fashion a sling. With that done, she asked, "Where are the others?"

I do not know.

Ying's taunt echoed in her head. Had he been right? Was everyone dead?

The grief threatened to overwhelm her and she shut it down. She didn't have time for this.

She shuffled back to the edge of the overhang. The sun hovered just above the horizon, spreading its light across the steppes, making everything golden. Below, Lake Tolui shimmered, and the forest was a carpet of green. The perfect resting spot for the Great Khan, overseeing his beloved land.

Now her land.

And she would protect it to her last breath.

The ledge below was too far away and too narrow, barely jutting out from the wall. One mistake and she'd join Ying's body so far away. She couldn't climb down by herself.

But how had the Rhoran got the khan up here in the first place? There had to be another entrance.

She limped back into the cave. A tunnel was hidden behind a wall. Maybe she could walk out. The corridor grew darker and darker and she stretched her good arm out in front of her.

Let me help. Manalin's jet of fire illuminated a wall of boulders. Her heart sank. She couldn't move it.

She shuffled back to the tomb and reviewed the items. The lid of the stone tomb was out of alignment.

The artefact.

Could it be inside?

Or was it one of the treasures scattered around the cave?

Lien scanned the silks, embroidery, threads and cooking implements. She frowned. A female would normally be left those kinds of items, not a khan. Though there were many weapons as well.

She peered inside the tomb. The body inside was well preserved, the yellow of the dress still clear.

Lien's eyes widened. Dress?

She examined it more closely. She would almost guarantee the Great Khan was female.

Why hadn't anyone said?

Her mind whirled. If that was the case, perhaps there wasn't an artefact at all. Perhaps the Great Khan had been the first to have the gift and passed it down to her family.

She would have to speak to Solongo—if Solongo had survived.

It was time to go.

"Manalin, can you help me fix the lid?"

He and Dhalin used their forelegs to push the lid back into position. The khan could rest peacefully now.

And Lien would have to go out the way she came.

She unwound the bolt of silk, but it wasn't long enough to reach the overhang if she anchored it to the tomb.

She peered over the overhang, focusing on the ledge and not the deadly drop below.

What are you doing? Manalin asked.

"I have to get down." Could she use her speed to get to the ledge? Or would it be too much and cause her to overshoot? A foothold there, and maybe one there. She examined the cliff face for alternatives.

We can help, Manalin said. *Hold the silk.* He projected an image into her head of them holding the silk at one end while she stood in a loop at the other and then lowering her to the ledge.

Were they and the silk strong enough? Her options were limited.

"All right." She tied one end of the silk into a loop and handed the other end to Manalin. She had to be quick and it would be agonising—more so if she made a mistake.

The dragons moved into position, hovering above her.

"Ready?"

Yes.

She squatted down, the pain reminding her she was alive. Gripping the silk, she stepped off.

And fell, the ledge rushing up to her.

Lien's heart leapt to her throat as her feet hit the ledge, and she let go of the silk, clutching at the loose dirt of the wall. The force of the impact unbalanced her. She fell backwards, away from the cliff, reaching desperately for the wall, her nails scraping down the surface, pain screaming through her chest.

She wouldn't make it.

Chapter 26

Lien's hands left the cliff, gravity pulling her body down.

Suddenly Manalin shoved her back towards the rock face. She grabbed a rock jutting out and adjusted her footing, her ribs screaming in protest. The dragon hovered next to her for support.

She'd made it. Her head spun and she closed her eyes. "Thank you."

You must keep moving. The ledge is not stable.

Underneath, rocks rattled down the cliff, their echo bouncing back to her. She had no time to recover. Opening her eyes, she moved fast as the ledge disintegrated beneath her. Every step was pure torture, but she had no time for hesitation, for caution. She focused on speed and balance, but exhaustion chased her.

The ledge crumbled with every step and the distance to the ravine was endless.

Jump!

At Manalin's shout, she used the last of her energy for a burst of speed. The ledge fell away as she lunged for the solid ground just in front of her.

She hit the earth, landing hard on her broken arm and ribs, sliding across the rocky ground, the stones ripping through her pants and her legs. Her whole body was in agony, pain not leaving a single cell untouched.

She lay still, panting, head spinning and fighting the desire to fall into the darkness calling her.

She'd made it.

Tears blurred her vision. She had to keep moving, had to embrace the pain. Her tribe needed her.

She rolled on to her back as Manalin and Dhalin landed next to her. *Are you all right?*

Hysterical laughter bubbled up inside her and she fought it back. "I will be."

Let me check if I can help. Dhalin mentally probed her body but the pain didn't alter. *There is nothing I can do.*

"Help me up." She reached out a bloodied hand. Gravel embedded deep inside her palm stung as she clutched Manalin's tail.

With Dhalin pushing and Manalin pulling, she made it to her feet. She stumbled to the rock wall, using its hard face to support her while she gasped for air. The sling fell useless around her neck, so she adjusted it to support her arm again. Everything was blurry and her head pounded.

She needed a second to rest until it stopped so she could walk in a straight line. She opened her eyes. The ledge was gone. Not even a toehold was left in the wall. The Great Khan would no longer be disturbed.

"Will you guide me back?"

Yes. We shall protect you.

Kun and his men were still out there somewhere.

Lien trembled, but she blocked it ruthlessly. She couldn't think about Temur now. She had to find a safe place to recover in order to defend herself from the next attack.

Her leg shook as she placed her foot down, but it held. The next step was a little better. She focused on the pebbles on the ground. If she saw the distance she had to travel it would overwhelm her. She had to trust the dragons to protect her.

Light came slowly to the pass, illuminating the dirt and rocks. She stopped mid-way to rest. A few dragons watched her from the caves, wary but not aggressive. *Thank you.*

Without the dragons' support, she wouldn't be here.

After what seemed like hours, she reached the meadow. Agonising pain had become normal. Leaning against a rock at the entrance, panting at her body's torture, she tried to focus on the trees.

They split into two and then three, before merging again into one.

She blinked.

She needed to see clearly so she could map her path.

Let me help, Manalin said.

"Thank you." Forcing herself away from the rock, she pressed on. Manalin guided her, telling her where to step. She shuffled, her concentration pinpointed on the next step, and then the next.

Eventually the meadow gave way to rock again. She looked up. The crevice she'd climbed the night before was right in front of her, too steep for her to see down its length.

Propping herself up against a tree, Lien stared at it, helplessness swamping her. She couldn't climb down. Not with one arm in a sling, and her other hand too torn to be any use. Her ribs wouldn't take the further punishment.

It is not far now.

Yes, it was. Even if she made it to the bottom, she'd have to face the possibility of finding Temur's body, and somehow get her men back to the horses. Her boots were nearly worn through and every stone she trod on felt like she was being stabbed by pottery shards. She had no more energy.

Tears flowed down her face.

Something nudged at her mind. "Go away, Manalin."

It is not me, it is Kew.

Her brain slowly comprehended the information. Her dragon was alive!

She opened her mind and images flashed through her head, too fast to make any sense. Was Kew in danger?

With a surge of energy, she moved towards the crevice. She could make it. She had to. She had to help Kew.

Wait. Manalin and Dhalin stood in front of her so she couldn't start down the rocky slope.

No. They wouldn't stop her.

Behind them stones rattled down the slope, too many to be just Kew. She froze. Someone was coming towards her up the crevice. She had to hide, had to surprise them, but the only hiding place was the trees in the meadow. She turned.

"Lien!"

Was that Temur's voice? Hope filled her, but her mind could be playing tricks.

Forcing her legs to move, she stumbled as she turned around, drawing her sabre.

She spotted Kew first and stared. Kew was all right. Safe.

Her eyes raised and she caught sight of Temur. Dirt and blood smeared his face, strands of hair had come out of his braid and his leather armour was scratched. But he was alive.

Temur's eyes widened. "My *bayar.*"

Lien's vision blurred and she shook. "Temur?" She stumbled forward into Temur's arms, inhaling his scent.

It was him.

She smiled as pain dragged her into the darkness.

~*~

"Lien, wake up."

The voice was much too loud, piercing Lien's consciousness. She tried to block it. She didn't want to wake. It would be too painful. Someone squeezed her hand.

"Come on, my *bayar*. You need to open your eyes."

Temur.

Memories flooded into the void. The fight with Ying, the journey to the meadow, seeing the man she'd thought was dead.

She opened her eyes, blinking until the blurred light came into focus.

"Welcome back." Temur's smile was the sweetest thing she'd ever seen.

"You're alive," she whispered, her throat dry and disused.

He nodded. "You scared me to death when you collapsed in my arms."

She frowned. What had happened?

"Get her to drink this." Amslan handed Temur a cup.

She didn't want to sit, didn't want to feel. She lifted her arm, the splint now removed, and there was no pain. Amslan must have healed her bones, though the rest of her body was still battered and bruised.

Temur placed an arm under her back and helped her to sit. They were at the edge of the meadow, though shadows were falling. The Rhoran warriors sat around a fire, sharpening their weapons. All had cuts, bruises or bandages to show they had fought Kun and his men.

She took a small sip of the sweet liquid and it

warmed her insides. "What happened?"

"That's what we'd like to know." Amslan laughed. "You look as if you took on an entire army."

She shook her head. "No, I meant to you. Why didn't Kun kill you? I thought he had the gift."

Temur shook his head. "Not that we saw. What made you think that?"

Her brain was still kind of foggy. "If Fen had it, then Kun could too. Ying said he trained Kun, that he was the best, so I just assumed…" She sighed. Thank the ancestors she'd been wrong.

"They fought fiercely," Temur said. "And the ground was rough. If Riltien hadn't separated us with fire, we might not have got away with so few injuries." He squeezed her hand. "We could only use our arrows and it took time, and the dragons' help before we'd killed the majority. When Riltien told us Ying had been killed, Kun retreated with his remaining men."

We will tell you if he approaches, Manalin said.

Tears welled in her eyes. They were safe for the moment. Safe, and Temur was alive, here with her.

Wait. "What about Sukh?"

He will be protected.

She sighed.

Temur stroked her forehead. "How are you feeling?"

Happy. Absolutely joyous he was still with her, but that wasn't what he was asking. She moved her limbs. She ached all over. "Like someone has used me as a punching bag."

"You were in a bad state," Amslan said. "I healed all your critical injuries and will attempt the rest tomorrow." Amslan handed her some dried meat, the dark rings under his eyes prominent.

"Thank you. I will be fine." He needed to rest. "Have you eaten?"

Amslan smiled and held up his own portion. "Just about to, Mother."

"What am I going to do about you two?" Temur asked. "It's as if you both have a death wish."

Lien stiffened. Although a smile played around his mouth, she was too exhausted to find it funny. Her mind growled at her, demanding she protect her honour. "Everything I have done is to protect my people." She struggled to her feet, shaking off his attempt to stop her. He had no concept of how terrified she had been. "I do not wish to die." She strode away before the anger could take hold. Emotion drove her now and in this instance, the Bonamese reserve was far better. She didn't want to say something she would regret.

"Temur, give her some time," Amslan said.

She didn't want time, she wanted his love. Everything she had done had been for her new family, her new tribe, for him. She kept to the edge of the meadow and sank to the ground amongst the grasses, hugging her knees, her tears flowing. Emotions battered around inside her, desperate to get out.

She loved this barbarian, with his ready smile and his determination to do what was best for his people. She loved the way he challenged her, the way he invaded her space to touch her hand or her shoulder in a gesture of understanding, the way he had shown her another way to live besides the cold, emotionless household she'd been raised in. The Rhoran and Temur respected her as a woman, as a warrior and as a friend.

She should be happy with that.

But she wanted his love as well.

Kew bumped her head against Lien's shoulder and blew smoke on her face.

She winced in pain, but drew Kew close, needing her

comfort.

Lien hid her head against Kew's scaly side as heavy footsteps crunched through the grass.

No. She didn't want to see anyone.

"Lien, I am sorry." Temur crouched down next to her, but she didn't look up. "My attempt at humour wasn't funny. I didn't mean to hurt you."

She couldn't answer. Couldn't form words past the lump in her throat.

"My *bayar*, look at me, please."

The term of endearment only made her sob harder.

Temur swore and gathered her into his arms, stroking her back. "I know you don't want to die. I get so worried, knowing I can't do anything to protect you as is my duty."

She raised her head and whispered, "Is that all I am to you—a duty?"

"No," he stuttered. "You're my wife and the tribal Mother."

Roles, responsibilities.

Her heart squeezed and Lien couldn't bear to sit there next to him. She pushed him away and stood.

"Lien, wait."

If she'd had the energy to use her speed, she would have.

He grabbed her arm, stopped her.

Anger attacked like a pack of snarling wolves. "I thought you were dead," she yelled. "When Ying implied Kun had the gift, I was certain he had killed you. The grief almost overwhelmed me and I realised I loved you."

Temur opened his mouth, but she spoke over him.

"Then Ying attacked and I thought I would die. I almost gave up, almost decided there was no point in fighting." She closed her eyes briefly. "And then I remembered our tribe." She paused. "I fought with all I had inside." Sorrow filled her once more. "So, it upsets me that you still consider me a burden."

He stared at her and she couldn't stand there waiting for him to speak.

Before she could move away, his hand slid down her arm to clasp hers, his warm brown eyes looking into hers. "You love me?"

"Yes."

"Thank Qadan." He crushed her against his chest in a hug that took her breath away.

She winced as hope battled with confusion.

Temur brushed her hair from her face, kissed her lips. "My life has been crazy since you came into it."

His smile brought her hope. "You've taught me so much." His thumbs caressed her arms. "Patience and compassion for my enemy, new fighting techniques. You've opened my eyes to a different world, my *bayar*, and I love you for that and so much more."

Her heart stopped. "What?"

His grin lit her up. "I love you, my *bayar*, with all my heart." His lips were gentle as he kissed her. "I was in agony before we married. The idea you could be a spy for the emperor tore my heart in two. I had to keep my distance."

"I thought you didn't care."

"Didn't care?" He laughed. "I cared too much."

Her chest swelled as her sorrow dissolved, and her pain faded away. "I am pleased to hear it."

Temur laughed again. "As am I." He reached for her hand. "I look forward to spending the rest of my life with you."

She smiled. "Me too."

His smile was wide. "Come, let's rejoin the others."

As they rejoined the group, Temur pulled Lien down

to sit next to him, keeping her hand firmly in his. Both Amslan and Chinua grinned at them, and Lien's face heated. She had yelled at Temur. Perhaps she was becoming more Rhoran each day.

Kew flushed happiness and settled next to her.

A movement in the meadow had Lien tensing, but it was Solongo.

"What did you find?" Temur asked.

Solongo shook her head. "There's nothing there. No trace of the ledge to the tomb." She turned to Lien. "What happened?"

Amslan grinned. "We'd all like to hear your story."

"Of course." She glanced at Solongo. Some things she wouldn't confide in them. She told them about the long climb, the leopard, and how when she'd reached the tomb, Ying had been waiting for her. "Manalin helped to distract him so I could get into the cave."

"Thank you," Temur said to Manalin.

The dragon nodded.

Lien didn't want to go into the battle in detail. "I fought Ying and I used a shoulder throw Chinua taught me to send Ying over the edge."

Chinua grinned at her. "Well done."

"How did you get back here with all of your injuries?" Amslan asked. "You must have been in agony."

She nodded. "Manalin and Dhalin helped me tie a splint and Dhalin healed my lungs. They also lowered me to the ledge." She shuddered at how close she'd come to joining Ying at the bottom of the cliff. She would have to repay them.

"What about the artefact?" Solongo asked.

"I couldn't find it. Ying had opened the tomb, but the dragons helped me replace the lid."

Solongo's eyes widened. "Thank you, Mother.

Perhaps we can speak in more detail later?"

Lien nodded.

"Is there any way someone could get back into the tomb?" Temur asked.

"I don't believe so," Solongo said.

Lien wouldn't mention the tunnel. It was better if no one knew about it.

"That's one less thing for us to worry about," Temur said. "Tomorrow, if Lien has recovered, we will journey back to the steppes and the army."

Had the Rhoran defeated the Bonamese yet? Would there be more killing ahead?

Lien couldn't worry about it now. She had to take each day as it came.

That night she slept soundly, wrapped in her husband's arms.

~*~

In the morning, Lien woke, still embraced by Temur. She was tempted to stay there, but she shifted and pain swamped her, robbing her of breath.

"Are you all right, my *bayar*?" Temur murmured.

"I am sore."

Temur sat up. "Amslan, can you heal my wife further?"

She lifted her head and saw him over by the fire with Batzorig. He appeared well enough.

"Of course." Amslan smiled and walked over. It would take time to get used to this friendly version of him. "Lie down, Mother." He placed his hands on her and Temur took her hand. Shaking his head, Amslan said, "It's a miracle you survived." The heat of healing hit her and she squeezed Temur's hand, gritting her teeth.

"It will be better soon, my *bayar*."

The heat faded, as did some pain. "Thank you."

"You will need more through the day."

She got up and aches spread through her body but it wasn't agonising. She joined the others by the fire and after she had eaten, Solongo asked, "Could I have a word, Mother?"

"Yes."

"Don't go far," Temur said. "We'll leave soon."

They walked along the edge of the meadow until they were out of earshot. "Tell me about the tomb," Solongo said.

"Have you ever been inside?"

Solongo shook her head.

Lien described everything and then said, "I saw the body of the Great Khan."

Her eyes narrowed. "What was he like?"

Lien hesitated. "I believe the Great Khan was a woman."

"Then you truly have seen the Great Khan," Solongo said.

Lien frowned. "Why the lie?"

"It helps us distinguish who is telling the truth. And she didn't believe her gender was important, only her actions."

"So the gift may have come from her."

Solongo's eyes widened. "Of course. It wasn't an artefact at all, it was her." She smiled.

All that pain for nothing. She couldn't be upset. It meant Ying was no longer a threat to them.

"Lien, we need to go," Temur called.

They moved back towards the camp. "You will keep what you learnt to yourself?" Solongo asked.

"Yes."

The others had packed up camp and they descended the mountain, meeting up with Sukh and their horses by nightfall.

"It was a success?" he asked, hugging Lien.

"Yes, Father."

"We'll tell you about it after we find a place to camp for the night," Temur said, mounting his horse.

Sukh said goodbye to the black dragon with him. Lien looked around for Kew. She walked with Manalin, her skin bright red as she was pleased with whatever they talked about. Lien had never seen her so happy, not even when she played with the children. Perhaps she needed to stay here.

For the next two days, she watched her dragon, witnessed her blossom in the company of the older dragon. When they reached the lake, she took Kew aside, kneeling on the ground so Kew could climb on to her lap. She hardened her heart. *Do you want to stay here?*

Kew snorted, her distress clear.

There is much you can learn from your own kind. Perhaps this is where you should be.

Kew projected so much sorrow that Lien wrapped her arms around her friend. *You will always be welcome with me, Kew, but I understand if you need to be with other dragons.*

Are you certain?

Lien's eyes widened as her friend's voice sounded in her head for the first time. Kew had already learnt so much. Lien nodded, not trusting her voice.

Kew surrounded her mind with love. *I will return after I have learnt.*

Return when you are ready. Lien hugged her. *Take care.* She got to her feet as Kew trotted to Manalin and they both headed back towards the mountains. She brushed the tear from her cheek as her oldest friend walked away. Temur put his hand around her waist. "You did the right thing."

She nodded. "Will we camp here tonight?"

The lake was quiet, littered with the bodies of the dead Bonamese. Lien frowned. "Where are the Rhoran?"

"Mongke would have sent men to retrieve the bodies of our fallen." Temur looked around. "They could be far from here by now."

"At least a day's ride, if they haven't moved from where I saw them from the tomb," Lien said.

"If we camp here, we can have fresh fish for dinner," Batzorig said. "And there is plenty of water."

"All right. We'll rejoin the army tomorrow," Temur said.

They made camp at the top of the hill and that night Lien took her first turn at standing guard since she had fought Ying. Sukh monitored the steppe side of the camp and the only sounds were the occasional splash of fish in the lake, and the gentle snores of the men sleeping.

Lien scanned the forest and towards midnight a movement in the trees below caught her attention.

She focused on the area and waited. Behind her Sukh woke Temur and Amslan for their shift. The trees were almost a complete shadow except at the front and she had seen the movement there.

"Lien, you can rest now." Temur lay a hand on her shoulder.

She held up a hand. "There's something out there."

"Where?"

"Three trees to the left of that rock."

"I'll watch it," he said. "Probably just a wolverine."

She shook her head. "No, it was human."

Kun.

Chapter 27

Every muscle in her body tensed. "It's Kun." Or one of his men. It had to be.

Temur drew his bow and arrow. "Let's scare him away then."

He fired five arrows in quick succession, each one hitting the tree Lien had pointed out.

The figure moved back into the trees.

"He's gone."

"Are you sure?"

"Yes." She checked her knives and picked up her bow.

"What are you doing?" Temur asked.

"I can stop him and his men." Fatigue hovered over her like a cloud, but she could kill them without risking anyone else's life.

"You need to rest."

"I will rest when we are safe."

Temur growled his displeasure. "No. You're too exhausted. Sukh, wake everyone. We're moving to the steppes."

"I can fight them, Temur." Lien kept her eyes on the tree line.

"I know you can, *bayar*, but you are tired. It will be easier if we put some distance between the remaining Bonamese and ourselves. And we'll have less distance to travel tomorrow."

Around them the warriors packed up camp.

"We can't leave them here."

"They can do little damage now."

She didn't like the idea of Kun getting away. It was so unlike Temur not to go after him. "Temur, is that wise?"

He turned to her. "Kun will return to the emperor and tell him what happened. Hopefully the emperor will think twice before attacking Rhora again."

Lien hoped he was right. She scanned the forest, waiting for Kun and his men to appear.

"We're ready, Lien," Temur said.

She mounted Batu and rode with an arrow notched as she scanned for any movement in the darkness.

It wasn't until the forest faded into a line on the horizon that she loosened her hold. Her shoulders relaxed. They weren't being followed.

Temur rode over to her. "Are we clear?"

"Yes." She replaced her arrow and swung the bow onto her back. "We should ride hard for longer."

He nodded and they galloped across the steppes in a thunder of hooves, until Temur called a halt.

Kun and his men couldn't sneak up on them. They were safe.

For now.

Lien slid off Batu and brushed her.

Temur took the brush from her hand. "I'll do that. You need to sleep. We don't know what tomorrow will bring."

She was too tired to protest. She unrolled her bed and the moment she lay down, she fell asleep.

In the morning they followed the trail left by the armies. They moved fast, occasionally passing dead bodies, until late in the day they crested a rise and found a sea of people.

Lien pulled Batu to a stop and scanned the camp. No one was fighting. In fact the Bonamese army was camped in the middle.

Chinua laughed. "They've surrendered. That didn't take long."

There would be no more killing. Thank the ancestors.

Temur greeted the guard at the outskirts of camp.

"Glad you're back, Temur," the guard said. "The command tent is over there." He pointed.

As Lien dismounted, Geriel ran up. She let out a deep breath and flung her arms around Lien. "I'm so glad you're safe." She turned and hugged her father.

"Ying is dead," Lien told her.

"Good. I want to hear all about it."

"I must first go with Temur, but we will eat together later."

Geriel nodded and Lien handed Batu's reins to Sukh and followed Temur to the tent.

"You've made it back alive," Mongke said. He hugged his son.

"And you've caught yourself some trespassers." Temur grinned.

Mongke hugged Lien and she squeezed him. He was safe.

"It wasn't difficult." Mongke gestured for them to sit at the table with the other older warriors. "We let them chase us for a day, and then attacked. They had too many people trying to take charge and it was easy to overwhelm them. They surrendered before the day was out."

Temur patted him on the shoulder. "Well done. Have they chosen a leader now—someone we can negotiate with?"

Mongke laughed. "No one wants the title now."

They would be terrified of what the Rhoran would do to them.

"We gathered up our dead and sent word to the camp of our success," Mongke continued. "We haven't heard from Muunokhoi yet, but it's probably too early for that."

Her brother. She'd forgotten about him.

"We'll give him a few more days," Temur said. "In the meantime, we need to decide what we want to do about Xue."

She smiled. This would be interesting.

~*~

A half moon later Lien sat on Batu, facing the Bonamese border. The emperor and his retinue stood several hundred yards past the treaty pavilion, in front of the forest which marked the border between their lands. She scanned the group for Kun, who had evaded capture, but they were too far away. She tugged her tunic straight, her stomach a whirl of nerves.

Temur reached out and brushed her arm. "There is no need to be nervous, *bayar*. Our ancestors and especially the spirit of the Great Khan will protect us."

Xue would not take the defeat lightly. He'd lost his honour and he'd have to win it back somehow. "The emperor may have more gifted soldiers."

"Xue would be foolish to try anything when we have half of his army."

Before she could answer, Manalin landed in front of them. *It is time.*

At Temur's signal, she nudged her horse forward and a group carrying a palanquin walked forward from the Bonamese side.

That wasn't part of the agreement. Only three were allowed to approach the treaty tent. "Temur…"

I sense only one person inside, Manalin said.

That may be so, but the palanquin bearers could all be soldiers.

Fifty yards from the tent the party stopped and the emperor climbed out, his voluminous yellow silk robes accentuating his girth rather than hiding it. He walked ahead of his two ministers and the bearers stayed behind. Lien studied the man who she had held in such high regard for so many years. His eyes were cold and focused on Temur.

Lien fingered her knives, checking they were in place.

No one would harm her husband.

At the pavilion, she dismounted and walked hand in hand with Temur underneath the shelter with Manalin beside them. They sat on the cushions, not waiting for the emperor to sit first. Prime Minister Cong fussed around Xue, and Qing, the minister for defence studied them.

The emperor didn't acknowledge her, keeping his gaze on Temur. To his side Cong stared at her in outrage. No one was meant to look directly at the emperor, least of all a woman. She smiled at him.

"We have arranged this meeting to discuss the terms on which we shall return your soldiers to you," Temur said. "They invaded our land, killed our people and caused much destruction."

"State your terms," Qing said.

They weren't even going to deny it.

"We want the release of all Rhoran prisoners who have been captured unlawfully." Lien passed Qing the list of names they had gathered.

"We want the immediate removal of the wall which

is on our land." Temur indicated the wall in the distance.

We want the mountains to the west of your city for our breeding ground as was always the way, and the immediate return of our stolen babies.

The emperor's eyes widened. "You cannot have my dragon," he growled. "We have done nothing to the dragons."

The man you called Ying invaded our land and stole our babies, forcing us to move from our home. Then in the last moon he again invaded our land and disturbed the new nesting grounds.

Qing and Cong looked at each other in surprise.

What had the emperor told them about his true mission into Rhora?

Temur continued. "You will continue to provide us with the yearly tribute, with the additional provision that these goods come from Bonam land only and are delivered to us at this place."

The emperor's face grew dark. "Is there anything else you want?"

"No." Temur held out the document they had prepared.

"Wait a minute," Qing blustered. "We have a right to disagree with these terms."

"You lost any rights when you invaded our land." Temur was quiet and calm. "You will either agree to our terms or we will kill the captured men and ensure your people understand their fathers and sons are dead because the emperor wouldn't give up property he stole in the first place."

"What proof do we have that any of our men are still alive?" Prime Minister Cong demanded.

I vouch for what Temur and Lien say.

Cong and Qing exchanged a glance. "At least show us a general, perhaps Ying," Qing said.

"Ying is dead," Lien said. "As are the others like him."

Xue flinched more in anger than in sorrow. He didn't care his daughter was dead. Anger hardened her.

"We expect our people and the dragons here at our borders within the half moon," Temur said. "For every day you are late, we will kill fifty men. Within six months we expect the wall to be gone. The dragons' breeding ground will be immediately declared a sanctuary."

Xue's right eye twitched. He picked up the quill, signed the parchment and stood. Without a word, he spun around and left the tent, his ministers following him.

"That went well." Temur grinned.

"Don't celebrate yet. Not until he has fulfilled his promises." Lien's stomach churned. She didn't trust him. "He has a way of twisting words."

"I'd like to see him try." Temur laughed.

Lien didn't.

~*~

The sun shone brightly on the day of the prisoner exchange. Lien inhaled to calm her nerves as she sat on Batu, scanning the forest, waiting for the first movement. The emperor may still attempt something even though a large contingent of the Rhoran army stood behind her.

A flash of colour revealed several dragons, those who had belonged to the imperial family, trotting towards the steppes. Manalin swooped down to greet them.

Then the first of the Rhoran staggered out of the trees.

They need your help.

They had arms around each other, some limping, some shuffling, all of them beaten. Lien gestured to the healers and kicked Batu into a gallop. The man at the front of the freed prisoners looked up through a bruised face and met Lien's gaze. He yelled a warning and turned to run.

Lien pulled Batu up short. Of course. The Rhoran didn't know who she was. They thought it was a trap.

As the group turned, Temur yelled, "Wait, Unegen! You are safe."

Lien stayed where she was while Temur galloped after the prisoners. She scanned the forest and moved behind the group so she could protect them from attack.

The prisoners were a mess. Not a single person was without bruises and torn and bloodied clothes. Many had pathetic makeshift splints to support broken bones. All were fearful and dazed as they helped each other walk.

Fury and helplessness coursed through Lien as the healers tended to them. She couldn't help her people, not yet. The Bonamese had beaten them and as far as they were concerned she was the enemy. She had to keep her distance until they felt safe.

As the carts arrived with more people to help, a man broke away from the group, his steps slow.

Muunokhoi.

She jumped off Batu and hurried to him. "Muunokhoi, where have you been?"

"I've been in a Chungson prison."

Her mouth dropped open. "Anming lied?"

He shook his head. "No. It's quite a story. I'll tell you back at camp."

She wanted to demand he tell her now, but he needed rest. "Take Batu." She handed him the reins.

"I'll find you when everyone has been cared for."

"Thanks, Mother." He mounted and joined the others heading for camp.

Temur rode over to her. "Most of these injuries occurred in the last half moon," he growled.

"We never said what state the prisoners should be returned in." That had been a mistake, one she wouldn't repeat. "Are there any who may die?"

"No. Xue made certain the maximum amount of pain was inflicted without killing anyone."

"Then we need to be thankful."

Temur scowled.

Lien checked over her shoulder to ensure they weren't being followed. What other tricks could he have up his sleeve?

Manalin landed next to them. *Amslan has said he does not require our services. I will take these dragons to their home in the mountains.*

Temur nodded. "Thank you for your help. If the emperor goes against his word, come to us."

We thank the Rhoran for their kindness. He turned to Lien. *Kew sends her love. She is learning quickly.*

She smiled, a slight pang in her heart. "Send her my love as well."

Manalin inclined his head and then took to the air, with the other dragons following him along the ground.

Temur held out his hand and she mounted behind him. Together they headed to the first healers' tent. She hung back as Temur greeted the patients and asked about their injuries. To one side Amslan healed a broken leg, his face pale.

Lien walked over to the food table and took some cheese over to her brother-in-law. When he opened his eyes, she handed it to him. "Eat this."

He smiled and took the food. "Thank you, Mother."

The person he was healing opened his eyes and jerked back in fright.

"Qorchi, let me introduce you to Temur's wife and our tribal Mother," Amslan said. "This is Lien."

"You are Bonamese," Qorchi hissed.

"I was," Lien corrected him. "I used to be State Princess Lien, niece to Emperor Xue—until he tried to kill me." She paused. "Now I am just Lien, tribal Mother, warrior and wife. Can I get you something to eat?" She checked with Amslan.

Qorchi glared at her.

"Amslan can tell you how much he disliked me when I first joined the tribe while I get the food." These Rhoran would not welcome her after their treatment.

But she could wait.

"Lien, can you see to the release of the Bonamese prisoners?" Temur asked.

She nodded. It was best if she gave her people space. She found Batu with the other horses and it didn't take her long to reach the Bonamese prisoners. They had been divided into smaller groups and a warrior would ride from group to group giving the order to free them.

As she rode in, Batzorig came over to her. "Are we ready?"

"Yes."

Batzorig gave a command and the soldiers were given leave to go. Most hurried towards the border without looking back.

So relieved to be alive.

Would they sweep their wives and children into their arms when they returned home, tell them how much they loved them? Or would they protect their honour, show no emotion, at least until they were in private?

She didn't know.

But that wasn't her life anymore.

She no longer had to behave in the manner becoming of an imperial princess.

She could laugh, cry, and yell if she wanted to. She could tell people she loved them. Which reminded her. "Muunokhoi was with the prisoners," she told Batzorig.

He frowned. "That must be an interesting story."

"Why don't you join us to hear it?"

They travelled back to the camp and after the healers had checked Muunokhoi, they gathered in Temur's tent. She lay out food, and Temur pushed a drink into Muunokhoi's hand.

"What happened?" Lien asked.

"It was an adventure for sure." Muunokhoi laughed. "Jie and I made it into Chungson, but ran into a Bonamese envoy just outside the city."

Lien stiffened. "Jie?"

"He's fine. The envoy didn't recognise him and set him free. I was taken to the palace and Anming threw me in jail."

"But I thought…" She'd been lied to again.

"He had no choice," Muunokhoi said. "The Bonamese were staying for a moon and would be suspicious if he set me free. He came down to question me with Jie, and they treated me well." He glanced at Lien. "Your brother brought me food."

Tears welled in her eyes. "He's alive?"

He nodded. "Been masquerading as a servant since he arrived. It was the safest way to hide him in the palace." He chuckled. "They're a strange people."

"So what now?" Temur asked.

"Anming and Bao would welcome Rhoran support. Bao suggested you come to Chungson for further discussions."

"People will notice a group of Rhoran on the roads,"

Batzorig said.

"Not if we go through the mountains. Jie is taking some of Anming's most loyal soldiers to the mountains to teach them about Bonamese strategy. We could meet them there, near the dragon sanctuary."

He'd thought about it a lot. "Do you support overthrowing the emperor?" Lien asked.

"I never thought I'd say this, but yes," Muunokhoi said. "I learnt a lot being with them. We should set up a cultural exchange. We can teach each other and stop the fighting."

Temur chuckled. "Being in jail has softened you."

The man laughed. "It opened my eyes."

"Very well. We'll take it to tribal council." Temur squeezed Lien's hand. "But whatever they decide, we'll reunite you with your brother."

Her chest swelled. "Thank you."

As Muunokhoi continued to speak about his time in Chungson, Lien sat back and smiled. Muunokhoi was right. They needed to get to know their neighbours, share and communicate, break down the myths between them.

Her whole life had changed being with the Rhoran. She could thank Xue for that, for enabling her life to be so complete.

The Rhoran would constantly challenge her and embrace her.

They were her family, the camp was her home.

No matter what happened in the future, she was Rhoran.

Thank you for reading!

I hope you enjoyed The Assassin's Gift. It would be wonderful if you could leave a review wherever you bought it. Reviews help other readers decide whether to give the book a chance, and I love to hear what you thought of the story.

Acknowledgements

I started writing The Assassin's Gift back in 2011, but when it wasn't picked up by publishers I turned my attention to writing contemporary romance. But fantasy has always been one of my favourite genres and I knew eventually I would come back to Lien, Temur and the Rhoran. So I'm thrilled that this year will see The Emperor's Conspiracy finally released.

A huge thank you must go to Lana Pecherczyk for the absolutely gorgeous cover she designed. It is so much better than I dreamed of. Also a big thank you to my editors, Ann Harth and Teena Raffa-Mulligan who help polish the words into the best they can be.

Finally I must thank you, the reader, because without you I could not continue to write the stories I love.

The Healer's Curse

The Emperor's Conspiracy #2

She's their only hope. If only she could wield the power to save them...

Geriel hates that she's the weakest healer in her tribe. And when a deadly disease sweeps through her village, she despairs she's not good enough to rescue her people. With the outbreak spreading and her gift unstable, she's sent on a desperate mission to locate the herbal cure deep in enemy territory.

Seeking to better control her powers with guidance from a skilled dragon, she falls in with a ragtag band of freedom fighters. But even with her mentor's mystic teachings, villagers are still dying. And as war closes in, Geriel fears she's losing the race against time.

Will Geriel find the cure and unlock her talents before her kind fall to the blight?

The Healer's Curse is the second book in the action-packed Emperor's Conspiracy fantasy series. If you like Far Eastern-inspired settings, magical creatures, and breathtaking suspense, then you'll love Claire Leggett's captivating tale.

Buy *The Healer's Curse* to reverse the deathly disaster today!